UNDENIABLE #5

MADELINE SHEEHAN

To the man in the faded photograph with the wide,
handsome smile
and the little girl in your lap.
This one is for you both.

PROLOGUE

I STORMED OUT OF THE ELEVATOR AND INTO THE FOURTH-floor hallway of Queens City Hospital in New York City, NY. Ignoring the glances I attracted from the staff standing behind and milling around the nurses' station, I quickly spotted what I was looking for—a group of familiar men clustered together down the hall—and began marching toward them.

Behind me—quite a distance behind me, actually—my husband, Cole "Deuce" West, better known as "Prez" to his fellow bikers in the Hell's Horsemen Motorcycle Club, was shuffling along slowly, obviously not in any hurry to catch up with me. Not that I could blame him. I'd done little else but yell, scream, and cry at him since finding out about my father's rapidly declining health, something I'd come to discover Deuce had known about all along and had purposely hidden from me.

But my anger with Deuce stemmed from more than just that.

In all the years we'd been together, through the good and the bad, the thick and the thin, he'd still yet to figure out how to react to me when I was upset. He was a man through and through, and in my experience, men like Deuce, men like my father, they dealt with their own emotions by using their fists, emptying a bottle of whiskey, or losing themselves between the thighs of a willing woman. Forget dealing with the upsets of their own women; at that, these men were all utterly clueless.

As for this latest turn of events, "upset" was putting very, very mildly what my tumultuous emotions were doing, and Deuce's cluelessness was only furthering my anger.

My father, my beloved father, was dying of cancer—cancer that had spread quickly throughout his entire body. On top of that, no one had told me—not my father himself nor my husband, nor either of my uncles, all of whom had known about his condition for quite some time now. Instead, a Silver Demons club whore, a woman half my age, had thankfully taken it upon herself to call me and give me the devastating news.

I was furious at them all. And on top of my fury, my heart was breaking.

I was losing my daddy. It didn't matter that I was a grown woman with children of my own. He would always be my daddy, and the thought of losing him…

No. I wouldn't think on that now. Not when my father was still here and I was spitting mad.

"Joe!" I yelled, pointing an accusatory finger at my

uncle, forgoing the formality of calling him "Uncle Joe" as I usually did. I was just *that* pissed.

A shorter and stockier version of my father, Joe shrank beneath my angry stare, at least having the decency to look suitably guilty. Yet beneath his guilt, I could plainly see his pain, so much so that when I reached him, instead of slapping him across the face like I'd planned, I collapsed in his arms and burst into tears.

"How could you not tell me?" I demanded hoarsely, grabbing fistfuls of his shirt. Looking up at him, I squeezed the threadbare material between my fingers, twisting and bunching it until I could hear the fabric tearing. "How could you keep this from me?"

Tears forming in his eyes, Joe couldn't seem to find the words to answer me. It was my other uncle, Max, also known as Dog, who spoke.

"He made us promise, Eva. You know how he is, didn't want no one fussin' over him."

Of course he didn't. Damon "Preacher" Fox was as self-sufficient as they came. He was one of a dying breed of men who only knew one way to live, headstrong to the point of stupidity, selfless to the point of selfishness, and so accustomed to taking care of everyone else around them, they usually forgot to take care of themselves. Or just plain didn't give a damn what happened to themselves, as long as their loved ones were provided for.

"Eva." A heavy arm came down over my shoulders, pulling me away from Joe and turning me. I glanced up at Douglas "Tiny" Williams, a Silver Demon and my father's best friend since childhood. I noted the dark circles ringing his eyes, the way his mouth was turned down sorrowfully.

Of course he was hurting. They were all hurting.

"Doctors say he ain't got much time… maybe a few days," Tiny said, his breaking voice heavy and breathless.

I swallowed hard, nodding, and as Tiny's arm fell away, I took a tentative step toward my father's door but stopped. I couldn't go in there, not yet.

Glancing over my shoulder, I found Deuce and went still. I said nothing, and he said nothing. We just stared at each other, me silently apologizing for my earlier anger, and him holding me captive with those icy blue eyes of his.

Something struck me then. Deuce was only a handful of years younger than my father and had not all that long ago suffered a heart attack. True, I was vigilant, making sure he ate right, took his medication, didn't smoke or drink excessively, and did cardio exercises instead of simply lifting his preferred weights, yet… never before had our eighteen-year age difference seemed so vast. After all, age was nothing but a number… until your number was closing in on its expiration date.

Knowing me better than anyone ever had, Deuce seemed to understand my unspoken fears. He stepped toward me, reaching for my hand. Threading his fingers through mine, he placed our joined hands on his chest, over his heart.

"Still beatin' strong, darlin'," he said quietly.

And as his heart continued beating steadily, mine skipped a beat. Even advancing in years, he was still the most fearsomely beautiful man I'd ever laid eyes upon. His shoulder-length hair, blond and heavily graying, and his beard, also gray and trimmed short and neat, framed a face full of innately masculine, ruggedly cut features that one both feared and yet was inexplicably drawn to.

Ours had been a connection that defied the laws of man, a bond that formed for me at the tender age of five and Deuce at twenty-three. Kindred spirits, a timeless friendship that, as the years continued to pass, had turned into something so much more. And now here we were, nearly half a lifetime later, with two children and still together. Still going strong.

And it was that very strength I needed now to face the pain of losing my father.

"I love you," I whispered.

Deuce didn't answer—he'd never been one to verbalize his feelings publicly—but he didn't have to. His eyes said it all. Icy blue, piercing in their intensity, they stared back at me, right through to my very core. Protecting me. Loving me. Always.

With a deep breath and a full-body shiver, I reluctantly pulled away from Deuce. Then I looked over the men in the hallway, pausing to look at each of them before turning toward the door.

I found my father lying asleep in a railed bed, IV stands and machines surrounding him, periodically beeping and flashing. I didn't know what any of it was for, only that the sight of it scared me, chilled me straight through to my bones.

Slowly approaching the bed, I nearly gasped in shock at the sight of him. It hadn't been that long since I'd last seen him, maybe a year, and yet he looked like a shriveled-up shell of his former self. His gray hair, what was left of it, had turned white. His skin, a mass of wrinkles, seemed to be barely hanging on to his body, a body that had lost nearly all its muscle and fat.

It was the first time in my life that my father actually seemed "old." Never before would I have ever described the once handsome, tall and lanky, yet packed-with-muscle president of the Silver Demons Motorcycle Club as fragile. Not when this particular man had headed a worldwide criminal organization comprised of men who made a living by making other men shit themselves.

But that was exactly what he appeared to be—fragile and breaking. Just like my heart.

"Daddy," I whispered, reaching out to place my hand over his. Resting on his stomach, his hands felt small beneath mine.

Holding my breath, I watched as my hand rose and fell with the rise and fall of his stomach, and my eyes filled with fresh tears.

It didn't matter that I was a grown woman with children of my own. It didn't matter that I had strands of gray in my brown hair and fine lines around my gray eyes. This man was my father, *my daddy*, and no matter his age or mine, losing him made me feel like a child all over again. A child who was losing the only parent she'd ever had.

Even as accustomed to tragedy as I was, as anyone who lived in the world I'd grown up in was, I couldn't imagine ever being truly prepared for this loss. My father was my rock, my foundation, and everyone else's. And if he were gone... well, it would feel like my once unbreakable house came crumbling down around me.

"Baby... girl..."

My head jerked up, and I immediately wiped away my tears. Sniffling, I tried to smile. "Daddy," I whispered, squeezing his hand. "You are such an incredible asshole."

The corner of Preacher's mouth turned up, his brown eyes shining with adoration. He'd never looked at me with anything but love, even when I'd disappointed him.

He loved me regardless of my mistakes and transgressions, and in return, I gave him the same unconditional love. No matter what my father had done, and I knew his sins were many, he would always be the first man I'd ever loved, and the man I still measured every other man against.

"Why didn't you tell me?" I whispered, my expression crumbling. How could I be strong when I was losing him? How could I be strong when he had always been the strong one?

"Why should I?" Preacher asked, sounding indignant and more like himself than he looked. "You've got a life out there in the middle of fuckin' nowhere." He made a face. "And you got people dependin' on you, babies you're raisin'. Didn't need you rushin' home only to sit around and watch me die."

I released his hand with a gasp and straightened to my full height. Glaring down at him, I snapped, "That's my damn decision, Daddy! And my babies aren't babies anymore!"

Again, he attempted a smile. "They'll always be your babies."

A sob and a sigh fled my lips simultaneously, and I turned away, squeezing my eyes tightly shut. Damn him. Damn him, damn him, *damn him*.

"Lived a long enough life, Eva," he continued, sounding exasperated, "and ain't nobody lives forever."

I knew that, of course I knew that, and I knew I had no

choice but to accept it. But that didn't mean I had to like it.

"Enough of this shit," he said. "Come give your old man a goddamn hug."

Blowing out a breath, I turned back to face him. Mindful of the bedrail and careful of his IV lines, I bent down and laid my cheek on his chest, noticing right away that he didn't smell like himself. There was no aroma of cigarettes, no hint of motor oil and exhaust fumes. Instead, he smelled like clean, warm skin and something else sharp and bitter.

Preacher wrapped his arm around my back and gave me as much of a squeeze as he could muster, which was weak at best. Feeling his lack of strength and hearing his lungs rattle and wheeze, I felt my eyes fill again.

"Thank you for always taking care of me, Daddy," I said hoarsely. "For doing the best you could. For stepping up even when *she* ran off."

The "she" I was referring to was my mother. Deborah "Darling" Reynolds had been a sixteen-year-old runaway and a junkie my father had met on a run. She'd taken off shortly after giving birth and was never seen or heard from again.

My parents' relationship had been a whirlwind, short but chock-full of emotion, and Preacher had never quite gotten over the loss of Deborah, never taken any interest in another woman other than for momentary pleasure. He rarely spoke of her, but on the rare occasions that she was mentioned, I'd seen in his eyes and heard in his words how much he cared for her. Even after what she'd done to him, done to us both.

"Eva." Preacher's voice was strained. I lifted my head,

meeting his eyes, finding them bloodshot and full of tears.

"Daddy?" I stood up, reaching for the call button at his bedside. "What's wrong? Are you in pain?"

Taking my hand, Preacher brought it back to his chest. "No," he said softly. "No, baby girl. No pain."

"Are you thirsty?" I asked. "Tired?"

He shook his head. "No, no, I'm just… I'm proud of you, baby girl. So damn proud of you. She woulda been proud of you, too."

I blinked. "Who?"

Preacher looked to the windows as a tear slid down his cheek. "Your mother."

My regret was instantaneous. I shouldn't have brought her up. My only intention had been to stress to my father how grateful I was for him and what an amazing job he'd done, especially having to do it all as a single parent. But now, seeing him still crying over a girl who'd been too immature to take responsibility for her own actions, I hated her even more.

"Daddy, no," I said. "Don't get upset. Let's talk about something else."

Preacher's sorrow-filled eyes found mine. "I lied to you," he whispered.

I squinted at him. "I don't understand. You lied to me about what?"

His eyes closed for a moment, and when they reopened—full of regret, full of guilt—my heart began to pound. All at once, I knew what he'd lied about, *whom* he'd lied about.

"Your mother," he croaked. "I lied about your mother. She wasn't no junkie. Her name wasn't Deborah… and she loved the hell outta you. Loved us both…"

I pulled my hand out from under his and took a small step backward, suddenly breathless. "What?" I whispered, my voice shaking.

"I didn't lie about everything," Preacher said. "She was a runaway. That much was true."

He turned away, his gaze on the window once again. As he stared, looking off into the distance, more tears rolled down his cheeks. And as the minutes continued to tick by, I could only assume the worst.

"Did she die?" I heard myself ask.

He turned back to me, his expression conflicted.

"I gotta start at the beginning. Lemme start at the beginning, baby girl. Lemme tell you the whole damn story."

Wrapping my arms around my middle, I glanced wildly around the room, not really looking at anything and unsure if I wanted to hear this or not. Yet I couldn't deny the hundreds of questions that I found myself wanting to ask, or the sudden desperate need to know the truth about my mother. Starting with, why the hell had my father lied to me?

Blowing out a breath, willing my emotions to stay in check, I forced myself to take a seat at the edge of Preacher's bed. Our eyes locked. "Okay, Daddy. Let's hear it."

Closing his eyes, he let out a hoarse sigh. "I'd gotten locked up at twenty-two, did two years for possession. I'd only been out a couple of months when I met her…" He chuckled softly. "When she tried to steal my wallet," he added.

"Pretty little thing," he continued. "Long brown hair and damn big eyes." His eyes opened and focused on me. "Lookin' just like your eyes, Eva, 'cept hers were brown.

Fact, you got a lot of her in you, only you got some of your grandma, too."

As he continued describing her, I found my own eyes closing as I tried to picture her. Trying to picture... my God... *my mother.*

PART ONE

*"I've never particularly liked the idea of looking back;
I'd rather look forward."*
—Jane Asher

*"At the end, we should all go back to the beginning,
if only to remind ourselves that we once lived."*
—Damon "Preacher" Fox

CHAPTER 1

Back to the beginning

IT WAS HIS LAST DAY.

Two long years he'd spent reading more books than he could count, pacing in his six by eight cell, wearing the same gray shirt-and-pants uniform, day in and day out.

Two years of eating shit food, having his every move monitored, forced to defend his right to simply exist.

Two years of his life… fucking wasted.

He'd never thought it would happen. Being behind bars has a way of making an hour feel more like a month, but it had finally come to pass.

He'd come through those gates a twenty-two-year-old cocky son of a bitch, the heir to a highly profitable criminal organization, the Silver Demons Motorcycle Club, thinking his lawyer would have him out in six months, maybe less.

And he'd thought he would rule this place—that his fellow inmates would hear the name Damon "Preacher" Fox and drop to their knees in respect. He'd come through those gates thinking nobody and nothing could touch him, that he was above them all, a force to be reckoned with. He'd come through those gates thinking he was a god.

He'd come through those gates a fool.

And now he didn't want to leave.

Correction. He did want to leave; who the hell wanted to stay in prison? What he didn't want to do was go back to the life he'd come from.

Prison changes people. It's inevitable. It will change anyone who passes through, whether it be a year-long stint or a life sentence. Once you leave, *if* you leave, you won't exit those gates the same person who'd been escorted through them.

Prison had been a painful wake-up call for Preacher. It had taken the man he'd been, beaten the holy hell out of him, flushed him down the shitter, and sputtered and spit him back out a ravaged and shameful shell.

But he'd persevered. Lived through the beatings, educated himself on prison politics, the self-serving guards and the prison gangs, both of which consisted of men who found inflicting pain on others, both mental and physical, an enjoyable pastime. For a time, Preacher had struggled just to get through a single day without worrying for himself and without some sort of altercation. As a result, he'd hardly slept for several seemingly unending months.

Eventually he'd found a niche for himself within a small group of like-minded men, allowing him to ride out his remaining sentence in whatever the prison equivalent of peace and quiet was. But the peace had come at a price; he was no longer the same man he'd been.

Yeah, prison had changed him.

But if anything, prison had made him a better man than he'd been. Breaking him had only served to make him stronger, harder, full of determination and self-preservation. It made him appreciate the smaller things, things he'd once taken for granted.

From his seat on the bottom bunk, his cellmate Mickey looked up at Preacher solemnly. Mickey was in his sixties, had been in prison since his thirties, but had been transferred here about twelve years back after killing a guard at his last place of residence. He looked a great deal older than he was, his long hair and beard nearly all white, his teeth rotted, and his face a mass of deep wrinkles and scars.

Oftentimes, when he would look too long at Mickey, Preacher would start to see himself, old and decrepit, knowing these cold stone walls would be the last thing he'd ever see.

"Don't come back here," Mickey said gravely, his voice hoarse and grating like a hundred miles of bad road. "I fuckin' mean it, don't you walk out those gates and hop right back into the life. You're young, only twenty-four. You can have a life out there—a good woman, some kids, a job that ain't gonna get you killed. Don't fuck it up."

Preacher just stared back at him.

Don't fuck it up.

Don't fuck it up.

This time it had been a deal gone bad. Preacher had been carrying enough cocaine on his person to get thrown

3

away for life, but thankfully he'd stashed most of what he'd had before his arrest and ended up getting charged solely with possession. He might have been able to lighten his sentence even more if he'd agreed to rat out his club, but Preacher wasn't a rat.

And so he'd ended up a casualty of his father's secret war against society, a war Preacher was no longer sure he wanted to continue waging.

Yet he had nothing else to go back to but the life. His father had all the money, the resources, everything. He'd slap Preacher's Silver Demons vest on his back, and in return, Preacher would be expected to resume service as vice president, utterly devoted to the club and to his father.

But it would never be the same. There was no returning to life as it once was. As happy as he was to be free, he knew now he wasn't really free. He was simply trading one cage for another.

"Number eight-five-seven!"

Preacher recognized the deep, booming voice as belonging to Pat, one of the guards, and the clanking clatter of a nightstick being dragged across steel bars. All over the cell block, fellow inmates began to stir, some shouting curses, others whistling. Someone began to bark like a dog.

As Pat's booted steps drew closer, Preacher's stomach flip-flopped.

Mickey jumped to his feet and crossed the cell. He gripped Preacher's shoulders and pulled him into an awkward hug that caught Preacher so off guard, he almost didn't reciprocate.

"I don't wanna see you again, Damon," Mickey said. "I fuckin' mean it."

Sentimental old fool.

"Let's go, Fox! You can fag it up on the outside from now on!"

Mickey pulled back, his tired old eyes full of cold, hard truths. "Get the fuck outta here," he growled, shoving Preacher toward the waiting guard.

"You gonna behave?" Pat asked. A pair of handcuffs dangled from his hand.

Preacher nodded.

"Get a move on, then. That sunshine is callin' your name."

Reaching up, Preacher quickly tied back his long brown hair, shot Mickey one last look, and then dutifully turned around and put his hands behind his back.

As Preacher was led through his cell block, he caught the eyes of the men he'd been forced to live side by side with for two years. In the pairs of eyes that met his, he found a variety of emotions. Jealous sneers, genuine smiles and congratulatory nods, and knowing stares—stares that seared straight through him, making him feel like those men knew something he didn't.

When they left the cell block and entered the bowels of the prison, Preacher released a breath he hadn't realized he'd been holding.

"You gonna tell me now why they call you Preacher?" Pat asked. "You said you would on your last day, and it's your last day."

Preacher smiled faintly. "I don't know when to shut my fuckin' mouth. Got an opinion 'bout everything, always preachin' 'bout this and that."

Pat was silent for a moment. "Maybe that was true two

years ago, but things sure have changed, huh?"

Preacher didn't bother answering. Yeah, things had definitely changed. He'd lived the last two years being told when to sit, stand, eat, sleep, and take a shit. At first, he'd had quite a bit to say about it, but he'd since learned his place.

"Park it over there," Pat said as they turned into the booking room. Leading Preacher to a far corner of the room, he removed his handcuffs and pointed to a rundown wooden bench.

Taking a seat, Preacher glanced around the room, rubbing his wrists. It was the same room he'd been brought into two years ago, the beige-colored walls lined with dark gray file cabinets, the same three guards manning separate desks, their heads bowed as they looked over various paperwork.

It was the same room where all his belongings had been taken away, where he'd been stripped and searched, put into a stiff gray jumpsuit, and shuffled off to his cell block. The same room where'd he'd become a nameless, faceless nobody, the equivalent of a maggot, just one among thousands forced to live off the garbage they were thrown into.

"Fox!" Pat called. The guard was gesturing toward a chair beside a desk and the bored-looking guard seated behind it. "We need your John Hancock. Get'cher ass over here."

When all his release forms were signed, dated, and sealed away, when his belongings—a pair of ratty old jeans, a white T-shirt, a leather jacket, a pair of riding boots, a wallet, and a small gold chain—were returned to him, when he was dressed and ready to walk out the door marked EXIT in big bright bold lettering, he paused.

"Problem?" Pat asked.

Still staring at the exit sign, Preacher shook his head. Was there a problem? He didn't know.

"What the fuck are you waiting for? You're maxed out, Fox. Free. You got your ride waiting on you. It's a new beginning, a fresh start. Get your ass going and stay the hell outta trouble."

A free man. According to the law and the state of New York, he was indeed a free man. But in reality, he wasn't free at all. He belonged to the Silver Demons body and soul, for better or worse. And if he stayed on this path, this wasn't going to be the last time he went to prison.

Pat slapped him on the back and shoved him forward, and then Preacher was moving, one foot in front of the other, through the exit door and down the long corridor. Another guard, standing at his post near a set of double doors at the end of the hall, nodded at him. Then Preacher was through the doors and stepping out into the warm sunlight...

He was free.

CHAPTER 2

HER GAZE FLICKERED FROM THE OLD MAN BEHIND THE wheel to the world outside the window, a blur of bright greens, blues, and grays. The rickety old truck smelled like stale cigars and feet, thanks to the many cigar stubs overflowing in the ashtray and the well-worn work boots lying on the truck's floor.

Turning back to the man, who'd muttered somewhere around fifteen miles ago that his name was Dave, she clutched her pocket knife a little tighter. He seemed kind— kind enough—and he was hardly in peak physical condition, but you could never be too careful. She'd learned the hard way exactly what sort of evil could lie simmering inside a well-dressed man with a kind smile.

Dave, in his torn denim coveralls, could hardly be considered well-dressed, and he hadn't smiled at all, not once.

In fact, every so often when the radio station would break from the steady stream of country music, Dave would glance her way, his body hunched over the steering wheel, his thin lips pressed in a firm, disapproving line. Having lived like this for some time now—on her own, on the road—this was nothing new. She was well versed in the judgment of strangers. More than likely he guessed she was rebelling against her parents, or society, or something else equally frivolous. But whatever it was he was guessing, she didn't see any malice lurking in his faded blue eyes. Still, she'd strategically placed her large canvas army pack between them while keeping her knife clutched tightly at her side, ready to strike if need be. Nobody got to take from her anymore... at least not without a fight.

Her careful stare meandered back to the window. Large, cultivated farms, looming barns, and the occasional tractor hard at work were all there was to see. In fact, this was exactly what most of America looked like when you watched it fly by from the highway.

Eventually a mile marker came into view, boasting in big white lettering that they were now four miles from the New York border. A rush of excited air escaped her. This was the closest she'd ever been. Briefly closing her eyes, she envisioned all those crowded sidewalks, could almost hear the constant rumble of traffic and the unending blare of car horns.

Her goal was New York City, and maybe she could have made it there much sooner if she hadn't had an entire country to traverse, coupled with the daily worries of food and shelter and bad weather. Not that time mattered in her world; she didn't live by a clock anymore, and no one was waiting on her.

And New York City, from what she'd gleaned from television and books and word of mouth, was the ideal place to disappear. It was a city teeming with people—enough people to panhandle from and pickpocket without having to worry about going to sleep hungry ever again. It was somewhere she could live in plain sight while still hiding. It was somewhere she could become someone new—anyone she wanted to be. She could start over, maybe have a real life again. In New York City, the possibilities would be endless.

The radio clicked off abruptly and her daydreams evaporated. Finding the old man watching her, the fingers curled around her blade twitched.

"This is as far as I go," he muttered, jerking his chin toward the truck stop seated on the approaching horizon. As they drew closer, she leaned forward in her seat and looked around, noting with disappointment that it was a smaller truck stop with only a handful of rigs in the lot.

Dave pulled to a stop a short ways away from the diner and turned to face her. He said nothing. Grasping the door handle, she pushed the heavy slab open and slid across the seat, dragging her bag with her.

"Girl," he called out, and she paused. "Get yourself a hot meal." He tossed a handful of dollar bills across the bench seat, sending them fluttering in all directions. Lunging for the money, she caught the bills before any could be lost to the breeze. Wadding them into a ball, she shoved them quickly into her jeans pocket.

"Thank you," she said, lifting her eyes to his, resenting the pity she found there.

She had enough pride left that being forced to rely on

the pity of strangers still stung. At the same time, she realized that without that pity, she wouldn't have survived nearly as long as she had. It was a double-edged sword, this life.

Dave opened his mouth, then closed it. His ancient eyes scanned the parking lot behind her. He appeared to want to say something else. She'd come across this type before—the individual who thought a few kind words or a good stern talking-to would send her back in the right direction, back to her home where all good girls belonged. If only they knew what home had been like for her.

Rubbing a hand over his bald head, Dave clicked his tongue once, then gestured at the door. She slammed it shut and quickly stepped back, watching as the truck rumbled slowly back toward the highway.

Alone now, she glanced up at the sky, more gray than blue, and inhaled deeply, tasting the thickening moisture in the air. The mild summer day was quickly growing dark and humid, which meant only one thing—rain was headed her way.

Readjusting her heavy pack, she turned in a circle, taking in her new surroundings. As far as truck stops went, it was disappointingly small and sparse. This one offered no bathhouse, no general store, nothing save a small diner and a refueling station.

There were other truck stops, bigger and always busy, running like small cities, so lucrative that most had their own set of working girls and a constant presence of panhandlers and thieves. But there were no hookers here, and there was no one begging for money. Only two men could be seen seated inside the diner, as well as an older woman standing behind the counter. Near the fuel island, a young man puttered around with a box of tools. The few rigs scattered around the lot were still and quiet. Farther back beyond the truck stop, was a tree line.

She sighed heavily, absentmindedly twisting the ring on her index finger—a small band of silver with a tiny butterfly in the center. No people meant no money to be made, and no money to be made meant that this place was a waste of her time.

Heading for the side of the building, she eyed the garbage bins as she passed them, the sickly smell of spoiled meat tingeing the breeze. She was hungry—she was always hungry or tired or both—but she wasn't *that* hungry. She'd been that desperate before, but not today. Today she had some stale chips in her pack and a few dollars in her pocket.

Approaching the trees, she headed into what looked to be a fairly dense forest. It was considerably cooler beneath the heavy canopy of towering oak trees, the humidity of the open air not quite as thick. The ground was soft beneath her worn sneakers, thick with weeds and the rotted remnants of fall saplings.

She paused beside a dried up creek bed and set her bag down. Settling herself on the edge, her legs dangling among the weeds below, she began rummaging through her belongings—everything she owned in this world. She pulled a flannel shirt free, a men's size large that she'd come across draped over the back of a bench at a bus station. Rolling it into a ball, she set it aside. The rest of her clothing, all filthy and in need of a good washing, was wrapped tightly inside her coat. Everything else wasn't much at all. A few cans of tuna fish she'd swiped from a market a couple of days ago, a half-eaten bag of chips, an old army canteen three-quarters of the way filled with water, a ragged coin purse filled with loose change, mostly dirty pennies, and a tattered composition notebook, a stub of a pencil shoved between its pages.

She flipped open her notebook, briefly skimming the hand-drawn faces of the people she'd met in her travels. An elderly woman in Oregon who'd given her fresh vegetables from her garden. A young couple, newly married, who'd offered her a ride through Utah. The good-natured truck driver who'd picked her up on the side of the highway in Kentucky.

A small photograph fluttered free from between the pages and she quickly straightened, snatching it before it could blow away. Gazing down at the picture, she rubbed the pad of her thumb over its smooth surface. Her father had been such a handsome man, with dark hair and eyes, and a smile nearly a mile wide.

She gave herself a moment longer than usual to lose herself inside what few happy memories she had before carefully tucking her photograph away.

Leaning forward, elbow on her thigh, chin in her hand, she closed her eyes and pictured Dave.

Opening her eyes, she pressed the dull tip of her pencil to a fresh page and began to draw.

She emerged from the forest as the last bit of light was slowly leaching from a violent-looking sky. Even with the late hour the air was still uncomfortably thick, made worse by the heavy flannel she wore. Not that she would take it off. The more skin she showed at a place like this, the higher her chances were of being mistaken for a working girl.

Buttoning her shirt all the way to her chin, she rounded the corner of the diner.

More trucks had appeared in her absence, rigs of various sizes and colors. She paused, chewing on her bottom lip, debating whether or not to check out the rigs. Certain truck cabs were surprisingly easier to break into than most cars. A quick flick of her blade inside the rubber gasket surrounding the little window located in the passenger side door and she was in.

Most truckers were careless, leaving their belongings strewn across their seats and dashboards. Sometimes there was money to be found, mostly change, and there was almost always food. An occasional piece of jewelry or pewter belt buckle. It was never worth much at a pawn shop, but five dollars for a watch was better than nothing. When she was feeling bold, she'd steal a CB radio to resell at the next truck stop.

A raindrop splashed against the top of her head. Glancing up, another splattered on her cheek. A web of lightning shimmered above her, followed by a rolling clatter of thunder. Her decision made for her, she headed for the diner.

The bells hanging from the door jingled loudly as she pushed inside the dimly lit building. Two young waitresses shuttled back and forth behind a counter lined with exhausted-looking men, some of whom turned on their stools to glimpse the new arrival. Finding a girl with long, ratty hair and dirty, worn clothing, most instantly dismissed her.

But there was always at least one whose gaze would linger just a bit too long. The owner of the eyes currently fixated on her sat alone at the counter. A scraggly beard mostly masked his features, with the exception of his dark, beady eyes. His calculating and hungry gaze was one she knew all too well. Patting the pocket containing her blade reassuringly, she continued on.

The beady-eyed trucker wasn't the only one watching her. Two waitresses stood behind the counter, wearing matching tight-lipped expressions as they watched her cross the diner. With an irritated huff, one of the waitresses shoved away from the counter and headed her way.

The woman paused at the end of her table, jutting her hip to one side, peering down her pert nose at her. An unnatural blonde with long red fingernails and a plastic nametag that read "Susan," she held a pen and pad in her hands, but she made no move to lift them.

"Coffee, please," she said tightly, feeling the weight of Susan's scrutiny, "and…" Her gaze scanned over the pie plates lining the countertop. "A slice of pie."

Susan's heavily made-up eyes flicked to hers. "This ain't no soup kitchen, girl," she said, "This here is a paid establishment."

Her jaw locked. She may hate the pity she sometimes received, but she hated the outright condemnation even more. Susan knew what she was—homeless and hitchhiking—and assumed she had no money.

Teeth still clenched, she reached into her pocket and pulled out the wad of bills Dave had given her. Susan's gaze snapped to the money, and her lips pursed. "Apple or pumpkin?"

"Apple, please."

With Susan's departure, she let out a breath, relieved that she wouldn't be asked to leave. A good thing, too, as the rain was fast picking up outside, and she vehemently hated spending the night in the rain. It wasn't the cold that bothered her, but she almost always got sick afterward.

Susan reappeared with a mug of steaming black coffee and two exceptionally large slices of apple pie. Surprised, she glanced up, but Susan had already turned away. She looked back at her pie, breathing in the warm, spicy scent… and almost smiled.

It wasn't often, but sometimes people surprised her.

CHAPTER 3

IF HE COULD HAVE, PREACHER WOULD HAVE STRANGLED Mother Nature. He would rip that dirty bitch straight from her throne in the sky, shake her until her brains scrambled, and squeeze her until her bones ground together. This rain—if you could call this...*this monsoon...* rain—hadn't just forced him and his motorcycle off the road, it was unending.

At first, he'd attempted to wait it out beneath a small cement overpass until hours had passed with no sign of it letting up any time soon. Pissed off and chilled straight through to his bones, he'd recalled passing a truck stop a few miles back. Figuring a short walk in the rain was better than being stuck outside all night, he'd set out on foot.

Only five minutes into his trek he'd lost the tie he'd been using to keep his hair off his face. Now his hair was sopping wet and whipping in every direction, lashing uncomfortably across his face. Every step was a hard-fought battle against the wind and rain, and after riding all day, all he wanted to do was take a hot shower and fall face-first into a mattress.

Readjusting the duffel bag slung over his back, Preacher felt an unwelcome wave of cold wash over his feet. Glancing down and realizing he'd just stepped into a fairly deep puddle, he shouted curses into the night.

He'd thought putting some miles between him and the city would do him some good. Just him, his bike, and the road, and he'd be back to his old self in no time. He snorted. If anything, his bad mood had worsened.

When he'd first been released from prison, he'd figured there'd be a small adjustment period as he settled back into the real world, but as the days had turned to weeks and the weeks to months, he'd found himself drunk more often than not, wanting to do little more than sleep most days.

When awake, he was constantly agitated or outright angry. Nothing seemed to help—not booze, not drugs, not women. And beneath the anger, he felt… empty, for lack of a better word. Like a gaping hole had taken up residence inside his fucking chest, and everything he did to try to fill it, to fix himself, only seemed to make him feel that much worse.

Another blast of whipping wind and cold rain circled around Preacher, causing him to falter, lose his footing, and nearly trip. Growling, he pulled the collar of his leather jacket up over the lower half of his face and pressed on.

By the time the flickering lights of the truck stop came into view, Preacher was drenched from head to toe. His soaked hair clung heavily to the sides of his face. Water sloshed inside his boots, and his jeans felt heavy, the denim sticking uncomfortably to his legs. Beneath his leather, his skin felt cold and clammy.

Three steps into the parking lot and the rain suddenly stopped. Preacher halted. Nostrils flaring, he lifted his middle finger to the sky and waved it around, hoping like hell God had a bird's eye view of him.

The truck stop was a sad-looking little place. A slash of concrete semi-filled with trucks bordered a small, squat building. Flickering lampposts surrounded the entire space, sending shadows bouncing across the otherwise dark area. A fueling station sat unattended to his left, and to his right stood a set of pay phones.

Reaching into his pocket, he jingled the change inside. He should call home. He'd left without saying goodbye and had been gone a while now without sending word. And his mother was a worrier. His father, however, was half the reason he'd left.

Gerald "The Judge" Fox was a grumpy old asshole on his best day. And a goddamn hurricane on his worst.

Preacher and he had never seen eye to eye. While Preacher had once preferred late-night partying and a different woman every night, The Judge was his polar opposite. He'd never strayed from his wife. He didn't drink to excess, and he certainly didn't use drugs. Every night he went to bed late, woke up far too early, had the work ethic of a honeybee and the personality of a pack mule. Stodgy. Determined. Unwavering.

Since Preacher's release from prison, their tenuous relationship had only grown more strained. Preacher couldn't be bothered to get out of bed most days, something The

Judge couldn't relate to.

I've been to war, he'd lectured Preacher. *I've seen horrible things happen to good people, I've done things I can't take back, and I've never felt like shirking my responsibilities and sleeping my life away.*

Preacher recalled telling his father exactly where he could shove his so-called responsibilities. And the black eye he'd gotten because of it.

His father wasn't the sort of man you could have a heart to heart with. You did what you were told, end of story, or you got a fist to the face. The Judge only understood three things—the club, loyalty, and family, and in that particular order. The club was his whole world, built from the ground up after he'd served in World War II. In the beginning, it had consisted of only Gerald and a few of his war buddies, drinking beer and fixing up bikes, but after dipping their feet into the sleazier side of life, they had since become a fairly profitable business.

The Judge didn't look at what the club did as criminal. In his mind, their illegal dealings were a way of keeping money in the pockets of war veterans—men who'd put their lives on the line for an ungrateful country and gotten nothing in return.

A criminal with a steady moral compass. That was The Judge.

Whatever Preacher was, it wasn't that.

Blowing out a frustrated breath, Preacher approached the pay phones. He dialed his parents' line first, and when no one answered, he called the club phone. A familiar voice picked up on the fourth ring. "Yelllowwww."

"Hightower," Preacher muttered. "What's doin'?"

There was a moment of silence and then, "*Preacher*?"

Hearing the combined joy and relief in Hightower's voice caused guilt to well in the pit of Preacher's stomach. "Yeah man... it's me."

"Brother, shit, we've been wonderin' about you! We thought—fuck, we didn't know what to think! Where are you? You comin' home?"

Unsure of what to say, Preacher said nothing at all.

"Preacher, you still there?"

Swallowing, Preacher eyed the night sky. "Yeah man, I'm still here... hey, I know it's late, but is my mom around?"

"Naw, brother, everyone left this mornin'. You forget the date? They're all headed to Four Points."

Preacher's brow shot up. Four Points? Jesus, he had completely lost track of time out here.

Held in upstate New York, the Four Points Motorcycle Rally was a two-week-long excuse for bikers from all over to get together and show off their rides, and The Judge never missed an excuse to tout his choppers or his high standing in the motorcycle community. Back before he'd been locked up, neither had Preacher.

"What about Tiny?" Preacher asked, knowing how much his friend hated camping. "Frank?"

"Yeah man, Tiny went with 'em. He's been on a tear lately 'bout how he don't ever get laid in the city, so he might as well try the country. Frank, no. Frank went... *to Philly...*"

Hightower trailed off, his implication clear. If Frank was in Philadelphia, that meant The Judge had sent him there on club business.

"Tiny can't get laid anywhere," Preacher said with a hint of a smile. Tiny was as big as a house and usually sweating profusely, even on a cool day. Finding a woman to take an interest in him had never been an easy task. It usually required a hell of a lot of alcohol and a lot of cash up front.

Feeling a sliver of homesickness, the first he'd felt since he'd been on the road, Preacher asked, "How's everyone doin'? Things good?"

"Things are good, brother, real good..." There was a pause. "... and we're all wondering when the hell you're comin' home. You're comin' home, right?"

Unsure of what to say, Preacher remained silent.

"Preach—"

A robotic feminine voice took over the line, asking for another twenty cents. Reaching into his pocket, Preacher fingered the change inside. The voice asked a second time and Preacher pulled his hand from his pocket. Taking the phone from his ear, he looked down at the receiver and... hung up.

Blowing out a heavy breath, his gaze fell on the diner, and Preacher absentmindedly scanned the mix of bodies inside. While the food at truck stops left a lot to be desired, lately he much preferred the company of truckers over everyone else.

Two years up the river doesn't seem like a whole heck of a lot of time until you find yourself back on the streets among people who aren't half mad. Suddenly surrounded by normalcy, and feeling out of place in a world in which he'd once thrived, had been a brutal shock to Preacher's system. It was easier for him in places like this, around those who lived on the fringes, who barely gave you a first glance, let alone a second.

The diner door opened, the bells on the door jingling,

and a dark figure stepped outside. The man's lowered head lifted and his gaze connected with Preacher's. Recognition was instantaneous.

"Dickie," Preacher greeted him as they briefly clasped hands. "How the fuck have you been?"

"I'm cookin', cat, I'm cookin.'" Dickie snapped his fingers together and pointed at Preacher. "I heard you were doin' time. You break out? Am I dealin' with an honest to God fugitive right now?"

Richard "Dickie" Darvis was a longtime friend of Preacher's father and the club. Tall and wiry, his jeans cuffed at the ankles, his dark hair slicked into a jelly roll, the self-proclaimed lone rider still looked every bit the 1950s greaser he'd been in his youth.

Preacher attempted a laugh. "I maxed out a few months back. Been out on the road." He shrugged. "Needed to clear my head."

The joy in Dickie's expression vanished. "Don't gotta tell me, cat. Been behind bars more times than I care to remember. You get enough miles behind you, and soon you'll be poppin' that clutch, gettin' back to it."

An ache in Preacher's neck flared to life, and he reached up to rub it. "Yeah well, it is what it is, right? Anyway, whatcha doin' on the east coast? Last I heard you were headed out west to play cowboys and Indians."

Dickie barked out a rough, grating laugh, a painful-sounding testament to the two packs a day he smoked. "Was as bored as a blind man at a peep show out there. Just got back this way, was actually thinkin' about heading to the city and dropping in on Gerry."

Preacher shook his head. "He ain't there. He's at Four

Points. You know he wouldn't miss the chance to show off his favorite girls."

Dickie's eyes lit up. "Yeah? Don't blame him, cat. Don't blame him one bit. Those are some rare beauties he's put together. Speakin' of… what are you riding these days?" Dickie's eyes scanned around the lot.

Preacher closed his eyes briefly. "She's not here." And when Dickie cocked an eyebrow in question, Preacher shook his head. "Don't ask. It's been the day from hell."

The wrinkles around Dickie's eyes deepened, his dark eyes shining with amusement. "First rule of the road, cat, you never try and outrun the rain."

Preacher sighed noisily. He'd been so lost in his own miserable thoughts, he hadn't even realized there'd been rain clouds looming. Lost. Amazing how one four-letter word could sum up his entire life.

"You joinin' Gerry upstate?" Dickie asked.

The pain in Preacher's neck doubled. He shrugged. "Maybe… haven't made up my mind yet."

"Maybe I'll see you there." Dickie waggled his thick, salt-and-pepper eyebrows. "… after I check in on a couple of my dollies up in Buffalo."

Preacher snorted. "A couple of 'em, huh? Still breakin' hearts across the country, Darvis?"

Winking, Dickie reached out and gave Preacher another hearty clap on the arm. "Is there any other way to live?"

Another grin, another slap on the arm, and Dickie was striding across the parking lot. Several minutes later, still standing in the same spot, Preacher watched as his friend's glowing taillight disappeared into the darkness.

That's when he felt it: an unnatural shift in the air around him; the presence of someone else. One of the many things prison had taught him was the necessity of awareness—awareness of the space around you—so that no one could catch you off guard.

Preacher spun and grabbed, snatching hold of a slender arm. Slim fingers, nails bitten to the quick—they held his wallet captive.

The girl let out a small, surprised squeak and tried to wrench her hand from his grip, but Preacher easily held her in place. In her other hand, a small blade flicked free from its sheath, glinting as it caught the light from the diner. Preacher took a moment to eye the weapon: a flimsy, rusted little thing he'd bet his bike wasn't sharp enough to do more than clean his nails.

"What's that you got there? A toothpick?" He smirked at her.

Long, limp hair framed a face smudged with dirt. A pair of tired brown eyes, flashing fear and resentment, met his. Her juicy-looking lips twisted bitterly.

A sense of familiarity slithered through Preacher—he knew a street rat when he saw one. Life on the road curses everyone, young and old, male and female, with the same expression—one part weary, one part bitter, two parts desperate.

But for a road-weary thief, she sure was cute.

He slid his gaze down her figure, taking in her flannel shirt and dirty jeans, worn straight through at the knees. The baggy clothes mostly hid her, but not so much that he couldn't see the outline of feminine curves beneath. An army-issued sack, bulging with her belongings, was slung smartly across her back.

"That's mine," he said. Plucking his wallet from her grasp, he released her wrist.

She jumped backward and stepped to the side, keeping her gaze locked with his. He remained where he stood, making a show of tucking his wallet inside his jacket's inner breast pocket. Still smirking, he gave his pocket a firm pat.

The fear in her gaze was nearly gone now. Through narrowed eyes she assessed him, her expression conveying that she didn't quite know what to make of the situation. Thoroughly amused now, Preacher was contemplating giving her a few dollars when a gruff shout interrupted his thoughts.

"Found her! Over here, boys, over here!" A broad-shouldered, heavyset man was storming toward them. His red face bulging with fury, he was making a big show of waving around a baseball bat.

Unimpressed, Preacher eyed him beneath furrowed brows. "Friend of yours?" he asked the girl.

"I saw you, you little bitch!" the man growled, pointing his bat at the girl. "Hand over the bag!" He angled the bat in Preacher's direction. "You too!"

"Hey now," Preacher started to say, "I didn't…"

"Gimme the bags, you thieving shits!" the man bellowed.

There was no way in hell Preacher was going to hand his bag over, and judging by the look on the girl's face, she wasn't going to be giving hers up either. Not without a fight.

Preacher rolled his shoulders. Fine. A fight was just fine with him. Growing up with brothers had left him well acquainted with solving problems with his fists. And if things got really out of hand, he had a blade in his boot big enough to send Red here crying back to whatever rig he'd crawled out of.

Jaw locked, fists clenched, Preacher was ready to step forward when he heard the clatter of footsteps approaching. A quick glance over his shoulder showed him two more men had joined their group, one brandishing a tire iron.

Cursing under his breath, Preacher glanced briefly up at the sky. First the rain and now this shit? Someone up there must really have it out for him.

"We'll be takin' the bags," the man holding the tire iron spat. "Make it easy on yourselves and hand 'em over." All three men were slowly advancing, creating a triangle formation around him and the girl.

"You need to run," Preacher breathed.

Panic-stricken eyes met Preacher's. "What?"

Red lunged and swung, and Preacher barely had enough time to duck. Grabbing the girl's arm, he thrust her forward just in time to duck another swing of the bat.

"Run!" he shouted. He ducked again, spinning around, and exploded back upright. His fist cracked the face of the man now closest to him—the one without a weapon. Propelled by Preacher's punch, he staggered backward as Preacher turned his attention to the man holding the tire iron. With a shout, Preacher barreled into him, sending them both sprawling on the wet cement. They hit the ground hard, the man beneath him taking the brunt of the fall while Preacher wrenched the iron from his grip.

He'd managed to bring himself to his knees when pain suddenly exploded in his shoulder.

"You scum-sucking lowlifes!" Red shouted, readying his bat.

His arm burning, fighting to keep hold of the iron,

Preacher dropped to the ground and rolled away, narrowly avoiding the next swing of the bat. Wood met concrete and Red let loose a string of curses.

Preacher jumped to his feet. "Back off," he growled, raising the iron, poised to swing. The two men glanced at one another and neither moved.

Realizing they were one man short, Preacher halted. As if on cue, a shrill cry sliced through the dark lot, and Preacher's eyes swung toward the noise. Sandwiched between two 18-wheelers, some sort of struggle was occurring.

Son of a bitch. Apparently he hadn't punched the asshole hard enough.

Seconds ticked by while Preacher wondered how wise it would be to just barrel straight into Red and his friend, hopefully knocking them both flat, allowing him to take off running.

"I called the police!" a woman shouted. A waitress poked her head out the door, and half the diner's occupants were congregated around the window.

Preacher released a string of muttered curses. The cops were the very last people he wanted to deal with right now. Once the local law got wind of him having served time, there was no doubt in his mind that they'd pin the full blame for this debacle on him. He'd just barely gotten out of prison, and he wasn't inclined to go back anytime soon.

With the threat of being put behind bars looming, Preacher threw caution to the wind and rushed forward, clipping Red in the gut with his elbow as he blew past him. A hand grabbed at the bag on his back, and he threw all his weight into shoving the man aside. He felt the swish of air as the bat swung and managed to spin around, catching Red in his meaty middle. Grunting, Red lost his momentum.

"Behind you! He's comin' up behind you!" The warning shouts followed Preacher as he tore across the parking lot.

Still grappling with the girl, the man attempted to turn toward the noise, but Preacher was already upon him. Skidding to a stop, gripping the tire iron with two hands, Preacher sent the metal bar swinging into the man's lower back.

Roaring in pain, the man spun around and toppled over. A quick glance behind showed Preacher Red and company were headed their way. Grabbing the girl's arm, he yanked her to him. "We need to go!" he shouted.

"My bag!" She screamed, thrashing in his grip. "Where's my bag?"

He tightened his hold on her. "They called the cops!" he bellowed. "We've got to go!"

"No!" She tried to pull free again. "I need my bag! Where's my bag?"

"Fuck your bag! Are you deaf? They called the cops! *We have to go!*"

She paused, barely breathing, and looked up at him with wide, savage eyes. A trail of blood trickled from her swollen bottom lip down to her chin. Her flannel shirt was hanging open, and the T-shirt beneath was torn and gaping at the collar. Then she blinked.

"But...my bag..." It was barely a whisper, all her fight gone.

Preacher was done listening. The moment she'd gone limp, he'd started running, dragging her along beside him.

They'd just hit the highway, swallowed up into the darkness when the skies opened up again.

CHAPTER 4

FRANKLIN DELUVA SR. SLIPPED HIS HANDS INTO HIS pockets and glanced up at the starless sky. Better known to others as "Frank," or "Ghost" for his uncanny ability to slip in and out of places unseen and unheard, his black leather riding boots pounded a nearly silent rhythm on the rain-dampened sidewalks. The darkened streets of Philadelphia were quiet and nearly empty at this time of night, and his business had wrapped up hours ago.

He should have been thrilled that everything had gone according to the book; he'd delivered the goods, and all money owed to the Silver Demons had been paid in full, right down to the last red cent. But he was far from thrilled. There were other things weighing heavily on his mind, shrouding his thoughts beneath a dome of static—static that would grow louder and louder until it would be all

Frank would hear.

Frank was a man who liked order. He liked everything in its rightful place. He liked his hair just so, his clothing to fit a certain way, his wallet always in his right back pocket, and his keys in his front left pocket. Everything in its rightful place. Everything and everyone.

Frank liked his wife at home, caring for their young son. He liked coming home to a clean house and a hot meal. And he liked his club and all their business partners in their respective roles, working in perfect sync, the cogs turning like a well-oiled machine.

This madness inside him extended to all facets of his life. His clothing had to be folded a particular way, the different foods on his plate could never touch, and then there was his unexplainable aversion to even numbers. He typically did certain things in groups of threes—looked at something three times, said a word three times, usually silently, or touched something three times. It was a never-ending cycle of constantly counting, enough to drive a sane man mad... or keep a mad man sane.

He'd often speculated that growing up as a ward of the state, never having had a place to call home, might have caused this incessant, demanding need for order in all things. If it hadn't been for his friendship with Preacher, the only constant in his hectic young life, who knew what kind of person he would have turned out to be?

Preacher.

Frank picked up his pace as the buzzing in his head grew louder, his heart pounding as a surge of anxiety-fueled adrenaline coursed through him. Preacher was not where he was supposed to be. Something was leaking inside

Frank's well-oiled machine. Cogs were rusting, and one had stopped turning altogether.

Frank hadn't exactly minded when Preacher had gone and gotten himself locked up. In fact, in a lot of ways, he'd preferred it. For the two years Preacher had been in prison, Frank had known exactly where to find his friend when he'd needed him, and had been secure in the knowledge that, once Preacher's sentence was up, things would return to normal.

Only... they hadn't.

Preacher had been released from prison, and right off the bat, everything had been different. Angry and sullen, Preacher had refused to come to the club, refusing anything and everyone. He drank incessantly, slept constantly, and when he wasn't drinking or sleeping, he was fighting with everyone. Then one day he'd upped and left. Vanished in the middle of the night without a word to anyone.

Weeks had passed, then months, and with every passing day without word of his whereabouts or his return, Frank had felt the crack in his control begin to splinter in every direction. His moods had been unpredictable lately. His usual methods for keeping control of himself weren't working properly. Preacher consumed his thoughts day in and day out.

Where was Preacher?

Was he ever coming home?

Frank didn't want to lose control. He liked being in control.

His hands clenched into fists, his short nails pressed painfully into his palms. His pace continued to increase.

He needed his fucking control. Because if his world

couldn't stay together, he couldn't stay together.

If he was a drinking man, Frank supposed he'd be drinking right now, but he wasn't. Booze, drugs... he didn't like anything that messed with his head. If a man couldn't think clearly, he wasn't useful, and if a man wasn't useful, that man had no business breathing.

What he needed was to figure out how to get Preacher home. Hell, first he needed to find Preacher. Without Preacher...

Blinking, Frank shook his head quickly. One, two, three, four—

He cursed and tried again.

He was already fraying.

A door slammed closed, echoing across the quiet street. Frank went instantly still, blending into the shadows as he observed a young black woman descend a nearby stoop. Wearing a slinky red dress and matching heels, she paused on the last step, rummaging through her purse.

Frank cocked his head to one side, a burst of excitement and anticipation heating his chest. It hadn't been all that long since his last, and he knew he shouldn't be craving it again so soon, but—

Frank calculated the distance between them, wondering if the door she'd just come from was locked. He glanced to a small alley some twenty feet away and wondered about the apartments above. Were they occupied? Were the windows open? He wasn't a man who particularly liked taking chances. He liked plans. Carefully crafted, calculated plans. Spur of the moment shit like this was just further proof that he was losing his grip on control.

Unable to ignore the relentless beat of need pounding

inside of him, Frank moved closer to the stoop. The move freed him from the shadows, and the woman looked up, her gaze widening.

Fear. That was fear gleaming brightly in her eyes. Another craving rippled through Frank.

The door opened again. A young man in a suit jogged down the stoop, offering his arm to the woman. Frank veered away quickly, crossing the street at breakneck speed.

Sloppy, he thought to himself. *Sloppy, sloppy, sloppy.*

He turned down another street, still silently berating himself. A yellow cab blew past him, splashing his pants with water. Gritting his teeth, Frank quickened his stride.

Everything was wrong. The noise in his head was building to a crescendo. He could feel the beat of his heart in every part of his body. Even his skin felt wrong, too tight. His insides too cold.

Noisy. Everything was so goddamn noisy.

He slowed his steps to run a hand across his stubbled jaw. He needed to shave. He needed to shave right now.

The noise in his head intensified, so loud he could feel it. Pulsing and expanding, it pushed painfully against his skull. Frank slowed as he rubbed furiously at his temples. Amid the panic, rage—hot and white and quivering—was building low in his belly. He couldn't control it; he couldn't control anything anymore!

The sudden sharp, biting sound of heels clicking the pavement brought his spiraling thoughts slamming to a halt. Everything froze and then slowly started back up, sluggish at first, as if he were stuck inside a slow-motion action scene. The footsteps grew louder, faster, and then all at once everything suddenly sped back up, came into clear, crisp focus.

His breathing shallow and his heart racing, he started to jog. Anticipation was building again. That delicious warmth was filling him. His hands twitched. He turned the corner—

"Shit!" A slight woman teetered precariously on her heels before him. Frank reached out and grabbed her arm, keeping her upright. The smell of her hit him like a brick to the face. Stale beer and unwashed skin and something else—an underlying rot.

She was a working girl who looked to be in her late twenties, wearing a tiny little yellow number that left very little to the imagination. Not that there was very much of her to see.

She was too thin, wasting away. Black hair hung thin and limp around an angular face. Bloodshot eyes were ringed in smudged eye makeup. Red lipstick had smeared pink across one jutting cheekbone. There were dirt stains amid small scrapes up and down her pale legs, as if she'd spent the entire night on her knees in back alleyways.

She had been pretty once, maybe even beautiful, but the years hadn't been kind to her. He turned her arm, eyeing the track marks along the crook. She hadn't been kind to herself either.

"How much?" he asked.

She attempted seduction as she smiled limply. "Depends on what you want," she slurred. "You want my hand, that'll be ten. You want my mouth, that's twenty. You want my pussy, that's gonna run you a solid fifty."

Excitement surged and Frank's fingers flexed, digging into her arm. She didn't appear to notice.

"I'll give you a cool hundred to do whatever I want," he said.

She blinked. "You an ass fucker? Or you wantin' to piss on me?" She shook her head and sighed noisily. "Man, I want the money up front." Dirty fingers, topped with cracked and broken fingernails, beckoned him to pay. A thin gold chain glinted from around her wrist, a small charm in the shape of a heart hanging from it. He took a half second to eye the jewelry. It looked real, and he wondered why she hadn't pawned it. Did it hold some sort of emotional value, or had she stolen it?

Releasing her, Frank dug his wallet from his back pocket and drew two bills from inside. She made a grab for the cash, and he quickly flicked it just out of her reach and jerked his chin toward the small walkway between two nearby buildings. "In there."

Following behind her, Frank observed the drugged sway of her gait, the way the straps of her dress kept falling down her arms, and wondered how many men had used her tonight. Not that he particularly cared, but he believed himself to be something of a people person. That is, when he could stomach the messy, unpredictable way so many people chose to live their lives, Frank enjoyed observing them. Often times it was his speculation that made what was going to come next all the more enjoyable for him.

For instance, Frank guessed that this whore had been working these same streets for the last decade or so, the last few years of which she'd started shooting junk. He surmised that her prices were cheap for two reasons. One, because she worked alone—there was no pimp holding a gun to her head, wanting his cut. And two, cheaper prices were more appealing to your average schmuck who wanted to get off and get home. Cheaper prices meant more customers, and more customers meant she'd be able to keep herself good and stocked with her daily dose of poison.

Partway down the alley the whore paused and swayed, turning to face him, half eclipsed in darkness, half lit by the moon. Frank approached her and pushed her into total darkness. His thoughts slid to the thick blade strapped to his belt, and a shudder of excitement rippled through him.

She'd had a family once, he supposed as he looked down at her. But whoever and wherever they were, they'd long since forgotten about her. There'd be no one to care, no one to grieve her. Hell, chances were she'd end up unclaimed, left to rot away in a nameless city grave.

Or maybe there was someone left. Maybe a grand-mother or a sister. Maybe she'd taken off in the middle of the night, maybe they hadn't seen or heard from her in years, and once they got word of her death, they'd—

Frank's thoughts flickered, then dimmed, and then flickered again as an idea began forming in the deepest, darkest regions of his mind. At first he shoved the thoughts away, instantly dismissing them, and then…

He veered back and studied them, wondering…

"Pay up," the whore said, her hand outstretched. Frank set the bills on her palm, watching as she tucked them swift-ly down the front of her dress.

"How you want me—"

He grabbed her neck, cutting off her words and most of her air. While her eyes bulged with surprise and she clawed at his hand, he carried her the remaining several feet toward the alley wall, her shoes dragging noisily along the cement.

As he pushed her back against the wall, her legs flailed and she tore at his hand, gauging thin slices into his skin with her jagged nails. Frank hardly felt it. He was too focused, too ready, too excited for what was to come to care about half-assed scratches made by a dying whore. With his free hand, he gripped the handle of his blade and slid it from its sheath.

Staring down at her, his insides were on fire, his skin twitching, his gut burning with hot anticipation. But it was even more than that. What he was feeling, it was more than just some cheap thrill.

Slowly he dragged the tip of his knife up her side, savoring the precise moment that she realized she was going to die. Frank often wondered what went through their minds at that moment. Regrets, maybe? Did they think of someone they'd be leaving behind? Or were they simply consumed with fear?

One, two, he counted, and when he reached three, he plunged the blade into her side.

With each thrust of the blade, Frank's breathing quickened. He breathed in through his nose, out through his mouth, watching with rapt delight as the flicker in the woman's protruding eyes began to dull.

There was something so personal, so intimate, about watching another person die, even more so when you were the one to steal the life from them. Much like birth, death was every bit as beautiful, if not more so. And to be the reason… it was almost as if… almost as if you weren't just witnessing a miracle, but causing one.

His head clear, his thoughts in perfect order, he released the whore, and her body folded quickly to the ground, her insides spilling out of her. Sheathing his blade, Frank bent down over the body and studied his kill, smiling faintly. Carefully lifting her hand so as not to disturb the rest of her, he yanked the gold chain from her wrist and slipped it into his pocket.

As he exited the alleyway, he began to whistle softly. The noise in his head was all but gone.

Frank had figured out how to bring Preacher home.

Even better, he knew how to *keep* Preacher home.

CHAPTER 5

S HE DIDN'T CARE THAT HER LIP WAS THROBBING FROM where the beady-eyed trucker had slapped her. She'd been slapped before… and worse. She didn't care that she was cold. She'd been cold many, many times before—freezing, even. She didn't care that she was sopping wet, soaked straight through her clothing. She'd been wet before, too. And she didn't care that she had only a crumbling, leaky overpass for shelter, which was doing very little to quell the rain-laden wind whipping around her. It wasn't the first time she'd been stranded in the elements with nowhere else to go and nothing to do except wait it out.

She'd survived much worse than this, something that might seem impossible to those who didn't live the way she did. Quite often, when her only shelter was the lip of a roof or a tree top, and she was forced to sleep up against a solid wall or a bark-roughened tree trunk, she would close her eyes and pretend she was in a warm bed, cocooned inside thick blankets, a fluffy pillow cradling her head. It didn't always work, especially in more extreme weather conditions, but it worked enough that, even if it didn't result in sleep, it served to occupy her mind.

What she *did* care about was that she'd just lost everything. Every single thing she had in this world—her canteen, her food, her money, her coat, all her clothing. They were all hard-won items to someone like her. Items that were now...just...*gone.*

Her heart fluttered, her chest filling with panic. *What was she going to do?*

If only she'd left well enough alone and hadn't pushed her luck by searching through the rigs in the lot. She'd known this particular truck stop hadn't been ideal. If only she'd stayed put inside the diner and waited out the night. Eventually she would have hitched a ride, New York City-bound.

She'd still have her bag, too.

She took a shuddering breath, a piss-poor attempt to calm her thundering heart, and began twisting the butterfly on her finger.

If she were a different girl, she guessed that maybe she would be crying right now. But she'd learned at a young age that tears didn't change anything. Tears didn't bring back the people you'd lost, they didn't heal you when you were hurt or wipe away the ugly memories festering inside you. And they certainly didn't replace bags that had gone missing.

The rainwater dripping from her sopping hair and rolling down her cheeks was as close to tears as she was going to get.

The flick and flash of a lighter drew her attention to the man beside her. Crouched on his heels, smoking a cigarette, he stared out across the dark highway.

He was hurt, too. He'd been favoring his left arm since they'd run from the truck stop, but he hadn't mentioned it. He'd said very little to her actually, leaving her wondering if he blamed her for his current situation.

As if he could feel her eyes on him, his gaze found hers. He was half hidden in shadows; she stared at the only discernable feature she could see, the whites of his eyes. Brown eyes, she recalled. A dark brown that matched the rich shade of his hair and beard.

"Smoke?" Reaching across the space between them, he held out his cigarette in offering. She considered taking it—she could use a cigarette right now—but made no move to do so.

"I don't bite," he said, a hint of amusement in his tone. She didn't respond and neither did she believe him. Everyone could and would bite. And she didn't know him. She didn't know what he was capable of.

A gust of wind blew suddenly through their small hiding space, and as a shiver tore through her, she snatched his cigarette quickly and turned away. Taking a long, hard pull, she closed her eyes, relishing the warm burn in the back of her throat, wishing it would spread to the rest of her.

The wind continued to blow. Above, the rhythm of the rain seemed to intensify and echo against their cement shelter. She wiggled her toes, hating the feel of wet socks against her cold feet. Hating even more that she didn't have a dry pair to change into.

"Nice weather we're havin," he said dryly. The man was staring off into the darkness again, idly flicking his lighter.

She said nothing.

"Name's Damon," he continued. "But my friends call me Preacher."

He paused, and she assumed he was waiting for her to introduce herself.

"So what do I call you?" she asked, "Damon or Preacher?"

"She speaks." Feigning shock, he chuckled. "Saved your ass back there, didn't I? I'd say that makes us friends."

Wondering what exactly his definition of "friends" was, she began to question what he might want in return for saving her. Her hand jerked, reflexively reaching for her blade, only to recall she no longer had one.

"Thank yo—" Her voice cracked as her anxiety spiked. She cleared her throat, took a breath, and tried again. "Thank you… for what you did."

Preacher shrugged, then hissed. His features pinched with pain, he slowly rotated his shoulder, rubbing the area just above his bicep.

"Are you hurt?" she asked.

He shook his head. "Naw. Banged up is all."

Flicking his lighter, he held the flame up between them. Scanning her face, his gaze paused on her mouth. "Are *you* hurt?"

She guessed her lip was swollen. She'd tasted blood, and she could feel her pulse pounding beneath the thin, sensitive skin. But hurt? *Ha.* If he considered a split lip worth a second thought, he must have a very rosy view of the world.

"I'm fine." Finishing her cigarette, she flicked the filter

into the rain.

A round of thunder rumbled above them; a bright white flash zigzagged across the sky. Another shiver tore through her body and she squeezed her eyes shut.

"Soon as the rain stops I can give you a lift some-where…" Preacher trailed off, leaving his offer hanging be-tween them.

She glanced at his motorcycle, eyeing it with trepida-tion. She'd never ridden on one before, but she'd never re-fuse a ride. Her gaze moved to the duffel bag strapped across the handlebars, and she wondered what was inside—what might be of use to her.

Her first priority was to replenish her supplies. Empty-handed, she'd take whatever she could get: clothing, money, food. Some things, such as her canteen, were going to be harder to replace. Others were irreplaceable.

The photograph. Knowing she would never see it again, her heart seized.

She took a breath. Released it. Took another. Released it. She didn't need the picture. Her father's face was forever burned into her memories. She had only to close her eyes to see that wide, handsome smile. And once she had the paper and pencil to do so, she would draw it from memory.

CHAPTER 6

PREACHER PULLED HIS MOTORCYCLE OFF THE QUIET highway, slowing to a stop. Toeing his kickstand down, he pushed his goggles up over his head and eyed the nearly empty parking lot. Aside from a beet-red Plymouth Avenger, they had the place to themselves.

Glancing up at the dark gray sky, he guessed it was around four or five in the morning. His thoughts wandered back to his apartment, where his watch was sitting on top of his dresser. He hadn't bothered putting it on before he'd left. Time was for men who had something to do.

Shivering violently behind him, the girl gripped his shoulders and attempted climbing down. She hadn't ever ridden on a motorcycle before; her death grip on his middle had told him as much. And with her wet and torn clothing and lack of protective eyewear, he couldn't imagine a less enjoyable first ride.

Slim, wind-reddened hands removed the helmet he'd given her to wear, revealing a matted mass of messy, knotted hair. Wrapping her arms around herself, she turned in a slow circle, surveying the area with a calculating, determined eye.

He'd been right about her—there was no doubt in his mind that she was a street rat. And if he hadn't already guessed as much at first glance, the fact that she'd sat on the side of the road in the dead of night, in the pouring rain no less, and hadn't complained once would have told him she was used to shit conditions such as this.

"I'm gonna get a room," he said. Standing, he swung his duffel over his shoulder. "You want to grab a shower and some shut-eye, you're welcome to it."

The motel offered your standard middle-of-nowhere room, with dark brown wall paneling and a yellowed popcorn ceiling. Two beds were stationed to the right, with a small night table nestled between them. A lime green rotary phone, a small flip clock, and a cheap-looking lamp covered the table.

A square, squat table sat on the left side of the room with one rickety-looking chair. A short ways back stood an antique-looking desk with a small television on top. And near the very back of the room, by the bathroom, was a six-drawer dresser that looked nice enough to have been taken straight from someone's home.

Keeping the door propped open with his boot, Preacher tossed the key onto the bed closest to him and gestured for the girl to enter.

She turned sideways as she slid inside, being especially careful not to brush up against him.

Jesus, did she think he was a half-crazed lunatic just waiting for the right moment to pounce on her?

"You want the first shower?" he asked. Taking a seat, he kicked off his boots. Next, he peeled off his waterlogged socks and grimaced at the sight of his cold, red feet.

"You go ahead."

Preacher glanced up and found the girl pressed against a wall, arms wrapped around herself. Catching her gaze, he lifted an eyebrow, and she looked away quickly.

Whatever. Preacher didn't need to be told twice. Cold, wet, and miserable, he headed for the bathroom.

Shut inside the tiny space, he carefully slid out of his jacket and began cautiously probing around his shoulder and arm. He could move it well enough, bend it just fine, but he had one hell of an ugly bruise starting to form. He continued poking the swollen skin, guessing that he had some minor muscle damage, too. He rolled his eyes. It was a good thing Red swung like a girl or else he'd be nursing a broken bone right now.

As he moved toward the shower, he caught sight of his reflection in the mirror and paused. Bloodshot eyes and a menacing scowl stared back at him. His riding goggles were half hidden in his mess of tangled hair.

His scowl bled slowly into a smile.

He did, in fact, look like a half-crazed lunatic.

CHAPTER 7

WRAPPED IN A TOWEL, SHE TOOK A SEAT ON THE EDGE of the tub and sniffed at her shoulder, inhaling the fresh, sharp scent of her skin. Then her hair, breathing in the citrusy scent. Quick cleanups with bars of soap in public bathrooms could hardly compare to hot showers and actual shampoo.

On the shower rod above her dangled her freshly scrubbed clothing. Most of the buttons on her flannel were missing, and her T-shirt had been torn open several inches down the middle. Two pathetic strips of stained cotton covered in holes were all that remained of her socks.

That was it—this was all she had left.

Moving to the door, she pressed the side of her face against the wooden surface, listening.

Earlier Preacher had strode from the bathroom in dry

clothing with his long, wet hair combed, looking clean and refreshed. He'd barely spared her a second glance as he'd flipped on the television set and settled himself on one of the beds. Feeling awkward and uncomfortable, she'd wasted little time hurrying inside the bathroom.

She'd been so anxious to get away from him, anxious to be clean, excited for a hot shower, that she'd given little thought to what she'd wear afterward.

Glancing down at her towel, she blew out a heavy breath. She supposed it didn't actually matter what she was wearing, as she was already planning on taking it off.

From the moment Preacher had offered her his room, a plan had begun to take shape. She had nothing but the torn, stained clothing hanging over the shower rod. In all her time on the road, she'd never been quite this desperate. So desperate, she was finally willing to do something she'd promised herself she would never do.

Swiping her hand across the fogged-over mirror, she leaned forward to inspect herself. Though there was nothing outwardly off-putting about her, there was nothing remarkable, either. And she certainly didn't look anything like the puffed-up prostitutes always hanging around truck stops.

She couldn't even remember the last time her hair had been cut. Dark brown, it hung in a straight line down her back. And she had no makeup to cover the smattering of freckles over her nose and cheeks, nothing to help her appear more polished, more feminine. More desirable.

Realizing she was procrastinating, she dropped her hand and turned to the door. The moment she gripped the doorknob, her heart quickened.

Straightening her spine, she took a deep breath and released it slowly. What did she have to fear? It wasn't as if she were a virgin. She knew exactly how to spread her legs and let a man do his thing between them—how to lay there with her eyes squeezed shut, pretending she was someone else, somewhere else.

She opened the door.

The noise from the television grew louder as she padded across the rough carpet. Preacher was sprawled across a bed, pillows stacked up behind him, with his hand inside a bag of potato chips. At the foot of the bed, his open duffel bag revealed several more bags of snacks. She stared at the food a moment, her stomach twingeing in response.

"Hungry?" Preacher asked around a mouthful, glancing sideways at her. He pushed the chips across the bed. "Help yourself."

Hungry and exhausted, she wanted nothing more than to eat and sleep and forget the wretchedness of her current situation for a little while. Except she couldn't. She had more than just right now to worry about.

She took a small step forward, bringing her flush with the side of the bed. She swallowed hard and took an imperceptible breath.

"It's thirty dollars for a fuck." The words toppled from her mouth in a hurried rush.

Pausing mid-chew, Preacher turned to face her, his brow shooting halfway up his forehead. The next several seconds ticked by slowly in agonizing silence. Worried he was going to reject her offer, she steeled her shattered nerves once more and dropped her towel.

Preacher's gaze dropped with her towel, unabashedly

traveling down the length of her and back up again, where he lingered on her chest. Her face grew hot; her entire body flushed. Unable to watch him look her over, she turned her focus on the olive green curtains covering the window.

Oh God, was she really doing this? Offering herself to a stranger in return for money?

"Sorry baby, I don't pay for it." Her eyes shot to his. His words were gently spoken, his expression curiously blank, as if he were concerned about offending her.

Too late for that. Hot humiliation flooded her. Mortification churned nauseatingly in her stomach.

"Twenty," she whispered, desperate. Her hands clenched into fists at her sides. "Or ten if you want me to just… you know…" She swallowed quickly. "Just use my mo—"

"How old are you?"

She stammered to a stop. "What?"

"How old are you?" he repeated. He was no longer looking at her body. Instead, his eyes were fixed on hers, which somehow made her feel twice as naked. Hurriedly she scooped the towel off the floor and quickly wrapped it around herself.

"Nineteen," she mumbled.

The corner of Preacher's mouth twitched. "You'd make a terrible poker player," he said. "Forget that I don't pay for it. It doesn't take a genius to know you ain't a whore. You ain't nineteen, either."

Grabbing his duffel bag, he dug around inside, pulling free a ball of red and black flannel. "Take this," he said, tossing it. Clinging to her towel, she caught it one-handed.

Preacher pointed at the bag of chips. "And eat something."

Half of her, her emotional half, wanted nothing more than to run back to the bathroom. But the logical half of her, the half that knew clothing and food were far more important than her dignity, dug her heels in.

She slid Preacher's shirt around her, his scent engulfing her—a combination of cigarettes, soap, and leather.

Listen," Preacher said. He'd moved to the edge of the bed, his feet on the floor. He ran his fingers idly through his short beard. "You just lost all your shit, and I'm not unsympathetic to that. Why don't you tell me where you're headed? Maybe I can give you a ride there?"

"Why are you helping me?" she blurted out. Nobody had ever been this kind to her before. No one had even been half as kind, not without wanting something in return. And yet he didn't seem to want anything from her.

Preacher's almond-shaped eyes regarded her, an indecipherable expression steeling his striking features. She couldn't read him, couldn't discern what she was seeing inside those dark depths. Men, she'd come to believe, were usually simple creatures, almost always some variation of three distinctly obvious things: angry, tired, or horny. Only this man seemed far more complicated than that.

"I've got nowhere I need to be right now." Simple, direct.

"I grew up on and off the road," he continued with a shrug. "Not too many places I haven't been, know a lot of people just like you.

"Fact, my mom was a grifter." His mouth was twitching again. "She was workin' at a traveling circus when my old man found her."

"The circus?"

Snorting softly, Preacher shook his head. "The damn

circus. Tattooed ladies, strongmen, a two-headed man. Some real freak show kinda shit."

Enthralled, she found herself sitting on the bed. "What did your mom do?"

"She was a fortune teller. Had a goddamn crystal ball and everything, swindling people out of their money in return for some lies about findin' love or makin' it rich." He paused to laugh, a rich baritone rumble that made her feel equal parts warm and uncomfortable.

"She's got a way about her, ya know? The woman could sell a glass of water to a drownin' man. My old man likes to say that's how she got her hooks in him; told him he'd never find another woman as beautiful as her. But he says it's the best fifty cents he ever spent."

"They sound really great," she said quietly. He'd painted a very captivating and colorful picture of his parents, especially his mother, in only a few short sentences.

"Yeah, well, that's a story for another day..." His expression hardening, he trailed off and glanced at the television.

She used the moment to study him. Unbound and nearly dry, his hair was well past his shoulders, thick with loose waves and as dark as his short beard. Dark, oval eyes sat atop a proud nose, just slightly crooked. Smooth, suntanned skin molded tightly over arms bursting with lean muscle. He was so very male and yet... beautiful, too.

"Speakin' of stories..." Preacher faced her. "What's yours?"

Her eyes dropped to her bare feet, and she traced a circle into the carpet with her big toe. "No story."

"Everyone's got a story. How about you start with your name?"

She waited a moment, the space of one breath and two heartbeats—just enough time to decide who she wanted to be today. She glanced up. "Debbie."

Preacher folded his arms over his chest. Head tilted slightly to one side, he stared at her, watching her so intently she had to fight not to squirm. "Debbie what?"

Her mouth opened and instantly closed. She blinked several times quickly. No one had asked her for her last name in… she couldn't even recall the last time someone had asked. Most people she encountered didn't even ask her first name.

"I—uh. Reynolds." She said the first name that she could think of.

"Your name is Debbie Reynolds?" Preacher's expression was a mixture of disbelief and hilarity. "America's sweetheart, huh? Nice to meet ya, Debbie darlin', I'm Fred fuckin' Astaire."

Her stomach dipped down low and her cheeks flamed hot. *Debbie Reynolds?* Her eyes closed briefly.

It had been so long since she'd engaged in a real conversation with another person. Not that she'd ever been any good at talking to people. Thinking about it, she couldn't seem to a recall a time in her life when she hadn't preferred to blend into the background, going unnoticed by all.

"My mom was a fan—she thought she was being clever," she muttered, hating the way the truth tasted on her tongue. Her mother loved the silver screen and worshipped the men and women who brought her favorite films to life. So obsessed, she'd named her daughter after one of her beloved actresses… it just hadn't been Debbie Reynolds.

Her stomach twisted at the memory of her beautiful

mother, feeling both the sharp sting of betrayal and the dull throb of longing, all rolled into one horrible ache.

She blew out a shaky breath. Ugly things often came in beautiful packages, and her mother had been the single loveliest monster she'd ever met.

CHAPTER 8

EBBIE REYNOLDS. THIS CHICK WAS A LIAR, LIAR, PANTS on fire. And a horrible one, at that. Preacher could detect a liar a mile away, could easily spot the extra blinks, extra swallows, and the avoidance of direct eye contact. Although with this girl, none of that had been needed. She was by far the worst liar he'd ever encountered. The worst hooker, too.

She had never spread her legs for money before, that much had been painfully obvious. And would have been comical if she hadn't looked so damn scared.

Amusement aside, he hadn't realized exactly how much her baggy clothing had hidden. She had a nice figure, good-sized tits, a decent curve to her hips, too—even if the rest of her was a little on the thin side. Most eye-catching, though, were the sleek lines of her muscles. Her arms and legs had been toned nicely from what was undoubtedly a hell of a lot of walking.

"Debbie Reynolds," he muttered, snickering.

The girl's—Debbie's—nostrils flared wide. The patches of red that had taken up residence on her cheeks began to spread. Preacher continued to smirk. *Debbie fucking Reynolds.* Hell, if she wanted to lie about something as useless as her name, that was fine with him. In fact, why not play along?

"Our moms have something in common. *The Singing Nun* is her favorite."

Debbie cleared her throat, another sign she was lying. "I prefer *The Rat Race*," she mumbled, refusing to meet his gaze.

"Yeah? Your mom have a thing for Tony Curtis, too?" Preacher might be entertaining Debbie's lies, but he wasn't lying. His mother really did have a thing for Tony Curtis. Recalling how her face would flush at the mere mention of the actor, and his father's irrational jealousy, Preacher laughed outright.

Debbie still wouldn't look at him. Chewing anxiously on her bottom lip, her shuttered gaze was glued to the floor.

Studying her, he fell quiet. He wasn't an idiot—whatever was going on inside her head more than likely wasn't anything good. Having grown up the way he did, knowing a large variety of people, he knew that most of them—the drifters, the grifters, the pavement pounders, the scammers and con-artists, and what was left of those goddamn piece-of-shit hippies—almost always had one thing in common.

They were all running from something. Always with some sad story trailing a million miles behind them.

His own mother was a perfect example. Her mother had died young, and her father had been a drunk who'd spent more time at the local tavern than he had at work. They'd had very little money and almost no food, but it wasn't until he'd started beating on his daughters that Preacher's mother had decided enough was enough. She'd packed a bag for herself and her sister and they'd hit the road together, eventually taking up with the circus.

Even decades later, his mother found it hard to talk about her childhood.

"Where you headed? Anywhere in particular or just driftin'?"

Debbie's eyes lifted; her bottom lip popped out from beneath her teeth. "New York City."

Preacher's brow shot up. "Yeah? You got friends there? Family?"

She shook her head, and he sighed noisily. New York City. The glittering city on the coast, the island that never slept, a city that gave birth to unattainable dreams in the minds of young people all across the nation—and then systematically crushed each and every single one of them.

Preacher would be the first to admit that his home-sweet-home was more cesspool than not. The streets were filthy. Crime was on the rise. Drug use was rampant, as were prostitution and homelessness. Hilariously ironic was that his club was one of those facilitating the flow of drugs into the city, and therefore was partly responsible for the crime that inevitably followed.

"I live there," he said. His revelation caused those unnervingly big eyes of hers to grow even wider.

"Born and raised... and I've seen people comin' and

goin' all my life. I know what you're thinkin'. That a city like New York, with all those people everywhere, all those dark corners to hide in, all those wallets to grab and purses to snatch, that you're going to be raking it in." He paused to shake his head. "You ain't the first street rat to think it, and you ain't gonna be the last. Believe me when I tell you that you're gonna have some serious competition out there. With no family, no friends…"

He trailed off, choosing his next words carefully.

"And you're young… and female… and good lookin'…" Preacher trailed off again, hoping his implication would be clear without having to spell out all the gory details.

"You don't know me," she said quietly, too quietly. There was anger simmering beneath her softly spoken words.

Preacher felt like laughing. He did know her. He knew her type: lost little girls and boys who packed up their bags, said a prayer and hopped on a bus or a train, big city-bound. But once they arrived in the Big Apple, they usually lost everything—including their dignity and sometimes their lives. There was just too much competition in New York, too many crazies, too many whores, too many junkies, all wanting the same damn thing and usually fighting each other for it. Bodies were found every day, John and Jane Does—robbed, raped, beaten to death, stabbed or shot—the possibilities were endless. Too many of those bodies were never claimed, either because no one knew who they were, or no one cared to find out.

Looking at Debbie, lost little thing that she was, he could see exactly how wrong it was going to go. She was going to trust the wrong person, or find herself in a bind nearly identical to the one he'd just helped her out of, and that would be it.

"It's not the paradise everyone seems to think it is. And trust me, I've been everywhere. You're better off out here."

An assortment of emotions passed over Debbie's face—disappointment, embarrassment, anger. Preacher almost felt bad. Almost, because he didn't want to crush her dream; but not quite, because he wanted to help spare her from those who would try to take advantage of her.

Debbie slowly stood, her white-knuckled fist clutching tightly to the front of his flannel shirt. Unblinking, she glared at him. "You don't know me," she repeated coldly.

"I do know you," he said evenly, holding her stare. "I've seen a million just like you. Little girls who don't have a clue. What are you? Sixteen, seventeen? Baby, you are prime real estate for some of these scumbags. I give you a week in the city before one of 'em sinks their hooks into you, has you workin' the corner, droppin' your towel for every Tom, Dick, and Harry."

Unmoving and barely breathing, Debbie's eyes were flashing fire.

"Your best bet," he continued, "is to keep doin' what you're doin'. Sticking to small towns. Less people, less police, less problems. Maybe find yourself a job under the table. Hell, I don't know your story, but maybe goin' home would be—"

Debbie suddenly spun away and hurried across the room. The bathroom door slammed behind her, the force reverberating throughout the walls.

Preacher stared after her, one eyebrow cocked, wondering why women were all so damn irrational. Sighing, he sprawled backward on the bed.

What he'd told Debbie had been for her own benefit, and in response, she'd decided to throw a temper tantrum? And therein lay the problem with the fairer sex—they were always falling victim to their emotions. Acting like the sky was falling when someone was only giving them some damn good advice.

The sitcom on the television let out a peal of laughter. Preacher turned and blinked, barely registering what he was seeing on the screen. Wave after wave of exhaustion swept through him, until his limbs felt heavy and his thoughts grew muddled.

Goddamn, he was tired.

He glanced at the bathroom and frowned. Did he just leave Debbie in there, or... what? Hell, he didn't know, and at the moment, he didn't really care. He hadn't slept in over twenty-four hours and was suddenly struggling to keep his eyes open.

He had just enough sense to grab his duffel bag and stuff it under his pillow before sleep consumed him. If anyone—mainly the overly emotional pickpocket in the bathroom—tried to rob him while he slept, he'd wake right the hell up.

Debbie stared at her reflection in the bathroom mirror, watching as her throat bobbed with each hard swallow. A heavy mass of self-pity churned in the pit of her stomach, expanding, growing, until her abdomen outright ached. She was feeling all sorts of things she wasn't prepared to feel in the face of Preacher's revelations. But she mostly felt foolish. Foolish and deflated. Like a child who'd discovered that

Santa Claus wasn't real before they were emotionally prepared to handle it.

No friends. No family. Little girls who don't have a clue.

His judgment was like a razor blade to her wrists, slashing her open, revealing all her shortcomings.

It wasn't as if she weren't aware of her situation. It had just sounded so pathetic, so pitiful coming from Preacher's mouth—a perfect stranger. She was used to the judgment and condemnation of strangers, but coming from Preacher it had felt worse than usual, and much more personal.

All this time she'd thought she'd been working toward something, and that goal had made this life just a bit more bearable. She'd thought that someday she'd have something again, something resembling an actual life… only to come face to face with the bewildering blow Preacher had just delivered to her. A blow that had caused all her ugly truths to rise to the surface. One by one, combined and crushing, they smacked her in the face. This was who she was—no one, and with nothing—and it was all she would ever be. There was nothing more for her out there, nothing better waiting around the corner. And everything she'd been so desperately seeking were nothing more than the pipe dreams of a foolish girl.

He hadn't even wanted to fuck her, not even for ten dollars. She couldn't even sell herself for ten measly dollars.

She touched a fingertip to her still stinging and now quivering lip, hating, *despising* everything that was looking back at her, wishing the world away. Wishing the floor would open up beneath her and swallow her whole, taking her far away from here. To the ends of the Earth, to heaven or hell, anywhere really. It didn't matter as long as it wasn't here.

To make matters even worse, Preacher had suggested she go home.

Home.

Just the thought of it, the mere suggestion—

Debbie's hands balled into fists as she tried to breathe through the outpouring of uninvited memories. One after another, they flashed in her mind—a slideshow of horror.

A flash of a face she'd tried so hard to forget. Black hair. A neatly trimmed mustache. Thick fingers. The glint of a gold wedding band. A crisp, clean shirt, always with the top few buttons undone. An expensive leather belt, the silver buckle gleaming as he pulled it from his pants. The smell of expensive liquor and Cuban cigars on his breath.

The hard press of a hand over her mouth.

The heft of a body over hers.

Unwanted touches, unwanted kisses.

The confusion, the pain, the self-doubt, the desperation, the fear. Oh my God, the constant fear.

And yet her treacherous body had allowed him inside of her, time and time again. No matter how vehemently she'd hadn't wanted it, no matter how hard she'd fought him.

She hated herself for that. But more than anything else, she hated her mother for doing nothing to stop it.

The disappointment. And isolation. And sorrow.

Debbie's skin was quivering, her muscles straining with the effort to keep from smashing her fists into the mirror. She'd spend a thousand nights in the rain, sleeping in the mud, wet and cold, before she'd ever go back there.

She'd rather starve, wither away to nothing.

She'd rather die before she ever went back.

Preacher blinked sleepily. A stream of sunlight warmed his left cheek, and for a moment, all he could see were the dust motes floating up the stream, all the way to the gap in the curtains. His neck ached, his pillow hard and lumpy beneath him. Groaning, he rolled over, away from the light.

He'd been having the most incredible dream—dreaming of homemade lasagna, of Polish sausage, and heavily buttered rye bread. Chocolate cake drenched in frosting. It had been so vivid, he swore he could still smell the sausage grease sizzling in the pan. Jesus, what he wouldn't give for a slice of homemade cake.

His eyelids flickered closed, and he began to drift off again.

His eyes burst open. Cursing under his breath, he pushed at the pillow beneath his head, feeling nothing but hard, unforgiving lumps. He pushed at it again and again, trying to fluff it, until realization suddenly dawned—he was sleeping on his duffel bag.

Sitting up, he surveyed the small motel room through blurry eyes. Where was he? What time was it? And where the hell were his cigarettes?

Recalling Debbie, he glanced to the bathroom, finding the door wide open. The other bed was empty, still made. Had he dreamed her? A quick assessment of his body, revealing the still-tender bruise on his bicep, told him he hadn't.

He needed a drink of water. No, scratch that. Before anything else, he needed a cigarette. His gaze darted to the bedside table—no cigarettes. Narrowing his eyes, he did another survey of the room. *Where the fuck was his jacket?*

Rolling out of bed, he searched the floor. His jacket nowhere to be found, he stormed across the room and flipped the bathroom light on. Empty.

Nostrils flaring widely, he spun around and stared at the room, eyes darting to and fro.

"Son of a bitch," he breathed. She'd taken his jacket, *his leather-fucking-jacket*, and his cigarettes, and—

Eyes wide, he quickly patted down his body and, as he'd expected, found his back pocket empty. She'd taken his jacket, and because he'd forgotten to take his wallet out of his jacket, she'd also gotten his wallet. As luck would have it, his wallet would have never been inside his jacket if she hadn't tried to steal it in the first place.

"You little mother-fuckin'-bitch," he spat, giving himself another once-over. His necklace, a slim gold chain, was still hanging around his neck, and his keys were still clipped to his belt loop.

Fuming, he darted across the room, grabbed his duffel bag, and dumped out the contents. Finding everything accounted for, most importantly the roll of cash he'd stuffed inside a dirty sock, he sank down onto the bed beside his belongings and glared at the wall.

It could have been a lot worse. He still had plenty of money and an extra jacket in his bag. Still, she'd pulled the wool over his eyes. Him, outsmarted by a street rat.

He continued glaring at the wall, his jaw clenched and twitching.

"Females," he muttered, "give 'em an inch, and they take your fuckin' wallet."

CHAPTER 9

DEBBIE PULLED A PINKISH-PEACH TANK TOP OFF ITS hanger and added it to the growing pile in her arms. Moving along, she looked over the shelves in dismay. The store's selection was a far cry from anything she actually needed, and none of it would hold up for very long. But since beggars couldn't afford to be choosers, she grabbed several more items and moved on.

Sweat beaded on her forehead. Grimacing, she swiped her face with the back of her hand, wishing for a cool drink. The hours-long walk in the sun had been arduous. She was overheated and thirsty, and wearing Preacher's heavy leather jacket inside this poorly ventilated building was only making her feel worse. Yet she couldn't take it off; not when the pockets and sleeves were brimming with stolen goods.

This was her second time today venturing off the

highway. The first attempt had been fruitless; she'd only come across a gas station that had had little to offer. When she'd chanced another exit, she'd found a town, and this Five and Dime.

"Did you just climb out of a mud pit?" Blonde and slim, a teenage girl was eyeing her with obvious distaste. Her two companions, a curvy brunette and a boy wearing a letterman's jacket, stood nearby, their faces screwed into ugly sneers.

"Poor, dirty little piggy," the brunette laughed.

Snickering, the boy pushed up his nose and began to snort.

Cheeks burning, Debbie spun away.

"Run away, little piggy!" one of the girls called after her. "Run away!"

While the group howled with laughter, Debbie ducked down the next aisle.

She hated towns for many reasons, but people were the first and foremost. When cities were few and far between, she stuck to the highways and the truck stops and the mom-and-pop shops scattered along the way. Places where people were always coming and going, where she went largely unnoticed.

Having to deal with the occasional judgmental truck stop waitress paled in comparison to the sort of scrutiny she received in towns like this. Typically, the smaller the town was, the worse she was treated.

Plucking a pair of sunglass off a display, she slid them discreetly inside her jacket, latching them onto the torn collar of her T-shirt.

Passing a rack of pretty summer dresses, she reached

out to finger the gauzy material. She used to look like those girls. She used to wear things like this. Better than this, even. Her clothing had always been current, her hair always cut in the latest style, her nails manicured. On the outside, Debbie had looked perfect, pristine. Her mother had insisted upon it because, in her mother's mind, appearance was everything.

Debbie released the dress with an angry sneer. Fuck those girls. And fuck her mother, too.

Her arms full, Debbie started toward the front of the store, had nearly reached the counter when the front door opened with a groan. Debbie halted, her eyes going wide. Tall and broad shouldered, a police officer in full uniform stepped inside. Removing his hat, he flashed a friendly smile at the elderly man managing the cash register.

"Afternoon, Wendell!"

A wave. "Mike! Hello! It's a hot one today!"

Debbie backtracked, disappearing down an aisle and behind a bin filled with flip-flops. Her heart pounding, her breath shallow, she quickly ticked through her options. Half of her wanted to simply drop everything and leave, while the other half balked at that idea, knowing it could be quite a while before she found another store.

As it was, she'd been shopping for long enough that up and leaving would look suspicious. She already stuck out like a sore thumb. Filthy, her clothing torn, she was wearing a bulky leather jacket several sizes too big for her, in the summer heat, no less. Once that police officer got an eyeful of her...

She swallowed thickly. Sweat trickled down her forehead. She could suddenly feel every stolen item she'd hidden inside the jacket biting uncomfortably into her skin.

Familiar giggles erupted several aisles over, and Debbie recognized the noise as the group from earlier. Peeking over the top of the display, she found the police officer had paused to speak with them.

Debbie's eyes darted back to the front of the store. What if she could check out before the officer found his way back? The old man behind the counter looked to have one foot in the grave already—she didn't foresee him giving her much trouble. And what the store lacked in width, it certainly made up for in depth. There was a good chance she could cash out and be halfway up the road before the officer was the wiser.

She took precious seconds to mull it over before deciding she didn't have any other options that made sense. Hurrying toward the front of the store, she kept her head down as she placed her items on the counter, and the old man behind it regarded her curiously. Pushing his thickly framed glasses up his nose, he folded his arms over his chest.

"You're not from around here." It wasn't a question, therefore Debbie didn't answer.

"You here for the county fair?" he continued. "My grandson's pigs are being featured, you know? He's got the best hogs in the entire county."

Debbie forced herself to make eye contact and attempted a smile.

"Yes," she said, her voice cracking. She cleared her throat. "I'll make sure to check them out."

With a satisfied nod, the old man finally turned his attention to her items. He spent several long minutes poking through her pile, sorting her things, and five more minutes examining each one.

"Best doughnuts in the whole state, too," he said, giving her a gummy smile.

Debbie attempted another smile as a fresh layer of sweat formed on her forehead and dampened her armpits. Could he be any slower? She chanced a glance over her shoulder, searching for the whereabouts of the officer. Her inability to locate him through the numerous bulky displays sent her stomach somersaulting. Panicking, she turned halfway around, and as she did, one of the many items stashed inside her jacket's sleeve slid down her arm, precariously close to the opening at her wrist. Horrified, she cleared her throat and quickly shook her sleeve, sending the stolen item back into hiding.

"$42.95." The old man pushed a brown paper bag, brimming with her new purchases, across the countertop.

Her heart racing in anticipation—*my God she was so hot and uncomfortable*—she pulled her money from her pocket, quickly counted out what she needed, and placed it on the counter. As she slowly withdrew her fingers, she heard a shuffle behind her.

Don't look, don't look, don't look.

The old man slid a nickel across the counter and tapped the coin twice. "Don't forget about the fair," he said.

Feeling like she might vomit, Debbie quickly pocketed her change and grabbed her bag full of purchases. She kept her head down as she turned away, hurrying toward the door.

Outside she didn't dare pause to catch her much-needed breath. Gulping down warm, sticky air, she darted through the small parking lot and jogged across the street. She retraced her steps, stopping once she'd reached the small strip of forest that separated the highway from the town.

Safely ensconced among the trees and tall overgrowth, she quickly shed Preacher's heavy jacket. Sighing in relief as the warm breeze hit her overheated skin, she sunk to the soft ground on her back. Breathing deeply, her heart rate slowing, she blinked up at the clouds, recalling what the old man had said.

Best doughnuts in the state.

Only six dollars and five cents remained from Preacher's wallet—only enough for something to eat.

A county fair would definitely draw a good-sized crowd. Lots of people, lots of wallets.

First things first, though.

Sitting up, she rummaged through her purchases, excited to have a toothbrush again and clean clothes to change into. After swapping outfits and freshening up, Debbie settled herself against a tree, flicked open her newly stolen pocketknife, and began sharpening a pencil.

Then she opened her brand-new composition notebook to the first page and closed her eyes. She'd stared at that photograph so often that every line, every curve, had been engraved into her memory.

Her eyes opened.

The first thing she drew was her father's smile.

CHAPTER 10

STANDING BESIDE HIS MOTORCYCLE PUFFING ON A cigarette, Preacher stared up at the brightly lit entrance to the fairgrounds, wondering how the hell he'd ended up at the Wayne County Fair. He'd jumped off the highway only for cigarettes, fuel, and a bite to eat. Three cups of coffee, a stack of pancakes, two fried eggs, and a bowl full of hash browns later, the sun was setting on the horizon. Which left him with two options—to find a nearby motel or get back on the highway and ride through the night.

Of course he'd chosen neither.

His father's voice echoed in his head. *As useless as a glass hammer.*

Yeah, Preacher was feeling pretty useless. Useless seemed to be how he operated lately, utterly clueless and with no direction.

"When in Rome," he muttered. Flicking his cigarette away, he pulled on his denim jacket and joined the stream of people heading inside.

Set up on a large stretch of land typically used for public recreation, the Wayne County Fair was filled with rows of colorful vendor booths with front men loudly hawking their wares, and food stands scenting the air with a hundred different flavors of grease. Decorative lights had been strung from tent top to tent top, brightly countering the black night sky. A carousel, bumper cars, a rickety looking roller coaster, and a Ferris wheel were just a few of the rides the fair's skyline boasted.

Preacher stood in the center of it all, weighing his options. A ways off, a petting zoo had been erected, and past the zoo he could make out a cordoned-off area where stunt men were performing on motorcycles for a cheering crowd. He stepped forward, immediately drawn to the unmistakable roar of hard-working engines, until the farmyard stench had him recoiling.

Mud and manure didn't smell much better than a New York City alleyway, yet Preacher preferred the devil he knew. The open road made for a good mistress, but the city held his heart. If it didn't smell like exhaust and someone wasn't trying to steal it, Preacher wouldn't be staying long.

Forgoing the trek through the farm animals, he headed for the vendors instead.

Walking idly through the aisles, browsing without actually seeing any of it, Preacher lit cigarette after cigarette, content to just soak up the atmosphere. Every now and then a pair of nicely tanned legs or a smooth, bare midriff would catch his eye, but nothing that warranted more than a brief, appreciative glance.

At a food booth, Preacher paused to order a burger. Leaning against the makeshift counter, waiting for his order, he surveyed the crowd. It had been a while since he'd been surrounded by so many people at once, the hum of too many voices. In a way, it reminded him of home.

His languid stare snagged on a passing pair of bare legs, sleek and muscular, and then on a familiar scrap of leather tied around the waist above. He blinked and his eyes widened. That was *his jacket*—he'd recognize that jacket in the middle of a snowstorm, blindfolded. And wearing it was most definitely *Debbie Reynolds*—those gorgeous legs were proof enough. A crisp new bag hung from her back; her clothing was clean, also new. His eyes narrowed, knowing he'd paid for all of it.

"Son of a bitch," he muttered, pushing away from the counter. Forgetting his food, he hurried after her.

He entertained the idea of grabbing her from behind, yanking her between vendors, and demanding that she return his things. Only as he drew closer, his anger began to wane.

She was working. And Debbie "*Liar, Liar, Pants on Fire*" Reynolds was quite a sight to behold.

Not wanting to draw attention to himself, Preacher slowed his gait, allowing more space to build between them.

It only took a few moments of observing her to identify her preferred marks—young couples with children. She'd wait until the parents were distracted by their kids, then strike and quickly slip away.

She made the act seem effortless, though Preacher knew otherwise. It took quite a bit of skill to lift something off the body of another without them noticing *anything*. But Debbie was pulling it off. No one who wasn't actively looking at her, studying her every movement as Preacher was, would be the wiser.

She was so damn good at what she did, watching her in action felt like live entertainment.

If he hadn't been accustomed to watching his back for even the smallest of threats, she would have gotten the drop on him back at the truck stop. He never would have noticed her; his wallet would have simply vanished, leaving him wondering what the hell had happened to it.

He continued after her, even as she wandered into the petting zoo, full of braying mules and bleating goats and stinking to high heaven. Preacher hardly noticed the stench; he was too busy enjoying Debbie, his grin growing with each theft.

Something soft squished beneath his boot, and Preacher glanced down to find his right foot half submerged in mud. When he looked up again, Debbie had disappeared. Cursing, he rushed forward, his eyes darting in every direction, scanning the clusters of people milling about.

He lurched to a stop only minutes later and burst out laughing. Debbie was standing in line for the Ferris wheel. With his jacket tied around her waist, her new clothes clean and fitted, her hair pulled neatly away from her face, she appeared utterly innocuous, every bit an average teenage girl. Not at all like the lying, thieving little minx she really was.

As the line began to move and Debbie ascended the small set of stairs, Preacher moved forward, an impromptu plan forming. He cut several people in line, jumped up the stairs and onto the platform, slapped a ten-dollar bill across the chest of the teenage boy manning the ride, and darted quickly across.

He slid into the swaying cart just as Debbie was sitting down. Her head jerked up, her eyes going wide as he sat down on the bench across from her. She glanced toward the exit, and Preacher swiftly lifted his legs, placing his muddy, booted feet up on the empty seat beside her, effectively caging her in.

"Shit." A breathless declaration of defeat.

The cart lurched, groaned, and then the Ferris wheel began to turn. Like a cat cornered by a bulldog, Debbie scrambled backward, her hackles raised.

And Preacher grinned.

Frozen in the corner of her seat, Debbie gaped at Preacher. The sounds of groaning metal, whirring motors, and shrieking people winked out of existence, leaving behind only the furious rhythm of blood pounding in her ears.

How had he found her here? Had he been following her? Or was this simply an unlucky case of wrong place, wrong time? Debbie swallowed several times, an attempt to calm her racing heart.

"You know," Preacher drawled. Head tipped to one side, arms draped over the back of the cart, he studied her intently. "Debbie don't really suit you. Debbie's a nice girl's name, and you really ain't so nice. You're more of a..." Preacher trailed off.

He snapped his fingers. "Hell on Wheels! That's what I'm gonna call you. Wheels for short!"

Still stunned by his appearance, Debbie only continued

to stare.

"I woulda given you a ride, you know." The humor in Preacher's expression vanished. "Some cash, too. You didn't have to steal my shit." He was frowning at her now, and while Debbie's outward appearance remained frozen, she was shrinking inside.

Although her pride told her she'd owed this man nothing—that in this life everything was up for grabs, no matter how kind you were—her guilt was screaming the opposite. She could feel his heavy leather jacket wrapped around her waist, a weighty reminder of what she'd done.

But it was neither her pride nor her guilt that had her untying his jacket from her waist. It was common sense. Regardless of how she felt, she knew she was no match for this man physically, and in her current situation, dangling from a Ferris wheel, she had nowhere to run.

Pulling the leather from her waist, she leaned forward in her seat and held it out in offering. Preacher eyed her shrewdly a moment before quickly snatching it away. He was patting down his coat when his eyes flashed with surprise.

His booted feet hit the floor with a thud, sending the cart rocking. He pulled his wallet from the coat's inner pocket. "You didn't toss it."

She shrugged. She'd meant to chuck it; she'd never kept a stolen wallet before, only the cash inside.

"I'm guessin' it's empty?" His smirk returned.

Debbie worried her bottom lip, unsure of what to do should he ask for his money back. His money was long gone, though she'd since stolen more than enough to pay him back.

But he never asked for it. He only continued to watch her with an infuriating all-knowing look on his obnoxiously handsome face, leaving her feeling as if he could see straight through her.

He didn't look away until their cart came to a rocking stop.

They both turned, peering out over the fairgrounds. They were nearly on top of the wheel, giving them a spectacular view of everything below. Debbie could see the entirety of the fair and beyond, patches of forest and quaint little neighborhoods. Streets lined with glittering street lamps and rows of homes, their lit windows letting off a soft golden glow.

Debbie's chest expanded, drinking in the sweet air. The higher she was, the more untouchable she felt. Nothing could reach her up here. She was a goddess among men. As opposed to what she really was. A speck of mortal nothing. A thing to use. Forsaken.

When the Ferris wheel began to move again, she turned back to Preacher. He'd since traded his denim jacket for his leather and was currently transferring the contents of his pockets. Balling up the faded blue denim, he tossed it onto Debbie's lap without warning.

Startled, she only half caught it and glanced up at Preacher, puzzled.

"Keep it," he said, nodding at the jacket in her clutches.

She stared at him, a hundred questions burning on the tip of her tongue. Why was he still helping her? Especially after what she'd done?

"Are you sure?" Unable to look him in the eye, she posed the question to the stretch of starlit sky over his shoulder.

"You need it more than me."

Debbie's attack of conscience intensified. No one, literally no one, had ever been this kind to her. Her guilt flamed hot once again, Preacher's continued generosity making her petty thievery feel a thousand times worse than ever before.

"I'm sorry," she blurted suddenly, finally facing him. "For, um, taking your stuff, and—"

Preacher laughed outright. "Liar." He laughed again, shaking his head.

Cheeks heating, Debbie clamped her mouth shut. Her guilt evaporated, replaced by indignant embarrassment. If she didn't need his jacket so badly, she would have thrown it in his laughing face.

If Preacher noticed her shift in mood, he didn't appear bothered by it. Still smirking, he placed his elbows on his knees and leaned forward. "Speakin' of. How'd a girl like you get so good at pickin' pockets?"

"A girl like me?" she bit out.

He shrugged. "You aren't a typical street rat. For starters, you got good teeth. And you're smart, too." He tapped two fingers against his temple. "Pretty easy to tell the difference between someone who's been to school and someone who hasn't. So I'm curious how a girl like you ended up so slick. I'm guessin' someone showed you the ropes?"

She wanted to hate him for figuring her out so perfectly. For knowing so much about her without knowing her at all. For being an all-knowing arrogant ass whose overly confident smirk was grating on her nerves. For laughing at her apology.

But for all her irritation, there was an odd sort of warmth blossoming inside of her. Preacher had seen straight through her. Through the grease and the dirt, through her torn, dingy clothing. Through the lies she'd told him.

No one, not one single soul, had ever done that before.

Debbie took a breath. "Sunshine. Her name was Sunshine."

Early on in her travels, Debbie had found herself stuck in Nashville, Tennessee. Out of money and without a plan, she'd spent most nights sleeping along the Cumberland River under a bridge, and most days rummaging through city garbage cans for something to eat. Out of options, she'd been trying her hand at panhandling on the Boulevard, typically with very little luck, when she'd happened upon Sunshine.

Tall and slim, her hair the color of ripe wheat, her skin glowing a tawny gold, a young woman had expertly strummed her guitar, crooning to a crowd of people. Debbie had stopped to listen, partially transfixed by the haunting quality of her voice, but mostly jealous of the ever-growing pile of money being tossed into her guitar case.

Hours passed, the crowd dispersed, and still Debbie remained—she'd had nowhere else to go. She'd watched the woman pack up her guitar and get ready to leave. But instead, she'd turned to Debbie and smiled.

"Ride's over."

Startled, Debbie blinked at the pimply-faced teenager standing outside their cart. Mouth downturned, eyes glassy, he stared blankly back at her.

"Ride's over," he repeated, deadpan. "You two have to get out."

"Here, kid," Preacher said, handing the teen a folded bill. "Buy yourself a personality. We're stayin' on."

Turning back to Debbie, Preacher folded his arms over his chest and quirked a brow. "You were sayin'?"

Debbie looked at her lap, where she was still clutching Preacher's denim jacket. The butterfly ring on her index finger—a gift from Sunshine—glinted in the moonlight. As she often did, she began to twist the silver band around her finger. "She taught me everything I know."

Sunshine had been born on a commune, the unclaimed result of her mother's many bed partners. She'd run away at thirteen for reasons she'd never disclosed to Debbie. By her twenties Sunshine had learned more than a few tricks for surviving on the road, pickpocketing being one of them. Surprisingly enough, Debbie had excelled at it.

Still twisting her ring, Debbie took a breath and met Preacher's gaze. "And then one day she was gone."

"She ditch you?"

Debbie nodded. Those few weeks had been the happiest of her life. She'd thought she'd found a companion, someone to share the burden of her lifestyle with. She'd thought her bad luck had finally taken a turn for the better.

She'd thought she'd found a true friend.

Finding her suddenly gone one morning, Debbie had broken down in tears. And she hadn't cried since.

"It wasn't anything you did." Shaking his head, Preacher's gaze wandered away.

"Known chicks just like Sunshine. Guys, too. They got the bug. Gotta keep movin', you know? Can't sit still, can't stay in one place too long. Bet my ass she stayed longer than she would have if she hadn't met you. And I'm guessing she left while you were sleepin' 'cause she didn't want to have to say goodbye."

"It's easier for 'em that way. Somethin' is broken up there, in there." He tapped a finger to his temple and then over his heart. "They can't face staying, and they can't face leaving either."

Debbie took a moment to consider his words. It made sense, more sense than anything else. And for the first time since Sunshine had left her, she felt maybe not quite so miserable about it.

"Was your mom—is your mom like that? Like Sunshine?"

"Nah. She was just makin' do. Just getting by until she found somethin' better, somethin' permanent… like you." His eyes settled on Debbie, those dark depths quickly sharpening.

As uncomfortable as she was in the face of his scrutiny, Debbie held his gaze, even as her stomach twisted anxiously. This was the most she'd spoken to another person in quite some time, and by far the most truth she'd divulged in twice as long. She also assumed Preacher had already guessed as much, given how obnoxiously perceptive he was.

And then he smiled. Not a smirk. Not a laugh. A generous curve to his mouth that lifted his cheeks, reaching all the way to his eyes. In that instant, he appeared younger than he looked. Sweet, even. And achingly handsome.

Debbie's lips twitched. The unease in her stomach began to ebb. Instead of clammy, she felt warm—a sort of comforting warmth, a sensation that was completely foreign to her.

"Anyway," she mumbled. She glanced out across the fair. They had nearly reached the top again, and the view was no less beautiful than before.

"Stealing is easy when you're practically invisible.

Hardly anyone even notices me." Unlike Sunshine, whose beauty and style had all but commanded attention, Debbie was plain in comparison.

Even before she'd set out on her own, she'd gone virtually unnoticed by her peers. She'd been the girl in the background, finding comfort in the shadows. And to her mother, she'd been only an accessory—a pair of polished pearl earrings worn only to complement the much larger, much more extravagant necklace.

Unfortunately the only person who had noticed her had been a monster.

"I noticed you."

Debbie's eyes darted back inside the cart, colliding with Preacher's.

I noticed you.

Those three words took flight, finding and nudging awake long hidden places inside of her.

Throat bobbing, she turned away. Why would someone who had spent her entire life hiding suddenly find being noticed so incredibly appealing? She didn't like being noticed. She worked hard to ensure she went unnoticed.

So what had changed so suddenly?

Unable to stop herself, Debbie's gaze shifted back to Preacher.

It was Preacher. She liked being noticed by Preacher.

CHAPTER 11

PREACHER FOLLOWED DEBBIE DOWN THE PLATFORM, observing the rigid line of her shoulders, the restless way she was glancing around as if she couldn't get away from him fast enough. Since telling him about Sunshine, she seemed suddenly agitated and twice as uncomfortable.

He didn't much like the way he was feeling, either.

Here he was, angry at the hand life had dealt him, pissing and moaning over his strained relationship with his father, wandering aimlessly without a clue—all because he could. He had more than enough money and more where that came from. And whenever he got sick and tired of wandering aimlessly? He had a home waiting for him. A family. Friends. The whole nine yards.

And here was this girl. With nothing. Day after day, fighting for her next meal, braving the weather, robbing truckers, and risking everything just to reach a city that, more likely than not, was going to eat her alive.

Yeah, he felt like a first-class asshole.

Debbie spun around suddenly, forcing Preacher to a lurching stop. He nearly reached out to grab her to avoid falling straight into her.

"I'm really sorry for taking your stuff," she rushed to say. She peered up at him through thick lashes. Her expression twisted. "I was just, um... I was..."

Having steadied himself, Preacher lifted his hand, signaling her to stop. "I get it. I ain't even mad."

He wasn't mad—not anymore. And he did get it. Her story had struck a chord in him. If anything, he wanted to do more for her. An old denim jacket and the paltry sum she'd taken from his wallet didn't seem like nearly enough.

"So, uh, I'm gonna go... thank you...um, for everything." Debbie tucked her thumbs beneath the straps of her backpack and offered him a tiny smile. He watched, somewhat transfixed, as a dimple appeared high on her left cheek.

She really was a good-looking girl, and sweet, too... when she wasn't stealing his shit.

Hesitantly she turned away.

Jamming his hands in his pockets, Preacher watched her go, her steps heavy and slow. Something continued to niggle at him; he really wished he could have done more. Offered her a hot meal or a ride. Something. Anything.

Pulling his hands from his pockets, Preacher stepped forward. He was lifting his arm, about to call out to Debbie, when a figure stepped in front of him.

"Demon." The tone was gruff, commanding. Downright cold.

Stiffening, Preacher dropped his arm to his side and met the gaze of the man blocking his path.

Dark hair, dark eyes, a thick mustache, he wore a denim vest covered in patches, the most noteworthy of which were the PRESIDENT patch above his left breast and the 1% patch above that signified him as a one-percenter—an outlaw.

99% of motorcycle clubs consisted of men who enjoyed riding, or whose hobbies included chopping bikes. Riding was more of a pastime for them, not a way of life. Then there were the criminal clubs; a small percentage of men who embraced a very different sort of life and set of rules.

Men like Preacher. And whoever the hell this guy was.

A Caucasian male of average height and average weight, he was older than Preacher by at least ten years. He wore no name patch, and there was nothing particularly remarkable about him, no distinct features that identified him. And although Preacher was younger, taller, and fitter, he didn't doubt the man was dangerous—not for a single second. You didn't become the leader of a group of outlaws without good reason.

Most outlaw clubs were a volatile bunch on a good day, and with Preacher being who he was—the vice president of one of the more well-known and infinitely more lucrative criminal clubs—his elevated position in the Silver Demons earned him respect from other clubs. But there were always those few that preferred the mayhem of the life over the business side of it, and it was those clubs that Preacher knew to watch out for. They would take him on for pure sport.

A glance over his shoulder and a quick look around

showed Preacher what he feared—several men rapidly approaching, all wearing identical denim vests.

Preacher's hands flexed into fists. They were boxing him in.

"You don't remember me, do ya?"

Preacher met the president's smug expression with a bored look.

"Should I?" His tone lazy and uninterested, Preacher lifted a single, speculative brow. If he remembered anything The Judge had attempted pounding into him, it was that you never showed weakness to your enemy. Preacher might not have the upper hand here, but you wouldn't think it to look at him.

A sly smile split the president's lips. "Trick," he called out, gesturing with his hand. A denim-clad man jogged forward, pulling something dark from inside his vest. Recognizing his leather cut, Preacher's nostrils flared wide. What was with today and everyone stealing his shit? It should be in the Bible, an eleventh commandment: thou shalt not take another man's leather.

"You always leave this just lyin' around?" The President flashed him a smile twice as shrewd as his last.

Preacher regarded him coolly. He hadn't left anything *just lyin' around*. His club cut had been inside his duffel bag, and his duffel bag had been tied to his handlebars with a sequence of complicated stopper knots.

But instead of tearing his vest away from the asshole who'd dared touch his shit, Preacher took a breath. He wasn't getting out of this with his fists or the lone blade in his boot. This, *whatever this was*, was going to require his wits.

The president continued to study him. "Name's Rocky. Was at your clubhouse in the city 'bout four, maybe five years back. Knocked a few back with you and your boys. Wouldn't expect you to remember, though. You'd just gotten VP, barely outta diapers back then. Didn't have that pathetic excuse for a beard you got now."

Rocky paused and laughed, though he didn't appear any more or less amused than he'd been moments ago. It was all an act. Every smile, every frown, every move this man made was a well thought-out, calculated plan. Nothing he did was without purpose.

Preacher stayed silent, waiting for Rocky to get all his bullshit mocking and posturing out of the way and get to the point. He didn't bother trying to recall when exactly the man had been to his clubhouse. The Silver Demons had entertained a lot of people over the years. Preacher could hardly be expected to keep track of them all.

"Preacher?"

Everyone turned toward the interruption. Preacher's eyes widened when he found Debbie approaching, and growing wider still when one of Rocky's men moved into position behind her. Heavily muscled, eyes vacant, he looked to be all brawn and very little brain.

She was aware of the man flanking her, but she kept her eyes on Preacher—big eyes full of questions and, *oh hell*, full of concern too. He silently cursed her, taking back every nice thing he'd thought about her. She was a stupid girl, walking straight into quicksand thinking it was the beach.

Another man moved to stand in front of Debbie, and like vultures surrounding their prey, both men began to circle her. The shift in positions allowed Preacher a glimpse at the backs of their vests. The top rocker identified them as Road Warriors, and below it was a center patch—a crude and childish rendition of a Viking warrior holding a spiked club. A bottom rocker proclaiming their location was noticeably absent.

Preacher knew them—or rather, he knew of them. The original Road Warriors had been based out of Virginia, but in recent years, they'd become more of a roving band of gypsies. They had no real business dealings unless you considered creating chaos a business. They were usually found working security at bars and concerts, but they were best known for their parties. There was a running joke about their club: no man left a Road Warrior party without getting knocked out, and no woman left without getting knocked up.

"You my dinner, sweetheart?" One of the men circling Debbie paused in front of her, laughing.

Debbie quickly sidestepped him only to be blocked by the second man. "She ain't big enough to be dinner," he mocked. Grabbing his crotch, he sneered at her. "This here's what you fuck *before you fuck*."

Debbie looked pleadingly to Preacher, and Preacher whirled on Rocky, all pretense gone. "Call your dogs off, Rocky," he growled. "Right the fuck now."

Rocky glanced between Preacher and Debbie, the calculating gleam in his eyes glowing brighter. He shrugged. "They gotta blow off steam somehow. If not..." Another shrug. "They end up turnin' on one another."

Struggling for calm, Preacher took a step toward Rocky, enough of a movement to command the attention of every Road Warrior present. Everyone stilled; all eyes shot to Preacher.

"Give. Her. To. Me." Preacher's quietly spoken words were punctuated with rage.

Rocky studied Preacher. If he was bothered by Preacher's proximity, he didn't show it. "Or what?"

"Or whatever the fuck you want, you won't be gettin' it."

"You think you're in any position to make demands?"

Preacher bared his teeth and nearly snarled. "Yeah, I do. We wouldn't be here if you didn't want somethin' from me. And whatever that is, I ain't gonna give it 'til you *give her to me.*"

Though it was slight, hardly noticeable, Preacher glimpsed a flash of anger in Rocky's eyes, a subtle hardening of the man's expression—the first glimpse of the man behind the carefully executed façade.

Composed once again, Rocky turned a cunning smile on his men and gestured. Grumbling, they moved reluctantly, just barely clearing a pathway from Debbie to Preacher. She wasted no time in hurrying forward. When she was standing beside him, her big brown eyes full of apologies, Preacher turned his focus back to Rocky.

"Now what?" he asked flatly.

"We've got a camp nearby. Some of my boys work the stunt circuit. Gotta make a livin' somehow. Why don't you and your friend here join us for a beer?" Rocky paused, his eyes on Debbie. Stroking his jaw, he ran his gaze up and down her body, a slow, deliberate grin spreading across his face.

Preacher recognized the threat for what it was. Either he cooperated, or Debbie became collateral damage.

His protective instincts flaring, Preacher wrapped his

arm around Debbie's shoulders, hauling her up against him. He looked to Rocky then, daring the man to try something.

Rocky only continued to smile.

Teeth clenched, Preacher tightened his grip on Debbie. "Lead the way."

Tucked neatly against Preacher's side, Debbie studied her surroundings. She was memorizing the exact route they were taking as the Road Warriors herded them through the fairgrounds.

She shouldn't have looked back. And she definitely shouldn't have interfered. She'd only wanted to see if Preacher had been watching her walk away.

At first glance, she'd thought Preacher had known them but had quickly gathered that the meeting wasn't a friendly one. There were too many of them, she'd realized as they'd circled around him, fists clenched, their eager eyes and twisted smirks promising violence. And only one of him.

She wasn't so foolish as to think she could take on a single one, let alone an entire gang, but she'd felt she had to do something. After all, Preacher had done the same for her.

Their group entered a roped-off area between two tents marked EMPLOYEES ONLY and were greeted with a bustle of activity. Men in stained aprons hurried to and fro. A woman wearing a pink cowboy hat and matching boots strode by, leading a pair of horses. A group of clowns in full costume sat smoking atop a stack of wooden crates.

Further back sat a stretch of land peppered with trailers and tents, small bonfires scattered throughout. It was quieter here, the air was cooler, the smells not quite so overwhelming. Somewhere a Tom Jones song was playing.

"Follow my lead," Preacher growled softly, squeezing her arm.

Debbie took a breath and glanced up, her gaze tracing the lines of worry creasing his forehead and the grim set of his mouth. Preacher didn't seem like the type to scare easily, and if he was worried… Debbie swallowed back a wave of fear.

Their group stopped at the far end of the clearing, at a campsite that grazed the forest line.

There was no trailer, no tents, no table and chairs. Only several sleeping rolls, a pile of backpacks, and a couple dozen empty beer bottles scattered around a low-lit bonfire. Two women sat shoulder to shoulder near the fire, their heads bent over a magazine, while a third stood nearby, a beer in her hand, a cigarette dangling from between her lips. All around them tall, thick trees loomed, shrouding them in near blackness.

"You can give her to the girls." Rocky jerked his chin to the fire before giving Debbie another long look, imbued with insinuation. A look that left her feeling naked and exposed.

She stared back at him, a chill sliding up her spine, half expecting to see fangs protruding from his mouth. She knew this sort of look all too well. She'd run from a look just like it. She was still running from it.

"Pretty little thing," Rocky murmured. Seconds passed, feeling more like minutes the longer he watched her. Expert, unwavering focus shone in his dark gaze. Wave after wave of anxiety rolled through her. This was not a man you wanted focused on you.

"Nobody touches her," Preacher said quietly, but not without an edge. Though low, his tone was cold, hard steel, mirroring the stiff, unyielding contours of his body.

Debbie glanced up to find Preacher's face had darkened, his expression thunderous as he stared at Rocky, then he turned slowly, meeting the eyes of each and every Road Warrior. Gone was the kindhearted man who'd saved her last night. Gone was the forgiving man who'd joined her on the Ferris wheel.

Her gaze ricocheted between Preacher and Rocky. There were similarities, not in appearance, but in demeanor. In the way they held themselves, in the authority exuding from both of them.

And despite Preacher not giving her the same uneasy feeling Rocky did, she couldn't help but think these men were cut from the same cloth.

An oily smile formed beneath Rocky's thick mustache. "She's yours then?" he asked, his awful eyes once again on Debbie.

Preacher didn't hesitate. "She's mine. Lay a hand on her and we've got a problem. You want a problem with the Demons, Rocky?"

Though it hadn't yet reached his eyes, Rocky's smile remained. "You've got my word then," he said, and shrugged. "No one touches her."

Debbie's eyes were still on Rocky when Preacher suddenly shifted her in his arms, bringing her flush against his front. One of his hands moved to cup the back of her head while the other gripped her lower back. Their eyes collided, the look on his face indecipherable when suddenly his hand on her back dropped, squeezing her butt. Debbie startled, and Preacher's head bent, his mouth covering hers. His tongue swept past her parted lips like a tidal wave, swiftly drowning her squeak of surprise.

Follow my lead. Preacher's words echoed in her thoughts and shock turned soon to understanding.

Still… nothing could have prepared her for… *this kiss.*

While Preacher's mouth was insistent, he wasn't at all sloppy. He kissed her with a cool precision that made Debbie think he probably kissed quite often. Then faster, harder, and with less finesse, his tongue plunged roughly into her mouth, the coarse hairs in his short beard scraping softly against her cheeks and chin.

Debbie's stomach plummeted to her feet as utterly unfamiliar sensations assaulted her. Not terrible, not at all terrible, but definitely foreign. Soft, warm sensations. But also hectic and fraying around the edges—a quickly expanding ball of electricity.

She was kissing him back now, meeting him stroke for stroke. Her thoughts muddied, her other senses sharpened, she became overly aware of every single place their bodies were touching, and all the places they weren't.

And then just as soon as it had begun, it was over.

Breathing hard, Debbie blinked up at Preacher. He was staring past her, his expression hewn from stone. Realizing she was gripping his arms, she quickly released him.

"Wait for me over there." His tone hard, Preacher pointed to the campfire. He still hadn't looked at her. Why wasn't he looking at her? He was unfazed, not even a little out of breath. It was as if nothing had happened, especially nothing as earth shattering as that kiss had been.

Ignoring the leering Road Warriors, Debbie stepped

away and hurried across the campsite.

Approaching the bonfire she slowed, hesitating as one of the women approached her, hostile energy rolling off her slim frame in thick waves. Frizzy blonde curls, bleached one too many times, framed an angular face with sharp, masculine features.

"So you're what a Demon bitch looks like, huh?" The blonde smirked, long, downturned lines highlighted her too-thin lips. "Can't say I'm impressed." Her voice matched her face—both were worn and cracking.

"Sorry, what?"

She made a face, an ugly mix of irritation and disdain. "You slow or somethin'? Your old man is VP of the Silver Demons, ain't he?"

Eyes narrowed, Debbie's gaze shot to Preacher. Surrounded by Road Warriors, only a sliver of his profile was visible. She looked to Rocky, specifically to the denim vest he was wearing, and then again at Preacher. She hadn't been wrong when she'd marked their similarities.

"Yeah, sorry," Debbie muttered, turning back to the blonde. "It's been a long day."

The woman took her time dragging her contemptuous gaze up and down Debbie's body. "Not sure what he sees in you, honey. Ain't got much in the looks department, and you bein' young ain't gonna sell ya forever."

Debbie blinked. Young? Bitterness squeezed her insides. She wasn't young anymore. She certainly didn't feel young. She'd never get to do the things that other people her age did. She wouldn't be attending her prom, she wouldn't be graduating from high school or applying to colleges. Young, old, and in between, none of it applied to her anymore. She wasn't anything anymore. She was little more than a ghost who slipped into the land of the living only long enough to scrounge for scraps before being shooed away, forced back to the edge of society. Time didn't matter. Age didn't matter. There was just right here, right now, your wits, and a bit of luck.

Debbie's eyes slid to Preacher. And the kindness of strangers, too.

"Lawd, Sissy, give it a rest, will ya?" A pair of dark eyes peeked out from beneath a thick fringe of inky black bangs. A young woman climbed to her feet, gracefully unfolding a tall, slim body.

Her fair skin shone white beneath her fall of sleek black hair, and as she stepped forward and smiled, Debbie guessed she wasn't much older than herself.

"Ignore Sissy." She gave a flippant wave of her hand. "She's just jealous. She's fucked her way around the country trying to find an in with any club that'll take her. She finally managed to nail down Duke over there, only 'cause poor Duke is too dumb to know any better."

Air whistled through Sissy's clenched teeth. "Fuck you, bitch!" she seethed.

"I'm Angela," the girl continued, unbothered by Sissy's outburst. "But my friends call me Angel." Smirking, Angel winked at Sissy. "And I'm Rocky's girl."

"You're Rocky's whore," Sissy shot back.

Debbie glanced warily between the two. Angel didn't seem at all upset by Sissy's jibe; if anything she appeared amused. Sissy, however, glared at Angel, fury sparking in her eyes. Several tense seconds passed before Sissy huffed loudly and whirled away.

Watching her storm off, Angel threw her head back and laughed loudly, as if she didn't have a care in the world.

"You've already met Sissy." Angel turned her attention to the woman still buried behind a magazine. "And this is Fat Becky."

Fat Becky, an average-sized woman whose only visible feature behind the magazine was a head of messy brown hair, grunted and lifted a hand in greeting.

Debbie began to introduce herself and suddenly stopped short. Preacher, Rocky, Duke, Angel… Fat Becky? Was it some sort of motorcycle club requirement? Preacher's words—*follow my lead*—echoed in her thoughts again.

"I'm Wheels," she said.

"Wheels?" Angel arched one slim, black brow. "You've got to tell me the story behind that."

Debbie shrugged. "Short for Hell on Wheels."

"Nice," Angel said, looking suitably impressed. "So, how long have you been riding with him?"

Debbie took precious seconds to wonder what the right answer would be.

"I'm not sure," she finally said, mimicking Angel's carefree, rather flippant tone. "Never really kept track of stuff like that, you know?"

Head bobbing in agreement, Angel reclaimed her seat next to Becky. Holding up a gleaming silver cigarette case, she patted the ground beside her. "Come sit. Smoke with me." She beckoned Debbie with the case.

Debbie spared another glance at Preacher, still surrounded by Road Warriors, before reluctantly taking a seat.

"You're lucky, you know? Your old man is a real fox." Angel's eyes were on Preacher as she placed a joint between her lips and lit it. "Rocky ain't too easy on the eyes, but he knows how to get down." She shivered excitedly. "And I'll take a big Johnson over a pretty face any day."

Becky glanced up, her freckled face and light blue eyes illuminated by firelight. "Too thin," she said dryly, and disappeared back behind the magazine.

Debbie took the joint Angel offered her, distractedly puffing on it while her gaze turned back to Preacher. She'd felt the hard slabs of muscle layering his abdomen when seated on the back of his bike, her arms wrapped around his middle. She'd seen the twin bulges of his biceps. Even now, surrounded by several big, burly men, Preacher looked like he could hold his own.

Debbie's eyes narrowed with indignation. Fat Becky was wrong.

He was long and lean, yes, but Preacher definitely wasn't thin.

CHAPTER 12

ROCKY UNFOLDED HIS ARMS, OPENING THEM WIDE. "You see? I'm not unreasonable. All I'm askin' for is a piece of the damn pie. What your old man refused to give me."

The tension had dissipated. The rigid posture and threatening expressions from earlier had been replaced with relaxed shoulders and a surprisingly expectant expression.

The Road Warriors were sick of being gypsies. They wanted to stop wandering endlessly and put down some roots. Only roots required money, and money required work. And if nothing else, the Silver Demons excelled at work.

Nevertheless, Rocky approaching Preacher was pointless. The Judge didn't employ or work alongside men like Rocky. He already knew what his father would say. That you couldn't trust the Road Warriors—that they were nothing more than homeless thugs. That there had to be honor among thieves, or your house of cards was going to come crashing down around you.

It didn't matter that The Judge's way of thinking was hypocritical and self-serving; he would never change. He wasn't just set in his ways, he was half blinded by his own superiority complex and firmly entrenched in his unwavering, half-mad convictions. In layman's terms, a working relationship with the Road Warriors *was never gonna happen.*

Even as vice president, Preacher held very little sway over the wheelings and dealings of the Silver Demons' business machinations. It was The Judge, and only The Judge, who opened and closed those doors. Everyone else only offered suggestions or followed orders.

But Rocky didn't need to know any of that, and what Rocky didn't know, Preacher had used to his benefit. He'd promised to put in a good word with The Judge, assuring Rocky he'd detail the benefits of a working relationship between the Silver Demons and the Road Warriors.

The latter hadn't been a ruse. Rocky had an impressive network of men, nomads who were scattered all over, ready to ride or work at a moment's notice. Only an idiot wouldn't realize the benefits of having eyes and ears across the nation.

Of course, if it were up to Preacher, the Road Warriors would have to agree to strip their colors and patch in as Silver Demons.

Preacher practically salivated at the thought of a Silver Demons clubhouse in all fifty states and the ability to control distribution not only along the east coast but nationwide. If done right, bringing the Road Warriors into the fold could create a highly profitable business relationship.

Hell, Preacher envisioned The Judge's business becoming a veritable empire.

Rocky motioned to Trick—the man holding Preacher's cut and Preacher stepped forward and snatched it from him. Shrugging it on over his jacket, the leather molded comfortably to his body like a second skin.

Rocky gestured to the bonfire. "Knock a few back with me?"

Preacher reluctantly agreed. No matter how badly he wanted to leave, refusing a drink with Rocky would be bad form—the equivalent of spitting in the man's face.

As they made their way toward the bonfire, Preacher's eyes were on Debbie. She was slumped forward, her hair hiding her face, fiddling with something on the ground in front of her. Frowning, he picked up his pace.

"Hey." He bent down and tapped her knee. "You okay?"

Her head lifted slowly, her long hair parting to reveal a pair of bloodshot, unfocused eyes.

Her mouth stretched into a wide smile.

"Hi," she whispered, then giggled.

He grinned at her. "Debbie Reynolds, *you are baked.*"

"Yes," she whispered, shrugging. "You said to follow your lead."

"You wanna smoke? It's my own blend." The proud declaration came from a raven-haired girl shaking a silver cigarette case at Preacher. Flicking the case open, she revealed several neatly rolled joints.

Holding up a hand, Preacher shook his head. Things might seem amicable at the moment, but the Road Warriors had still coerced him into a meeting. A head full of drugs was the last thing he needed while among men he didn't trust.

The girl glanced at Debbie. "Wheels seemed to like it."

Brows up, Preacher looked to Debbie, who quickly turned away. Her cheeks had gone pink and her bottom lip had disappeared beneath her teeth.

Chuckling, he sat down beside her and nudged her shoulder with his. "*Wheels*, huh?" he whispered, and Debbie ducked her head, burying her face in her hands.

"We've got whiskey and moonshine." Rocky stepped forward, a bottle in each hand. He shook one of them. "Right outta the backwoods of West Virginia."

Knowing better than to put himself in a moonshine coma, Preacher gestured for the whiskey.

"Turn some music on!" someone demanded. Someone else complied, and a country song filled the space between idle chatter.

Some of the Road Warriors headed back to the fair while others found seats around the fire. One Road Warrior cozied up beside a woman with her face buried in a magazine. Another, gripping a large hunting knife, was sharpening the blade on a nearby rock. Several yards away Rocky had tugged the black-haired girl onto his lap, and his hands were all over her.

Preacher took a swig of whiskey, grimacing at the bitter taste.

"So you're the vice president of a motorcycle club?"

Out of the corner of his eye, Preacher noticed Debbie studying his leather cut. He grimaced through another swallow of whiskey before answering. "That's what they tell me."

"What does the vice president of a motorcycle club do?"

"Whatever the president tells him to do."

"What does the president tell you to do?"

"You should have left," he said, veering her away from questions he couldn't answer.

Debbie blinked. Confusion flickered across her features as she glanced around the campsite. "But… I thought I was supposed to wait here for you?"

"I'm talkin' about earlier. You shouldn't have gotten involved."

"I thought they were going to hurt you," she whispered. "I only wanted to help."

As ridiculous as it was—this slip of a girl thinking she could somehow protect him from the Road Warriors—Preacher also found it admirable.

"I took on all those guys at the truck stop. You don't gotta worry about me."

She shook her head. "This was different." Her eyes slid to the Road Warrior sharpening his blade. "*They're different.*"

Preacher paused, unable to dispute her reasoning. The men from the truck stop weren't good men by any stretch of the imagination, but he doubted they were killers. Preacher didn't doubt for a single second that a man like Rocky had a body count.

"I'm blamin' it all on you, you know," he said eventually. Facing the fire, he lifted the whiskey to his mouth. "You're a whole lot of bad luck. Got me slapped with a baseball bat, stole my wallet and my goddamn jacket—"

Before he was able to drink, Debbie grabbed hold of the whiskey bottle, threw her head back, and took a stunningly long swallow. Amused, Preacher watched as she began to sputter and cough.

"Holy shit," she breathed, thrusting the bottle back into his hand. "That was horrible!"

A drop of whiskey slipped down Debbie's chin, and before Preacher could think twice about it, he wiped it away. Her eyes shot to his, and his thoughts took a tire-squealing turn back to earlier—back to their kiss. A claiming kiss he'd given her only to ensure the Road Warriors would keep their hands to themselves.

He hadn't expected her to kiss him back like she had. If anything, he'd expected her to be mostly unreceptive. And she had been… at first. A little shaky, too. But then, out of nowhere, she'd been on fire, kissing him with a wild eagerness he hadn't experienced since he was a teenager. Back when Preacher had been about girls, girls, and more girls. Any girl he could get his hands on, he most definitely put his hands on. He'd been all too eager and therefore messy, lacking in the skill and finesse that would come later, with time and experience.

He'd forgotten what that felt like. To be so enthusiastic about something or someone that you temporarily lost yourself and just… *lived in the moment.* Just thinking about kissing Debbie again, experiencing her energy and enthusiasm again, had his dick twitching.

It certainly didn't help that he'd already seen the beautiful body beneath her clothing. Visions of her back at the motel—dropping her towel and offering him sex—suddenly consumed his thoughts.

"Are you going to kiss me again?" Debbie whispered, gazing up at him unabashedly. Eyes shining expectantly, cheeks flushed innocently.

He stared down at her, marveling at the way she could

hide nothing, not one single thing she was thinking or feeling, while also feeling a bit dumbfounded by his reaction to her.

"How old are you?" he asked quietly.

"Seventeen," she said quickly, averting her eyes.

He snorted softly. "Lie."

Her eyes found his again, dark brown and full of frustration.

"It isn't," she insisted. "I'll be seventeen soon. My birthday's in a few weeks... I think." She glanced down at her hands, her fingers ticking a silent countdown.

He stared at her.

Sixteen. Six-fucking-teen. He supposed it could be worse. But still... *sixteen.*

Preacher hadn't been with a woman since he'd left New York City and hadn't given them all that much thought. Yet here he was, suddenly giving all sorts of thoughts to a thieving teenager. *How fitting*, he thought, rolling his eyes. It was just his fucking luck, that the woman to drag him out of his dry spell... wasn't even a woman yet.

And it wasn't just her age that bothered him. He had only to look at her to know that the last thing this girl needed was his hands on her. She needed a warm bed to sleep in, three square meals a day. Someone to look after her.

Preacher gave his head a small shake and started pouring whiskey down his throat.

Yep. It was definitely going to be a long night.

It was the headache that woke her.

Head pounding, mouth uncomfortably dry, Debbie

cracked one eye open. A pile of embers glowed a brilliant orange several feet away, still hot enough that she could feel the heat warming her arms and legs. There were noises— crackling embers, muffled sounds of movement, the low hum of a radio, someone snoring.

Opening both eyes, she peered into the semidarkness, scanning the bodies lying around the fire pit. There was a weight on her back—comforting confirmation that her backpack was still exactly where it was supposed to be. Beneath her cheek was something firm. She blinked several times, finally registering the outstretched leg in front of her, and then stiffened as she realized she was sleeping on someone. Alarmed, she shot upright, wincing as a spot above her left eye began to throb. Grimacing, she clutched her head.

It all came back to her in a confused and cluttered rush. The fair. The Ferris wheel. Preacher. The Road Warriors. The Kiss. Angel. But when had she'd fallen asleep? She couldn't remember anything else.

"Here. This'll help."

Scrambling to her knees, Debbie whirled around. Finding Preacher, she blew out a relieved breath and sank down on her heels.

Eyebrows arched, Preacher shook the whiskey bottle in his hand, and the remaining liquid sloshed back and forth. "For the headache. Hair of the dog."

As she took the bottle, Debbie was startled to realize that Preacher hadn't left her alone with the Road Warriors. He'd remained by her side, watching over her while she'd slept.

"Th-thanks," she whispered and sipped. The liquor burned a hot path down her dry throat, waking her further.

She took a second swallow, and a third, and eventually the sharp pain in her forehead was no more than a dull ache.

"I can't believe I fell asleep..." Catching sight of movement in the distance, Debbie's words fell away.

A short ways off in the grass, her pale skin glowing white in the moonlight, Angel was straddling Rocky, who was mostly hidden by grass and shadows. Debbie could make out his hands, his tanned skin stark against Angel's light, repeatedly brushing up and down the length of her.

Angel suddenly threw her head back, her long mane of hair like a sheet of black silk swaying across her back. Mouth open, lips parted in a soundless moan, her hips began a frantic, furious pace.

Breathy pants filled Debbie's ears. The soft slap of skin on skin. A low groan. A high-pitched whimper that speared through the quiet night.

And Debbie couldn't seem to look away. She'd never seen anything quite like it. So uninhibited. So beautiful and free. It was nothing like the truck stop hookers and their johns—cold, sometimes callous acts between unfeeling strangers.

It was certainly nothing like she'd ever experienced.

Captivated, barely breathing, she bit down hard on her bottom lip. She wanted to grab her notebook and draw them, capturing forever the intensity, the fervor between them.

"Wheels."

Debbie's gaze flicked to Preacher, breath shuddering from her lungs as their eyes met. Spellbound, she recalled their kiss. A hard, hungry kiss. Hungry like the way Angel was fucking Rocky. Hungry like the way Preacher was looking at her now.

Debbie felt her entire body come alive and take notice of this man. The smooth arches of his cheeks. The curve of his mouth. The hard edge of his jaw. The loose strands of hair that had slipped free from his ponytail. The urge to reach out and touch him, run her fingers over his lips, tuck his hair behind his ears, was a commanding presence.

Unused to these feelings, Debbie sucked in a sharp breath, and Preacher's gaze zeroed in on her mouth. Reflexively she licked her lips and watched as his eyes flared. In response, everything inside her grew warmer, softer, and she could suddenly feel her heartbeat in places she didn't realize you could feel a heartbeat.

Preacher suddenly snatched the bottle from her hand and took two consecutive slugs, emptying it. Tossing it aside, he jumped to his feet. The spell holding Debbie captive broke and the warm, butter-soft sensation that had settled low in her belly evaporated instantly.

"You wanna get the hell outta here?" Preacher's tone was low and biting, matching his expression. All traces of hunger had vanished from his expression, and Debbie wondered if she'd imagined it.

"What?"

"Never did like sleepin' in the grass. Gonna find a motel." He shot her a look as hard as his tone. "You promise not to hijack my shit again, you got yourself a bed."

Then he turned on his heel and started walking—a fast-paced, long-legged stride, leaving Debbie scrambling to her feet and hurrying after him.

CHAPTER 13

SEATED ON THE EDGE OF THE BED, PREACHER PUFFED ON a cigarette, staring daggers at the back of Debbie's head. The curtains covering the motel windows were parted, letting in a thin shaft of moonlight that stretched far across the room, highlighting her sleeping form.

She slept with his jacket on, her backpack and sneakers too—as if she didn't trust him with her belongings. And if Preacher hadn't been in such a shit mood, he'd laugh at the irony of it all.

Still glaring, he brought the cigarette to his mouth. It crackled and hissed along with the steady rhythm of Debbie's heavy breathing and the muted sounds of a television left on in the room next door.

He was so goddamn angry he couldn't sleep.

Angry because his duffel bag had been shredded,

reduced to ribbons by the Road Warriors when they'd stolen his cut. And not all of his belongings had fit into Debbie's backpack, forcing him to leave a third of his clothing behind.

He took another searing hot drag off his cigarette, feeling his lungs recoil in protest. Coughing, he blew out a breath thick with smoke that billowed and swirled in the moonlight.

The loss of his duffel bag wasn't his only bone to pick with the Road Warriors. Today's unplanned meeting had stirred up some shit inside of him, picked a scab that had only just formed. The life he'd been running from? It had just slugged him in the gut tonight.

Preacher stubbed out his cigarette and quickly lit another. Forget the Road Warriors. He was horny—really, irritably horny. Months had gone by with barely a twitch below his belt. One kiss with a teenage pickpocket and he was suddenly flying at full mast. *One goddamn kiss.*

He'd kissed a lot of women. So many that he'd gotten bored with kissing years ago. He couldn't even remember the last time he'd paid attention to a woman's mouth other than to direct it to his lap.

And the way Debbie had looked at him after spotting Angel and Rocky off in the grass...

Preacher's nostrils flared. *I want to be fucked right here, right now, and just like that,* had been all but engraved onto her expression.

All of it had been playing on repeat in his head for the last several hours, his dick trapped in this agonizing, semi-hard state that he didn't quite know what to do with.

The guy he'd been before? That guy would have already enjoyed the hell out of Debbie. He wouldn't have given a single shit about her age or what would become of her after he was done with her. But this new Preacher, this infuriatingly indecisive half-man, was sitting here thinking about how there were consequences to every action—something he'd learned the hard way. And a meaningless fuck was not worth hurting this girl, especially a girl who had nothing and no one.

Jesus-fucking-Christ. If he wasn't going to fuck her, what was he still doing with her? He'd already fulfilled and surpassed his good deed quota for the entire year. Whatever the hell he was doing now bordered on philanthropy. Or self-flagellation.

Once the sun came up, he needed to cut her loose. She could resume her trek to New York City and he could get back to wandering.

Except, the longer Preacher stared at Debbie, the less comfortable he felt with that plan.

She was too good for the streets, too good for the shit life she was living. And not nearly hard enough to hold her own in New York City.

He sighed angrily. Why did he care? What was it about this girl?

He liked her—that much was clear. But why?

Was it because she made him laugh, and it had been a very long time since anyone had?

Or was it because he recognized something in her—something that spoke to that empty hole that had taken up residence inside his chest? They were both out on the road, running from their lives, weren't they? And even though Debbie claimed to be running toward New York City, Preacher knew a lifeline when he saw one. That's all New

York City was: a goal to keep her going, even when the odds were stacked against her.

Rolling his eyes, Preacher shook his head. Maybe she was nothing more than a distraction—a reprieve from the self-doubt he couldn't seem to shake.

Whatever it was about this girl, it was just one more thing to add to the ever-growing list of things taking up space inside his overcrowded head.

Lying back on the bed, Preacher stared up at the ceiling until his eyes began to close. His last coherent thought before he drifted off to sleep was that, come hell or high water, he would not be spending another day in or around Wayne County.

This place was cursed.

Turning, he cracked an eye at Debbie.

Either the place was cursed… or the girl was.

Sitting cross-legged in bed, elbows propped on her thighs and chin resting in her hands, Debbie stared across the room. Snoring loudly, Preacher was sprawled across the center of his bed, one arm slung across his face. He was shirtless, and staring back at her was the face of a horned demon—a dark tattoo inked onto his bicep.

He'd been asleep when she'd woken, was still sleeping long after her shower and her not-so-shabby job of turning her torn jeans into cutoff shorts.

It was nearly noon now, and she had debated waking him several times. Only… she wasn't sure what waking him might mean for her. When it came to Preacher's generosity, Debbie knew that she'd already overstayed her welcome.

That she should thank him and be on her way.

The only thing stopping her was a pesky bit of truth: she didn't want to leave.

It was weak and she knew it. Allowing the lonely solitude of her lifestyle to overshadow reason and sensibility.

She barely knew Preacher, yet she found herself liking him more than she liked being alone. She trusted him, too. How could she not? He'd proven himself half a dozen times already. It was she who'd been untrustworthy.

Conflicted, Debbie reached across the bed and plucked a cigarette from the pack on the nightstand. As she smoked, she resumed watching Preacher sleep. He continued to snore, the heavy rumbles in perfect sync with the rise and fall of his chest. Her gaze drifted to where his unbuttoned jeans sat low on his waist, exposing the tapered cut of his abdominal muscles and the trail of dark hair that disappeared beneath the denim.

Recalling their kiss, the demanding way Preacher's tongue had swept through her mouth, warmth began to spread through her. Curling low in her stomach, it unfurled up and down her body, heating every inch it touched. Breathing in deeply through her nose, Debbie's bottom lip disappeared beneath her teeth.

Chock full of feelings she didn't know what to do with and jittery with unspent energy, Debbie rolled out of bed. Leaving her cigarette burning in the ashtray, she rifled through her backpack. Notebook and pencil in hand, she settled back onto the bed and flipped to a clean page.

She drew Angel and Rocky first, using her imagination to fill in what the night sky had kept hidden. When she was satisfied with her sketch, she turned the page. Head tilted, pencil poised, Debbie began to draw all those hard lines and smooth planes she'd been ogling for the last two hours.

Eyes flicking from Preacher to her notebook, she drew him as he was—half naked and sleeping. She smoked cigarette after cigarette while she sketched, her pencil strokes as quick and precise as her breathing had become.

Lost in concentration, Debbie didn't notice when Preacher stopped snoring.

It was only when his leg twitched that she cast a glance to his face and found him wide awake and watching her.

Heat exploded in her cheeks and she quickly slapped her notebook closed, covering it with her hand. "Hi," she said lamely, hoping she didn't look as embarrassed as she felt.

"What's that?" Preacher gestured to her notebook.

She shrugged. "I draw sometimes."

"You any good?"

Another shrug.

"Can I see?"

"No." Debbie tightened her grip on the notebook.

"No?" Preacher quirked an eyebrow. "Why not?"

Because I just sketched you half naked and sleeping.

"Because."

"Because? That's it? That's all I'm gonna get?" His eyes were light; a teasing smile tugged on his lips. "After all we've been through together?"

Debbie started to smile—a smile she quickly squelched as Preacher sat up and swung his legs out of bed, a maneuver that dragged his jeans further down his hips. He reached for his cigarettes while Debbie struggled to keep her gaze above his waist, away from the evident bulge in his pants that hadn't been there earlier.

"Did you smoke all my cigarettes?" Frowning, Preacher shook the empty pack.

"Shit," she muttered, scrambling out of bed to hand him the half-smoked cigarette in her hand. "I'm sorry."

"Goddamn, Wheels, you are an expensive date." He flashed her a wry look. "Least I still got my wallet."

Debbie looked down at her lap, her bottom lip disappearing beneath her teeth. She deserved the jab, yet it still stung.

"Jesus," Preacher groaned. "'Bout to lose another day of riding."

Debbie's gaze shot to Preacher and found him scowling at the table clock. Angrily he stubbed his cigarette into the ashtray.

Realizing he would be leaving soon, the candy bar she'd eaten earlier turned to stone in her gut. There would be no more motel rooms, no more hot showers. She would be alone again with nothing but the road to keep her company.

Weak, weak, weak, she thought bitterly. After all she'd been through, all she'd survived? She shouldn't be this weak anymore.

But she could already sense all those unwanted feelings rising to the surface. And even as she attempted to steel her emotions, ready to battle them back down to where they belonged, she knew it was pointless.

She'd only spent a few strange moments with Preacher, but those moments had been enough. He'd given her beautiful glimpses of things she'd long gone without: protection, companionship, and conversation.

It was Sunshine all over again—a stranger unexpectedly

dropping into her life, filling all those secret holes inside of her, the ones that had been carved from loneliness and starved for companionship… only to end up leaving her.

Preacher climbed out of bed and Debbie's gaze lifted. Arm muscles shifted and rolled as he stretched, reaching for the water-stained ceiling. The movement caused his jeans to slide another half inch down his hips. Visually tracing the long lines of his body, Debbie's mouth went dry

The urge to touch him, to run her hands over his sun-tanned skin, to tug his jeans down just a little farther, was so palpable that her fingers began to twitch.

"You still headed to the city?"

Debbie jerked her eyes away from Preacher's gaping waistband and hurried to school her expression, hoping he couldn't read her and wouldn't know what she'd been thinking about.

Her hope died a quick death when she found him staring at her, his features tight, his eyes burning. Her breathing hitched. Her grip on her notebook turned crushing. A hundred butterflies fluttered inside her.

It took her several seconds to recall he'd asked her a question, and several more to answer as she made a concerted effort to keep her gaze away from his sagging jeans.

Swallowing, she nodded through the fog that had taken up residence in her brain. "Yes," she said quietly.

Despite Preacher's warnings, her plans hadn't changed. If not New York City, then where would she go? She couldn't live like this forever—moving from truck stop to truck stop, living out of her backpack and off the kindness of strangers.

This wasn't a life. At least not a fulfilling one. And Debbie wanted more.

Preacher cleared his throat. "You want a ride?"

Debbie blinked up at him, her eyes widening.

"But I'm gonna need to make a pit stop upstate before showin' my face in the city," he hurried to say. "If you're cool with that, you got yourself a ride."

Was she cool with spending more time with Preacher? Debbie pressed her lips together—an attempt to prevent the burst of excitement inside her from making a noisy escape. Her stomach somersaulting, she nodded happily.

The corners of Preacher's mouth lifted, his lips twisting into a small smirk. Idly scratching at his beard, he started across the room.

Pausing just outside the bathroom, he tossed her a glance over his shoulder. "Hey, so, you gonna tell me your real name?"

She floundered for a moment. She wanted to tell him. She wanted to be honest with him, genuine. But at the same time, she never wanted to hear that name again, be that girl again. She wanted *that girl* to disappear forever.

"I like Wheels," she finally said.

She truly liked the nickname. Maybe because Preacher had given it to her, and therefore it wasn't a lie. It was real, genuine—the latter being something she was not.

A slow smile split Preacher's lips. "Fair enough, *Wheels.*" He knocked his fist lightly on the wall. "Lots of people where we're going. Lots of wallets to steal. You'll love it." With a wink, he disappeared inside the bathroom.

Staring at the empty space he'd just vacated, Debbie bit down on her bottom lip, barely breathing. She remained that way until she heard the shower turn on, and then she propelled herself face-first onto a pillow… and grinned.

CHAPTER 14

Present Day

"**S**O YOU TOOK HER TO FOUR POINTS?" I ASKED.

"'Course I did," Preacher mumbled, yawning. "I guess I felt…responsible for what happened to her.

"Hell," he continued, "it ain't like I had anything better to be doin' anyway." He yawned again.

"I think you just wanted to kiss her again," I said softly.

Although his eyes were closed, he smiled. "That too, baby girl… that too…"

Seated on a hard plastic chair beside Preacher's hospital bed, my chin resting on the bedrail, I watched his ashen features grow slack with sleep. He'd been talking animatedly for almost an hour, and then suddenly he'd gone quiet, staring off across the room. Maybe it was the reliving of his memories that had exhausted him, after keeping them locked away inside him for so long.

God knew I was feeling exhausted myself.

Getting to my feet, I leaned over the bedrail and drew the blanket up to his chin, tucking it tightly around his shoulders. Then I smoothed a few wisps of hair away from his forehead and placed a soft kiss there.

Turning, I found Deuce standing in the doorway, leaning against the doorjamb with his arms folded over his chest. "You alright, darlin'?"

I nodded despite myself. Not only was I learning that everything I'd thought I'd known about my mother had been a lie, but the reality of how sick Preacher actually was, that I was indeed losing my father, was becoming more apparent with every passing moment in his presence.

If only I'd known how sick he'd been back when there would have been time to do something. Chemotherapy, radiation, something… anything! God, if only Preacher had just told me. *If only someone had fucking told me.*

"Did the boys leave?" I asked, peering around Deuce into the hall.

Deuce dipped his chin. "Most of 'em. Joe's around here somewhere. And Tiny, that fat fuck, is snoring up a storm in the waiting room, drooling all over himself, driving me fuckin' crazy."

Nodding, I shot a quick glance at my father and released a shaky sigh. When the time came, I knew Tiny would have to be dragged kicking and screaming from Preacher's side. Despite Tiny's less appealing tendencies, his loyalty and love for my father was unwavering.

"You know, she wasn't a junkie," I told Deuce. Shaking my head, I shrugged helplessly. "Did you hear what he said?" I gestured at my father. "*She wasn't a junkie.*"

Suddenly awash with feelings, my eyes filled with tears. I'd hated my mother—a supposed teenage junkie who'd abandoned me—for my entire life, only to find out I'd been hating a lie.

"She was just a kid," I whispered, my voice breaking. "And she was out there all alone…"

Guilt squeezed my chest. Guilt for hating her. Guilt for never questioning the lies I'd been told.

"Babe." Deuce held out his arms to me. Feeling drained, both physically and emotionally, I crossed the room quickly and collapsed into them. He held me tightly, crushing me to him.

"If she was livin' on the streets, she damn sure wasn't a fuckin' kid anymore. You know this shit. Ain't no use in beatin' yourself up for somethin' that happened a fuck of a long time ago." He pulled back just enough to peer down at me. "You feel me?"

I knew he was right, but it wasn't as if I could help how I was feeling. This was all new information to me, and it was going to take time to process and come to terms with it. Then there was still the matter of what exactly had happened to my mother.

My father was acting as if it were imperative I know all the details leading up to the truth. And I didn't want to rush him because I wanted to hear all those details, too. But at the same time, I also wanted to skip right to the end.

An overwhelming desire to see my children suddenly swept through me. To see their faces, hear their voices.

Squeezing my eyes shut, my gathering tears slid free.

"We should have brought the kids," I whispered, pressing my nose to Deuce's shirt, breathing in the familiar, comforting smell of him. "They should be here to say goodbye."

"There's still time, darlin'." He smoothed a work-roughened hand down the long length of my hair. "You say the word and I'll get 'em here."

I tilted my head back and looked up into his eyes. Twin pools of icy blue stared back at me.

"Get them here," I whispered. "Cage and Danny, they should be here. And Kami, too… she'll never forgive herself if she doesn't say goodbye."

"Done. You thirsty? Hungry?"

"I should eat," I said. Pulling out of Deuce's embrace, I wiped my tears from my cheeks and glanced at my father. "But I'm afraid to leave him."

"I'll bring somethin' up for you." Before I had a chance to respond, Deuce disappeared into the hallway.

"Wait!" I cried, rushing after him. Deuce stopped short and swiveled on his boot heel, causing a passing nurse to nearly trip trying to avoid crashing into him. The young man's eyes grew wide at the sight of Deuce, a veritable wall of a man, and he hurried off down the hall.

Grabbing Deuce's hand, I tugged him back inside Preacher's room.

"The Four Points Rally upstate," I said. "Did you ever go?"

Deuce scrubbed a hand over his grizzled jaw. "Yeah, I think—yeah, I went a few times back when I was a kid."

"She was there," I hurriedly told him. "At Four Points. My dad and my mom were there together the summer before I was born—were you there that year?"

"Darlin', slow down." Deuce shook his head. "That was a long-ass time ago, and your old man always had more than one piece of ass hangin' off him."

Internally I groaned. Of course he had. I'd never known Preacher without at least one leggy blonde on his arm.

"I know, I know," I muttered. "But I'm talking specifically about the year before I was born. Think back to that summer. Were you there?"

"Eva… back then I was—" Deuce cut himself off and glanced to where Preacher lay sleeping. "The summer before you were born?" His eyes narrowed and then flicked to me, his expression turning grave. He shook his head. "Wasn't that the summer The Judge was…"

When he didn't finish his thought, I felt my stomach flip-flop. "What?" I demanded. "Wasn't that the summer The Judge was *what*?"

Looking bewildered, he shook his head. "Eva, what the fuck? Don't you know what happened that summer?"

Confused, I shook my head. "What do you mean? What happened?"

"You motherfucker." Deuce sent a seething glare in Preacher's direction. "You dirty, lyin' motherfucker—"

"Deuce! Focus!" I grabbed his arm and shook it. "What the hell happened that summer?"

Nostrils flaring, Deuce finally faced me. His jaw was clenched tight, making his cheekbones more pronounced. Angry grooves lined his forehead. "That was the last year they held the rally in Four Points," he bit out, "because that was the summer The Judge and his old lady were put to ground."

"What?" I whispered, backing away from him. I shook my head. "No. *No*. The Judge and Ginny… they died in a car accident."

Deuce cursed several times. "No, Eva, they fuckin' didn't. I thought you knew this shit. They're *your* fuckin' grandparents."

Shock zinging through my body like mini electrical surges, I fell silent. The Judge and Ginny were about as familiar to me as my mother was. They were almost never discussed, and on the rare occasions I had asked about them, nobody had ever had much to say. Eventually I'd stopped asking.

"God, they were…*murdered*? At the rally?" Feeling disordered and overwhelmed, I continued shaking my head.

"Everyone was questioned," Deuce said. "I don't remember much, just that no one seemed to know jack shit."

"They never… they never figured out who did it?"

Deuce took a deep breath, his chest rising noticeably, then blew it out slowly. "Wish I knew, darlin'. But all I remember from back then is after the boys in blue told us we were free to go, we got the fuck outta Dodge."

Wanting answers, Deuce left Eva sitting by her father's bedside, googling Four Points on her cell phone. He marched past the elevators and into the small waiting room, finding Tiny exactly where he'd left him—stretched out over a loveseat, sound asleep and snoring.

Deuce sent the toe of his boot into Tiny's shin. "Wake up," he growled. Nothing. Tiny continued to sleep, his large head lolling side to side with every earth-shattering snore.

Deuce kicked him harder. "Wake the fuck up!"

Tiny jerked, blinked twice, and then started snoring again.

Muttering curses, Deuce gathered the collar of Tiny's sweat-stained T-shirt in his fist and yanked him upright. "Wake the fuck up, you useless piece of shit!"

Tiny's eyes flew open. "What? Where?" Breathless, Tiny frantically scanned the waiting room.

Deuce released him with a light shove. "Who killed The Judge and his old lady?" he demanded.

There was no sense in beating around the bush. The Hells Horsemen and the Silver Demons were more than just business partners. While still technically two clubs, they both operated under one umbrella and functioned as one unit—a unit both Deuce and Preacher presided over. Soon though, all of that power would be going to Deuce's eldest son, Cage, and who-the-fuck-ever the Demons chose to replace Preacher. Long story short, Demon business was Horsemen business and vice versa, and so Deuce figured he had every goddamn right to know who the fuck killed the former president of the Silver Demons.

"Wh-what?" Sputtering and wide-eyed, Tiny glanced nervously around the room.

"You heard me," Deuce growled, his irritation mounting. "Who killed The Judge?"

Tiny pushed himself into as much of an upright position as his overly round body would allow. "Ain't nobody ever figured that shit out, and why the fuck you bringin' this up now? Ain't it bad enough my Prez is—"

"Your Prez is on his fuckin' deathbed spillin' his guts to

Eva. Tellin' her all about Debbie and the summer he met her."

Placing his hands on the loveseat's armrests, Deuce leaned down into Tiny's personal space. His next words were spoken softly, but with deadly intonation. "I'm guessin' you remember that summer, yeah?"

Tiny's eyes grew rounder, wider, and he began to shake his head, his heavy mass of gray curls bouncing riotously around his shoulders. "You're lyin'!" he shouted, and Deuce quickly straightened in order to avoid the mist of spittle flying from Tiny's mouth.

"You're lyin'!" Tiny repeated as he attempted to stand.

It took him three tries to gain enough momentum to lift his giant body from the couch. Panting with exertion, Tiny glared angrily at Deuce. "Ain't nobody talks about Debbie, you hear me? Ain't nobody talks about The Judge and Ginny, or that summer! Those are Preacher's rules and he wouldn't be breakin' 'em!"

"*His rules*, genius," Deuce said flatly. "And he's dyin', remember? So I'm guessin' he doesn't give two fucks about breakin' 'em."

Tiny, his face a mass of angry red blotches, went still. The rage in his expression quickly shifted to shock. "Shit," he muttered, wiping his brow. "Eva's gonna know. She's gonna know we all lied to her. She's gonna know *I* lied to her."

Deuce felt a pang of pity for Tiny, and for all the Silver Demons that had been around long enough to have been wrapped up in Preacher's web of lies. Eva wasn't just the love of Deuce's life; she had an entire club full of old men who'd watched her grow up, who'd helped raise her. Men who'd rather shoot their own faces off than ever see her hurt.

"The Judge," Deuce pressed. "Who killed him?"

Tiny's features pinched and twisted. "You don't under-stand—it ain't as easy as all that. Things weren't never black and white. Preacher, he was different back then, and this was…"

Tiny threw his hands up in the air helplessly. "You don't know how bad he beat himself up for so many things. But he didn't know! He didn't know until later, until it was too fuckin' late and everybody was already long gone."

As Deuce tried to make sense of his nonsensical decla-ration, Tiny collapsed back onto the sofa and dropped his head into his hands. His next words were muffled and full of grief.

"He never forgave himself."

"Who did it?" Deuce slammed his fist on the arm of the sofa and Tiny's head shot up, his eyes filled with tears.

"Did the club vote?" Deuce demanded. "Did the fuckin' gavel go down? That means whatever went down was club business, and seein' as how our clubs are—"

"West."

One-Eyed Joe's boots pounded an agitated rhythm as he crossed the room. And damn, the man could still glare. Even with only one eye. In fact, it was the eye patch that made him look even more menacing—like an angry old pirate.

"Leave him be," Joe snarled. "It ain't his story to tell."

"Yeah? Whose fuckin' story is it then?" Deuce straight-ened to his full height and folded his arms over his chest. He matched Joe's one-eyed glare with a two-eyed scowl that usually sent his own boys running for cover. Joe, however, didn't bat an eye. He wouldn't though, not with a man like

Preacher for a brother and boss.

The stare-down dragged on for several more tense seconds until Tiny let out a nervous laugh. "You two ain't gonna fight, are you? 'Cause I don't wanna get kicked out of the hospital."

Stone-faced, Deuce turned to Tiny and stared him down until Tiny had enough smarts to look away. How the rest of the Demons could stand the blubbering idiot, Deuce had no idea.

"They were my parents, too." Some of the anger faded from Joe's expression. "So I'm thinkin' it's my story to tell." Joe gestured with his chin. "Walk with me."

Neither Deuce nor Joe spoke as they headed down the hall. The elevator ride to the main floor was tense and silent, punctuated by Joe's irritating tendency to suck loudly on his teeth. By the time they'd reached the first floor, Deuce pushed ahead of Joe and practically burst outside—only to be greeted by stale, pungent air and the obnoxious sounds of too much traffic.

"I know my niece has got you on a tight leash, God love her." Smiling and shaking his head, Joe offered him a cigarette. "But brother, you're gonna need this."

Eyeing the cigarette, Deuce hesitated. His cravings had never really gone away entirely. And now, stuck in this concrete hellhole, dealing with Preacher's bullshit, they'd doubled.

"Fuck it," he muttered, and lit what was undoubtedly going to be his very last cigarette in life after Eva smelled it on him—and promptly killed him.

"How much do you remember of that summer?" Joe asked.

Deuce shook his head. "Not a whole fuck of a lot."

He'd racked his brain, trying to remember anything else other than what he'd already told Eva, but it was half a lifetime ago. The older he got, the more everything began to blur together—murders included.

Joe stared out across the street, smoke filtering slowly through his nostrils. "Some of us thought it might have been Reaper," he said quietly.

"He didn't kill women," Deuce replied tonelessly, hoping he didn't sound as if he were defending his father—a man he'd hated all his life, a man he'd personally paid someone to kill. He was simply speaking the truth. Reaper West had treated the fairer sex like shit on a shoe, but had only ever killed people he'd considered a problem. Seeing as how Reaper hadn't thought much of women to begin with, hadn't had a use for them other than to fuck them, he wouldn't have thought they were worth the trouble or the resources.

"They were good people." Joe faced Deuce. "My old man started the club to help vets get back on their feet, you know? And my mom, hell, she woulda given you the shirt off her back and whatever else you needed. That woman had a heart of gold."

Deuce scarcely remembered them. He'd met The Judge way back when, but it had been during a time in his life when his main concern had been trying to survive having Reaper as a father. That unlucky lot in life had included incessant name calling, and dodging punches or taking them so his little brother didn't have to.

Joe flicked his cigarette away, earning him a nasty look from a passer-by—a young man wearing skinny jeans with thin red suspenders and a matching red bow tie.

Jesus Christ. Deuce really, *really* hated New York City.

"Did anyone ever tell you how it went down?" Joe asked.

"Heard some shit through the grapevine, nothin' solid."

"It was some real sick shit." Joe tapped another cigarette out of his pack and lit it up. "They were mutilated. Sliced and diced. Blood everywhere. My old man... a few of his fingers had been cut off. And my mom... she... she..."

Joe's mouth snapped shut and his lips pressed together, and Deuce turned away and got busy enjoying his cigarette.

Growing up, Deuce didn't have the sort of close-knit family Joe had, but he'd improvised well enough. Once upon a time he'd had a little brother he'd loved fiercely, and other men he'd looked up to and depended upon. He knew what it felt like to give a fuck about someone and then to lose them one day unexpectedly.

Loss didn't care how much time had passed. It didn't care that you were getting on in years, half staring down the barrel of a gun yourself. Loss like that stuck with you, all the way to the bitter fucking end.

Eventually Joe let out a long, hard sigh and scrubbed a grease-stained hand over his face. "Preacher always thought it was the Italians. That was their thing back then—cuttin' off the fingers from any poor son of a bitch who took somethin' that didn't belong to 'em.

"But for me... man, that shit didn't ever add up. Back then the Demons were good business for the syndicate. We did all their grunt work, got our hands dirty so they didn't have to. Didn't make sense for them to cut ties. And The Judge? He woulda never bit the hand that fed him. He didn't work that way."

A sad smile twisting his lips, Joe nodded to himself.

"My old man was loyal to a fuckin' fault."

Letting out another hard sigh, Joe looked at Deuce. "Truth of the matter was, none of us knew who the fuck did it… or why."

"But you found out, didn't you?"

"Preacher did."

"And?"

Joe smiled cruelly, his one eye gleaming with renewed retribution. "You know my brother."

Snorting, Deuce shook his head. He sure as shit did. Preacher was a shoot-first, ask-questions-later kind of guy.

And Deuce had two bullet wounds to prove it.

PART TWO

"When I do good, I feel good.
When I do bad, I feel bad."
—Abraham Lincoln

"When I do good, I feel good.
When I do bad, I feel fucking great."
—Damon "Preacher" Fox

CHAPTER 15

THE SUN HAD ALREADY BEGUN ITS DESCENT ONLY FOUR hours into their travels, and by the time Preacher crested the small hill that signaled their arrival in Four Points, it was little more than a half moon, glowing gold as it disappeared behind the high peaks of the Appalachian Mountains.

Today the normally quaint and quiet lake town was anything but. Cars, trucks, and motorcycles lined both sides of Main Street, a narrow two-lane road brimming with bikers and their families. Four Points didn't have much to offer, only a small market, a laundromat, a movie theater, and a handful of mom-and-pop shops, but what it lacked in consumerism, it made up for with one hell of a beautiful view.

Traffic thickened, forcing Preacher to a full stop in the middle of the road. Further back someone laid on their horn, and the response from the crowd was instantaneous. From one end of the street to the other, men and women stopped what they were doing and started shouting and jeering.

"Nice ride, man!" A slim man clad head to toe in leather paused in front of Preacher, his eyes gleaming with envy.

He wasn't the only one who'd stopped to stare. She was a rare beauty, his '69 chopper, with her deep blue tank, matching raked frame, extended fork tubes, and drag bars on dogbone risers. And glistening in the setting sun like she was, Preacher would fault a man for *not* looking.

Behind him Debbie released his middle and straightened. Stretching her suntanned limbs, she gave Preacher a primo view of the nicely toned legs that had been hindering him for the past several hours. Initially she'd worn jeans for the ride, but after it had rained briefly, she'd changed into shorts.

She'd chosen a small thicket of trees on the side of the highway to change behind that had done very little to hide her. Preacher had caught fortuitous glimpses of skin every time she'd moved and a flash of one very firm ass cheek. And when she'd switched her top, Preacher had gotten another eyeful—a frustrating peek at her left breast. He'd outright stared, the recollection of her fully naked and offering him sex once again mocking him.

Sixteen, he chanted silently, fumbling for his cigarettes. *Sixteen, sixteen, six-fucking-teen.* Where the hell were his goddamn cigarettes?

Finding out her age should have been the equivalent of a cold shower. Instead, it'd had the opposite effect on him, and he'd spent nearly every moment since trying not to think about her... *like that*. Which had caused him to think about her twice as much.

Neither did it help when the person he was actively trying not to think about was pressed up against him, her arms wrapped around his waist, her breasts crushed against his back, her bare legs cradling his hips. All of it making it twice as hard to hear reason and sensibility over the roar of blood rushing straight to his dick.

Still searching for his cigarettes and looking anywhere except at Debbie's sixteen-year-old legs, Preacher eyed the crowded street and paused on a woman strutting down the sidewalk. She was his type to a tee—blonde, tan, with hourglass curves and legs for days. Noticing Preacher, the blonde shot him a knowing smirk and put a little extra swing in her hips. Appreciating the show, he continued tracking her movements. There'd be more just like her at the rally, and he was planning on taking one to bed as soon as possible.

Because that's all this bullshit with Debbie was—an urge to fuck. He was finally feeling a little bit like his old self again, and after months without a woman, he needed to blow off some steam.

Traffic began to move again, and Preacher revved his engine, pulling forward. Debbie's arms slid back in place, her hands coming to rest inside his open vest and settling low on his hips.

He blew out a breath of smoke through gritted teeth, then flicked away what remained of his cigarette. *Sixteen, you horny asshole, she's only six-fucking-teen.*

As they continued down Main Street, the smells of the rally preceded the view of the park—a thick blend of exhaust and campfire smoke, along with cooking meat and freshly cut grass.

Preacher turned right at the third light, and then made an immediate left onto Lakeside Drive. He knew these streets like the back of his hand; he'd been coming to Four Points for years—until he'd been locked up. This would be his first summer back after two years away.

The realization that he was about to come face to face with The Judge caused his neck muscles to tighten. He'd been so preoccupied thinking about Debbie all damn day, thoughts of his father had slipped his mind. His old man was going to have quite a lot to say to him, and none of it was going to be good.

As Preacher turned slowly into the state park's gravel entrance, the ache in his neck flared hot, accompanied by shooting pains above his eyes. Fighting the urge to rub his forehead, he continued on, slowly weaving his way through the overcrowded picnic area.

He felt Debbie twisting in her seat behind him and wondered at the expression on her face. Did the crowd un-nerve her? The rally had twice as many people as the Wayne County Fair. Or was she gleefully plotting how many wallets she could grab before dinner had ended? Preacher's smirked at the thought, and the pain in his head began to ease.

His mother was going to love Debbie. Ginny Fox wasn't happy unless she was sticking her nose in someone else's business and rearranging their entire life. She was a one-woman reform mission in their neighborhood. Feeding the homeless, counseling the addicts, volunteering at Father Evan's home for boys. Preacher had once caught her trying to be a go-between for feuding hookers.

The moment Ginny sensed the street on Debbie, she'd come barreling in like a bat out of hell on a mission to save the girl, and Debbie wouldn't stand a chance against her.

He drew in a deep, anxious breath... just like he wouldn't stand a chance against The Judge.

Preacher slowed his bike to a stop at the end of a long line of motorcycles and toed the kickstand down. Pushing his goggles over his head, he looked around. Nothing had changed since the last time he'd been here—with the exception of him. Behind the picnic area sat the campground, filled with a variety of tents and trailers, all shapes and sizes. And beyond the campground, there was a waterfall that emptied into a swimming hole. During the day the area would be bursting with children and families, but after dark, the young adult crowd would congregate there. Preacher had many fond memories of after dark at the waterfall.

Debbie dismounted and turned in a circle, drinking it all in. She appeared nervous yet curious.

"You weren't kidding," she said. "There's a lot of people here."

Preacher smirked at her, a smartass joke about pickpocketing on the tip of his tongue when a whistled catcall drew their attention.

"You get sick of her, you give her to me!" a burly man shouted, raising a bottle of beer in salutation. "What I wouldn't do to ride a beaut like that-a-one!"

"The bitch ain't bad, either!" one of his companions called out, laughing.

"I'll fuck 'em both!" a third man stated loudly, crudely grabbing his crotch. At that, the entire group burst into hysterics.

Preacher sent a two-finger salute in their direction, dismissing them. Debbie's gaze slid to Preacher. "Bitch?" she asked, brows raised.

Laughing, he set to work untying her backpack from his handlebars. "Welcome to my world, Wheels."

"Welcome to another world," Debbie muttered under her breath.

Trailing closely behind Preacher, she'd glimpsed campsites crowded with families—moms and dads playing with their children, older people snoring in lawn chairs while younger generations manned the grills. In others the music was turned up loud, the picnic tables littered with bottles of booze. Young men and women danced in the grass while others were pressed up against one another, engaged in another sort of dance.

Debbie hadn't bothered to ask Preacher any questions about where they were headed, and therefore she hadn't known what to expect. But never in a million years would she have guessed something like this.

It wasn't that the place felt unwelcoming; quite the opposite actually. This place, these people, gave off a similar vibe to the people she sometimes encountered on the road. People like Sunshine. People like Preacher. People who didn't adhere to the same social standards as everyone else and who didn't look at you sideways if you didn't look or act a certain way. Here she didn't feel like a fish out of water... but instead, just another fish in the sea.

"Shit." Preacher stopped and glanced around, his gaze bouncing from campsite to campsite. Debbie came to stand beside him. "What's wrong?"

"Lookin' for my parents. They usually park right around here."

His parents? Debbie's eyes widened. Preacher's parents were here?

"Preacher? No fuckin' way! *Noooo fuckin' way!*"

All of a sudden, a very large, very round young man barreled into Preacher, sending both men sprawling onto the ground. Startled, Debbie leaped backward and continued backing away as two more men were fast approaching.

"Holy shit! Preacher!" The younger of the approaching pair rushed forward, his brown eyes shining with excitement—eyes that Debbie noticed were very similar to Preacher's. In fact, the more she studied him, the more similarities she found between them. She suspected they were related, though this man was slimmer than Preacher, clean-shaven and with a much shorter hairstyle. And unlike the others, he wasn't wearing a leather vest.

Preacher rolled away from his assailant and jumped to his feet, pulling the younger man into a hug.

"Do Mom and Dad know you're here?" the younger man asked, confirming Debbie's suspicion.

"Naw," Preacher drawled, and gave him a friendly punch on the shoulder. "Hightower told me you'd headed up here." He shrugged. "I was in the neighborhood. Figured I'd swing by and see what you sorry bunch of assholes were doin'."

"Preacher." The remaining man stepped forward. A great deal older than the other three, he had short dark hair with thick, graying sideburns. Low on his nose sat a pair of small round bifocals that were in sharp contrast to his worn leather vest and dirty jeans.

"Doc," Preacher greeted him, clasping his hand, and Debbie's gaze was drawn to the extensive scarring covering his hands and forearms—a road map of raised white lines. As their hands pulled apart, she counted only three fingers on Doc's right hand.

"Who's the broad?" Red-faced and breathing hard, Preacher's attacker gestured to Debbie. And to her absolute horror, all eyes were suddenly on her.

Preacher looked at her, his eyes glittering with amusement.

"Wheels," he said. "Meet my littlest brother, Max. And this here's Doc." Preacher nodded at the older man. "And this shithead—is Tiny."

Preacher tossed Tiny a carefree smirk. "Found her poundin' pavement on 89. She's headed to the city, so I offered my... *services*." He said the word "services" in such a way—drawing out each syllable, and imbued with insinuation.

Everyone but Debbie laughed. Feeling mildly incensed, she crossed her arms over her chest.

"Her name is Wheels?" Tiny asked.

All eyes were still on Debbie—Tiny and Doc's were filled with questions, while Max unabashedly stared at her in a way that made her wish for her jacket despite the heat.

Laughing, Preacher hooked an arm around Tiny's neck and tugged him forward. "It's Hell on Wheels. I call her Wheels for short."

CHAPTER 16

PREACHER'S FAMILY'S CAMPSITE CONSISTED OF THREE successive sites. A lone pop-up trailer sat in the center, and behind it, a robin's-egg blue Chevy van was parked amid a handful of motorcycles. Tents had been erected in every direction, ranging in size from single-person to large enough to house a family of four. A short distance from the trailer several picnic tables had been pushed together, their benches currently brimming with bodies.

Debbie swallowed back her surprise. Even after realizing Preacher's family was here, she hadn't anticipated that a bona fide army awaited her.

As their small group neared the picnic tables, Debbie's anxiety reached its boiling point. She envisioned more eyes on her, studying her, judging her, wondering who she was and what she was doing with Preacher. Her late lunch swirled inside her gut and her palms grew sweaty.

A young man with long blond hair shot up off a bench. "Preacher!" he shouted, and the campsite went silent as everyone swivelled in their seats, turning their shocked and gaping expressions toward Preacher.

The picnic tables exploded. People jumped to their feet, cursing and shouting his name. A woman darted across the grass, her hand over her heart. "Damon!" she cried. "Oh God, Damon!"

She was a tall woman with wavy brown hair that hung thick and heavy to her waist. As she hurried across the campsite, her generous curves swayed and bounced beneath an orange and yellow sundress that billowed and swirled around her bare feet. Large, ornate earrings dangled from her ears, and a stack of silver and gold bangles lined each of her forearms. She was naturally beautiful and stunning in a way that reminded Debbie of Sunshine.

Who was this gorgeous creature? And why did Preacher look so happy to see her?

"Mom." Preacher packed so much emotion into the lone word as he folded the woman into his arms. Debbie blinked, startled. This striking, bohemian woman was Preacher's mother? She didn't look like a mom, at least not any mom Debbie had ever known. Certainly not her own.

Debbie watched them embrace—a hug that seemed never-ending—and it caused swirls of envy to stir beneath her skin. The tiny twisters roused a maelstrom of emotions that swept through her like an unforgiving wind and sent her staggering back a step.

Her mother had never greeted her like that, never looked at her like Preacher's mother was looking at him—with her hands on his cheeks, looking up at her son with such adoration, as if the sun rose and set in his eyes.

Hands clenched into fists, Debbie took another step back and released a shaky breath. It wasn't that she was unused to seeing families. She saw them often quite often in passing and paid them the same amount of attention they paid her—next to none. Certainly not to the point where she'd allow herself to become overwhelmed with feelings.

Deep breath after deep breath, Debbie slowly but surely steeled her emotions, forcing them back down to the darkness where they couldn't hurt her.

"So, uh, are you and my brother, you know…"

Debbie's head swiveled to find Max beside her, grinning slyly. He might share his brother's good looks, but there was a world of difference between the two. Max's gaze was too bright and full of youthful mischief, whereas Preacher's was much darker, heavier, and filled with things Debbie recognized, things she'd glimpsed in her own reflection.

"He's just giving me a ride," she mumbled, turning away. She searched out Preacher, finding him surrounded by nearly everyone in camp. Only one man remained by the picnic tables—older, of stocky build, he was heavily muscled with salt-and-pepper hair cut into a high-and-tight. Thick arms folded over his broad chest, he watched the happy reunion through narrowed eyes.

He was Preacher's father, she decided. He had the same distinctive jawline, the same proud nose and broad shoulders as his son. *As both his sons*, she silently amended, glancing sideways at Max. The resemblance was uncanny, despite Preacher and Max's taller, leaner frames.

"And you are?" A touch to her arm startled Debbie. A

spicy, sweet scent filled her nostrils.

Swallowing her surprise, she blinked up at Preacher's mother. "I, uh… Debbie. My name is Debbie. But, um, Preacher calls me Wheels."

The woman's dark brows shot up, and Debbie was entranced by her eyes. Surrounded by fine lines, ringed in thick, dark lashes, they were a deep shade of gray reminiscent of the sky just before it rains.

"Wheels? Any particular reason he chose Wheels?"

Debbie lifted her shoulder. "He says it's short for Hell on Wheels."

Chuckling, the woman shook her head and placed a heavily bejewelled hand on her chest. Stacks of gold and silver rings encircled her fingers. "Oh my dear, on behalf of my son, I'm so sorry. Wheels… good grief, these boys and their nicknames."

She continued on, still shaking her head. "I'm Evangeline. But you can call me Ginny—everyone else does. Or little Ginny, if you can believe that." She laughed loudly, and Debbie decided that even her laugh—a deep, throaty feminine rumble—was nearly as beautiful as the woman herself.

"Preacher met her on 89," Max interjected. "She's headed for the city and hitched a ride with him."

Ginny's eyes widened, brightening with curiosity. "You'll have to tell me more about yourself, Debbie. And you'll have to forgive me for not calling you Wheels." She winked at Max. "She's much too pretty for a name like *Wheels,* isn't she Maxwell?"

Grinning impishly, Max's eyes slanted in Debbie's direction. "Yeah, Ma. Way too pretty."

Five minutes in Max's presence and Debbie was already tired of him. She attempted a smile, managing only a slight baring of teeth—a reminder of just how rusty and untried she was when it came to interacting with other people.

But neither Max nor Ginny seemed to notice. Max continued to grin obnoxiously, leaving Debbie to wonder if it was the teenager's only expression.

"Come, Debbie darling," Ginny said, offering Debbie her arm. "And meet everyone."

The introductions felt endless, and Debbie's mind was soon spinning with names and faces. Aside from the three men she'd already met—Max, Tiny, and Doc—Ginny introduced her to Preacher's other brother, Joe, and his pregnant wife, Sylvia. Joe, who was shorter and stockier like his father, wore a black eyepatch over his left eye and had been aptly nicknamed One-Eyed Joe. Debbie had hardly had time to wonder how he'd lost his eye when she was turned around to meet the others.

Palms clammy, heart pounding an uneven beat inside her chest, Debbie reluctantly allowed Ginny to parade her around the campsite, introducing her to person after person.

She met Doc's wife June—a slim woman with indistinct features who seemed as quiet and reserved as her husband. And Whiskey Jim, an older man with a head full of white hair, and his much younger wife, Anne. Blonde and beautiful, Anne looked as if she'd stepped off the pages of a fashion magazine.

Best friends with Anne was Louisa. And the two

women couldn't have been more different. Whereas Anne was tall and slim, polished and well-dressed, Louisa was much shorter, curvier, and covered in tattoos. Wearing a ratty band tee and jeans, she was cuddled up to a biker named Crazy-8. Also heavily tattooed, Crazy-8 had a rough and tough appearance, contrasted by an easygoing smile.

She met Smokey and Knuckles next. Smokey, a middle-aged widower who had a look to him that gave Debbie the impression that he'd seen and done it all. And Knuckles, twenty-two years old with an unruly mass of blond curls framing his flirtatious smile, he wore a T-shirt that read in big, bold lettering: FUCK HAIRCUTS.

Faking smiles and shaking hands, Debbie began feeling strange and desperate. Everyone was mostly kind, if not overly so, but made no effort to hide their questions. They stared at her with blatant curiosity, their thoughts clear. Who was she? And what was she doing with Preacher?

Each new face added to her growing anxiety, worse because Preacher seemed to have abandoned her to Ginny.

Eventually Ginny led Debbie to the picnic tables, where Preacher's father still stood at the head, stone-faced and unmoving. He was an intimidating-looking man, his stiff, unfriendly demeanor making him seem all the more threatening, even more so up close.

And he practically exuded authority, so much so that Debbie didn't need to read the PRESIDENT patch on his leather vest to know that, among these people, this man was king.

"Gerald, honey." Ginny placed her hand on her husband's arm. "This is Debbie. She arrived with Damon."

Gerald looked her up and down with a critical eye, as a

buyer might look over a car they were considering purchasing. Finished, he glanced over at his wife, his mouth pressed into a thin, grim line, leaving Debbie feeling not quite sure she'd passed his inspection.

"This is what he's been doing all this time?" Gerald bit out. "Messin' with girls? He couldn't have done this shit at home?"

"Gerry," Ginny admonished quietly. "Don't start."

"Don't start?" Gerald shot back. "He can't just waltz back in here like nothin' happened!"

Unsure of what to do, Debbie glanced down at her hands, suddenly very interested in her nails. She was contemplating slinking away when a familiar arm came down around her shoulders.

"You doin' okay, Wheels?" Preacher gave her a crooked smile. "You look a little green."

"I'm fine," she whispered through clenched teeth. She glanced longingly at her pack on his back, feeling naked without it. "Can I have my backpack?"

"Lie," he retorted softly, giving her shoulder a squeeze. "And no. Can't have you runnin' off with my stuff."

She met his gaze, ready to tell him exactly where he could shove his stuff if he didn't give her the bag back, only to find his attention was elsewhere. His eyes were locked with Gerald's, and both father and son were wearing identical scathing expressions.

"The prodigal son returns," Gerald said flatly.

"The prodigal son is just visiting," Preacher amended tersely.

Gerald's nostrils flared, his fists clenched, and if Preacher's arm hadn't been wrapped around her shoulders,

Debbie would have backed away.

Clearing her throat, Ginny glanced nervously between her husband and son. "You must be hungry, Damon," she said. "We have—"

"Yeah," Gerald loudly interrupted, "you must be hungry. And while you're eatin' my food, why don't you tell us what your plans are? Will you be comin' home with us, or headin' back to God only knows where to do God only knows what with God only knows who?" At that, Gerald gave Debbie a pointed, disapproving look.

Beside Debbie, Preacher had gone stiff. His arm resting on her shoulders grew rigid. All around them, the campsite fell quiet, and Debbie didn't need to look to know that all eyes were now on them.

"Gerry," Ginny snapped quietly, "please. He just got here."

Gerald's hard stare remained fixed on Preacher. "Still doesn't change the fact that he just up and took off on us, been gone for months now with no word."

Debbie looked to Preacher, a dozen questions brewing. If Preacher noticed her eyes on him, he'd didn't show it. His attention remained on his father.

"Well?" Gerald growled. "What have you got to say for yourself, boy?"

Preacher's arm fell away from Debbie's shoulders, his angry expression turning downright murderous.

"This ain't the army." Preacher's voice quivered with rage. "And I ain't your fuckin' soldier."

Gerald's thick salt-and-pepper brows drew together, deep grooves appearing between them. His nostrils continued to flare, faster and faster like tiny hummingbird wings.

His suntanned skin appeared to darken, reddening with anger. And just when Debbie thought Gerald was going to quite literally explode, he spun away and stalked off across the campsite. There were several slams as he disappeared inside the trailer, followed by a worrisome crash and several shouted curses.

Also cursing, Preacher marched away in the opposite direction. Biting down on her bottom lip, Debbie stared blankly after him. What was she supposed to do?

"Damon!" Ginny called. She gestured wildly with her hands. "Dammit, someone follow him!"

"I got this!" Tiny declared, waving at Ginny as he hurried out of camp.

Debbie eyed the rest of the group. Knowing glances were being exchanged. Others shook their heads and rolled their eyes. It seemed this wasn't an uncommon occurrence where Preacher and Gerald were concerned.

"Lord help me with fathers and sons," Ginny muttered. Pulling a leather pouch from her dress pocket, she flicked it open, revealing the dark brown cigarettes inside. Long and slim, they smelled both spicy and sweet once lit.

Sighing, Ginny gave Debbie a small, strained smile. "You must be hungry." She gestured to the picnic tables. "Let me make you a plate."

CHAPTER 17

"WAIT UP, WILL YOU?" TINY CALLED OUT breathlessly.

Preacher picked up his pace, weaving in and around campsites without looking where he was going and barreled straight into a young couple holding hands, forcing them apart. Muttering apologies, he made a quick right and ended up clipping a leather-clad man on the arm. He plowed through another few campsites before finally finding the dirt path that would lead him to the swimming hole.

"Five fuckin' minutes," he hissed under his breath. Five minutes was all it had taken for The Judge to start in on him. He hadn't seen the man in months—he could have at least said hello before laying into him. But no. The Judge was all business, all the fucking time. Nothing else ever seemed to matter.

Jesus Christ. Why had he come here? Had he really missed any of this? Shaking his head, he let out a derisive snort. The Judge would never be capable of seeing anything other than his own obscured judgment.

"Preacher, man! I said, wait the fuck up!"

Fists clenched, jaw locked, Preacher forced himself to stop. Seconds later Tiny reached him, sweat dripping down his forehead and both his cheeks. Leaning forward, hands on his knees, Tiny wheezed through his next several breaths.

Preacher glared down at him. "You need to mind your own business."

Still bent over, Tiny nodded jerkily. "Yeah...brother," he rasped. "I know...it. Just couldn't...let you...run off... again."

Preacher instantly felt bad. He hadn't been thinking clearly when he'd taken off, hadn't given much thought to how his sudden disappearance would affect the others. Looking at his friend now, he realized how incredibly selfish he'd been.

But then again... if memory served him correctly, everyone had seemed to think his release from prison had been just another goddamn Tuesday, and business as usual. Tiny included.

Straightening, Tiny placed his hand on Preacher's shoulder. "You know The Judge won't ever admit to it, but he's been worried sick about you. He's been makin' calls, checkin' in with everyone, tryin' to find you."

Rolling his eyes, Preacher turned away and stared off across the park. He didn't doubt The Judge had been looking for him, but he doubted his reasons. If The Judge had been worried, it was only worry for his club and Preacher's role in it.

Moving off the pathway, Preacher dropped down beside a cluster of trees. The jagged backdrop of the Appalachians loomed in the distance. The sun was barely visible now, a quickly fading haze of oranges and reds.

Tiny sat down beside him, breathing hard and smelling strongly of body odor.

"You fuckin' stink."

"Yeah? You look like a caveman with that beard."

"Man, you're as wet as they are." Preacher gestured to Tiny's T-shirt, soaked through at the collar with sweat, before jerking his chin toward a group of bikini-clad young women heading down the path. Hair wet, wrapped in towels, they'd clearly been swimming.

"Not as wet as they're gonna be once I get my hands on 'em."

Preacher started to laugh, and so did Tiny. And *shit*, even with Tiny stinking to high heaven, Preacher realized how much he really had missed his friend.

"Get a couple a' drinks in 'em and we'll be in like Flynn," Tiny suggested, waggling his eyebrows.

Preacher spared the group of women another quick, dismissive glance. Shrugging, he turned back to the sunset and lit a cigarette. Minutes passed in silence.

"He really was worried," Tiny said eventually.

Preacher didn't answer him.

"You stupid or something?" Tiny asked irritably. "He blamed himself the entire time you were locked up! And then you come home and you ain't actin' right! Next, you up and take off in the middle of the night and nobody knows where the fuck you are! And now you've showed up here outta nowhere? Man, you can't blame him for wonderin' what the fuck you're gonna do next. Hell, brother, I'm wonderin' the same damn thing and I can guarantee you so is everyone else."

Sighing, Preacher flicked his cigarette away. He didn't want to talk about this shit, not with Tiny, not with anyone. He didn't like the way it made him feel—guilty and pissed off, and angry with everyone, himself most of all.

His frustration mounting, feeling suddenly uncomfortably warm, he shrugged out of the pack on his back and started removing layers. Once he felt cooler and less like punching someone in the face, he glanced down at the bag in front of him and froze.

Shit.

He'd been so pissed off, he'd left Debbie alone with his family. She was probably cursing him to hell and back.

"You gonna tell me where you been all this time?"

Preacher glanced at Tiny and shrugged. "Nowhere. Just... on the road."

"Doin' what?"

"Nothin'."

"Okay, fine. Who's the broad?"

"Just some chick."

"She ain't exactly your type."

"I don't have a fuckin' type," Preacher muttered, despite knowing full well that he most definitely had a type. And Debbie was so far removed from the loud, flashy women Preacher had always preferred. But even as he pictured them—the well-built blondes he'd once thought he'd never get enough of—his thoughts immediately veered back to Debbie.

Tiny snickered. "Brother, you've got a type, and she is the exact opposite of it!"

"It ain't like that," Preacher snapped. "I'm just helping her out, is all."

"Is that what you're callin' it now?"

"Dumbass, I'm not fuckin' her." Preacher punctuated each word with every ounce of irritation he was feeling regarding Debbie. Irritation because all he could seem to think about was how he wasn't fucking her.

"You're not fuckin' her?" Tiny sounded confused.

Preacher glared up at the sky. "I'm not fuckin' her," he growled.

"You're really not fuckin' her?"

"I'm really not."

"Are you sure you're not—"

"I'm not fuckin' her!" Preacher exploded, grabbing the attention of a passing group of campers. Shooting Preacher a disapproving look, an older woman covered a young girl's ears and hurried off down the path.

Beside him, Tiny was chuckling. "Man, maybe you should be…"

"She's sixteen," Preacher muttered. *Almost seventeen*, he silent added.

Tiny didn't appear concerned. "Ain't sixteen legal… somewhere? Didn't Fore-Face get hitched at sixteen?"

Fore-Face was the nickname given to a neighborhood girl whose forehead had been abnormally large. They'd all gone to school together, where she'd been picked on mercilessly. It was no wonder she'd spread her legs for the first piece of shit to come calling—a man twice her age.

"Fore-Face got knocked up and her parents made her

marry the chump. And just 'cause the only chicks you can talk into bed are too young to know better don't make it right."

"Didn't realize you'd become such a fuckin' pillar of righteousness, brother."

Preacher opened his mouth to snap back, then quickly closed it. Just because he didn't currently recognize himself or know what the fuck he was doing didn't mean he should take any of it out on Tiny.

Fiddling with the straps on Debbie's backpack, Preacher stared off across the park, thinking about... *mother-fucking-Debbie.* Why was that exactly?

Although very pretty, she was no great beauty.

Not that being beautiful had ever been a requirement Preacher had sought in a woman. He had his preferences in the looks department, but he'd never discriminated. A fuck was a fuck, usually made better if the girl knew what she was doing. If Preacher had enjoyed the fuck, that's what brought him back for more, not her looks.

Yet Debbie? He hadn't even fucked her and he was giving her lots of thought—all his goddamn thoughts, even.

Who the fuck are you? he wondered, flicking open the flap on her backpack and peering inside. Digging beneath his own belongings, he found hers. She didn't have much— some clothing, toiletries, and a composition notebook. Pulling out the notebook, he flipped it open.

Well, shit. She wasn't half bad. In fact, the sketch he was looking at was really very good. Preacher tilted his head, studying a drawing of a little girl seated on a man's lap. Staring into the little girl's doe eyes, he was reminded of Debbie.

Flipping to the next page, Preacher's brow shot to the top of his forehead. She'd drawn Angel straddling Rocky in the grass, Angel's back arched, her mouth open... and hot damn, the drawing did more for him than any *Playboy* spread ever had.

Itching to see what else she'd drawn, Preacher turned the page and... *holy fucking shit.*

She'd drawn him. Shirtless, stretched across the motel bed, Preacher's arm was flung over his face, his mouth hanging slightly agape.

Did his arms really look that good? Preacher's eyes flicked to his bicep and he flexed the muscle. Yep, not bad. Not bad at all.

The detail was incredible. Looking closer, he noticed every fold in the fabric, every scar and freckle on his skin. Where the light had hit him, highlighting him in places, shadowing others.

How long had this taken her? How long had she been staring at him? Most importantly, had she liked what she'd been drawing? Had it turned her on?

"What's that?" Tiny leaned against him, craning his neck.

Preacher slammed the notebook closed and elbowed Tiny away from him. "None of your goddamn business."

Shoving the notebook back inside the bag, Preacher quickly packed up his things and shot to his feet.

"I gotta get back," he muttered and rushed off without waiting for his friend.

Arriving back at camp, Preacher found the crowd had

considerably thinned.

Doc was in the process of building a bonfire, while June and Smokey chatted nearby. Around the picnic table sat Ginny, Joe, and Sylvia on one side, while Debbie and Max sat across from them. Half-eaten plates of food and bottles of beer were scattered across the table.

Someone had brought out the tape deck and Ginny was singing along to Billie Holiday. Eyes half-lidded, her chin resting in her hand, a clove cigarette smoking between her fingers, she swayed gently from side to side.

The Judge, thankfully, was nowhere in sight.

As Preacher drew closer to the picnic table, Ginny was the first to notice him. She smiled, and he felt that smile wrap around him like a warm blanket.

A flicker of light turned his attention to Max. His brother had lit a cigarette for Debbie and had used the opportunity to slide himself closer. Max, with his usual dopey-as-shit smile plastered across his face, leaned into Debbie and whispered something in her ear.

Preacher's eyes narrowed into slits. *That stupid little fucker likes her.*

Although Max wasn't quite so little anymore. It was yet another thing that had changed while he'd been locked up. Joe had married Sylvia, and Max had gone from a gangly fourteen-year-old obsessed with pinball and *Planet of the Apes* to a taller, thicker version of himself, and with a five o'clock shadow.

Max was nearly a man now, and it wouldn't be all that much longer before The Judge patched him into the club.

Preacher frowned. *Man or not, Max should know better than to encroach on his girl.*

He paused, his forehead wrinkling. What the hell? Debbie wasn't his girl. Debbie wasn't his anything. But as he resumed his trek toward the picnic tables, watching Max continue to try and coax Debbie into conversation, he found himself growing more and more irritated.

So irritated in fact that, when he reached them, he hooked his arm around Max's neck and forcefully dragged him, flailing and cursing, down the entire length of the bench and deposited him onto the ground. While Max continued to curse, Joe burst into a fit of laughter, pounding the table with his fist.

Preacher took Max's seat beside Debbie and placed her backpack between them. "Whatever he was sayin' about me, it ain't true."

She attempted a smile, but her eyes were shuttered as she looked up at him, and her bottom lip was wet and swollen as if she'd been chewing nervously on it the entire time he'd been gone.

Dropping an arm over her shoulders, he bowed his head to hers. "You okay?"

She faced him fully, bringing their faces nearly flush, and his gaze dropped again to her mouth. Man, this girl had some seriously great lips. Kissable lips. Lips that begged to be sucked on. Lips that he knew firsthand tasted both salty and sweet. Lips that he wanted to—

"Damon? Earth to Damon?"

Preacher's eyes snapped to his mother. "What?"

"I was saying that I had Max set up your tent for Debbie—"

"Found a *Playboy* in it," Max interrupted, and Preacher could hear the smirk on his little brother's face. "December issue," he continued. "Big ole titties and—"

Preacher reached behind him to where Max now sat, grabbed a fistful of his brother's shirt, and shoved him off the bench. Max hit the ground with a loud "oomph," and again Joe roared with laughter.

Stubbing out her cigarette, Ginny shot Preacher a look that made him feel like he was twelve years old again. "As I was saying," she said pointedly, "I had Max set up your tent for Debbie, and you can share with Joe."

Joe's laughter abruptly cut off. Horror-stricken, he faced Ginny. "What? Mom, no!"

Preacher, feeling equally horrified, jerked his thumb at Sylvia. "What about Sylvie? Shouldn't Joe be sleepin' with his wife?"

Preacher had been forced to share a room with Joe until he'd moved out on his own and knew better than most that Joe snored at a decibel level very few could reach—a horrible combination of braying mule and table saw. Joe also came with his own unbearable stench, a cross between stale beer and dirty socks.

When it came to sharing sleeping space with another man, Preacher would choose anyone over Joe.

Sylvia shot Preacher an annoyed glance. "In case you haven't noticed, you idiot, I'm pregnant with your nephew. And I'm too big to be sleepin' on the ground. You put me on the ground and I won't ever get up again."

"She's been sleeping in the camper with us," Ginny added.

"Nephew?" Preacher asked, glancing at Joe. "It's a boy?"

"We don't know." Joe rolled his eyes. "Just last week she was sayin' he was a she."

Sylvia glared. "Well, I have to call it something, don't I?"

"She's carrying low." Ginny gestured to Sylvia's swollen belly. "My guess is it's a boy."

Sylvia beamed. "See! We can call him a he!"

Joe ran a hand through his short dark hair and mumbled something that sounded suspiciously like, "How 'bout we call him a life-ruining cock block?"

"Joseph Fox!" Ginny snapped, her eyes wide.

"What did you say?" Sylvia demanded, thrusting a finger at Joe, the nail painted bright red.

"Nothin'," Joe muttered.

"It wasn't *nothin'*!" she shot back. "I heard you!" Sylvia slowly lifted herself off the bench. Standing over Joe, she glared down at him. "You apologize!"

Joe, refusing to look at his wife, only scowled at the tabletop.

"What about Max?" Preacher had to raise his voice to be heard over Sylvia. "Why can't he double with Joe?"

"Hell no!" Max chimed in, "I'm sharin' with Knuckles! You couldn't pay me to sleep in that stink-hole!"

No one paid either Max or Preacher any attention. Sylvia had graduated to shouting while Joe looked like he wished a lightning bolt would strike him dead. Ginny had moved to stand between them and was attempting to calm Sylvia down with hand gestures and softly spoken words.

Preacher sighed. Didn't his mother know by now that her attempts were futile? A bat to the head wouldn't shut up a Jersey girl—let alone an Italian. The only chance anyone had at peace was walking into traffic.

Eventually Sylvia burst into loud, exaggerated tears and shuffled away. Joe looked momentarily relieved until Ginny snatched his arm and dragged him along after her.

"Is it always like this?" Looking bewildered, Debbie stared after Ginny and Joe as if she didn't quite know what to make of his family.

"Yup." It was Max who'd answered. At some point, he'd taken Sylvia's seat across from Debbie. Leaning forward on his elbows, a cocksure grin on his face, Max said, "Sometimes it's worse. You should see them when—"

"Go away," Preacher interjected. He really, *really* did not like the way Max was looking at Debbie—like it was his goddamn birthday and she was a present he couldn't wait to unwrap.

Max faced Preacher, his eyes narrowed into angry slits. "Man, what is your fuckin' problem?"

"You are. So go away. Right now."

Eyes flashing, Max shot to his feet and slapped his palms down hard on the table. "You're just like Dad!" he accused, before storming off.

Preacher watched him go, more perturbed that Max had likened him to their father than anything else.

"That wasn't very nice," Debbie remarked.

He snorted. "*Nice*? Do you have any brothers—or sisters?"

She shook her head. "My dad died when I was really little. I was an only child."

Preacher was reminded of the drawing in Debbie's notebook—the man with the little girl on his lap.

"My mom... remarried," she continued, her words clipped and strained. Then her features tightened. "But they... didn't have any kids."

He stayed silent a moment, studying her, waiting to see

if she was going to elaborate further. When she didn't, he replied, "Truth."

Her eyes shifted, their gazes colliding. Those big, beautiful eyes of hers, boring into his, looked darker than usual. He glanced at her mouth again, her seriously sexy mouth, then down her body, to where the thin material of her T-shirt was pulled tight over her breasts, and then further, all the way down her bare legs and back up again.

Another maddening vision of her dropping her towel and offering him sex crept into his thoughts, only this time, instead of turning her down, he tugged her forward and pulled her onto the bed.

His body hardening, Preacher shoved her backpack off the bench and shifted closer.

"Your mouth is so crazy sexy," he heard himself saying, reaching for Debbie. He ran his thumb up her finely-carved cheekbone, and when she didn't jerk away, he continued on, stroking a path down to her chin and across her jaw. He paused beneath her full bottom lip and glanced up.

Her expression was changing—her eyes widening, her lips parting. Her breaths were coming quicker—sharp bursts of air in rapid succession that told Preacher she was either scared or eager. Judging by the way she was looking at him, he'd bet his life on the latter.

Debbie wanted to be kissed again.

And *fuck him*, he was going to kiss her.

Sixteensixteensixteensixteen.

Preacher covered her mouth with his. His tongue jutted past her lips, roughly tangling with hers. She gripped his arms, and he pulled her closer. One hand went into her hair, the other slid down her back.

She was kissing him like she'd kissed him last night, messy and desperate, and it was spurring him on, firing him up, driving him half mad with wanting.

He wanted more. He wanted her closer—on his lap, her legs wrapped around his middle, grinding herself over his—

"I got special brownies!" There was a loud thump and the picnic table bounced. Startled, Debbie released Preacher and jumped halfway down the bench.

Tiny was sitting across from them, a shit-eating grin stretching his chubby cheeks straight across his face, clutching a brightly-colored tin to his chest.

"Snagged these babies off Marcie." Tiny gave the tin a loving caress. "You remember Marcie, right? Her old man wrecked a few years back. Get this, Preacher, the woman started her own club! Can you believe it? A club full of fuckin' chicks!"

Debbie got to her feet. "I, uh, I..." she stammered, refusing to look at Preacher. "I'll be right back."

Grabbing her backpack, she shot off across the camp like a bat out of hell. And Preacher watched her go, his erection throbbing in his jeans.

"Something I said?" Tiny asked.

Preacher turned to him, deadpan, and wrenched the tin of brownies from his grasp. "Gimme those," he growled.

CHAPTER 18

DEBBIE WOKE BEFORE THE SUN, A RESULT OF FREQUENTLY sleeping outside. Shoving Preacher's jean jacket off, she sat up and unzipped the tent's nylon door flap. Greeted with the same gray sky and chirping birds that always preceded the sunrise, she leaned forward and pressed her hands into the damp grass, peering around the quiet campsite.

She wondered which tent Preacher was in and if he was awake yet.

After wandering around the park last night, exploring and spying on other campers, Debbie had returned to the camp with little fanfare. Only a small group had remained seated around the bonfire, Preacher among them. As if he'd been waiting for her, Preacher's fire-lit gaze had found her slinking through the dark. Turning in his lawn chair, he'd tracked her as she'd hurried across camp.

She'd slipped inside the tent Ginny has assigned her, half hoping he would follow her. When he hadn't, she'd set up a makeshift bed using her bag as a pillow and Preacher's jacket as a blanket and eventually fell asleep.

Had she screwed everything up by running off? Did Preacher now think her an idiot child?

Debbie's gaze meandered over to the picnic tables. She pressed her fingertips to her lips. He'd kissed her again. And it had been different than the first time. Better, even. Rougher. Frantic.

Your mouth is so crazy sexy.

She'd replayed that declaration in her head at least a million times since he'd said it. His voice had been deeper than normal, gruffer. As if his words had been torn from a place that he rarely exposed.

The statement alone had been enough to make her melt.

Dragging in a slow, dizzying breath, Debbie rolled onto her back and stared up at the arched ceiling. She didn't just like kissing Preacher. She liked *him*.

Last night she hadn't realized exactly what had made her run off like she had. Why she'd felt so flustered. So overwhelmed.

Now she knew.

She never thought she'd feel this way about a boy—*a man*. Actually, she'd never realized she could feel this way. Debbie hadn't fit in with the girls she'd gone to school with. She'd never understood their incessant talk of boys, their obsession with them. The last thing she'd wanted to do was go to second base with Roger Campbell beneath the bleachers.

The last thing she'd wanted was anyone touching her.

She supposed that things were different for those who had a say in who got to touch them.

But here, with Preacher, free from the things that had haunted her back home and while alone on the road, Debbie was free to feel… whatever she wanted to feel.

And what she feeling was a lot. Too much, really. Dozens of feelings all at once, none of which she had a name for, let alone knew what to do with.

It was more than just Preacher. Meeting his family, his club, had made her feel even smaller than she was used to feeling. Ginny and Gerald, Sylvia and Joe, even Tiny, they each had such a strong individual presence. But combined?

Debbie pressed a hand to her belly and blew out a breath. Jealousy was a bitter pill to swallow.

What she wouldn't give for a family just like this one. A loud and joyful, angry and messy… family. Imperfect, yes. But also perfect in their imperfections.

Feeling inspired, Debbie rolled over and rifled through her bag. Pulling out her notebook, she propped herself up, flipped to a clean page, and began to draw.

First she drew the picnic tables, then she began to sketch the people seated around them. She drew Gerald at the head and Ginny beside him. She drew them all as best as she could recall.

The sky lightened as she drew, illuminating the inside of the tent with a soft, golden glow. Debbie chewed endlessly on her bottom lip, eager to scratch out the image in her mind.

Finally she drew Preacher approaching the gathering. She drew him as if she were a spectator, standing behind him, unable to see his face.

And when she finished, she did something she'd never done before: she titled it. In the bottom corner, in scrolling cursive, she penned: FAMILY.

For some time she simply stared down at her work. It was far from her best. She'd drawn it much too fast. And she'd most certainly screwed up a few features drawing the faces of people she'd only glimpsed briefly.

But it was also one of her best.

Because there was more to it than serving as a mere visual reminder of the people she'd met that day. From the frown on Gerald's face as he watched Preacher approach, to the joy on Ginny's as she shot up in her seat, it was chock-full of everything that made this family what it was.

With a heavy sigh, Debbie put her notebook away and grabbed her things. While exploring last night, she'd discovered showers inside the bathhouses, and she meant to get in as many hot showers as possible before they weren't possible anymore.

The bathhouses were two-room brick structures. The first room was filled with toilet cubicles and sinks, and the second housed showers. There wasn't much privacy in the shower room, no doors or curtains, only partial stalls within a small alcove that did little to hide you. It reminded Debbie of her school locker room, where everyone had been forced to change and shower in front of their classmates. Back then she hadn't wanted anyone to see her naked.

She didn't mind so much anymore; she was simply glad for hot water.

Freshly showered, Debbie had just finished dressing and was finger-combing her wet hair when she heard a noise and turned.

"Oh!" Sylvia paused mid-step and blinked at her. "I know you... Debbie, right?" Her large belly preceding her, Sylvia looked exhausted and bedraggled. Dark circles ringed her eyes, and her shoulder-length brown hair stuck up in all directions.

"I haven't been able to sleep a wink since we arrived," Sylvia complained as she moved toward the shower stalls. Pausing by a bench, she set down a large purse and began pulling out the contents one by one.

Biting down on her bottom lip, Debbie's gaze touched covetously upon each of the items Sylvia had laid out—a towel, a bar of soap, a bottle of shampoo, and a bag full of makeup—and probably took for granted.

"This baby in here," Sylvia said, absentmindedly rubbing her belly, "is constantly movin', always kickin' me. I have to pee all the time, and everything aches.

"Ginny is right, you know? I'm carrying so low it has to be a boy. And I know Joey wants a boy so badly. And we already have his name picked out. Trey Joseph Fox. Trey after my granddaddy, and Joseph after Joey, of course.

"But on the chance he's a girl, I was thinkin' about naming her Marie. You know, after Marie Osmond? I just love her. Some people say I look like her. What do you think? Do you watch Donny and Marie? Speakin' of Donny and Marie, how's the water today? Is it hot? It was ice cold yesterday!"

Debbie stared at the young woman trying to decipher her east coast accent. It had taken her several seconds to realize that when Sylvia had said "wudder", what she'd meant was "water." Her accent was so thick, her D's sounded like T's, and vice versa. Her R's were harshly spoken, and extra A's were thrown in almost everywhere.

Sylvia didn't seem bothered by Debbie's prolonged silence and continued talking. She talked while she undressed, and was still talking even after she'd climbed in the shower.

"I'm so glad my morning sickness is finally gone!" she called out. "I thought it was going to last the full nine months. My gums are still bleeding, though," she continued. "Did you know pregnancy could do that? I didn't. My hair has gotten fuller, my boobs are bigger, and my skin has never looked better. But I'm as fat as Tiny, and my feet are swollen, and my gums are bleedin', and Joey won't...touch me..."

At that last announcement, Sylvia trailed off, growing quiet. Debbie glanced longingly toward the exit, wondering if Sylvia would care if she left—or even notice.

"He used to be all over me. Couldn't keep his hands off me. I was a virgin before Joey, only ever let Robbie Bianchi feel me up, you know?"

Debbie did not know. She had nothing to offer this woman, no words of wisdom. She was no relationship expert, having never had one. And neither had she ever been pregnant—thank God—or been close to anyone who had been. Her mother had certainly never discussed things like that with her.

"Debbie? Could you hand me my dress?" Sylvia emerged from the shower stall with a towel pressed to her front, far too small to provide her with much coverage. Debbie had no idea what Sylvia had looked like before she'd gotten pregnant, but she could imagine her as a slim, petite woman. Her limbs were still tiny, at least in comparison with her midsection. But her belly appeared even more monstrous now that she was naked, the large swell of it dwarfing her hips and breasts.

Debbie hurried to help her, unable to avert her eyes as Sylvia dropped her towel. Jagged, painful-looking red lines covered her belly where her skin had stretched. Debbie outright stared, cringing at the thought of ever being pregnant. Between Sylvia's talk of bleeding gums and swollen ankles and seeing firsthand what pregnancy did to your body, Debbie thanked her lucky stars she'd been fortunate enough to have avoided that fate.

"I was thinkin' about inducing early," Sylvia said. "I read that celebrities do it all the time. Everybody says Yoko Ono had a Caesarean just so Sean could be born on John's birthday. I don't know about all that though, and there's somethin' to be said about a natural birth, right? I bet Marie will have a natural birth. She seems the type, right?"

CHAPTER 19

"I HATE YOU," PREACHER MUTTERED OVER HIS shoulder. "You know that, right?"

Picking up his pace, Preacher hurried through the campground, Joe on his heels. They'd already combed through the west side of the park searching for Sylvia, and now they were searching the east.

They'd both been rudely awakened by Ginny, who'd been frantic with worry when she'd woken and found that her very pregnant and very emotional daughter-in-law had gone missing.

It was early, the park was still quiet, the sky streaked with the colorful beginnings of sunrise, and all Preacher wanted to do was go back to Joe's foul-smelling tent and sleep for another hour.

He'd had difficulty falling asleep last night, having spent

most of it listening to the devil seated on his left shoulder tell the angel on his right to go fuck itself.

At one point he'd spent almost an hour trying to convince himself that Debbie's age didn't matter because of her situation—there was no one in her life to care what she did or didn't do. If there was no one to care, then what did it matter? Then he'd felt like shit for thinking it and had spent another hour wide awake, telling himself what an asshole he was.

"This ain't my fault!" Joe protested. "I tried tellin' Mom that Sylvie just ain't been sleepin' good lately and she's probably off walkin' around somewhere."

"You shouldn't have brought her. What kind of man brings a pregnant woman camping?"

"You try tellin' Sylvie no! I told her no way in fuckin' hell was she comin', and you should have seen her, all pissed off and haulin' her fat ass up into Dad's van and givin' me that look!"

Preacher glanced sideways at his brother. "What look?"

"You know, the look. That fuckin' look a chick gives you, tellin' you that you ain't got a choice in the matter. It's do or die, man, do or fuckin' die. That's the look. I get that look every fuckin' day. I married that fuckin' look. That fuckin' look is gonna kill me."

Preacher glanced up at the sky and made a face. "Idiot. That ain't the look she was givin' you. She was givin' you the look that said she knew what the fuck you were going to be doin' up here if she *didn't* come."

Joe fell silent, and Preacher rolled his eyes. It was no secret to anyone who knew Joe that he wasn't a one-woman kind of guy. He hadn't been faithful to Sylvia when they'd been dating, and anyone with half a brain would know that marriage hadn't changed him. If anything, Preacher guessed Joe's new situation had only increased his brother's appetite for women—he was probably screwing every piece of ass he could get his hands on.

"I told you not to marry her," Preacher muttered, shaking his head. "Remember? This is your own damn fault."

Joe had come to visit him in prison to tell him Sylvia was pregnant, and Preacher had told him point blank not to marry her if he didn't love her—and that he'd regret it if he did.

But Joe had succumbed to The Judge's and Ginny's demand that he do right by Sylvia, and if Joe felt trapped now, it was his own damn fault and none of Preacher's concern. What *was* Preacher's problem was Ginny forcing him to share a tent with his idiot brother.

Gripping his arm, Joe wrenched Preacher to a stop, forcing him to turn around and face him.

"Mom made me," he seethed, his eyes wide and glinting with anger. "She said no grandbaby of hers was gonna be a bastard!"

"*Mom made me,*" Preacher mimicked. He shook his arm free from Joe's grip and shoved his brother in the chest, sending him stumbling backward. "Man, you know you sound like a little girl, right?"

"You weren't there!" Joe shouted, a vein in his forehead throbbing angrily.

Preacher knew Joe was seconds away from hauling off and slugging him. A recreational boxer with fists of steel, Joe wasn't someone you wanted to piss off. But the way Preacher saw it, a concussion and couple of black eyes were preferable to wandering around the park at the ass-crack of dawn bickering like a pair of old women. Balling his hands into fists, Preacher readied to duck and swing.

"Dad told me if I wasn't gonna do the respectable thing, he wasn't gonna have a place for me at the table!"

As Preacher's jaw went slack, so did his fists. "What?"

"Yeah," Joe hissed. "He was gonna take my patch. And then what?" Joe threw his hands up in the air. "And then I'd have nothin'!"

Preacher raked a hand through his hair. "Man, I didn't know. If I woulda known—"

"Joey?"

Both men turned and found Sylvia rounding the corner of a nearby trailer. Appearing freshly showered, she was wearing a blindingly bright polyester number that made Preacher wish for temporary blindness. Then he spotted who was turning the corner behind Sylvia and Preacher suddenly couldn't remember what he was doing out here in the first place.

Debbie's long dark hair was wet and messy in a way that looked sexy. A pair of aviator sunglasses hid her eyes. She wore denim cutoff shorts and the same yellow T-shirt she'd had on yesterday, only today she'd gathered the hem and knotted it off to one side, exposing several inches of flat, smooth stomach. Barefoot, she held her sneakers in one hand and her backpack in the other.

Debbie paused beside Sylvia and lifted her sunglasses, her gaze on Preacher. He found himself smiling at her and then grinning when she suddenly flushed pink and her bottom lip disappeared behind her teeth.

"Dammit, Sylvie," Joe growled, shoving past Preacher

and holding his hand out to his wife. "You can't run off like this! Ain't nobody gettin' any damn sleep!"

"You think this is what no sleep feels like, do you?" Sylvia's eyes narrowed dangerously. "What about when the baby comes? Then you'll see what no sleep feels like!"

Joe's arm dropped to his side. "Fuck this," he muttered, turning away.

"What did you say?" Sylvia shouted, hurrying after him. "Joey, did you hear me? I asked you a goddamn question! Don't you walk away from me! Did you hear me? Joey, you come back here right now!"

"She talks a lot," Debbie murmured, joining Preacher.

"You have no idea."

"She's nice, though. But sad, too."

Frowning, Preacher glanced over his shoulder at Sylvia's retreating form. "Sad? Really?"

"Maybe sad wasn't the right word. Maybe lonely."

"Lonely? Why do you say that?"

Preacher actually couldn't care less about the South Jersey chatterbox who'd trapped his brother in a shitty marriage. But because he liked hearing Debbie talk and wanted to keep her talking, he kept the dialogue rolling. Debbie was the polar opposite of Sylvia, and while he didn't like overly chatty women, he did appreciate *some* conversation.

Gazing off into the park, Debbie shrugged. "I don't know. I just got that impression. I think she and your brother are equally unhappy and neither of them knows what to do about it."

Preacher lit up a cigarette. "You know a lot about unhappy marriages?"

Her eyes found his, flashing fire, fire that was in direct

contrast to the vulnerable expression she was suddenly wearing. "A little bit," she said softly.

Preacher stared at her, wondering what she meant. And as his eyes roamed her face, he found himself noticing things he hadn't before. The high cut of her cheekbones, the dashes of gold shining in her big brown eyes. And her nose wasn't just small; it was straight and pretty much perfect. And her lips... shit, he just really fucking liked her lips.

He'd been wrong yesterday when he'd thought her no great beauty. She was beautiful—really beautiful.

And young. Too young for him.

"Preacher?"

"Hmm?"

"Why'd you run away from home?" The vulnerability in her expression had doubled, and Preacher got the impression that his response was important to her.

He took several pulls on his cigarette before answering. "It's gonna sound stupid," he said, and shook his head. "But I couldn't breathe. I couldn't think." Dropping his cigarette, he crushed it beneath the toe of his boot. "I felt like the goddamn walls were closin' in on me."

Debbie placed her hand on his forearm. "That doesn't sound stupid," she said, breathless. "I couldn't breathe either."

Their eyes collided, and what Preacher saw in her face gutted him. He'd already guessed there was pain in her past, but he hadn't speculated the extent of it. Looking at her now, he knew someone had hurt this girl badly. And he didn't know what to feel first—pity or rage.

"Wheels," he started to say and then stopped. He didn't have a clue what to say; he just felt like he needed to say something, anything at all, to try and close that raw, gaping wound he saw in her expression.

A sudden crash caused Debbie to jump, and Preacher spun in a circle, seeking the source of the noise. There was a splintering crack, and Preacher watched as the entire face of a trailer bowed outward and then shuddered, rippling. Then a muffled shout, and the unmistakable thump of a fist hitting something solid—wood or bone—and then the trailer door flew open, the wall of metal quaking around it, and a body came flying through the opening. A man wearing a blood-soaked T-shirt and boxer shorts hit the ground on his back with an audible thump.

A young woman appeared in the doorway, blonde and beautiful, with legs for days and big, bouncy tits, the kind a man could bury his face in and fall asleep happy. Wearing only a bra and a pair of underwear half torn off her, she fled down the steps and dropped to her knees beside the man. "Oh my God!" she cried, horror-stricken. "Are you okay?"

"Get the fuck off me," the man hissed, shoving her away.

"It wasn't my fault!" Wrapping her arms around her middle, she rocked backward. Tears streamed down her cheeks, black rivulets of smeared eye makeup. "I was sleepin'! He attacked me!"

"You motherfuckin' stupid fuck."

Preacher jerked. He knew that voice—that unmistakable Midwestern snarl.

Robert "Reaper" West, president of the Hell's Horsemen Motorcycle Club, stepped out of the shadows of the trailer and into the growing daylight. With arms the size of tree trunks folded across an impressively built chest, and wearing a scowl forged in the bowels of hell, one couldn't help but get the impression that "Reaper" wasn't just a nickname.

Preacher instinctively grabbed Debbie's arm and shoved her behind him. Doing a mental sweep of himself, he quickly pinpointed the blade in his boot.

Hailing from Miles City, Montana, the Hell's Horsemen Motorcycle Club had been making quite a name for itself lately. It wasn't a new club by any means, but it was less well-known than the Silver Demons. And their president was suddenly, desperately trying to change all that. Within the last five years, the Hell's Horsemen had gone from making friends and forging alliances to acting like petty thieves and street thugs.

It had started out small—stealing business associates out from under the noses of other clubs and breaking the faces of anyone who tried to talk some sense into them. It hadn't made any sense at first, and they had been more or less dismissed as a bunch of country-bumpkin bastards with a collective Napoleon complex.

But then they'd begun to grow. Hell's Horsemen chapters had begun popping up all over the country, and as the club had tripled in size, so had Reaper's ego. They'd continued with their overbearing tactics, ostracizing themselves and making powerful enemies. It was now to the point where the mere mention of their name created a sense of unease among other clubs, and when people became apprehensive or afraid, especially when said people didn't work under the guidelines of a strict moral code, things tended to get messy. Or bloody.

The young man on the ground pushed himself upright. On his feet, his fists clenched, he straightened to his full height. Preacher blinked. *Holy shit.*

UNDESERVING

By Preacher's estimation, Cole West was still a teenager, although he hardly looked like one. He'd doubled in size since Preacher had last seen him, grown into a beast of a man, and was nearly as big as Reaper now. But not even Cole's size had stopped Reaper from giving his oldest son two black eyes and a bloody nose.

"Boy, you are as dumb as shit," Reaper snarled. "Fact, you're even dumber than shit. How many times do I gotta tell you, you don't stick your nose where it don't fuckin' belong?"

Cole, his jaw locked and ticking furiously, his legs spread apart, his fists so tightly clenched that his knuckles had turned white, took a menacing step forward. "Fuck you, old man," he gritted out.

Reaper smiled—a vicious showing of teeth. Arms raised, he tauntingly gestured his son forward.

Yep. Time to go. This was an explosion waiting to happen, and Preacher had no interest in witnessing it.

Still holding tightly to Debbie's arm, he slid his hand into hers, interlocking their fingers. They'd taken only a single backward step when Reaper's head whipped in their direction, his ice-blue stare catching sight of them.

"Well, well, well, what's this?" Reaper's gaze narrowed, then widened with cruel delight. "Preacher Fuckin' Fox, that you, boy? I'd heard you gone and gotten yourself locked up."

Preacher cursed under his breath. The next person to call him "boy" was going get spoon-fed his balls.

"Free as a bird, as you can see," Preacher drawled lazily, though he felt anything but lazy—or free, for that matter.

Reaper let out a laugh that was more of a sneer. "Prison finally make a man of you?"

Preacher shrugged. "Depends on your definition of a man."

If by man Reaper was referring to someone like himself, a madman who apparently ruled his kids like he did his club—with an iron fist—then no, Preacher wasn't that kind of man. And God willing, he never would be.

Reaper raised a menacing brow. "That so? Maybe you shoulda stayed locked up. Then that pussy-footin' daddy of yours wouldn't have to worry 'bout you fuckin' everything up. How much did that fuck-up of yours cost the club? I'm bettin' it was more than you're worth."

Preacher's heart rate picked up. "What are you tryin' to say?"

Reaper shrugged his massive shoulders. "Nothin'. Just that maybe you were safer behind bars."

Releasing Debbie, Preacher took a step forward. Reaper's insinuation wasn't lost on him—that was a threat if he'd ever heard one. And Preacher didn't back down from threats. If he'd learned anything at all during his twenty-four years on Earth, it was that men like Reaper didn't respect you for being the bigger man and walking away. Respect from men like him was hard earned, usually only after you beat it into them.

"Preacher!" Debbie hissed, grabbing his arm. "Don't!"

Shaking her off, Preacher growled at Reaper. "What the fuck are you really tryin' to say?"

Reaper grinned—one hell of a sadistic smile meant to egg Preacher on. And it worked. Preacher took another step forward, thinking only about how satisfying it would be to wipe that grin off Reaper's face. With his fists.

Instead, he found himself face to face with Cole.

"Walk the fuck away, Preacher," Cole ground out hoarsely between clenched, bloodied teeth. He lowered his voice. "He's mine."

Staring into the teenager's light blue eye, the one that wasn't swollen shut—an eye alight with so much anger, anger that needed an outlet—gave Preacher pause.

This wasn't his fight and it was none of his business.

Behind Cole, Reaper began to laugh, a deep, bloodthirsty rumble that would have sent lesser men running for the hills.

Cole's nostrils flared wide in response, his fists clenched tighter, and the muscles in his arms twitched, bunching restlessly. He was primed and ready to fight, and Preacher knew it was only a matter of minutes before father and son went at it again.

"Give him hell," Preacher said, dipping his chin and taking a step back. Finding Debbie where he'd left her—the stupid girl didn't seem to know when to run—he snatched up her arm and strode quickly toward the dirt pathway that would lead them back to their campsite.

Holy crap.

Debbie glanced at where her arm was being squeezed uncomfortably inside Preacher's unforgiving grip, then up at his face, her gaze tracing the hard edge of his jaw all the way up to the tightness around his eyes. He was tense, practically vibrating with unspent energy and aggression.

She didn't blame him. That had been intense. And those men? She didn't really know how to describe them. Combined with their encounter with the Road Warriors, intense didn't even begin to scratch the surface of the type of people Preacher knew.

"Friend of yours?" she asked, hoping some humor would lighten his mood.

He glanced down at her briefly, his dark eyes nearly black. "I'm gonna tell you right now, stay the fuck away from those two and anyone else wearin' a Hell's Horsemen cut."

Debbie's eyes narrowed. Did he really think she was as stupid as all that? She liked to think she was a somewhat decent judge of character. Maybe she hadn't been at first, but she'd gotten smarter as time had passed. Just like she'd learned where to look for the things she needed, she'd learned to read people, figuring out who she could and couldn't scam, who was safe to hitch a ride with and who was not.

"Can't be pullin' stupid stunts like you did with the Road Warriors," he continued to mutter. "Gonna find yourself in a world of shit."

Debbie gaped at him. "Are you kidding? I was trying to help *you*!"

Preacher stopped suddenly and turned to face her. He lifted one dark, questioning brow. "Help me? Seems to me like you've been in nothin' but trouble."

With a huff, she pulled her arm free from his grasp. "You're the one who knows all these—these crazy people! You're the one who's—*who's been in prison*!" She hadn't so quickly forgotten that juicy revelation.

Shadows swirled in Preacher's gaze. His eyes narrowed, his expression turning cold, hard. "That scare you?" he asked evenly. "You think I'm the next Son of Sam or somethin'?"

Debbie didn't appreciate his twisted humor. Glaring up at him, she snapped, "I don't know, are you?"

They both fell silent as an elderly couple passed by, regarding them curiously. All around them the park was waking up. People were puttering around their campsites, while others headed to the bathhouses.

Flashing the passing couple a quick smile, Preacher grabbed hold of Debbie's arm and pulled her off the path into a small grove of maple trees.

"Don't seem to me like you've got a single fuckin' clue what you're doin' out here." His hand on her arm flexed and squeezed. "What would have happened if I hadn't saved your ass at the truck stop?" he demanded.

Debbie dropped both her bag and her sneakers and, with a hard shove to Preacher's chest, broke free from his grip. "What would have happened?" she spat. "Nothing that I couldn't handle!

"You don't know me," she continued, shaking her head furiously. "I can take care of myself!"

Eyes flashing, Preacher opened his mouth, and then promptly closed it. Unmoving, he breathed deliberately slow, as if he were fighting something back. The violent storm brewing in his eyes began to fade. Sighing, he ran a hand down over his mouth.

"Shit," he muttered. "Shit, Wheels, I'm sorry... I didn't mean that. That asshole back there had me all worked up. I shouldn't have taken it out on you."

He sighed again. Looking at her, he held up his hands in defeat. "You're right. You can take care of yourself. I watched you in action. I'm only sayin'... you shouldn't have to."

Debbie sucked in a sharp breath. That statement, *you*

shouldn't have to, had been both a punch in the gut and a soft caress. What did he mean? Was it a well-intentioned observation or… something more?

"Drugs," Preacher said suddenly.

Debbie blinked. "What?"

"Drugs," he repeated. "Dope? Junk? That's why I went to prison. Got caught with some shit, did two years. Got out a few months back." He gave her a crooked smile. "So you know I'm not some maniac killer."

Though Debbie's body was still buzzing with adrenaline, it was quickly waning, and she offered Preacher a small smile. "I didn't think you were. But that guy back there…" She made a face that drew a chuckle from Preacher.

"Is that what you do, then?" she asked. "Is that what your club does?"

Preacher pressed a finger to Debbie's lips. "Me," he said quietly. "I went to prison for drugs. Not the club. *Never the club*. The club doesn't *do* anything. And don't ever let my dad hear you talkin' about the club."

Debbie stared up at him. For such a threatening statement, there was nothing currently threatening about Preacher. No longer tense, his shoulders were loose. Even his eyes were soft as he gazed down at her.

And his finger? The one that was slowly tracing the outline of her mouth? Debbie stared up at Preacher, her body buzzing with an entirely different feeling.

He moved closer, close enough that Debbie could feel the heat from his body whisper across her skin. She felt her nipples harden, and a delicious ache flared to life low in her belly.

The pad of his thumb paused on her bottom lip. He was

going to kiss her again. He was definitely going to kiss her again.

Then Preacher's finger was gone, as was he. Bending down, he scooped up her sneakers and backpack.

"I'm hungry," he announced. "You hungry?" He didn't wait for her to answer before striding quickly back to the path. "Fucking starving to death..." he continued to mutter.

Debbie had to take a moment to catch her breath and find her composure, and then she hurried after him.

CHAPTER 20

A CIGARETTE DANGLING FROM HIS LIPS, PREACHER twirled the sharp tip of his dagger over the picnic table surface, watching the wood splinter beneath it.

He was avoiding everyone, especially his father, which was not a difficult feat since the old bastard was also doing his best to avoid him. The Judge had left the park entirely and gone into town with Doc and Smokey.

Complaining that the heat from the midday sun was getting to them, Ginny and June had retreated inside the trailer to listen to music. Preacher knew his mother well enough to know that "listening to music" was code for smoking weed, and he'd bet his life they were higher than kites right about now. Somewhere, Tiny and Crazy-8 were off engaging in similar activities.

Everyone else—Joe and Sylvia, Jim and Anne, Louisa,

Knuckles, and Max—had gone to the swimming hole to stave off the heat. And Debbie? It had taken Preacher nearly to twenty minutes to convince her to tag along with them.

She'd refused at first, and he'd understood that she was uncomfortable, that they were strangers to her, but he needed a breather. Debbie being out of sight didn't necessarily mean she was out of mind, but at least out of sight meant his hands were off of her.

All morning and all afternoon had been an exercise in self-control for Preacher.

After breakfast, Debbie had retreated to the fire pit where she'd curled up in a lawn chair with her notebook and pencil. The campsite continued to bustle all around her, and no one paid her any attention. She'd faded away into the background for everyone except him.

Like a blinking beacon in a thick fog, she consistently drew his eyes. He traced the shape of her legs as she swung them back and forth over the arm of the chair. He stared at the rise and fall of her breasts with each breath. He followed the movement of her hair every time the warm breeze lifted it. He watched the way she'd pause in drawing, absentmindedly chewing on the tip of her pencil.

Lifting his blade, Preacher drove the sharp tip down into the wood, causing tiny fissures to splinter in all directions.

Before prison, he'd lived a life of self-indulgence—women, drinking, drugs. He'd never wanted for anything; it had all been at his fingertips.

Everything was different now. He was denying himself. And maybe that's where this unusual interest and attraction to her began and ended. By telling himself no, he was only worsening the craving.

"What did that table ever do to you?"

Flicking his cigarette away, Preacher watched as Ginny slid onto the bench across from him. Her long dark hair had been pulled up into a thick bun, and just as he'd suspected, her smile was lazy, her eyes bloodshot and glossy.

Smoothing her hands down the front of her wrinkled white tunic, she produced a clove cigarette from her pocket and lit it. "Where is everyone?" she asked around a mouthful of spice-scented smoke.

He shrugged. "Swimming."

"Debbie too?"

Preacher nodded.

"And why aren't you swimming?"

Another shrug.

Puffing on her clove, Ginny's tipped her head to one side and studied him. "Damon, talk to me. What's the problem? Is it your father or the girl? Are you sleeping with her?"

Preacher internally groaned. Even doped up, his mother missed nothing.

Ginny Fox was most definitely prettier than her husband, nearly a decade younger too, and a hell of a lot nicer. But she had at least one thing in common with The Judge— neither of them beat around the bush. They were both as straightforward as they came.

Brows up, he gave his mother a look—the same look he'd given her every time she'd try to bring up his sex life. It was a look that said there was not a chance in hell he was going to answer her.

Talking sex with his father was one thing. His mother? Preacher would rather be strung up by his toes on a clothes-line and gutted with a dull blade.

Knowing he wasn't going to answer her, Ginny snorted out a small laugh and shook her head. Leaning forward, she placed her hand over his and squeezed. "Don't make that face at me. I'm your mother. I have a right to know what's going on in my baby boy's life."

"Not a baby," he muttered.

She laughed again. "Oh yes you are. You are my baby and always will be." She tapped the ash from her clove cigarette. "Furthermore," she whispered, her eyes darting around the campsite, "you're my favorite. Your firstborn is always your favorite."

A smile tugged on the corners of his mouth. Ginny had been telling Preacher he was her favorite for as long as he could remember. He was also fairly certain she fed both Joe and Max the same line of bullshit.

"Yeah? I thought the youngest was always the favorite."

Ginny's upper lip curled. "That little pervert has got the whole block in an uproar. He's chasin' everything in a skirt these days, even that homely little thing next door. You remember Cecelia? Alfonso's girl?"

"The butcher's daughter? What the hell? She's a little kid!"

Ginny smiled. "No baby. You weren't home long enough to get the lay of the land. She's the same age as Max. Terribly ugly, though. Looks just like her daddy." She paused to tap her clove again. "Anyway, these girls are just falling all over one another fighting for his attention, and I'm afraid he's getting a big head because of it. Not to mention all the angry fathers poor Gerry is having to deal with. Alfonso showed up at the club with a shotgun!

"Your father is furious with Max over it, too. Lord help

us all if he ends up like Joe. But the little devil doesn't seem to care. Just a few weeks ago Gerry caught him on the roof with a pretty little blonde thing, both of them nearly naked. And well, he dragged Max inside and gave him a good talking-to."

Shrugging, Ginny took another puff from her clove before stubbing it out on the tabletop and flicking it away. "Didn't do a lick of good. A week later I caught him in his bedroom with Sean Boyle's daughter bouncing away on top of him. And she's a little vixen if I ever saw one. Red curls as far as the eye can see and is she ever freckled! Even her ass has freckles! Tits, too!"

"So whaddya do?" Preacher asked, fighting laughter.

Ginny shrugged. "What could I do? I told her to get her freckled backside off my son and put some clothes on. Then I took her to the kitchen, gave her a slice of *Bienenstich,* and told her that if she didn't start keeping her knees together, her five minutes of fun with my Max was going to land her at Sister Agnes' home for troubled girls."

His shoulders quaking, Preacher dropped his face into his hands. His poor mother, having to go through this with each of her sons.

"You know I've been making *Bienenstich* every week? And I'm going to keep making it until you come home."

His laughter dying in his throat, Preacher looked up from his hands and into his mother's eyes. *Bienenstich* was his favorite dessert. Hearing that she'd been making it every week, hoping that would be the week he'd come home, felt like a fist to the face.

"Now don't go and look at me like that, Damon," Ginny said tenderly, her slate-colored eyes misting over, shining like liquid silver. "I'm not trying to make you feel bad. I only want you to know you're missed, and you're loved. And that's never going to change."

Preacher drew in a deep breath and opened his mouth to speak, but his mother stopped him with a wagging finger. "No, no," she said, "enough about that. Tell me about this girl—Debbie. What's her story? I couldn't get more than two words out of her."

Preacher blew out his breath. "Your guess is as good as mine. She won't talk about herself."

"And you like her?"

"… She's okay."

"And you're sleeping with her?"

Preacher glared at his mother, who smirked in return.

"Ahhh," Ginny mused. "So you're not sleeping with her. That's your tell, you know? I ask and ask, and if you get embarrassed, that's a yes. If you get angry, that's a no."

"*Mo-om*," he groaned, dropping his face back into his hands. "Please, for the love of fuckin' God, stop! I'm not talkin' to you about this!"

"But you like her," Ginny continued, unbothered. "And she's halfway in love with you. So what's the problem? Why are you sitting around here moping instead of spending time with her?"

Preacher glanced up. "She's what?"

"Oh Lord," Ginny sighed. "Don't tell me you don't see the way she looks at you, Damon. That girl is head over heels. Even your father noticed, and you know your father. If it isn't business, he'd be hard pressed to notice a falling anvil until he was buried beneath it."

He shook his head slowly. No. Well, yeah… he'd seen

the way she looked at him and he'd thought it was lust, same as him. But love? No way. They hardly knew each other.

"It ain't like that," he said quickly. "She's too young for me... and I'm just givin' her a ride."

"Then why'd you bring her here?" she asked. Several moments passed in silence while Ginny eyed him shrewdly. "You brought her to me, didn't you?"

Unwilling to admit to anything, Preacher only stared at his mother.

Ginny laughed softly. "You care about her, Damon. If you didn't, you wouldn't have brought her here—to me."

"Mom," he finally said, "I don't know, I really don't. I wasn't thinkin', haven't been thinkin' clearly for a long time now. My head's a mess, and I was just out there ridin', and I meet this chick and... I don't know. She's been on her own a while now, makin' a go of it on the road. But I just had this feeling that if I didn't help her out, something might happen to her."

Reaching across the table, Ginny placed her hand over his. "And?" she prompted.

"And what?"

"And you didn't want anything to happen to her because...?"

Blank-faced, Preacher stared at his mother. "Because... that would suck for her?"

Ginny slapped his head. "Because you like her, you dolt!"

Exasperated, Preacher rolled his eyes. "Yeah, Ma. You got me. I like her. So fuckin' what?"

A self-satisfied smile on her face, Ginny got to her feet. "Nothing," she shrugged, turning away. "Just wanted to hear you say it.

"By the way, you remind me of him," she called over her shoulder.

Preacher's eyes narrowed. "Who?" he growled.

Ginny's smile was downright wicked as she strode through camp. "Nobody," she replied in a sing-song voice.

Shaking his head, Preacher picked up his knife and resumed twisting the tip into the picnic table. He wasn't anything like his father. The Judge wouldn't know a good time if it bit him in the ass. He was all business, all the time. The man lived by a strict code of laughable ethics and deprived himself of every fun thing the world had to offer.

Only Preacher couldn't recall the last time he'd been able to let loose, either. And hadn't Max accused him of acting *just like Dad*?

Scowling, Preacher continued mutilating the picnic table, trying to think about something else—anything else. He thought of *Bienenstich*, and then of Max being chased down the block by a gang of angry fathers wielding shotguns. He started to smile… and then froze.

Max. Max was at the swimming hole.

Debbie was at the swimming hole.

Max, that little fucking gigolo, was with Debbie.

Preacher shot up out of his seat, slipped his blade into his boot, and headed out of camp.

The heat had brought half the camp to the swimming hole. Overflowing with people, it took Preacher a good ten minutes searching the small space before finding a familiar face.

He spotted Sylvia first, easy to identify by her bulging

belly and brightly colored sundress. Wearing a dark blue bikini top and white shorts, Louisa was sunbathing beside Sylvia, her nose in a book. Whiskey Jim and Joe were seated nearby, a pack of beer and Debbie's backpack wedged between them.

Preacher glanced around. But no Debbie.

Dropping down beside his brother, he snagged a beer for himself. "Where's everyone else?" he asked, scanning the area again.

Scowling, Joe shrugged. "Not bein' forced to sit here. Probably havin' fun."

Sylvia lifted her sunglasses only long enough to shoot Joe what Preacher assumed was *the look* Joe had referred to earlier, but thankfully she didn't say anything. Chuckling, Jim shook his head and pointed toward the swimming hole. "They're swimmin'," he said.

Preacher followed his finger across the water to the far end, where the waterfall flowed thick and heavy over the rocky outcropping. He spotted Anne first, wading through waist-high water in a skimpy red bikini top—just a tiny scrap of fabric that barely covered her. He saw Knuckles next, splashing and chasing two young women around. He followed their movements until he spied Max… but still no Debbie.

Just then a body broke through the water surface. Water droplets flying in all directions, Debbie shoved her sopping hair out of her face and smiled at Max.

Smiled.

At Max.

She fucking smiled at Max—his dirty dog of a little brother.

Frowning, Preacher straightened and shielded his eyes with his hand. Max was gesturing to Debbie, talking animatedly about something, and Debbie was... laughing?

Preacher stiffened, irritation prickling along his skin. Getting Debbie to talk was like pulling teeth, but making her smile was ten times more difficult. And yet here she was, smiling at and laughing with Max.

Preacher's frown continued to deepen as Max drew closer to Debbie. Max pointed at something off in the distance, and when Debbie turned to look, Max casually slid his arm over her shoulders.

Preacher shot to his feet. He was two seconds away from jumping into the water, jeans, boots, and leather vest be damned, and dragging Max out by the scruff of his neck. And he would have if Debbie hadn't immediately shrugged out from beneath Max's arm and swam away.

"What's it gonna be?" Joe asked, standing shoulder to shoulder with Preacher, peering out across the water. "Wedgie? Swirly? Purple nurple?"

"I'm gonna smash his fuckin' face in."

"Damn. You're really diggin' this chick, huh?"

Preacher shook his head, about to tell Joe that it wasn't like that when Debbie appeared on the grass, and his words died in his throat.

She'd gone swimming in her T-shirt and shorts, but she might as well have been topless. Preacher could see everything through the thin material—the outline of her full, firm breasts, the shape and size of her rock-hard nipples.

And he wasn't the only one noticing, either. For a girl who thought no one noticed her, she sure was catching a lot of looks.

"Nice," Joe muttered under his breath.

Growling, Preacher elbowed Joe in the ribs. "Shut the fuck up, asshole."

Debbie approached them, wringing out her wet hair, drops of water cascading down her sun-kissed skin, utterly oblivious to the half dozen erections she'd just caused.

"Are you going swimming?" she asked.

Beside him, Joe snorted. "He can't swim."

Preacher slowly faced his brother. "This ain't exactly the ocean. I think I can handle myself."

Joe smirked at him. "Don't change the fact that you can't fuckin' swim."

"And you wet the fuckin' bed until you were twelve, either," Preacher shot back. "But who's askin', right?"

Someone giggled, a high-pitched girly squeak, and Preacher jerked his gaze away from Joe to find Debbie with her hand over her mouth, a tiny dimple indenting her left cheek.

Taking a swig of warm beer, Debbie glanced over at Preacher. Seated beside her on the sun-warmed grass, he was alternating between scowling at Joe and outright glaring at Max. He'd been agitated all day, it felt like, but now he seemed even more so, leaving her wondering if he'd gotten into another argument with his father.

She nudged him with her elbow, and he turned his scowl on her.

"Are you okay?" she whispered.

His expression didn't change. "What was so funny?" he asked.

Confused, Debbie shook her head. "What was so funny... when?"

Preacher jerked his chin toward the swimming hole. "You were laughin'. With Max."

"Uh..." Debbie looked to the water, trying to recall what Max had said. "I don't remember," she eventually replied. "He made a joke about something, but I can't remember what." She turned back to Preacher. "So, you really can't swim?"

It was the wrong thing to say. Preacher's brows drew together, his already tense expression tightening further.

"My parents tried to teach me when I was little, but I was scared shitless. Didn't like the feeling of bein' underwater." He rolled his eyes. "Still don't."

Debbie couldn't stop her smile. After watching Preacher take on those men at the truck stop, and stand up to the Road Warriors and that terrifying man from this morning, the notion that he was afraid of something as harmless as water was laughable.

"Somethin' funny?" he growled.

Biting down on her bottom lip, squelching her smile, Debbie shook her head. "I just didn't picture you as being afraid of anything."

That had been the right thing to say. Preacher's mouth quirked and his strained expression began to ease.

"Not afraid anymore, Wheels," he said dryly, "Just don't like it."

She shrugged. "Well, I *love* swimming."

"Yeah?"

She nodded. "I used to live near the beach, and every day after school I'd stop there."

She paused to sip her beer. "I went to a private school and we wore these awful uniforms." Recalling the button-down shirt that had reached clear up to her chin and the heavy plaid skirt, Debbie made a face. "The socks were the worst. So itchy. My favorite part of the day was taking them off and walking in the water."

It had also been her least favorite part of the day because it had meant she was that much closer to having to head home. And home was hell—complete with Satan himself.

Feeling her stomach tighten, Debbie shuddered through her next breath and wished she'd kept her mouth shut. Even her happy memories always turned dark.

"Private school, huh?" Preacher laughed. "I fuckin' knew it." He tapped two fingers to his temple. "Smart."

Despite her roiling insides, Debbie forced a smile. But the smile didn't last and she began shifting uncomfortably, suddenly acutely aware of her wet clothes, the way they were sticking to her body, chafing her skin. And the way the prickly weeds beneath her were poking sharply against her. And the way the sun was suddenly too hot, shining too brightly overhead, leaving her feeling as if she was under a spotlight.

Quickly she swallowed the last of her beer and set the bottle aside. The warm brew sloshed uncomfortably in the pit of her stomach.

"I'm going to go change," she mumbled and shot to her feet. Grabbing her backpack, she whirled away and hurried off through the crowds of people.

Reaching the dirt path, feeling overwhelmed by stomach-turning images, awash in unwanted feelings, Debbie picked up her pace.

Why had she even brought up the beach in the first place? What had she thought was going to happen? Maybe some small part of her had begun to hate the constant lying. Maybe that same part of her had wanted to set free a sliver of her truth and unburden a bit of her soul in the process.

Her eyes burning, she released a bitter snort. Whatever the reason, she should have known better.

Debbie slowed her steps and dug her sunglasses out of her backpack. She didn't think she was going to cry—she hadn't cried in forever—but just in case she did, she didn't want anyone to see.

God, she wouldn't ever be normal, would she? How could she hope to let someone else in when she couldn't even let herself in? The burning in her eyes intensified. Beneath the tinted lenses, she blinked furiously. Her chest tightened. She would not cry. She would absolutely not fucking cry.

Noticing a bathhouse just ahead, she felt a small sense of relief. She would lock herself in a toilet stall and fall apart in private.

"Wheels!"

Debbie jumped, nearly tripping over her own feet. Whirling around, she found Preacher striding up a small incline, concern darkening his features. Her stomach flip-flopped. She didn't want him to see her like this. She didn't want him to look at her like that—with concern or pity.

"What's wrong?" he demanded.

Nothing is wrong, she wanted to scream. *I'm normal! Please, just look at me like I'm a normal girl!*

"I'm fine," she managed to squeak out.

"Lie," Preacher snapped and plucked her sunglasses from her face before she could stop him. She attempted snatching them back, but he held them just out of reach.

"You're fine, huh? Like hell you're fine. What the fuck happened back there?"

Standing in the center of the path, a large group was forced to part around them, and Debbie could feel their questioning, curious eyes on her as they passed by. Biting her bottom lip, she looked down at her bare feet.

"Wheels…" Preacher's hand brushed her cheek, and then he was cupping her chin, forcing her head up, forcing her to look at him.

His hand was cool, much cooler than her overheated skin, and she felt herself leaning into his touch. Her chest loosened, breathing becoming easier. Her stomach unknotted. Everything softened and slowed.

Debbie stared into Preacher's searching eyes. There were no shadows there, no storms brewing. Clear, dark-brown depths stared back at her without judgment, without pity, without… hunger.

Debbie, all of a sudden, desperately wanted the hunger.

She didn't remember going up on her toes or wrapping her arm around Preacher's neck. She hardly registered pressing her mouth to his. It all happened so quickly. One moment she was looking into his eyes and the next she was kissing him.

Harder and harder she kissed him, faster and faster. Their noses bumped, their teeth clacked, their breaths were infrequent, erratic bursts of air between the tangling of their tongues.

She hadn't meant to kiss him like this—so viciously.

One moment she'd been filled with ugly memories, haunted by the touch of a monster, and the next she'd been filled with wanting.

Want rolled through her body like molten lava, turning her insides into liquid fire.

She wanted to erase all the ugly. And replace it with this. With Preacher.

Preacher. Preacher. *Preacher.*

His name was her pulse. Was the thrust of her tongue. Was the throbbing ache building within her.

His hands were on her now, one on the small of her back pressing her closer, the other cupping her head, angling her face. Their kisses slowed as they adjusted to their new position and then sped up again, his beard grating across her cheeks and chin. Her hands were in his hair now, her body bowed to his, her breasts crushed against his lower chest.

And then, just as she'd gone from aflutter to flying, Preacher was gone. His kisses, his touches, just gone. Dazed and breathing hard, Debbie staggered back a step, much to the amusement of several giggling bystanders.

Then he was back, gripping her wrist and tugging her off the pathway. He led her around the corner of the bathhouse to an alcove partially hidden by several towering pine trees.

Standing there, half an arm's length away from one another, they stared. Preacher's eyes were wild, his breaths hard, his chest visibly expanding. His shoulders were squared, his legs spread apart, one hand gripping his belt buckle right above the unmistakable bulge in his jeans.

She wanted him back. Every bit of her he'd kissed and touched wanted more. And in that moment Debbie wasn't sure she'd ever wanted anything so badly before in her life.

He stepped toward her and stopped. "Ah, fuck, Wheels," he groaned, looking away. He scrubbed a hand down his face and across his beard. "We can't do this."

Still reeling, she pressed her lips together, forcing her heavy breaths through her nose. Adrenaline and lust were caught in her throat—a ball of hot and cold, making breathing difficult.

"Lie," she said after a moment, and his eyes shot to hers. "We can do this—*I want to do this.*"

His lips twitched "You're… sixteen. I'm twenty-four."

"I'm almost seventeen." The childish plea slipped free before she could catch it and lock it away.

When he still made no move toward her, she tried again, one last time. "Preacher… I'm not a virgin."

His nostrils flared. His eyes were liquid fire. But still, he didn't move. More seconds ticked by. Then, just as Debbie was feeling the faint stirrings of defeat infiltrate her haze of need, he was back.

An arm came down on either side of her, caging her in, and Debbie dragged herself up the wall onto her tiptoes, reaching.

His lips were on hers, her hands tangled in his shirt, and they kissed hard and fast until their breaths grew ragged and kissing was no longer enough.

Lifting Debbie off the ground, Preacher used his body to keep her flat against the wall. Legs around his waist, ankles locked at his back, she brought that desperate, aching place between her thighs flush with the bulge in Preacher's jeans. He ground himself against her, half growling, half groaning into her mouth, and if Debbie's eyes had been open, they would have rolled back.

She. Was. Melting.

Melting into nothing. Weightless. Writhing energy. A feather-light slave to the throbbing need between her legs.

Everything else... gone.

She'd finally found it—a place to exist without pain.

CHAPTER 21

HEAT.

Debbie was feeling intense heat all over her body that had nothing at all to do with the warm, sticky night air, the blazing bonfire before her, or the whiskey she'd consumed.

The heat was from the lean body she was tucked against, the muscled arm wrapped around her, and the calloused fingertips tracing invisible lines over and under her collarbone. Back and forth, up and down, Preacher lulled her into a place she'd never been before.

If she let herself, it'd be easy to forget that they weren't the only ones seated around the bonfire.

Everyone was here; even Preacher's father had chosen to join them. Seated in one of the few lawn chairs, Gerald stared somberly into the fire, while most of the others engaged in quiet conversations amongst themselves. Janis Joplin's *Summertime* was playing on the tape deck and Ginny and June were singing along. Across the way, Knuckles and Max were roasting marshmallows.

Preacher's fingers stilled as he bent his head to hers. "Tell me somethin' else about you, Wheels. Gimme more truth."

She shook her head. There was no way she was going to ruin any more moments with more of her truths. "Nope," she said, her tone intentionally light. "It's your turn. Tell *me* something about *you*."

"What else is there to know? You've already met my entire family."

Debbie angled her head toward Preacher. Firelight and shadows danced across his handsome face.

"How'd you get the name Preacher?" she asked.

"Same way you got the name Wheels." His lips twitched; humor glinted in his eyes. "Some asshole thought it was funny."

Giggling, Debbie sank down against Preacher's side and turned back to the fire. His fingers started up again, sliding back and forth across her clavicle before dipping down low. Preacher slowly outlined the swells of her breasts, sending jolts of sensation tearing straight to her core.

Feeling flustered and fevered, Debbie gulped down her next several breaths, then gripped the neck of the whiskey bottle propped between her legs and took a lengthy swig.

As if Preacher somehow realized the fiery thoughts running amok in her mind, he chuckled quietly, his warm breath tickling her neck and sending a heated shiver down her spine.

All day long, since the encounter at the bathhouse, Debbie had been able to think of little else. She hadn't wanted to stop. It had been Preacher who'd eventually pulled away, who'd said "*not here*" in a heavy, hoarse tone that belied his words. Who'd then taken her hand and led her back to the swimming hole.

And though he hadn't kissed her again, Debbie couldn't think of a single moment since that he hadn't been touching her. An arm around her shoulders. His fingers brushing against hers. A hand at her waist, sinking slowly down her hip. And in doing so, he'd kept her in this strange state of being, lost in a haze, teetering on the edge between reality and sensation.

"I'm the asshole who coined him Preacher."

Debbie's haze cleared. The gruffly spoken statement had come from Gerald. Leaning forward in his chair, hands steepled beneath his chin, his eternal grimace was focused on Debbie.

Feeling the weight of Gerald's scrutiny as if it were a crushing boulder, she attempted to straighten, but Preacher's arm across her chest only tightened.

"Like a goddamn preacher, he never did know when to shut his mouth," Gerald continued. "Had a damn opinion 'bout everything. Always buttin' his nose in my business, always thinkin' he was right and tellin' me how to do my job."

Gerald let out a low chuckle and his eyes slid to Preacher. "Ain't that right? Couldn't wait to get your hands on that gavel, could ya?"

Preacher's chin came down on Debbie's shoulder, refusing to even look at his father. Gerald's smile slowly flattened and he turned back to the bonfire, frowning.

"Don't know what happened, though," he muttered. "Don't even know my own boy anymore.

"I went to war, you know." Nodding, Gerald continued to frown at the fire. "Doc and Jim here, they went to war, too. And we've seen some shit, haven't we? Now that kinda shit… that can change a man." Gerald paused as if carefully considering his next words. "But prison…"

Preacher's head jerked up, and Debbie didn't have to see his face to know that his expression was murderous. She could feel it in the suddenly rigid lines of his body—every part of him that was touching a part of her had turned to stone.

"Gerry, no," Ginny whispered, her expression pleading.

"In prison," Gerald continued loudly, ignoring his wife, "you get a roof over your head, three square meals a day, clean clothes, and a nice warm bed to sleep in every night." Gerald glanced around the bonfire. "Sounds like a god-damned vacation if you ask me."

Ginny's eyes squeezed closed.

Though Janis Joplin still played and the fire continued to crackle and hiss, the campsite had fallen quiet. All eyes were on either Preacher or Gerald.

And Preacher, he was shaking. Not visibly, just a slight shudder with every breath he expelled, as if he were full to the brim with ugly things that he could no longer contain.

Debbie covered the arm banded across her chest with her own. Slipping her fingers between his, she squeezed his hand and waited for the explosion. The entire campsite waited.

Instead, Preacher reached around her, seizing the whiskey from between her thighs. Lifting the bottle to his mouth, he chugged the amber liquid. Having soon finished what was left, he tossed the empty bottle aside and gestured to Tiny. "Gimme that," he growled.

Tiny glanced down at the joint cinched between his fingers, and then quickly handed it over to Preacher. Puffing on the joint, thick smoke poured from Preacher's mouth, billowing around Debbie. Eventually, the arm around her chest began to loosen.

"So, uh, they're playin' *Taxi Driver* at the theater in town." Smokey glanced around the bonfire, a strained smile on his face.

"We should go," Max offered meekly. "Ain't nothin' else to do around here."

"Haven't you seen that already, Maxwell?" Ginny asked tentatively, her eyes on Gerald. "Back home?"

Knuckles, who seemed to have forgotten the tension entirely, gaped at her. "Are you kiddin', Little Ginny? You could see that movie a hundred times and never get sick of it!"

At that, Max perked up. Grinning, he turned to Knuckles and drew a finger-gun from his pocket. "You talkin' to me? *You talkin' to me?*"

Knuckles mimed drawing a gun from an invisible holster and pointed his own finger-gun at Max. "Don't try it, you fuck," he shot back, laughing.

"I'm in," Tiny announced.

"Count me and Anne in, too," Whiskey Jim added.

"I wanna go," Sylvia said, looking at Joe.

"You?" Joe snorted and shook his head. "No way. You'd hate it."

"God forbid I would wanna get outta this park for a

couple hours!" she hissed. "The bike fumes are makin' me queasy!"

Joe's teeth clenched. "You shoulda stayed home. I told you not to—"

"We should all go," June hurriedly interrupted, "Make a day of it. I've been wanting to head into town. And Ginny, you probably want to go to the farmers' market?"

Ginny glanced at Gerald before turning to June. "No, no, you all go." She waved her hand and smiled. "Take the van and go into town and make a day of it. Give... Gerry and me some peace and quiet."

"Wheels." Preacher's breath, smelling strongly of whiskey and marijuana, fanned her cheek.

Debbie turned, finding Preacher's face only inches from hers. His arm fell away from her chest, his hand cupped her cheek. Taking a drag off the joint, he closed the remaining gap between their lips and exhaled into her mouth.

Debbie drew in a hard breath and earthy-tasting smoke billowed inside her mouth, pouring down her throat. Preacher's tongue came next, sweeping through her mouth, while his hand slid into her hair, cupping her head. Smoke trickled out from between their lips as they kissed slowly, deeply. Debbie's thoughts grew fuzzy and muddled from either the drugs, or the man, or both.

"I haven't seen a movie since before I got tossed in the joint," Preacher whispered, after releasing her mouth.

"What movie was it?" she murmured.

He glanced away, considering. "*Jaws*," he finally said. "I think. Wait, no... coulda been *Death Race*. Don't remember which. What about you?"

Once upon a time Debbie had treasured going to the

movies. Before her mother had remarried, she'd worked odd jobs and strange hours, and with Debbie's school schedule they'd rarely seen one another, with the exception of Sundays. Every Sunday they'd go to their local theater for classic movie night.

Unlike most mothers and daughters, Debbie and her mother had never been close. But every Sunday it had felt as if she'd almost had a mother—at least for a couple of hours. The tradition had continued until her mother had remarried, and then Sunday movie nights were no more.

The only movie theaters she'd been inside recently had been ones she'd snuck into for warmth and to catch a few hours of sleep.

She shrugged. "I can't remember."

"You wanna go, then?" He watched her through lazy, half-lidded eyes, his pupils noticeably larger. He appeared relaxed, the only remaining sign of stress was the subtle tightening around his eyes. At some point he'd lain his hand on her thigh and was now toying with the hem of her shorts. His fingers started up again, dancing a drunken path up and down her leg.

"Sure," she breathed as she shivered beneath his touch. The movies, New York City, in that moment, Debbie would go anywhere with Preacher.

The corner of his mouth lifted, and any remaining strain in his expression vanished.

Being bad felt damn good.

This was something Preacher had learned from a young age. It had started out innocently enough, disobeying his parents or lying to a schoolteacher. Tiny acts of defiance that made a small boy in a world of men feel not quite so insignificant.

At ten years old he was shoplifting from the corner bodega and slipping money out of The Judge's wallet. At thirteen he was placing illegal bets in the back alley behind the neighborhood butcher shop.

And by the time Preacher was in high school, he'd graduated from shoplifting to jacking neighborhood cars and joyriding with his friends.

Even after his father had brought him into the club and illegal doings had become a way of life, Preacher had still found ways to get his kicks. Taking another man's girl to bed just because he could. Skimming money from business associates, or snagging some junk for himself. It was never enough to cause notice—just enough to satiate Preacher's appetite for rebellion.

In Preacher's mind, those tiny bits of rebellion had kept him fresh. Awake. Alive.

He'd since grown stale in prison. He'd forgotten what being him felt like. He'd forgotten how much he loved to push boundaries. To break rules. To bend them to his will.

He remembered now and he had Debbie to thank for that.

It wasn't that being with Debbie was necessarily bad, only that Preacher had deemed it not the right thing. He'd drawn a line.

And then he gave his conscience a swift kick off a tall bridge and dove headfirst right over that line.

And yeah, it felt damn good.

Crouched inside his tent, Preacher zipped the door flap

closed and turned toward Debbie. Seated cross-legged on top of the sleeping bag he'd laid out, she looked up at him with a nervous, expectant expression. Moonlight filtering through the tent's windows bathed her in an almost angelic glow, emphasizing the dark of her eyes.

Was that a little bit of fear he was seeing, too?

It might have given him pause... if he hadn't been so drunk. And high. And three times as keyed up as he could ever remember feeling before in his life—an uncomfortable combination of angry and horny that desperately needed an outlet.

Not bothering to kick off his boots or remove his cut, Preacher moved swiftly across the tent. Cupping the side of Debbie's face, he claimed her mouth. And as his tongue plunged past her lips, he used the weight of his body to push her onto her back and maneuver himself between her legs.

While his hands were busy skimming the length of her, Preacher thrust his hips forward, rocking himself over the sweet spot between her thighs. She jerked at the contact, gasping softly into his mouth. He continued mimicking sex until her legs were wrapped around his waist and she was grinding against him the same way she kissed him—absolutely inexperienced, but at the same time, so crazy into it.

This girl did not think, not when it came to him anyway, and Preacher fucking loved it.

A breast in one hand and a handful of ass in the other, he broke their kiss and moved to her neck, licking, sucking, biting his way across the soft skin there.

He traveled quickly down to her collarbone, pushing her T-shirt up as he went.

He didn't bother to take her top off—he'd already freed

the parts of her he wanted. He groped and kneaded and teased until Debbie was panting.

And then his mouth replaced his hands.

Debbie's hands went to his head, gripping handfuls of his hair. Soft, needy, sexy-as-hell noises filled his ears, and he went from straining uncomfortably against his jeans to nearly punching straight through them.

Heaving himself up over her, he took her mouth again, kissing her hard and fast.

Still wet from his mouth, her tits were in his hand; he palmed one and then the other before sliding his hand down her stomach toward her shorts.

He yanked open the top button.

"Preacher." Debbie turned her head, freeing her mouth. "Preacher... wait."

He continued fumbling with her shorts, pulling open two more buttons. Although he'd heard her, nothing had registered. His skin was too hot, his anger with The Judge was still simmering inside him. And his dick felt full to the point of bursting. He was sick of only wanting this girl—*he wanted to have her*.

Legs twisted beneath him, hands shoved at his shoulders. "Preacher, stop!"

Preacher froze and Debbie shoved at him again. He rolled off her onto his side as she scrambled to sit. Flushed and breathing hard, she wrenched her T-shirt down and quickly fixed her shorts.

"What's wrong?" Preacher asked, unable to hear himself over the rapid roar of blood pumping through him.

Biting her bottom lip, refusing to look at him, Debbie only shook her head.

Irritation rose inside him, and Preacher had to fight to battle it back down, to remain calm. Sitting up, he ran a hand through his unbound hair and blew out a breath.

"I'm sorry," he heard Debbie whisper. Her voice sounded small and timid, and Preacher heard real fear there. He blew out another breath, and with it, some of his frustration.

"It's cool," he muttered. "We don't gotta do it."

"It's not that." Debbie joined him at the door. "I do wanna do it. It was just…"

She trailed off and Preacher made the mistake of looking at her. Her hair was a mess, her lips wet and swollen. Her nipples were visible beneath her T-shirt, tiny torpedoes aimed straight at him. Inside his jeans his dick surged, the buildup of pressure quickly becoming uncomfortable. His hands began to twitch, suddenly desperate for something to do.

Grinding his teeth, Preacher moved quickly across the tent and opened the door. "You don't gotta explain shit to me," he managed to grit out as he fumbled to light a cigarette.

Staring out into the night, he puffed on his cigarette like his life depended on it, feeling like he might actually explode if he didn't fuck… *something*.

Debbie's hand appeared on his arm, her touch an electric surge to his already fried system. "I'm really sorry. I just got—I don't know. It was, um—it was just too fast." The hand on his arm began to quiver almost as much as her voice. "I don't know—"

Preacher cut her off by shoving a cigarette between her lips. "Shh," he growled, "and let me calm the fuck down."

They smoked in silence. Preacher lit one cigarette after

another until the mountain in his jeans was more of a semi-hard mound and his heartbeat had returned to normal.

When he eventually chanced another glance at Debbie, he found her with her arms wrapped around her legs, chin resting on her knees, nervously twisting a small silver ring around her finger. And now that he could think clearly, he felt like a first-class asshole.

"Wheels," he said, sighing. "Look at me."

Her big brown eyes lifted, full of riotous emotions that Preacher wasn't going to begin to guess at.

"Whatever bullshit you got goin' on inside that head of yours, it better not be because of me. I ain't mad. You don't gotta fuck me. Hell, you don't even gotta talk to me and I'll still get you to the city. A promise is a promise."

"What about you?" she asked.

"What about me?"

"After you get me to the city. Are you going to stay... or are you going back on the road?"

Preacher studied her. "You tryin' to ask me something specific?"

She stared at him a moment, then shrugged. "Just wondering."

It was too flippant a tone, too cavalier a gesture to be anything other than a lie. And Preacher wondered if that's why she'd stopped him. It made sense—why would a good girl like her want to sleep with an asshole like him, especially if he was just going to cut and run in a few days?

"I don't know." He rubbed his neck. "I got some shit goin' on with my dad."

"I know, but... why don't you just talk to him?"

Preacher snorted. The idea that The Judge would be

willing to hear anything Preacher had to say was a pipe dream at best. His old man was wired wrong. He couldn't actually listen to anything anyone said. He was built to give orders, nothing more.

"That ain't gonna happen."

"Why not?"

"Because if it doesn't have somethin' to do with him or the club, he doesn't give a shit. He was in the Marines and the Navy, Wheels. He thinks he's the biggest, baddest thing out there. He thinks he's seen and done it all, and only he knows best. And he thinks we're all his goddamn soldiers. He can't handle anyone questionin' him. He can't handle anything but blind fuckin' obedience." Preacher shook his head. "I used to look up to him. I used to want to be just like him. But now... " He trailed off, unsure of what to say, unsure of what he wanted.

"So what, then? You're just never going home again?"

He didn't answer her right away. He'd been asking himself the same question every day for months now and had yet to come up with anything even resembling an answer.

"I don't fit there anymore," he eventually said. "That's his world, not mine."

The statement was true. The Judge had always liked flat surfaces and straight, even lines. He liked all his soldiers lined up in a row, ready to salute. And Preacher didn't have straight lines anymore. He'd never had straight lines, but now... he was all over the place—a mess of jagged edges and incoherent scribbles.

"You're so lucky," she whispered, and Preacher was startled to find tears shining in her eyes. "You're so stupid, too. You don't even realize how lucky you are. You have this huge family, all these people, and they all love you." Shaking her head, she gestured passionately with her hands. "They love you so much that they're angry with you for taking off. And they're so happy you're back, and you're just going to leave them again because you're scared of your dad—"

"I ain't scared of him," Preacher interjected. "That cranky old bastard—"

"Wants you around!" Debbie snapped. A tear slipped free from the corner of her eye, glinting in the moonlight.

"You're so stupid," she continued, her voice cracking. "You're so lucky and you don't even realize it. I wish every day I had a family like yours."

Preacher stared at her, feeling a little bewildered, and ten times the asshole he'd previously thought himself to be.

"Jesus, Wheels, come here." He held out his arm to her, and she quickly tucked herself against him. She folded her knees to her chest, and he slid his arm around her back. Neither of them spoke for a long while, and he found himself marveling at how perfectly she fit beside him.

"I don't want you to disappear."

He glanced down to find Debbie's eyes on him—big, expressive eyes like vacuums, sucking all thoughts straight from him. Those eyes. That mouth. That vulnerable look on her face that made him want to tuck her inside his jacket and shield her from the world.

She was definitely a problem he wasn't accustomed to dealing with. On the one hand, he wanted to fuck her, and on the other, he wanted to save her. Were both possible? Or was one going to cancel out the other?

Cupping Debbie's cheek, Preacher ran the pad of his thumb over her lips. She stared up at him in a way that made him think that when his mother had told him Debbie was halfway in love with him, she hadn't been exaggerating.

It was a responsibility he wasn't quite sure he wanted and made him feel more than just a little uneasy. He could hardly fend for himself these days, let alone someone else.

But even as he thought it, it wasn't enough of a concern to deter his baser wants or to distract from the way he felt when he looked at her.

"Who are you?" he muttered. Then he kissed her, not bothering to wait for an answer.

If she didn't want to fuck, they didn't have to fuck. But Preacher still wanted his hands on her—blue balls be damned.

CHAPTER 22

THE FOUR POINTS FARMERS' MARKET WAS SMALL BUT plentiful, with rows of tables piled high with baskets full of seasonal fruits and vegetables—apples, peaches, and raspberries, as well as corn, beans, beets, and more. The veritable rainbow of colors reminded Debbie of the local farmers' market back home—a much larger market that had been open all year round. She'd wasted entire days wandering the market, happily lost among the feast of colors and smells.

And today was no different. Debbie strolled through the aisles, breathing in the crisp, fresh scents, returning the smiles of the men and women selling them. She took extra inhales when she came across a table laden with sugary baked goods and large loaves of fresh bread.

A short ways down the aisle, Debbie paused beside a

table covered in short stacks of used books and ran a finger over a coverless copy of *Anna Karenina*, the book stained and torn. She found herself unexpectedly frowning—a frown that had nothing to do with the tragic love story beneath her fingertips and everything to do with Preacher.

Last night had been… confusing at first. They'd been kissing, and that had felt amazing. And Preacher had been touching her, and she'd been touching him, and that had also felt amazing.

But then something unexpected had happened. Something ugly had wormed its way inside her happy haze. Only this time it hadn't been her past to darken her thoughts and fill her with unease. It had been her future.

Debbie hadn't ever factored someone like Preacher into her life. She especially hadn't considered all the feelings that had come with him. Turbulent, foreign feelings. Excitement and panic, sometimes to the point of fear. She felt as if her world had been rocked and then set on fire, but instead of burning her, the flames licking up and down her skin had left her soft and warm and utterly consumed.

I love him.

Those three words banged through her head like a gong, jarring and irrefutable. And completely ridiculous. She knew it was silly, and yet everything she was feeling told her otherwise. And what she was feeling? *Oh my God*. It was twice what she'd felt for him yesterday and triple the day before that. And she felt oddly hopeful, too. Hopeful in a way that made her chest ache. Hopeful in a way that scared her.

It had to be love.

What else could it be?

Moving away from the books, Debbie stopped in front

of a table covered in large wicker baskets overflowing with large green apples. Allowing her backpack to slide down her arm, she casually flipped the top flap open. Leaning far over the table, pretending to browse the selection of apples, she covertly rolled one straight off the top of the pile and into her bag. She did this several more times before finally selecting an apple to pay for.

Biting into the fruit, Debbie glanced over her shoulder and found Preacher where she'd left him—leaning against a wooden pillar just outside the market, hands shoved inside his jeans pockets. Wearing head to toe black, his dark hair was pulled tightly away from his face, giving his already stone-hewn features even more of an edge. Beside him, Tiny was talking animatedly, oblivious that Preacher's attention was elsewhere.

Having just witnessed her shoplifting, Preacher was smirking as he pushed away from the pillar. Taking another bite of her apple, Debbie watched him approach, and by the time she swallowed, he was beside her, his arm around her shoulders, his head bent to hers. She breathed in deeply, smelling leather and smoke—and since he'd showered this morning, faint hints of soap.

"Can't believe you're stealin' apples from a little old lady."

Debbie motioned him closer. Their faces almost touching, she whispered, "If you feel so bad about it, you could always pay her for them."

While Preacher was staring at her mouth, Debbie reached around him, slipped her hand inside the back pocket of his jeans and pulled his wallet free. He realized what she was doing at the last second, quickly straightened, and snatched her wrist.

Grinning, he plucked his wallet from her hand and stuffed it back in his pocket. "You tryin' to turn me on, Wheels?"

Debbie didn't know *what* she was doing, exactly. She was just reacting to Preacher and how he made her feel.

"'Cause it's workin'," he continued quietly, and Debbie watched the humor in his expression fade, his features tighten, and his eyes begin to burn. It was a look that, each time she saw it, left her feeling twice as desperate as the last time. Hot and needy, too. And Beautiful. Debbie felt beautiful for the first time in her life.

Beautiful not just because of the way Preacher looked at her, but because of the way he kissed and touched her, too— like he couldn't get enough. And beautiful because, despite what hadn't happened between them last night, Debbie had woken this morning and found herself tucked against his side, her cheek resting on his chest and his arm wrapped tightly around her middle.

Preacher tugged her closer and slapped his hand down on her ass. "You keep lookin' at me like that, Wheels," he murmured, "and that little old lady is gonna get a show."

Bursts of awareness zinged through Debbie. Awareness of Preacher's proximity, the location of his hand, the way he couldn't ever seem to keep his eyes off her mouth. Her breaths grew shallow and her heart began to race. The rapidly rising heat inside of her reached volcanic levels.

"Quit eye-fuckin' your girl, VP, and get your ass on your bike." Knuckles appeared beside them, glancing between them and grinning slyly.

Cursing, Preacher shoved him backward and started

advancing on him. Laughing, Knuckles nearly tripped over his own feet as he tried to scramble away.

"What was that, asshole?" Preacher demanded, his good-natured grin belying his tone. "You think I'm gonna let some scrawny little shitstain from the goddamn neighborhood talk to me like that?"

Knuckles made it to the edge of the parking lot just before Preacher tackled him. Both men lurched forward, lost their balance, and went toppling over one another into the dirt.

"I ain't scrawny no more!" Knuckles shouted. "Like my shirt says—pussy builds strong bones!"

"I second that, brother!" Crazy-8 called out. "Pussy gets me growin' every damn time!"

While the elderly woman selling apples looked on in horror, laughter erupted from the Silver Demons.

Shouldering her backpack, Debbie hurried to join the rest of the group in the parking lot. Standing beside Gerald and Ginny's van, Smokey turned to Debbie with a rare smile on his face. He was quite handsome for an older man, she decided, when he didn't look like he carried the weight of the world on his shoulders.

"Ginny tells me we've got you to thank for this." Smokey nodded toward Preacher and Knuckles.

Her forehead wrinkled. "Me?"

"Little Ginny said Preacher didn't want you headin' into the city not knowin' no one. So he brought you here to introduce you to his family—to all of us."

Debbie's heart skipped a beat. Preacher had... what?

"You see, we didn't know where he was," Smokey continued. "Didn't know if he was dead or alive or what, 'til now. You brought 'im back to us, and now we're in your debt. You ever need somethin', sweetheart, you come talk to me. I'll make it happen."

Speechless, Debbie could only nod, and Smokey turned his happy gaze back to Knuckles and Preacher. Both men were on their feet now, covered in dust and playfully shoving one another. A smear of dirt on his cheek, grass stuck in his hair, Preacher's eyes locked with hers.

Flushing from head to toe, Debbie took a bite of her apple.

And those three silly words continued to beat an undeniable rhythm inside of her.

Much like the park, the local movie theater was chock-full of bikers and their families, and as their own large group made its way to the ticket counter, Debbie couldn't help but roll her eyes at the nervous expressions of the townspeople and theater workers. If only they knew how sweet these men really were, how caring and giving too.

At the same time, she enjoyed the adverse reactions. She liked it when others averted their gazes or swallowed nervously as they passed. Beneath Preacher's arm, tucked against his side, she felt safe and protected in ways she'd never felt before—powerful feelings for someone who'd spent years living in fear.

Inside the screening room, Preacher broke away from their group and led Debbie to the back of the theater to the very last row, where there were less people, and very little light.

Preacher took the aisle seat, and as Debbie edged past,

he grabbed her hips and tugged her onto his lap. Quickly divesting her of her backpack, he captured her mouth in a kiss.

They kissed slowly at first—deliberate, leisurely strokes of Preacher's tongue, so slow, so perfect, and Debbie sighed into his mouth. She forgot entirely about the movie, forgot she was even in a movie theater. She forgot about everything but the lips moving hungrily over hers and the hands quietly roaming her stomach and hips.

Their kisses sped up—quick, hungry kisses in rapid succession—and Debbie felt Preacher grow hard beneath her. She started to squirm, the thick, firm feel of him beneath her causing a now-familiar ache to flare to life between her thighs.

Growling softly, Preacher wrapped an arm around her waist, holding her still. She attempted pulling away to complain, only he captured her cheek and held her in place.

Soon Debbie's kisses became distracted and messy. These feelings—the needy, pulsating knot low in her belly and the insatiable ache between her thighs—were all she could focus on. She wanted... no, she *needed* to be touched.

But Preacher seemed made of stone—the hand on her cheek remained firm, and the band of steel wrapped around her middle flexed and tightened.

It took all of Debbie's strength to pry his hand from her side. Frustrated and aching, she shoved it down between her legs.

As if he'd been waiting for this moment, Preacher promptly broke their kiss and spread his legs apart, unceremoniously dropping Debbie between them.

The disruption gave Debbie a brief glimpse of

reality—the movie had begun. Playing overhead, the bright screen highlighted the room full of people. Her cheeks heated, flushing with embarrassment, only to quickly realize that no one was paying them any attention. And that the people nearby were other couples engaged in the same sort of activities.

Then Preacher's mouth found her neck and his arm snaked around her middle, gripping her tightly. Situating one of her legs over his, he tugged open her jeans.

Debbie's breathing hitched, all other thoughts instantly forgotten.

His hand slid slowly down her midriff, the feel of his calloused palm against her smooth stomach causing delicious friction that sent a shiver spiraling through her.

His hand disappeared inside her jeans.

Her breath shuddered free, and Debbie sank back against Preacher and gripped his arm, her nails biting crescent moons into his skin.

This was… he was… *oh my God.*

Eyes rolling back, lids fluttering furiously, she was nothing more than a rolling boil of sensation, waves of heat rising and falling, but never quite cresting.

Afraid of making a sound, Debbie pressed her lips together tightly and turned her head. Preacher glanced down, his eyes dark, his expression hard, determined. Their eyes locked and her lips parted, dragging in a staggered breath.

And suddenly everything inside of her lit up all at once, her body drew up tight, and then… exploded.

Debbie sagged sideways, boneless and breathing hard, little more than a quivering bag of jelly.

Looking up, she found Preacher staring at her, his eyes

half-lidded, his nostrils flaring wide with each heavy, hungry breath he took.

Her hand moved of its own accord, cupping his cheek, her fingers twining through his beard. Arching her back, she pulled his face down to hers and kissed him gently on the lips. A soft rumble in his throat, he covered her mouth with his and deepened their kiss.

Yes, she loved him.

Holding tightly to Debbie's hand, Preacher veered quickly through the river of people leaving the theater. He wanted to get back to the park as soon as humanly possible. Back to camp, back inside his tent, and back inside—

He glanced at Debbie. Her bottom lip tucked beneath her teeth, her concentration was on the crowd ahead of them. His gaze traveled the rest of her, over all the places he wished he were still touching.

Her tank top was thin, she wasn't wearing a bra, and the night breeze that greeted them as they exited the theater was just cool enough for her nipples to stand up and take notice. Her high-waisted jeans were snug on her hips and thighs, emphasizing the curves Preacher liked best, but also baggy around her calves and feet, hiding her sneakers. She was both sexy and adorable and damn near perfect.

The following surge in his jeans was a visceral reaction, but it was more than just that. Preacher felt invigorated, and much younger than he had only a week ago. He wanted something again. He was looking forward to something instead of dreading it.

It had grown dark during the movie, the only remaining

light emanating from the streetlamps, the brightly lit storefronts, and the full moon hanging low and fat in the distance. A short ways down the street, Preacher spotted half of their group congregated around their motorcycles. The van was gone, meaning the others had already left.

"How'd you like the movie, Wheels?" he asked, glancing down at her. Still biting down on her lip, Debbie fought to contain a smile.

Laughing, Preacher released her hand and slung his arm around her shoulders, pulling her close. "It was good, right?" he teased. "My favorite part was when that guy did that thing. You know what I'm talkin' about, right? That thing?"

Truth be told, Preacher had very little idea what the movie had been about. He'd only managed to catch bits and pieces here and there when he hadn't been preoccupied with Debbie—which hadn't been all that often.

Debbie's blush deepened.

"What?" he asked, "you didn't like that part? Wheels, come on! That was the best fuckin' part!"

Bursting into giggles, Debbie turned and buried her face in his chest. Laughing loudly, Preacher squeezed her even tighter.

"Bunch of fuckin' slowpokes!" Knuckles called out. "Whaddya do—stick around for the cleanin' crew or somethin'?" Leaning against his motorcycle, Knuckles twirled a pair of women's pink panties on his finger.

Eyes wide and mocking, Preacher pointed. "Man, you forgot to put your underwear on!"

Seated on their bikes close by, Smokey and Jim began to snicker.

UNDESERVING

Knuckles stopped twirling and grinned. "Brother, I'm just workin' out my pussy finger for the next lucky lady."

Draped over Jim's back, Anne rolled her eyes and groaned. "Only one finger, huh? I'm guessin' you've left a lot of ladies feeling pretty *unlucky*."

"I only need one." Waggling his eyebrows, Knuckles flipped Anne off. "I got fat fingers, baby."

"And I'll break every single last one of 'em, if you ever talk to my ol' lady like that again," Jim growled.

Behind Jim, wearing a self-satisfied smirk, Anne stuck her tongue out at Knuckles.

His expression contrite, Knuckles folded his arms across his chest and muttered, "She fuckin' started it."

Smokey released a world-weary sigh. "Christ, kid. You sound like a broken record. Tits and pussy. Tits and pussy. You know there's more to life, right?"

Knuckles whirled on Smokey, his mouth hanging open. "Did you see that chick?" he demanded.

"How could I not?" Smokey's expression was as dry as his tone. "Hard to watch a movie when I got a goddamn ass bouncin' in my face."

Knuckles continued to look horrified. "Fuckin'-A, that was a piece of ass worth lookin' at!" He mimed smacking a woman's backside.

"You've seen one ass, you've seen 'em all."

"Man, what happened to you? You're, like, asexual or somethin' now?"

Amused, Preacher glanced between the two men. Smokey wasn't asexual; he was just a man who'd loved his wife and lost her. Growing up, Preacher couldn't remember a time when Maryanne hadn't been sick. As a diabetic, she'd slowly grown thinner, frailer, until her body eventually succumbed.

Before Maryanne's passing, Smokey had been a different man. He'd had a sense of humor, was hardly ever seen without a drink in his hand, and had often indulged in other women. He'd been a lot like Knuckles, actually. It wasn't until after Maryanne's death that Smokey had done a one-eighty in the personality department. Full of guilt and grief, the club's business became his sole focus.

Knuckles didn't understand this yet, how something could change a man so drastically. Truth be told, just two years earlier, neither had Preacher.

Just then, a police car flew past at top speed, lights blazing, sirens wailing, turning everyone's attention to the street. The response of the several dozen bikers still milling around was to thrust their fists in the air, shouting slurs and obscenities.

"Something's goin' on at the park," Jim said. "That ain't the first pig to blow by here."

Knuckles faked a yawn. "It's the same old shit every year. Last summer some dumb shit drank himself to death. Bunch of kids found him floatin' face down in the swimmin' hole, buck-ass naked, and the cops sent us all packin'. You ask me, they're just lookin' for an excuse to kick us out."

Preacher raised an eyebrow. When you put a large number of out-of-control people in a space together, it wasn't uncommon for things to get, well, out of control. Tempers flared and fights broke out. People drank too much booze, smoked too much grass, and then some dumbass kid goes and accidentally fucks the wife of a Hercules-sized bastard with a rare knife collection. Not that Preacher knew anything at all about *that*.

Smokey started his bike, revving his engine. "Whatever it is, it ain't got shit to do with us." He looked to Preacher and jerked his chin toward the road. "Come on VP, take your place up front and lead us back."

Jim revved his engine and Knuckles followed suit—all eyes were on him.

Preacher's neck muscles stiffened and began to ache, and his chest felt suddenly too tight. Smokey had been appointed temporary vice president while he'd been locked up. Now it appeared as if the man was handing him back his title.

Only he didn't want it. More, he didn't deserve it. A man like Smokey was far more qualified, and infinitely more deserving than he would ever be. Unlike Preacher, Smokey was loyal to both the club and The Judge and would never have abandoned either.

As he reached for his neck, Debbie stepped out from under his arm, plucked his helmet from his bike and placed it on her head. Fumbling with the chin strap, she offered him a small, encouraging smile that he found himself returning.

Mounting his motorcycle, Preacher waited for Debbie to climb on behind him before starting the engine. Her hands on his shoulders, she scooted quickly up the seat until her body was flush against his. Wrapping her arms around his middle, she slid her hands over his stomach, her fingertips pressing possessively into his skin.

It was a small, seemingly insignificant thing that Preacher might never have noticed had he not had the misfortune of having had very little human contact for two full years. And what contact he did have had been the glaring opposite of pleasurable.

But this—an unconscious gesture from his pretty-little-pickpocket, laying claim to him, telling him in no uncertain terms that she most definitely wanted him—filled Preacher with something he hadn't felt in a very, very long time. If ever. And almost instantly the pain in his neck began to ease.

Preacher covered her hands with one of his, and Debbie squeezed him tighter. His chest loosened and he blew out a breath he hadn't realized he'd been holding.

Five minutes later they were heading down the road, with Preacher riding point.

CHAPTER 23

"WHAT'S GOIN' ON?" PREACHER ASKED NO ONE IN particular.

An older woman with a head full of curlers scowled around her cigarette. "I look like the fuckin' news to you? Ain't nobody tellin' us nothin!"

The state park was a mob scene. Police cars and fire trucks blocked every entrance, forcing Preacher and the others to leave their bikes on the side of the road and head into the park on foot.

Crowds of rally-goers had amassed inside the picnic area, some spilling out onto the road. Park Rangers appeared to have herded them there and looked to be providing crowd control.

Everyone Preacher spoke to seemed largely confused—no two stories were the same. While one group was convinced a fight had broken out and someone had been injured, another group guessed there'd been a fire. A heavily intoxicated man stumbling about muttered something along the lines of aliens having come to Earth.

"Ain't that Sylvie?" Knuckles squinted through the darkness, pointing at a picnic table full of people.

"Hey, Sylvie!" Preacher shouted, his hands cupped around his mouth.

A head full of dark hair snapped up. Swiping at her cheeks, Sylvia pushed herself off the picnic bench and shuffled quickly toward them. Preacher jogged ahead, meeting her before the rest of the group.

"Something's wrong!" she cried, gripping his arms, her long red nails biting his skin. "We tried to get back to camp, but they got it all blocked off! Joey made me wait here, and he hasn't come back!"

Prying her hands off him, Preacher squeezed them gently. "Breathe, Sylvie. I'm sure everything is fine." He briefly scanned the crowded area. "Where's my mom and dad? They here somewhere, too?"

Sylvia shook her head, her eyes wet with tears. "I don't know! Everyone left me! I don't know where anyone is!"

"Alright, alright, calm down, okay?" He squeezed her once more before releasing her. Anne took his place beside her and slipped her arm through Sylvia's.

"I'll find out what's goin' on, Sylvie. You just sit tight." Preacher glanced around and found that the rest of the group had joined them. "Jim, you stay here with the girls. Knuckles, Smokey, you're with me."

He paused when he noticed that Debbie appeared nervous—her eyes were wide, and darting in every direction.

234

Taking hold of her chin, he lowered his head to hers. "You get asked any questions, give 'em that fake-ass name of yours and say you're with me—that you're my girl."

When she didn't respond, he growled softly, "Don't run off on me, Wheels. "Stay put, alright? I promise I'll be right back."

Debbie blew out a breath and nodded, and Preacher kissed her quickly on the mouth. Jogging back to the path with Knuckles and Smokey on his heels, he kept an eye out for a familiar face.

"Heads up," Knuckles muttered. "Five-O at two o'clock."

A small group of police officers blocked the path up ahead. They didn't appear to be doing anything other than standing guard.

"The swimmin' hole," Preacher whispered, and headed left. "We'll circle back around."

They forged a wide path around the campground. Once they'd reached the creepily empty swimming hole, they entered the campground from behind. As they cut through the quiet campsites filled with tents and trailers but no people, a knot began to form in the pit of Preacher's stomach.

"Stop it right there!" A flashlight temporarily blinded Preacher and stopped him dead in his tracks. Instinctively he put his hands up. The light lowered and he blinked rapidly. Tall and wiry with sharp pointed features, the fast approaching police officer was young, no older than Preacher.

"Our campsite's over there, officer." Smokey jerked his thumb left.

The officer shined his flashlight over Smokey and narrowed his eyes. "Which one is yours?"

Preacher stepped forward. "We got three sites. Brown

pop-up trailer dead center. Bunch of tents lyin' around and a couple picnic tables pushed together."

The officer's eyes widened only a fraction, but it was enough of a reaction that the knot in Preacher's stomach painfully expanded. He took another step forward. "What happened?" he demanded. "What's goin' on?"

"You need to go back." The officer gestured with his flashlight. "Go back to the park entrance and wait with everyone else. Someone will—"

Preacher took off running. Shouting erupted behind him, and he only increased his speed. The closer he came to his family's campsite, the noisier everything became. There was a loud clanging off in the distance, and someone was shouting. He recognized the voice. It was his brother—Joe was the person shouting.

Rounding a corner, Preacher skidded to a stop. Police and firemen were everywhere, crawling all over his family's campsite. Lights from a dozen or more heavy-duty flashlights lit up the roped-off area. Somewhere someone was crying—soft, feminine sobbing could be heard amid the angry shouting.

Preacher's gaze swept through the campsite, halting when he found Joe. Bent over the rope, Joe was nose to nose with an older man wearing plain clothes. Behind him, both Tiny and Crazy-8 struggled to hold him back.

"I don't give a flyin' fuck about your fuckin' protocol!" Joe shouted, his voice hoarse and strained.

Preacher blinked. Some several feet from the scene Max stood alone, his arms wrapped around his upper body, his gaze fixed on the ground.

"Who the hell are you?" an unfamiliar voice demanded.

Preacher blinked again. Another officer with another flashlight in his face.

"You can't be here!"

Preacher shook his head. "What happened…?" He trailed off as he caught sight of something in the shadows—the shape of a woman on her hands and knees, and another woman beside her, clinging to her. Two officers towered over them.

"Please let me touch him," the crying woman begged, her sobs tinged with hysteria as she attempted to reach around the officer's legs. "*Please, please…* I just need to touch him…"

June—it was June who was crying. And that was Louisa beside her, pleading with her, struggling to hold her back.

His heart pounding, Preacher's stare shifted to the human-shaped lump lying prone in the distance. Breathing became difficult.

Sudden noise drew his wavering gaze to the trailer where several figures had emerged. A heavyset man in uniform was staggering down the steps, a hand clasped over his mouth. The door hung open behind him and lights could be seen flashing from within.

Flash. Flash. Flash. Preacher blinked with each flash.

His vision tunneled, then widened.

Was that—was that blood on the trailer door? Not blinking, no longer breathing, Preacher stared at the blood smeared across the door until it became difficult to see. The painful knot in his gut was all he could feel.

"You can't be here," a voice said, muffled, sounding far away.

"My parents," Preacher attempted to say, not recognizing

MADELINE SHEEHAN

the sound of his own voice. His vision was blurring, his hearing fading—a quickly dying light bulb, Preacher was flickering before he blew out entirely.

A commotion broke out. Panicked shouts rang out across the camp as Preacher snapped to attention. He could see clearly, hear clearly, and think clearly once again.

"Don't you touch my brother! Don't you fuckin' touch him, you fuckin' pigs, don't you fuckin' touch him!" Behind the rope, Joe progressed from shouting to raging incoherently.

Guns were drawn, and all of them were pointed at Joe. "Back up!" an officer screamed. "Back up the fuck up, asshole! Back up right now!"

It was Max, Preacher realized belatedly as his gaze pinged between his brothers. Max had ducked beneath the rope and was running across the campsite toward the trailer.

Frozen in place, Preacher watched as six officers converged on his youngest brother and tackled him to the ground.

"Mom!" The gut-wrenching wail came from beneath the pile of bodies. "*Mom!*"

Feeling the pain in his little brother's words so acutely, Preacher lurched forward. He'd only managed a few steps when his arm was grabbed, and he was wrenched backward.

"You can't go in there!" a police officer shouted.

"Like hell," Preacher growled and swung. There was an audible crack as his fist collided with the officer's nose. The man staggered backwards, and Preacher took off running.

CHAPTER 24

DEBBIE TOOK ONE LAST LOOK AROUND THE QUIET MOTEL room as she shouldered her backpack. Sylvia lay in bed, holding her swollen stomach, and Anne curled up beside her. Neither woman had spoken in hours. Expressionless, Sylvia simply stared at the wall, while Anne cried softly.

The grief in the room was evident, and Debbie didn't know these women well enough to know what to do or say to help them. She figured leaving them to one another was the best thing she could do for them.

Quietly pushing open the door, she slipped outside. It was early morning, though the sun was nowhere to be found, and a heavy fog had settled over the surrounding area.

She couldn't recall which town they were in, only that

the motel they'd been directed to stay at was only three miles from the county sheriff's department—where all the men currently were. The women had been dropped at the motel, with the exception of June, who'd been taken to a hospital in a fire truck, and Louisa, who'd requested to stay with her.

Debbie sucked in another heavy breath. She still couldn't wrap her mind around it. Doc was dead. Ginny and Gerald were dead. And yet she'd seen them just yesterday. Gerald had been manning the grill, cooking up the hot dogs and hamburgers that Ginny was dishing out. All three had been alive and well when their group had left the park, only to return to find them… gone.

No, not gone. Murdered.

God, it all felt so surreal. Like a dream, or rather, a nightmare. She couldn't even begin to imagine how the others were feeling. More specifically, how Preacher was feeling.

Debbie sank down onto the curb, feeling utterly bewildered and helpless. The last time she'd seen Preacher he'd been frighteningly out of control, thrashing violently against the four police officers who'd been dragging him through the park. It had taken the officers nearly fifteen minutes and sheer brute strength to force him inside the back of a police car. Joe, who'd been equally enraged, had received similar treatment. And everyone else had been quickly gathered and given instructions to follow the police back to the station.

"Debbie," she had informed the questioning officer, her voice shaking. "Deborah Reynolds. I'm—I'm Preacher's, um, I'm Damon's girl."

Other than her name, the police had asked her where she'd been that day and who she'd been with, and then she'd been dismissed. Eventually Jim had been instructed to bring the women here.

Her arms wrapped around her shins, Debbie rested her head on her knees and stared off into the fog. She was well past exhausted and yet unable to sleep. Her worry for Preacher's wellbeing was too pressing, and dominating all her other thoughts.

All except for one.

Her eyes squeezed closed and her arms tightened around her legs. Was it selfish to hope Preacher wouldn't send her away? That he would still want her around? She swallowed thickly. Of course it was selfish. Self-absorbed and utterly contemptible.

Still, she continued to hope.

The sound of an engine eventually roused her, and Debbie blinked back the gathering sleep in her eyes as a familiar blue van pulled into the parking lot. A state police car followed closely behind the van, two officers inside. While the van pulled up to the building, the police remained across the lot.

One by one the Silver Demons climbed out of the van, each man looking some variation of strung out and bleak. Nobody paid her much attention as they trudged past her and entered the room. She paid them little mind as well, her sole focus on the van. The last to exit, Preacher's long legs preceded him. His boots hit the ground hard, and when he turned, lifting his head, Debbie both flinched and cursed.

Dark bags ringed his bloodshot eyes. His left cheek was swollen and mottled with blue and purple bruises. His bottom lip had been split down the center.

Shoulders drooping, sagging with exhaustion, Preacher dropped down beside Debbie with a pained groan. Panic rose inside her as she wondered what she should say. Nothing she came up with sounded right, or nearly enough.

"Just the one room?" he asked. His voice was rough as if he'd spent the last several hours shouting.

"Two. And mine." Debbie dug a key out of her jeans pocket and showed it to him. Jim had paid for two motel rooms before leaving with the van, after which she'd taken the initiative to purchase a third room with her own money.

"I didn't want to bother anyone," she finished softly.

Preacher slumped forward on his knees, and his eyes found hers. Seeing the suffering look on his face, her heart thudded painfully in her chest. Instinctively she wanted to reach out and touch him, and instead closed her hand tightly around the key, squeezing to the point of pain.

"Preacher." His name was a hoarse whisper on her lips. "I... I..." She trailed off, and her eyes filled with tears. Quickly glancing away, she silently cursed herself.

Debbie jerked when Preacher unexpectedly placed his hand over hers and gently pried open her fingers. Taking the key, he glanced over his shoulder. "Lemme tell them where we'll be."

Minutes later, inside Debbie's room, Preacher fell back against the door and stared across the room as if he were drugged, looking like he might topple over at any moment.

Debbie set her backpack on the floor and took a hesitant seat on a bed. She stared at Preacher, tears still burning in her eyes, and at a loss for how to help him.

"Doc was alive." Preacher's eyes blinked furiously,

and his voice was brittle and weak. "A woman found him crawlin' across the campsite, bleedin', tryin' to talk. She ran for help, but—"

He shook his head, let out a hoarse sigh, and slid down the door all the way to the floor "He was gone by the time the park rangers got to him."

Debbie continued to watch him, desperately wanting to touch him, hold him, comfort him in any way she could. Second-guessing herself every other second, and unsure of what he needed, she remained where she was, with her fists clenched tightly in her lap.

"Nobody saw anything," he continued. "Nobody saw anything, and no one knows jack shit." Preacher's head lolled back and rolled across the door. Their gazes collided. "How's that work? A whole fuckin' park full of people and no one saw a goddamn thing?"

"I'm sorry," Debbie whispered, and instantly wished her words back. Cringing, she closed her eyes. What was she thinking? *I'm sorry* wasn't good enough. *I'm sorry* was useless and trivial. People apologized when they spilled a drink or cut in line—not when someone's parents were murdered. Feeling wetness on her cheek, Debbie swiped her hand quickly across her face, wiping away the tears she had no right to cry.

When she opened her eyes again, Preacher was still staring at her. Just staring and breathing—harsh, ragged breaths that sounded as if his lungs were crumbling.

"I can't get it to stick," he croaked. "Every time I try to think it, it doesn't make sense. It won't stick."

He looked away, his haunted gaze finding a blank wall. "They're gone. But how the fuck can they be gone? I just saw 'em—how can they be gone?"

Filled with grief for Preacher, Debbie had to fight to keep from sobbing.

"How's that work exactly?" he shouted, and shot to his feet. "They were there, right fuckin' there when we left, and now they're just gone?"

Ashen-faced, his hands running violently through his hair, Preacher glanced aimlessly around the room. "How's that fuckin' work?" he demanded.

He turned and faced Debbie, desperation and agony further distorting his bruised and swollen features. And her heart wrenched at the sight of him.

Debbie stood and stepped slowly toward him. She didn't have any idea what she was going to say or do once she reached him; she only knew that she needed to reach him.

Preacher watched her approach, glancing from her face to the hand she was offering him when suddenly an anguished groan flew past his lips and he spun away, sending his fist barreling into the wall closest to him.

Debbie scrambled backward, her hand flying to her mouth, while Preacher continued to punch the wall. And then proceeded to tear the room apart.

When he reached her, a trail of destruction behind him, his chest heaving with heavy, labored breaths, blood gushing from his shredded knuckles, Debbie thought he might tear her apart, too.

Instead, he collapsed at her feet.

Debbie dropped down beside him and threw her arms around his neck. Half expecting him to push her away, she was surprised when he pulled her into his lap instead, buried his face in her neck, and began to cry.

"I'm so sorry," she whispered frantically. "Oh God, Preacher, I'm so sorry."

She curled her legs around his back, her arms around his quaking shoulders, and just held him as tightly as she could.

Preacher jolted awake. His head was pounding, throbbing in time to the beat of the heavy-handed knock at the door.

Sluggish and blurry-eyed, he untangled himself from Debbie and swung his legs out of bed. The movement caused the pressure and pain in his head to worsen and he spent several seconds only kneading his forehead with the heel of his palms. Everything hurt. His hands hurt. His face hurt. Breathing hurt. Thinking hurt.

Another round of knocking echoed through the motel room.

Cursing, Preacher shot to his feet, then cursed again when the pain in his head tripled.

"I'm coming!" he ground out and stalked quickly across the room. He threw open the door and found Joe, his fist hanging in mid-air. His eyes were bloodshot, puffy, and ringed in red. His usually tan skin was a sickly shade of pale.

Seeing Preacher, Joe shoved his hands into his pockets. "Hey."

"Hey."

"How's your face?" Joe's gaze dropped to Preacher's blood-encrusted hands and his eyes narrowed. Peering around Preacher inside the destroyed motel room, Joe's eyes widened. "Shit, man. That's gonna cost us a fortune."

Leaning back against the doorjamb, Preacher looked past his brother. "Yeah."

"We gotta be back at the sheriff's office in a few hours."

They both glanced to where the police cruiser was parked. They'd been told the extra company was for their protection, but they knew bullshit when they saw it. The law was here to ensure the Silver Demons stayed put.

"You gotta control yourself."

"Yeah."

"Ain't gonna be long before the Feds get wind."

Preacher nodded in agreement. He wouldn't be surprised to find out that the Federal Bureau of Investigation was already on their way. According to the law, the Silver Demons were considered a gang. But they weren't just any gang; they were a gang with ties to a well-known east coast crime syndicate. Because of that working relationship, the Feds had been breathing down their necks for quite a while.

So far they'd been unsuccessful at proving the Silver Demons' affiliation with the mob and their attempts to infiltrate the club. Desperate, they'd since resorted to picking off individual members. Preacher had been the third Silver Demon to be locked up for a low-level crime as part of the FBI's continued attempts to break them down.

"How's Max?" Preacher eventually asked. Yesterday Max had been inconsolable. He'd cried for hours, bordering on hysteria until out of nowhere he'd shut down. He'd stopped crying. He'd stopped speaking, too. He'd just sat there, his limp, unfocused gaze staring off at nothing.

"He's sleepin' now." Joe ran a shaking hand through his hair. "You know he's got another year of school left?"

"We'll figure it out," Preacher muttered.

Joe began to turn, then paused. "Hey, uh, do you think this was Reaper..." He trailed off, his throat noticeably bobbing.

Preacher gritted his teeth and closed his eyes, refusing to succumb to his rising emotions. He was well aware of what had transpired yesterday. Doc was gone. His parents were... gone. But for sanity's sake, he couldn't quite bring himself to think about the finality of it and hope to remain in any sort of control of himself. The mess he'd made in the motel room was proof enough of the edge he was teetering on.

Even now he felt precariously close to slipping into the black abyss that beckoned. And he knew that if he slipped, he wouldn't be crawling back out anytime soon.

"No," Preacher rasped. Clearing his throat, he straightened and forced himself to face his brother. "Reaper ain't that stupid."

Reaper West was a lunatic, but Preacher was positive he wasn't so insane as to exact a hit that would undoubtedly have the police looking his way. In fact, Preacher didn't think it was a rival club hit at all. It certainly didn't feel like one. The police, while questioning him, had revealed several particularly gruesome details that led him to believe this had been the mob's doing.

At the moment a mob hit was the only scenario that made any sense. The mob liked to deliver a message in the goriest way possible, and the mob certainly didn't have any qualms about taking out innocent family members.

His mother's face crept into his thoughts and Preacher nearly choked. Clenching his fists, he forced her away. He couldn't do this here. Right now he had to keep his shit together.

"You think the Rossis did this, don't you?" Joe pressed his fingertips over his eyes and scrubbed. His already blood-shot eyes grew even redder.

"I don't know," Preacher admitted. "But I'm gonna find out. Did Dad mention somethin'? Was he havin' trouble with anyone?"

"Not that I know of…you know how dad is with those guys. Everyone fuckin' loves him."

Yeah, everyone had loved The Judge. Respected him and looked up to him, too. Everyone except Preacher. More things to add to the list of stomach-turning things he couldn't think about right now.

Preacher?"

"What?"

"You're comin' home, right? Because I can't—I can't—" Joe took a breath and tried again. "I can't do this by myself."

Though Joe's voice was deep and gruff, that of a grown man, his shaky timbre reminded Preacher of when they were kids. Scared of thunderstorms, Joe would climb into bed with him when it rained and whisper timidly, "Make it stop." And he would cover Joe's ears with his hands, blocking out the noise until Joe was calm enough to fall asleep.

Nostrils flaring, eyes burning, Preacher nodded jerkily. "I'm comin' home."

Watching Joe walk away, Preacher wished it was that simple now. That he could just cover Joe's ears and make it all just fucking stop.

Closing the door behind him, Preacher locked it and then spent several moments just staring at it, noticing every crack, every scuff and scratch. He ran a finger over a partic- ularly long fissure in the paint, feeling the weight of every- thing that had just been laid at his feet.

His new reality.

The one in which Max would continue to cry for a mother he'd never see again. Where Joe no longer had a fa- ther to push him to do better, to be better. The reality where an entire club had just had their footing ripped out from under them, all their tethers sent scattering in the wind.

All they had now was… him.

Preacher knew what he needed to do—what his father would expect of him. He needed to pick up the burden at his feet and place it squarely on his shoulders. Only how? How did he—someone who couldn't get his own shit to- gether—take on the responsibility of everyone?

"Preacher?"

Turning, Preacher's eyes roamed the destroyed room before coming to rest on Debbie. Sitting up in bed, she was wearing only a tank top and her underwear. She stared back at him, her brow furrowed with concern.

Again he glanced around at his destruction. Then down at his swollen hands, covered in dried blood. Blood, just like the blood smeared on the trailer door. Had it been his fa- ther's blood or his mother's?

His stomach heaved, and Preacher scrubbed a hand down his face—a failed attempt to scrub the image from his mind.

"I'm gonna go clean up." Refusing to look at Debbie, he headed to the bathroom.

Turning on the shower, Preacher quickly divested him- self of his shirt and jeans and stepped inside. Bowing his head, he watched the water circling the drain turn pink from his blood. Blood, like the smear of blood on the trailer door. He squeezed his eyes shut, only to see it all again.

June on her hands and knees. Joe, red in the face, and shouting. The blood smeared on the door. Max running across the campsite. One after the other, as if someone was rapidly changing the channel in his mind, he flicked through the collection of unnerving images.

He opened his eyes, and the images evaporated.

Jesus Christ. He couldn't do this.

Cursing, Preacher grabbed hold of the shower curtain and tore it open. Debbie stood in the center of the bathroom, still wearing the same concerned look on her face. "I was... worried about you," she stammered.

He didn't respond. He didn't know what to say. To anyone. And neither did he know what to do—for anyone.

"You're bleeding again." Debbie hurried forward and he let her take his hand. Fresh blood welled at his knuckles and dripped onto the bathroom floor. Onto her hands. Onto her bare feet. Blood—*there was fucking blood everywhere.*

"Some of these are really deep. You need to wrap them."

Preacher only stared back at Debbie, wondering what the hell she was still doing here with him and this god-awful mess, and yet thankful that she was. He couldn't bear to be around the others, couldn't face another second of witnessing the devastation in their faces... but neither did he want to be alone.

"It's fine," he muttered, taking his hand back and turning away. Although his wounds throbbed angrily, the pain was insignificant compared to the storm raining down chaos and destruction inside of him.

Had they died quickly? The thought of his mother suffering was too much for him, and he slapped his forehead against the shower wall. Then again, harder. And again, harder still, wishing that his skull were an eggshell and easy to shatter. Easy to discard.

Preacher stilled when he felt a brush of soft skin against his leg. A hand touched his back, and tentative fingers trailed up his spine.

"Preacher," Debbie whispered. "Preacher, look at me."

He couldn't look at her. He couldn't even breathe. If he breathed, he was going to lose it.

"I don't know what to do. But I want to help. Just tell me what to do. Tell me what you need."

When he didn't respond, she continued. "I lost my dad when I was little. He was killed in a car accident and I—"

White noise exploded in Preacher's mind and he turned, grabbed hold of Debbie and pulled her beneath the water. Unable to speak for fear that he'd lose his feeble grasp on control, he only shook his head tightly.

Wide-eyed, she lifted her shaking hands to his face and laid them gently on his cheeks.

"I'm so sorry," she breathed. "So sorry."

She stroked his cheeks, his forehead, and tucked his wet hair back behind his ears. Then she rose up on her tiptoes, draped her arms around his neck, and pressed a kiss to his cheek, his jaw, his lips, his nose. Preacher let out a shuddering, ragged breath, and found himself leaning into her.

She was naked, he realized once they were pressed against one another.

Preacher's hands slid up her back, and she continued to kiss him. Soft, gentle kisses, as if she were afraid he might break.

The next kiss Debbie placed on his lips, Preacher returned. He kissed her painstakingly slow with long, deep, lingering strokes of his tongue. One hand cupping her jaw, the other slid down the side of her body. And as his mental machinations slid swiftly into a different gear, his body hardened.

Pushing Debbie up against the wall, Preacher lifted her leg and wrapped it around his hip. Lifting her, he used his body to hold hers to the wall and positioned himself between her thighs.

Debbie's eyes found his. Her pupils dilated. Her breaths sped up. Her breasts heaved with the rapid rise and fall of her chest. And Preacher resented her—he envied the single-minded need shining in her eyes.

He wanted that.

He wanted to not think about all that would be coming next.

He wanted to not see the smear of blood on the trailer door.

He wanted not to hear his brother screaming for their mother.

He wanted not to feel the shock, and the fear, and the pain.

Jesus Christ, he wanted just a moment even, *just one single fucking moment*, to be free of all of it.

Preacher slammed his hips forward and Debbie cried out. He pulled back, the tight, slick feel of her clenching around him tearing a groan from his throat. He thrust again, harder, and Debbie's answering cry echoed throughout the room.

He thrust again; she cried out again—a harsh, frantic sound, as hungry as the nails scouring his back.

Thrust, cry. Thrust, cry. Thrust, cry.

Hard and fast, Preacher fucked himself into oblivion. Skin-slapping strokes and a primal chorus of guttural groans, desperate cries, and breathless pants were the soundtrack to his manufactured bliss.

His mind was nearly blank, focused only on the body he was pressed against—soft in all the right places, firm in all the right places, and how he felt sheathed inside her—a warm, wet sanctuary where he could hide from everything that was coming.

Because he knew.

He knew what sort of hell lay in wait for him outside of her body. Outside of this room.

The kind that there was no coming back from.

CHAPTER 25

Present Day

Having grown quiet, Preacher took several shallow breaths and turned away. Leaning back in my chair, I wrapped my arms around myself and just attempted to process everything he'd just confessed.

I could count on two hands the times that my father had been noticeably emotional about anything over the course of my lifetime. Half of those moments had been about me, while the other half had occurred on the rare occasion that my mother was brought up.

I'm not entirely sure why I was so surprised to find out the true extent of his feelings for Debbie. I supposed knowing something as opposed to hearing a firsthand account of that same thing were two very different beasts.

I'd known he'd loved her, of course, even as brief as their relationship had been. He'd loved her enough that her disappearance had crushed him. However, I'd never realized the true depth of his emotions.

Having had Debbie by his side during the tragic loss of his parents, the extent of what he felt for her now made more sense. I knew well enough how tragedy tends to bring about heightened emotions, and usually only one of two possible outcomes: you either grow closer or farther apart. Debbie, it seemed, had quickly become Preacher's crutch, every bit as much as Preacher had become hers.

I would have thought these revelations might have had a soothing effect on me, but I found myself experiencing the opposite. My irritation was mounting, coupled with the anger of being lied to for so long, and about my own family no less. "Daddy," I snapped before I could squelch my rising temper. "What happened next?"

Preacher faced me and smiled sadly. "Baby girl, I'd be willin' to put good money on that being the day we made you."

"Not *that*," I said, making a face. "I meant what happened *after* that."

Behind me, Deuce snorted loudly, and I turned to find him smirking. Frowning, I asked, "What's so funny?"

Deuce shrugged. "*That* probably happened a few more times."

With an exasperated sigh, I turned back to my father. "I want to know what happened with the police. Did they have any leads? Was anyone taken into custody?"

I'd only managed to find one article about it online—the Four Points Massacre, it had been called. The article had been sparse on details, and instead fraught with warnings and accusations about the dangers of "motorcycle gangs".

A faraway look in his eyes, Preacher stared at something over my shoulder. "Wasn't long after gettin' back to the city that your mother started gettin' sick. Couldn't hold nothin' down."

"Daddy, the cops. What did the cops say?"

"It was your Aunt Sylvia who thought she might be pregnant."

Frustrated, I glanced back at Deuce and rolled my eyes. Now that I knew the truth about my grandparents, it was obvious to me what Preacher was doing. The same thing he'd done my entire life—refuse to discuss his parents. He'd never dealt with losing them, that much was obvious to me now.

"So you brought Debbie home with you?" I asked, resigned to just letting him talk. There would be no forcing Preacher Fox to do anything he didn't want to do. And I could always ask my uncles for specifics later.

Preacher's eyes flicked to mine. "Of course I did!" he huffed indignantly. "You think I'd leave her behind?"

"I don't know what to think!" I shot back. "Everything I thought I knew was wrong! I don't know what's true and what's a lie anymore!"

"There were good reasons I lied to ya, Eva."

"Like what?" I practically shouted, jumping to my feet. Gripping the bedrail, I glared down at him. So many feelings were coursing through me, too many, and every single one of them was unpleasant.

I jabbed myself in the chest. "Tell me why *I* couldn't know the truth about *my mother*!"

Preacher let out a hard sigh, and his chest let out a pain-ful-sounding rattle in response. "I will, I will… but I gotta tell you the rest of the story first."

My eyes bulged, and my grip on the bedrail tightened. I was about to let loose a string of curses when a familiar hand appeared on my shoulder.

"Fuckin' breathe," Deuce whispered.

I shook my head furiously. "But he—"

Deuce grabbed my wrist, pulled me out of my chair, and dragged me across the room and into the bathroom. Glaring at me, he kicked the door closed behind us and folded his arms across his chest. Regardless of his age, my husband still painted a formidable picture—his height, his breadth, and the way his eyes could turn bitterly cold in an instant, sucking all the warmth from the room.

Not that I was intimidated. "Move," I demanded, ges-turing angrily.

His arm muscles flexed, causing the dragons tattooed on his forearms to twitch restlessly. "Not a chance in hell, bitch. You need to calm the fuck down first. You start yellin' at your old man now, you're gonna regret it later."

I mirrored his stance—arms crossed under my breasts, legs spread apart—and scowled up at him. His lips twisted, and dimples appeared.

"Put your fucking dimples away!" I hissed. "He lied to me for my entire life! Not just about my mother, but my grandparents too! I thought I could do this, but now—" I threw my arms up in the air. "I feel like I don't even know my own father!"

I went from shouting to crying in the span of two heart-beats and collapsed to the cold floor with my face buried in

257

my hands. Of course Deuce was right—I couldn't lash out at my dying father, couldn't let him leave this world thinking I was angry with him. Even though angry was exactly what I was. Furious, even. Confused, too. And a whole lot brokenhearted.

"You can do this." Deuce's voice was firm, yet soft. "I've seen you weather worse shit than this and still come out swingin'."

I peeked up at him through my hands. "Worse than finding out everything I knew was a lie? Worse than losing my father?"

Deuce only stared down at me, stone-faced, those beautiful blue eyes of his suddenly ice-cold and swimming with ugly memories.

"Never mind," I quickly whispered. Wiping my eyes, I took several shaky breaths. I could do this. I could get control of myself and walk back out there and do everything in my power to ensure Preacher's last days were good ones.

Getting to my feet, I pressed a hand to my throat. "Deuce, the kids? Did you—"

"Taken care of. They're all on the next flight outta Billings. First thing tomorrow."

"Everyone is coming?"

"Every last one of them little assholes and all the damn fools they married." His eyes began to smile. "My grandbabies, too. They're all comin'."

I lurched forward into his waiting arms and sagged against him.

"I should be able to do this," I cried softly. "I'm a grown woman. Our daughter is practically grown. And I've got stepchildren with babies of their own. I should be able to keep it together!"

"Didn't really care much for my old man," Deuce said, chuckling darkly. "Hardly knew my mom. I think the closest thing I had to a real father was Blue. And darlin', there wasn't a goddamn thing on this Earth that could have kept me together when I found him sittin' there dead. Not a fuckin' thing.

"It ain't gonna be easy," he continued, "But I know you, Eva, and you're gonna be just fine. You know how I know?"

I looked up to find his eyes on me. "How?"

A corner of his mouth lifted. "'Cause I'm gonna make damn sure of it."

Tears welled in my eyes. *Sheesh.* I'd seen perfect couples before—like-minded people who shared the same interests and hobbies and who complemented each other in every way.

Deuce and I weren't that—we fought just as much as we loved, and to this day the hard times still occasionally outshined the good times. But despite it all, I was unable to recall a time when I wasn't either fascinated by him, turned on by him, or in love with him.

We were special, me and Deuce. All his sharp and jagged edges may not align perfectly with mine, yet I loved him anyway.

All my grief and guilt, all my shock and sadness, and all my anger suddenly took a very different path. Reaching up, I grabbed hold of Deuce's face and crushed my mouth to his.

For a full ten minutes, we kissed each another with more passion than either of us had put into a kiss in the last five years, a fact I'd only just realized.

Children, grandchildren, and an entire club's worth of lives to constantly care for and worry about had begun to dull what had once been such an ever-present and intensely demanding sexual connection. And wasn't that always the way of things? Life happened, and then happened some more, and kept happening until you were so caught up in life itself that you forgot to actually live it.

It was Eva who broke their kiss, and Deuce reluctantly let her. He let her because he knew if they kept going like this, he was going to pull her pants down and bend her over the fucking sink.

Breathing hard, she pressed her forehead to his chest. "I'm sorry. I don't know what's wrong with me."

He smiled at her. "Someone dyin' sure has a funny way of makin' everyone else want to get up quick and start livin', don't it? And darlin'? Don't you ever be sorry for fuckin' kissin' me."

Still clinging to him, Eva looked up at Deuce, her big gray eyes storming with emotion. And Deuce stared down into them, into the eyes of the little girl who'd charmed the shit out of him, the teenager who'd gotten him shot and the woman he'd fallen in love with. He still felt the same way about her; it didn't matter how much time had passed. Take away the fine lines that had taken residence on her forehead and beside her eyes, the strands of gray intermingled among her dark brown waves, and she was twenty-two again… and he was still too goddamn old for her.

"We could ride home," he offered. It had been far too long since she'd ridden on the back of his bike. And he was only now realizing just how much he'd missed having her there.

She nodded slowly. "I'd like that."

"Good." He released her with a hard slap on her ass. "Now go get some air. You've been locked up in this room with him all fuckin' day."

Eva started to protest.

"I'll sit with him," Deuce growled. "You go get some air, go smoke a damn joint. Fuck, bitch, just go do somethin'." He opened the bathroom door and shoved her gently toward the hallway. "Go. I'll call you if anything happens."

Deuce waited several minutes, ensuring Eva was gone, before coming to stand at Preacher's bedside. Preacher's eyes were closed, his shallow, labored breaths echoing noisily throughout the otherwise silent room.

Gripping the bedrail, Deuce stared down at one of the most powerful men in the criminal underground. A man who'd crafted his own signature execution styles. A man that other men had both feared and envied.

He didn't look like that man anymore.

"Preacher," he said. Preacher stirred, but his eyes remained closed.

"Preacher," he repeated, louder. "Everyone knows Deluva Sr. was hit by a fuckin' truck on the Long Island Expressway. So how's about you tell me why Joe is accusin' him of puttin' your parents to ground?"

Preacher's eyes flew open, as did his mouth, and Deuce wondered if getting straight to the point had been a bad idea. The last thing he wanted to do was give his already dying father-in-law a heart attack.

"What did you tell Eva?" Preacher hoarsely demanded.

"What the fuck did you tell her?"

Deuce shrugged. "Nothin' yet. But if you ain't gonna tell her, I sure as fuck will."

Preacher's sunken features contorted with anger. "Don't you threaten me, asshole. You think you know what you're talkin' about, but you don't. There's more to it—there's some shit I gotta explain first."

"It's true, then?" Disgusted, Deuce closed his eyes and shook his head. "You fuckin' knew that kid came from crazy."

Deuce was referring to Franklin Deluva Jr., better known as Crazy Frankie, the only child of the late Franklin Deluva Sr. and his wife, Maria, also deceased. Preacher had taken Frankie in after both his parents had died and raised him as his own.

"It might've been Eva who put that blade in Frankie's neck," Deuce continued angrily. "But it was because of you that she had to do it! You let that messed-up fuck into your house, into your club, and *into her mother-fuckin' bed*!"

Preacher gritted his teeth and attempted to push himself upright. "I don't need you to remind me that I failed my daughter," he growled. "But what you're not understandin', you self-righteous piece of shit, is why I didn't know what Frankie was doing to her. I was lettin' Eva be. I was lettin' her do her own damn thing, become her own woman. I was givin' her the chances my old man never gave me. Hell, I did everything I could to make sure she had friends outside of the life. I woulda paid for any college she wanted to attend, too, didn't matter if it was on the other side of the world. I gave her every out and she didn't take a single one of 'em. She refused to leave the city, refused to leave the club."

Preacher paused to catch his breath, and the painful-sounding rattle in his chest grew louder.

"I thought she was always hangin' around for Frankie. I thought someday I'd be handing the club to them both. I didn't know enough, I know that now. And because I didn't know enough, I never saw it. I never saw what he was doin' to her. I just thought... I just thought she was..."

Shaking his head, Preacher glared up at Deuce. "In hindsight," he spat, "I think maybe she wasn't leavin' because she was waitin' on you, Deuce. You ever think of that?"

It was an accusation meant to give Deuce pause, and it worked. But fuck if Deuce was going to let Preacher know he'd struck a nerve.

"She wasn't waitin' on me," Deuce shot back, "She knew she coulda had me. Hell, she did have me whenever the fuck she wanted me, and every damn time it was her who walked away."

Walked away and went right back to Frankie.

Deuce's heart rate shot up, and his chest grew uncomfortably tight. Just because he'd learned to live with Frankie's ghost, didn't mean he'd ever get over what that lunatic had done to Eva. Frankie's brand of crazy had left a mark on everything it touched. You could cover it up and ignore it, but that mark was always going to be there, just below the surface, burning a slowly growing hole through whatever peace you thought you may have found.

"Eva is just like us, you fuckin' asshole." Deuce pointed between him and Preacher. "She's lived and breathed the club from day fuckin' one. And not one of us ever had a fuckin' chance."

As the two men continued to stare at one another, the anger in Preacher's eyes began to slowly fade.

"You're wrong," Preacher said, sounding resigned. "I used to think that... but I was wrong. We had choices. I made the choice to bring Frankie into my home, and Eva chose to marry him. You made the choice to knock up another man's wife and then drag her off to Montana with you. We all made our motherfuckin' choices, and we've all been living with the consequences of 'em ever since."

Seeing red, Deuce's nostrils flared. *Drag Eva to Montana? Fuck that and fuck Preacher.* He hadn't dragged Eva anywhere. She'd come home with him because she was his. She had always been his.

"Preacher," Deuce growled, feeling like crushing someone's skull with his bare hands. "Forget fuckin' Frankie and tell me about Frank."

Preacher closed his eyes and let out a ragged sigh. When his eyes reopened, he stared out across the room. "Joe was tellin' the truth. It was Frank who killed my parents."

"Yeah, but when did you find out? Fuck, *how* did you find out? Was Frank at the rally?"

"He musta been. But no one knew he was there, no one saw him. As far as we knew he was in Philly."

"Why'd he do it?"

When Preacher finally spoke, his tone was pained, his every word sounding as if it were being physically pried from his insides with a rusty blade. "Took me a long time to figure that out." He swallowed thickly. "Even longer than it took me to find out it was him who'd done it."

When it didn't look like Preacher was going to elaborate further, Deuce switched topics. "The accident on the expressway. Was that your doin'?"

Preacher choked out an ugly laugh. "No. That woulda been too easy. Frank, that sick shit—he needed my hands on him."

Preacher's gaze suddenly swung to Deuce, glowering with the hate of a thousand deadly men. "My only regret is that I could only kill him once."

Had Preacher not been lying in a hospital bed, knocking on death's door, Deuce might have taken a step back. Because this was the Preacher who'd turned The Judge's motorcycle club into an empire that rivaled most mafias. This was the man who didn't think twice about taking a life—even the life of a friend.

This was the man other men both feared and envied… and with due cause.

PART THREE

"Pain is inevitable. Suffering is optional."
—Haruki Murakami

"Pain is power. It's what drives me.
Suffering is what happens to those that cause me pain."
—Damon "Preacher" Fox

CHAPTER 26

PARKED ON A ONE-WAY STREET IN EAST VILLAGE, NEW York City, seated in the driver's seat of a dirt-brown Monaco sedan, Agent Donald Willis of the Federal Bureau of Investigation glanced over at his partner. Thirty years Willis's junior, Agent James Parker was fidgeting in his seat, pulling irritably at the wool scarf wrapped around his neck.

"It's fucking cold in here," Parker complained. "My coffee's gone cold."

"Roll up the window," Willis replied. "You're cold because you're sitting here with the goddamn window down, letting all the cold air in."

"Wouldn't be sitting here at all if the cops did their fucking jobs."

Willis glanced across the street, eyeing their target—the

Silver Demons' clubhouse—and bobbed his head in agreement. It was no secret that the local police department tended to look the other way when it came to the Silver Demons. The Bureau had long suspected the Demons were paying off the police, but they hadn't been able to prove it… yet.

There was nothing Willis hated more than a dirty cop. A former police officer, Willis had taken his oath seriously and expected the same from his fellow peacekeepers.

"I don't blame them." Parker rubbed his hands together before blowing on them. "Someone offered me the right amount, I'd be looking the other way, too."

Willis glared at Parker and the younger man laughed. "Kidding. Take a fucking joke, will ya?" Rolling his eyes, Parker slouched down in his seat and resumed pulling on his scarf.

"Once we get these guys," Willis muttered, "then it'll be easy pickings. They'll be clamoring to tell us which officers they've got in their pockets, and their house of cards will come tumbling down right on top of 'em."

Parker shot Willis a skeptical look, silently conveying what Willis was already thinking—that the Silver Demons were too damn good at what they did. There were no holes in their operation—if there had been, the Bureau would have found them by now.

The telltale rumbling of a motorcycle approaching drew their attention to the street. The heavily bearded rider slowed to a near stop as he passed and flashed a grin—and his middle finger—at the agents.

Wearing matching sour expressions, Willis and Parker watched as the rider turned down the alleyway beside the clubhouse and disappeared from sight.

Willis didn't need to leaf through his stacks of files to identify the rider; he'd long ago memorized all their names and faces. This particular man was Robert M. Schneider, age 31, known to his family in Queens as 'Bobby' and to his brothers in the Silver Demons as 'Hightower'.

A former private in the United States Army and a Purple Heart recipient, Hightower had once been considered an American hero. He'd dragged several unconscious soldiers to safety after an explosion had detonated near their camp, an explosion that had left him with a severely mangled left leg and a nasty limp. Willis had seen the pictures—it was a miracle he'd ever walked again.

"No respect," Parker muttered, shaking his head.

"Of course they don't have any respect for us. They don't respect the law, they aren't going to respect the people enforcing it."

"I think he did it," Parker said, frowning at the clubhouse. "I think that son of a bitch offed his own damn parents. These guys are sick."

Parker was referring to Damon Fox, better known as 'Preacher', the eldest of the three Fox brothers, and recently appointed president of the Silver Demons. Six months earlier both of Preacher's parents and a fellow club member had been brutally slain at a state park in upstate New York. And the case had since gone cold. In fact, the case had started out frigid. Many people had been questioned, yet despite the sheer number of people in attendance, not one had come forward with any information. Without a murder weapon, without any witnesses, there'd been very little to go on.

Willis stared down the street, rubbing his chin, mulling over the facts. Did he think Preacher had killed his parents? Maybe. But he doubted it. A family of criminals was still a family. And Willis had observed the Fox family long enough to know that, despite the healthy amount of tension between Gerald Fox and his sons, not one of those boys would have ever harmed their mother.

"No," Willis eventually replied. "I was at the funeral. I saw them—they were grieving. My best guess is they pissed someone off, someone high up. Maybe the Rossi family, maybe even higher. Maybe whoever is bringing in the drugs from overseas."

Parker blew out a steamy breath full of frustration. "The Rossi family is who we should be going after, or the Columbos. Not these lowlifes."

Willis shrugged. "The U.S. attorney doesn't agree with you. These lowlifes are working for the Rossi family—we get them, we finally get a shot the Rossis."

Parker continued to huff. "There's no fucking proof they're even working for the Rossis!" His clenched fist came down on his thigh. "Both families are locked up tighter than a nun's pussy. We can't get a single one of these pieces of shit to turn rat. Hell, we still don't know where they're getting their dope from! We don't know a goddamn thing!"

Parker was right; they had no substantial proof that the Silver Demons were confirmed Rossi associates or vice versa. Yet it was still well known that they were. The Rossis owned several restaurants in all five boroughs, and the Demons had been spotted at almost all of them at one time or another, meeting with the Rossi underboss or other Rossi family affiliates. Furthermore, the Demons owned several small businesses of their own—a couple of gas stations in New Jersey and a garage in Brooklyn—that employed known Rossi soldiers. The Bureau had obtained warrants to raid the garage twice now, hoping to find something to charge someone with—the Demons or the Rossis—but had come up empty both times.

Parker was also correct in stating that none of these men were going to turn on one another. The Rossi crime family seemed impenetrable, as did the Silver Demons. Much like the mob foot soldiers, most of the Demons had been busted for one thing or another. In fact, one of the Demons' own, a biker named Gunny, was currently doing a 15-year stretch at Ossining. The Bureau had offered him everything under the sun, including his freedom, if he'd sing. Hands and feet in chains, the bastard had leaned across the table and told Willis to *"go fuck his mother."*

Willis released a heavy sigh. The Bureau had hit at a dead end. Having already exhausted all their usual avenues of investigation, they were left with surveillance.

Facing the clubhouse, Willis looked over the small group of people gathered on the front stoop. Despite the cold temperatures, Douglas "Tiny" Williams was dressed in only a T-shirt and jeans. Seated in a lawn chair, he was catcalling any woman who had the misfortune to walk by. Nearby, Sylvia Fox was talking animatedly with another young woman—Preacher's live-in girlfriend.

Willis elbowed Parker. "Did we ever find out who Preacher's girl really is?"

"Name's Deborah Reynolds," Parker said and snorted. "Goes by Debbie. Nineteen years old, from Akron, Ohio. Only Akron hasn't ever heard of her, and she's not in the system. Her papers are fake—bought and paid for by Preacher, I'm guessing. Not that it matters. We've been down this road before. They don't tell their women a damn thing. So unless we're going to charge her with forging documents, she's irrelevant."

They watched as Debbie gave Sylvia's infant son a quick kiss on the cheek, then as the two women briefly embraced. Then Tiny jumped up out of his seat and offered Debbie his arm. Arms linked, they started down the sidewalk.

Beside him, Parker was squinting. "Jesus, Don, she's got a bun in the oven."

Willis tilted his head to get a better look. Sure enough, there was a telltale bulge beneath her coat.

Quickly straightening, Willis started the car.

"We're gonna tail some broad?"

Pulling the car onto the street, Willis shrugged. "Why the fake papers? What's she hiding? I want to find out who the hell she really is."

"And then what?"

"She's pregnant, Jim. I'm willing to bet this one means something to him." He shrugged again. "Who knows... maybe we can use her."

CHAPTER 27

"**M**ORE COOKIES, PLEASE?"

Tiny fingers beckoned Debbie from just below the edge of the countertop. Leaning over, she found a pair of dark eyes framed in long, thick lashes blinking up at her from beneath a messy mop of brown hair.

"Frankie," she cooed, grinning at the toddler. She crooked her finger. "Come here, you."

Little legs, thick with baby fat, wobbled around the kitchen counter. Scooping Frankie into her arms, Debbie set him down on the countertop. After a quick glance toward the hall, ensuring no one would catch her, she slipped her hand inside a large metal tin and handed Frankie another cookie, which he promptly put in his mouth.

"Good?" she asked, ruffling his hair. Frankie smiled

around a mouthful of cookie. Eyes wide, he nodded vigorously.

"Aw, Debbie!" Storming into the kitchen, Sylvia sent Debbie a scathing look. "Those are for the church potluck tomorrow!"

Balancing her son Trey on her hip, Sylvia began checking through the numerous tins full of goodies she'd spent the entire weekend preparing. "God bless Ginny and this giant kitchen. Or thanks to you two, I wouldn't have any cookies left!"

The clubhouse kitchen was spacious, with ample counter space, wall-to-wall cupboards, and every appliance under the sun. It was also oddly mismatching, with country wooden cupboards, green tiled walls, and a red linoleum floor. Ginny's unique, colorful tastes had even extended to her kitchen.

"I could never do all this in my kitchen at home," Sylvia continued. "You hear that, Joey? Can't even cook a decent lasagna in that glorified closet you call a kitchen!"

Both Debbie and Frankie cringed as Sylvia's voice turned shrill. Trey only opened his tiny mouth in a wide, toothless yawn.

"I swear that man is hidin' from me," she muttered. "Only time I ever see him anymore is when he's crawling into bed at night wantin' somethin'. He gets his rocks off and all I get is pregnant."

Sylvia glanced sideways at Debbie. "Not that I need to tell you about *that*."

Reflexively, Debbie's hand went to her stomach. Whereas Sylvia was only two months pregnant and couldn't stop talking about it, Debbie was nearly six months along and still having a hard time coming to terms with the fact that she was pregnant at all.

She didn't want a baby. She was only seventeen and didn't know the first thing about being a mother. She couldn't even think about the birth or what would come after without feeling anxious and breaking out in a cold sweat. What if she was as horrible a mother as her own had been?

Debbie shuddered through her next few breaths. This pregnancy wasn't fair to either of them—her or the baby growing inside her.

Worse, she was alone in her feelings. Preacher seemed... almost happy about it.

Maybe because it served as a distraction from the ugly things that often plagued his thoughts. Most nights Debbie would find him wide awake and pacing the hallway in their tiny apartment. Debbie would go to him, and Preacher would pull her into his arms. Eventually, his hands almost always ended up on her belly, and his entire expression would shift—the shadows would flee his face and his eyes would brighten.

They never spoke of what bothered them—Preacher didn't talk of what kept him up at night and, not wanting to burden him further, Debbie kept her pregnancy fears to herself. They'd talk only about meaningless things—television sitcoms, whatever idiotic thing Tiny had done recently, and Debbie's frequent outings with the girls.

For the first time in nearly two years, her hair was styled, cut into feathered layers, and enhanced by her natural waves. And her nails were done, painted a soft pink that matched the color of the flower studs in her ears. Her outfit today was simple yet fashionable—a white, long-sleeved peasant top paired with a beige corduroy skirt. Dark tights and knee-high boots completed the ensemble.

Flicking a cookie crumb off her skirt, she couldn't help but smile. A year ago she never would have thought she'd be wearing clothing like this again. A year ago she'd never have imagined this was where she'd be—in New York City, in love with a man, and blessed with all the creature comforts she'd thought she'd lost forever.

And so Debbie took solace in how different things were now compared to a year ago. How incredibly lucky she was and, aside from her pregnancy, how good things were with Preacher.

"There you are!" Maria Deluva rushed inside the kitchen and gathered Frankie into her arms. "I was looking everywhere," she lovingly admonished her son and pressed a kiss to his cheek.

Maria was a small woman, slim and petite with olive skin and long jet-black hair, and one of the only people associated with the club that Debbie had yet to spend any real time with. Unlike the other wives and girlfriends, Maria was soft-spoken and reserved, and rarely made an appearance at the clubhouse. She was only here today because it was the first Saturday of the month, the one day each month that Preacher required everyone to gather for family day.

Even if Preacher himself wasn't currently here.

Three weeks earlier, Preacher had left for business reasons. The last Debbie had heard from him was almost a week ago, promising her he would be home two days ago. She wasn't worried yet; he often arrived later than he said he would. She simply missed him.

"More cookies, please." From Maria's arms, Frankie

beckoned Debbie.

"How many have you had already?" Maria asked.

"Just two," Debbie lied.

"One more?" Frankie asked, holding up four fingers. "Please, Mama?"

"Oh, alright," Maria laughed. "Just one—"

"No more."

Everyone froze as Frank's booted feet pounded a heavy, authoritative cadence across the linoleum. He stopped beside Maria and placed a possessive arm over her shoulders. Maria seemed to stiffen further beneath him. Even little Frankie appeared eerily still. It was as if Frank's presence had sucked the life straight from them both.

Frank wasn't an overly large man, his stature was fairly similar to Preacher's. But standing beside his wife and son, instead of giving the impression of a doting husband and father, he had the look of a king dominating his subjects.

Frank was an enigma Debbie hadn't quite figured out yet. Although he dressed the part of a biker, he hardly looked like his fellow Silver Demons. His short hair was always neatly trimmed and perfectly styled, and his face was always clean-shaven. And unlike the other men, whose hands and clothing seemed forever stained with grease, Frank's were always uncommonly free of grime.

"Ready to go?" Though Frank was addressing Maria, his calculating gaze was on Debbie. She often found him staring at her—his brown eyes so dark they appeared black. And each and every time it made her uncomfortable. Yet, Preacher considered Frank a good friend, so Debbie was inclined to keep her feelings to herself.

Maria nodded mutely, and as Frank led his family from

the kitchen Maria glanced over her shoulder and flashed Debbie a small, wooden smile.

"Say goodbye to Debbie," Maria encouraged Frankie.

Chocolate-covered fingers wiggled. "Bye-bye Debbie."

She blew the little boy a kiss. "Bye-bye Frankie."

Debbie remained inside the kitchen until she heard the front door open and close, signaling the Deluva's departure. Moving into the hallway, she stopped suddenly when she found Joe dangling over the side of the stairwell railing.

"Debbie!" he whisper-shouted. "Where's Sylvie?" His one eye darted nervously around the hallway.

Debbie only shrugged in response. She'd made a point to never get involved in Joe and Sylvia's sham of a marriage. Grimacing, Joe spun away and darted up the stairs. Rolling her eyes, she continued on, pausing briefly to glance into the stairwell Joe had been hanging from.

The Silver Demons' brownstone was an impressive five stories high, not including the rooftop patio and flower garden. The second-floor apartment was where Gerald, Ginny, and Max had lived, while the third and fourth floors contained rooms for the club members.

Max lived with Joe and Sylvia now, and Preacher had closed off the second-floor. As for Ginny's flowers on the roof, Louisa and Debbie took turns tending to them as best they could.

Debbie entered the living room—a large space lined with couches and chairs in a variety of sizes and colors. Mismatched rugs covered the in-between areas. Large, colorful pop art prints from the 1950s and 1960s hung on nearly every wall. Near the back stairwell a bar area had been set up, and on the other side of the room sat a wall-to-wall entertainment center.

Today Louisa and Anne were huddled together at the bar, while Whiskey Jim was stretched out over one of the sofas, snoring loudly. *Some Girls* by the Rolling Stones was buzzing softly through the speakers while a Silver Demon named Bullet browsed the records.

"What's your pleasure today, Debbie darling?" Bullet called out. "We got Queen, we got the Doobie Brothers… we got some Aerosmith…"

"Blondie," she replied with a smile. "Always Blondie."

He flashed her a gleaming white grin that accentuated his dark brown skin. "'Course," he drawled, "What was I thinkin'? I got your Blondie comin' right up, little mama."

Debbie headed for the bar and took a much-needed seat on one of the stools. Although her pregnant stomach was still measuring relatively small and had yet to become a bother, she was tired and sore almost all the time.

"Aw, honey," Anne cooed. "You look exhausted. How're ya feelin'?"

She shrugged. "I'm okay, I guess. Just wish Preacher was back."

Sighing, Louisa frowned down at the drink in her hand. "They were supposed to be back days ago."

"Preacher'll be back soon, don't you worry, honey." Anne wrapped an arm around Louisa's waist and gave her a squeeze. "Yours too, baby doll.

"I envy you both, though, you know?" Smiling mischievously, Anne tucked her long blonde hair behind her ears and leaned over the bar. "Jim's gettin' on in years, so he doesn't go riding as much. But when he did…" Anne's smile turned positively wicked. "Oh honey, the welcome home sex was some of the best I've ever had."

Debbie and Louisa glanced to where Jim was still snoring on the sofa and started giggling. "Gross," Louisa mouthed to Debbie and Debbie nodded vigorously in agreement.

"I saw that!" Anne snapped. "And all I gotta say is don't knock it 'til you try it."

"Speaking of gross…" Louisa's eyes darted suspiciously around the room, and she lowered her voice. "Did Frank leave?"

Debbie nodded. "A few minutes ago."

Brows up, Louisa looked at Anne. "Did you get a load of Maria wearing that big ol' neck scarf, lookin' like Mary Tyler Moore?"

"Mmhmm, sure did."

"He's hitting her again. I just know it."

Anne snorted. "Who are you kidding? He didn't ever stop."

"Hitting her?" Debbie repeated dumbly, her gaze darting between the two women. "Frank hits Maria?"

Louisa bobbed her head dramatically up and down. "Oh my God, Debbie, it's so obvious. This one time last year she wore sunglasses all through dinner. Like we wouldn't know what she was hiding underneath."

Anne nudged Louisa. "And remember when I saw the bruises on her arm?" Facing Debbie, Anne said, "I accidentally walked in on her in the bathroom. And I'm talkin', these weren't no small bruises. Her whole arm was black and blue."

Debbie's hand went to her stomach. Thinking of Maria, how quiet she was, and the way she always shied away from Frank's touch, made Debbie feel sick. "Does Preacher know?"

Anne shot her a disbelieving look. "Most men are oblivious to things like that. 'Sides, it ain't any of our business. It's *their* marriage."

Louisa nodded in agreement, and Debbie gaped at them both.

She couldn't believe she hadn't noticed it before—the painful secrets Maria was carrying around. Especially when she knew full well the burden of carrying around painful secrets. Debbie might have left the source of her pain on the other side of the country, but that didn't mean it wasn't still with her. It would always be with her.

"Someone should tell Preacher," she insisted.

"Honey, you know those two have been friends since forever, right? You tell Preacher and he says somethin' to Frank and Frank gets angry, and then who do you think gets the short end of the stick, hmm?" Lips pursed and twisted, Anne regarded Debbie.

Debbie recalled the one and only time she had tried to tell her mother what was happening to her. It hadn't gone well, and things had only gotten worse for her.

"Frank will take it out on Maria," Debbie whispered.

Anne nodded gravely. "You see? That's why we mind our own business. Now hand me the ashtray, will you?"

Sliding off her stool, Debbie reached down the bar and grabbed one of two glass ashtrays residing at the end. She slid one toward Anne, leaving the other where it had remained untouched since her arrival in New York City— with a half smoked clove cigarette still resting inside.

Debbie had hardly known Ginny and Gerald, but after

spending half a year with their family and friends, she certainly felt like she'd known them. Ginny most of all.

Debby felt Ginny's presence almost everywhere in the clubhouse—in the fun styles of the furniture and the colorful décor. Certain rooms even smelled like the clove cigarettes she'd loved.

"Alright, I'm heading home." Debbie glanced around the room. "Anyone seen Tiny?"

Preacher insisted that Debbie have a round-the-clock bodyguard whenever he couldn't be with her. Unfortunately for Debbie, her bodyguard was usually Tiny. Although he always meant well, the man was a public nuisance. He was loud, obnoxious, usually stinking to high heaven, and always drawing attention Debbie would rather not receive.

"Last I saw he was chillin' out front," Bullet called out. "Probably scammin' on chicks."

Anne choked on her laughter. "Unless he's offerin' money up front, that ain't never gonna happen!"

Keys jingling in his hand, Preacher bounded up the poorly lit staircase that led to his fourth-floor apartment—a dinky, dingy one-bedroom. All his furniture were hand-me-downs from his parents, and his decorations were sparse—only the bare necessities.

It had been perfect for him—a minimalist who'd never spent much time at home—but with Debbie here now and a baby on the way, he'd been meaning to find a bigger, nicer place.

He just needed to find the time.

He'd been gone three weeks this time. And three weeks

without Debbie was three weeks too long. If she wasn't pregnant, he'd be taking her with him. Although… not on this last trip.

The Road Warriors had more than lived up to their reputation for sex and violence, and sometimes both at once. He'd watched them pass around their own women to fellow club members without reservation. He'd seen brother pitted against brother in bloody boxing matches that almost always ended in an all-out brawl.

He'd also witnessed something far worse.

While meeting with a group of Road Warriors inside a highway bar in West Virginia, a young woman had been forcefully dragged up onto a pool table, stripped naked, and raped. Nearly every Road Warrior in the place had taken a turn with her, sometimes two at a time.

Almost two weeks had passed since the incident, and Preacher could still hear her screams, could still see her thrashing on the pool table every time he closed his eyes.

The Judge, had he still been alive, would have stripped his patch for that—for standing idly by and allowing a woman to be raped on his watch. Hell, The Judge would have punched his lights out for even associating with men like the Road Warriors.

But The Judge was gone.

There was only Preacher now. And his vengeance.

Without any other leads, he'd convinced himself that the Rossi family had exacted the hit on his parents. Only he had no proof, and he couldn't exactly go around accusing a well-known crime syndicate of murder and expect to keep his head attached to his body.

Instead, he'd decided to slowly rip the rug out from

beneath the Rossis. And once the Silver Demons were free of them? *Adios, you murdering mobster motherfuckers.*

But to accomplish everything he had planned, Preacher was going to need a big show of muscle and a hell of a lot more manpower than he had.

When it came to ending the Rossi family, Preacher figured the end would justify the means. Thanks to the Road Warriors, he now had the means.

Television static and slobbery snores greeted Preacher as he entered his apartment. Finding Tiny passed out on the couch, snuggled up to a half-eaten box of cookies, he pried the box from his friend's grip and switched off the television.

Inside his bedroom he found the lights on and Debbie curled up at the wrong end of the bed. Using her sketch pad as a pillow, she was also clutching a pencil in one hand.

Laughing softly, Preacher took a seat beside her and pulled the pencil from her hand. After tossing it away, he gently tugged the sketch pad from beneath her head and set it on the floor.

He brushed her long dark hair away from her face and caressed her cheek, then her chin, and finally the soft swell of her full bottom lip.

Staring down at her, Preacher felt his lungs deflate.

He wouldn't have made it the last six months without her. Those first few months after Four Points had been rough. There'd been so much to do, to sort through, and figure out. And so many awful feelings associated with all of it.

Somewhere in the middle of it all Debbie had become his anchor, and the only thing keeping him steady inside the raging sea that had become his life. With her, Preacher didn't have to be the president of anything. With her, he could still be him.

"Wheels." He bent down to kiss her, once on the tip of her nose, and twice on her mouth. Her eyelids fluttered.

"Preacher?" she mumbled sleepily and blinked up at him. "Preacher!" She shot upright and flung her arms around his neck. "When did you get back?"

"Just now."

He wrapped his arm around Debbie's waist and pulled her sideways onto his lap, a position that drew his eyes to the belly bulge beneath her nightgown. Smiling, he placed his hand on her stomach and was startled to feel a flutter beneath his palm.

His eyes met Debbie's. "Holy shit. Was that... him?"

The shift in Debbie's demeanor was instantaneous. Her brow furrowed, lines appearing. The excitement shining in her eyes faded fast into unease.

"Yes," she muttered, shoving his hand away.

Preacher exhaled noisily. He knew she was terrified. From day one she'd refused to talk about the baby, and whenever he brought it up, she'd either change the subject or leave the room. Unlike most pregnant women Preacher had known, Debbie balked at the idea of going shopping for the baby. What few things they did have, had been purchased by Sylvia.

He understood her fear. The pregnancy had been a shock to him as well, especially being so soon after his parents' death. And, *hell*, Preacher had no idea how to be a father and hadn't pictured himself ever becoming one. Still, it was just a matter of time before there was no choice but to accept his fate—he was becoming a father whether he liked it or not.

So instead of wallowing, he told himself that a baby was something to look forward to, something pure and good in a cruel world.

And lately, he needed all the good he could get his hands on.

Preacher bent his head and placed a kiss on Debbie's lips. "You smell like cookies," he mumbled. Traveling to her neck, he sniffed her skin.

"Somethin' you wanna tell me 'bout you and Tiny?" Sniffing turned to kisses, and he kissed his way back to her mouth.

"Ew, Preacher! Gross!" Laughing, she shoved at his shoulders until he released her. Moving off his lap, she leaned back against the pillows.

Preacher got to his feet and began undressing. "How's things at the club? Anything I need to know about?"

For a moment Preacher thought Debbie looked troubled, but the look vanished nearly as quickly as it had appeared, leaving him wondering if he'd only imagined it.

She shrugged and then grinned. "Same shit, different toilet."

"Jesus Christ, Wheels. No more hangin' 'round Hightower for you."

"But he's my favorite," she replied, her tone as sweet as sugar. Preacher paused in unbuckling his belt.

"How you gonna say that shit to me?" he demanded. "I thought I was your favorite."

Debbie smiled slyly. "Oh, you are... when you're here. And Hightower's my favorite when you're not." She shrugged again.

Preacher yanked his belt free from his jeans with a loud crack. Tossing it aside, he quickly finished undressing and climbed into bed.

Narrowed eyes on Debbie, he growled, "You wanna try that again, smartass?"

Debbie rolled toward him and slung her arm around his stomach and tucked her leg between his. "You could just never leave again. Then you won't ever have to wonder who my favorite is."

Already the stress of the last several weeks was beginning to wane. Preacher's head was clearing. The tension between his shoulders was evaporating. And his dick was waking up and taking notice of the beautiful girl on top of him.

Debbie had become Preacher's drug of choice. And when he was gone too long, like a junkie craving his next fix, Preacher craved his girl.

He rolled them over, flipping their positions. "I missed you."

"I missed this mouth." He nipped at her bottom lip.

"This ass, too," He slipped a hand beneath her and squeezed one perfectly round cheek.

Debbie wrapped her arms around his neck and slid her fingers through his hair, freeing it from its binding. Spreading her legs apart, she hooked her feet around his calves.

Gazing up at him through hooded eyes, she whispered, "What else?"

He shifted his hips, brushing himself against her. "This what you're lookin' for?"

Debbie made a noise—a sexy combination of a gasp and

a moan. Arching her back, she slowly dragged her pussy over the length of his dick. Grinning, Preacher pulled away from her only long enough to rid her of her nightgown.

He took his time entering her, watching with male satisfaction as her breath hitched and her eyes flared wide with every inch he claimed.

Ahhh, goddamn. Preacher dropped his face into the sweet-smelling space between her neck and her shoulder. Debbie's arms tightened around him. Her fingers dug into the skin on his back. Her body arched, she crushed her breasts to his chest. Then her hips began to move—small, jerky movements in an attempt to get him to increase his pace.

"Impatient," he grunted, and gripped her hip, stilling her.

"Control freak," she whispered, wriggling wildly beneath him.

With a growl, he increased his speed. And with it, everything quickened. His mouth on hers. Her breaths. His heartbeat. Her hands roaming his back and ass.

Debbie dragged her nails across his shoulders and moaned his name—a sexy-as-hell something she always did right before she came. Glancing at her face, he found her perfect features tightly drawn, and barely breathing. He watched, rapt, as her breath abruptly punched past her lips and her eyelids fluttered erratically. Gasping, she cried out his name twice more. And as she clenched and pulsed around him, he doubled his speed and finished only moments later.

Preacher collapsed on the bed beside Debbie and spent the next several minutes just catching his breath. Wiping the sweat from his brow, he turned to look at her. Her eyes were already on him, gleaming with satisfaction.

"I love you," she whispered.

"Yeah?" He started to smile. "That mean you're gonna take back that shit you said about Hightower?"

Preacher caught Debbie's hand before she could smack his chest, and quickly gathered her in his arms. Laughing, he buried his face in her neck.

"I can't believe Tiny slept through all that screamin'," he murmured, breathing in the salty scent of her sweat-dampened skin.

Debbie huffed. "I wasn't screaming."

"You were definitely screamin'."

"Was not."

"Was."

"Was not."

Eventually they fell silent, and Preacher soon grew drowsy. Untangling himself from Debbie, he rolled over and turned off the light.

"Preacher?"

"Yeah?"

"I know you can't tell me what you've been doing on the road, but... you haven't been saving girls at truck stops, have you?"

Although he couldn't see her face in the dark, and her tone was light, Preacher picked up on her underlying unease.

She worried for nothing. Yeah, he had opportunities to be with other women, but he always passed on them. Because he gave a shit about this girl. Loved her, even.

If there was anything losing his parents had taught

Preacher, outside of his newfound thirst for revenge, it was not to take the people he loved for granted.

Reaching out blindly, he pulled Debbie to him, tucking her tightly against him.

"Not a chance in hell," he said. "I learned my damned lesson the first time."

CHAPTER 28

"JOEY DIDN'T SAY NOTHIN' ABOUT A PARTY," SYLVIA hissed.

Seated inside Sylvia's cherry red Chevy Chevette, Debbie peered up at the looming brownstone. The music coming from inside was loud enough to be heard from the street. Both the street and the alleyway beside the clubhouse were littered with at least a hundred motorcycles.

Looking over the dozen or so people lounging on the stoop and walkway, men and women that Debbie didn't recognize, one thing in particular caught her eye: the Viking warrior emblem on the men's denim vests.

The Road Warriors were here.

Debbie bit down on her bottom lip. Was that why Preacher had insisted she stay away from the club?

For weeks neither Debbie nor Sylvia had been allowed

at the club. All the women had been ordered to stay away without being given any real reason why. It was club business, they'd been told. Worse, Preacher was always at the club now. When he did come home, he came home late and was usually gone before she woke in the morning.

Debbie looked at Sylvia. "Is this what they've been doing this whole time? Partying?"

Sylvia dark eyes flashed angrily. "Joey hasn't been home in two weeks. His last phone call was four fuckin' days ago."

A wave of anxiety rolled through Debbie and her hands flew to her stomach.

She knew she shouldn't compare her relationship with Preacher to Joe and Sylvia's unhappy marriage, yet she couldn't help but suddenly make those comparisons.

Joe resented Sylvia, and to some extent his son, for trapping him in a marriage he clearly never wanted—that was obvious to anyone who knew them. Yet Sylvia seemed oblivious.

Was that what was happening to her and Preacher? Was he sick of her already and slowly shutting her out of his life? Was that why she wasn't welcome at the clubhouse anymore?

Tears pricked her eyes. Had this god-awful pregnancy ruined everything?

"Move the fuckin' car outta the street, ya dumb bitch!" A passing taxi driver shook his fist at Sylvia.

Yanking the keys from the ignition, Sylvia shoved them into her purse and kicked the driver's side door open. "Fuck you, you fuckin' piece of shit!" she shouted after the taxi.

Debbie hurried to exit the vehicle and catch up to Sylvia as she stormed toward the clubhouse. Partygoers eyed them with amusement as they wove their way through the small crowd gathered outside. Ducking her head, Debbie could only imagine how they must look—both of them pregnant and at a party full of bikers.

"Jesus-fucking-Christ, Mary, mother of fucking God." Sylvia's New Jersey accent thickened with each muttered curse word.

The front hallway was dark, dense with smoke, and filled with people. A dozen different smells hung heavily in the cloudy air—cigarettes, marijuana, liquor, and sweat.

Debbie followed Sylvia's horrified stare into the kitchen and froze.

A blonde woman, utterly naked, lay spread-eagled on the same dining table where they ate their Saturday dinners. A man loomed over her, his hips pumping at breakneck speed between her thighs. Other men were gathered around the table taking turns kissing and groping her. Beyond them, a gathered crowd in the kitchen cheered them on.

"She needs a dick in her mouth!" a man shouted.

"She needs two!" someone else answered.

As cheers went up across the kitchen, bodies surged, converging on the table. A chair was thrown, dishes were shattered. Men toppled over one another as they scrambled to climb onto the table.

A large, burly black man emerged, towering over the crowd. He crossed the kitchen, pushing and shoving other men out of his way as if they weighed nothing. Coming up behind the man still pumping furiously into the woman, the burly man grabbed hold of the other man's neck, wrenched him off the table, and sent him flying into the nearby wall.

While the fighting continued all around him, he took

the other man's place between the woman's legs and unzipped his pants. And as he began to thrust, cheers and
jeers went up across the rowdy crowd.

Sylvia turned briefly to Debbie. "He's fucking dead," she
spat and spun away. Before Debbie could respond, Sylvia
darted down the hallway.

Taking care not to draw attention to herself, Debbie
pressed herself against the wall and followed it down the
hall. She slowly approached the living room where the
music was playing at near-deafening decibels and peered
inside.

Everywhere she looked she found more of the same—
more Road Warriors and more women in various stages of
undress, and almost all of them engaged sexually.

Her wide-eyed stare paused on a familiar shock of
blond hair. Knuckles was sagging against the far wall, his
eyes screwed shut, his mouth agape. In one hand he held a
beer and in the other a fistful of corkscrew curls. Debbie's
eyes dropped to the dark-skinned woman on her knees before him, whose head was bobbing steadily in his lap.

Heat exploded in Debbie's cheeks, and she quickly looked away, only to immediately spot another familiar
face.

On a couch crawling with naked and half-dressed bodies, Crazy-8 was snorting white powder off a topless woman's breasts. Finished, he used his tongue to lick off anything
that remained. When they started kissing, Debbie forced
herself to turn away from the hurtful scene. She didn't understand how he could do that to Louisa—a woman he
claimed to love.

Taking a quick, shaky breath, Debbie dragged her

sweaty palms down the sides of her dress and then fretfully continued her search through the room. Afraid of finding Preacher in a similar situation, she began frantically twisting her butterfly ring.

Debbie's search ground to a halt. Leaning back against the bar, Preacher stood alone, surveying the room with an impassive expression. As if there weren't drunken orgies happening all around him. As if there weren't two naked women dancing on the bar directly behind him.

Her heart pounding furiously inside her chest, Debbie quivered through her next breath. Now that she'd found him, she had no idea what on earth she was going to say to him. In her current state, shocked and disgusted, she wondered if returning to Sylvia's car would be better than confronting him.

She was still undecided when one of the women dancing on the bar dropped to her knees and wrapped her arms around Preacher's neck. Laughing drunkenly, the woman slumped forward, forcing Preacher to catch her.

When the woman moved in for a kiss, Debbie's breath turned to ice in her lungs.

He wouldn't.

Oh God, he couldn't.

Relief came quickly when Preacher all but dropped her. Grabbing her arm, he hauled her across the room and handed her off to a cluster of men.

Then Preacher returned to the bar and lit up a cigarette. Brow heavy, mouth grim, he continued to inventory his surroundings.

For all intents and purposes, he looked like the Preacher Debbie loved. His long brown hair was tied back in a knot at his nape and his short beard was in need of a trim. He was wearing his usual attire—a pair of black jeans, a Led Zeppelin concert tee, his black leather vest, and his riding boots.

But there was something startlingly different about him. An eerie stillness to him. A strange deadness in his eyes.

This man was harder and colder than she knew Preacher to be, and more detached than she'd ever seen him before. And she'd thought she'd seen him at his worst—grief-stricken, full of rage, and feeling helpless.

"I remember you." Hot breath, smelling strongly of whiskey tickled Debbie's ear and cheek. Jerking away, she whirled around.

Flat, dark, dispassionate eyes met her gaze. An oily smile full of malevolence twisted beneath a thick black mustache. If she hadn't already been flush against the wall, she would have taken several steps back.

"Rocky," she said, quickly finding her voice. "Hi."

Rocky's unnerving stare cruised her figure, halting on her protruding belly. "Well fuck." He laughed horribly, his black eyes flicking to hers. "That Preacher's bastard in there?"

Feeling an unexpected flare of protectiveness, Debbie's hands went to her stomach. "It's Preacher's *baby*," she countered.

Another cruel smile split his lips. "Yeah? He marry you?"

When Debbie didn't respond, Rocky's smile grew. "Didn't think so."

He pressed a hand on the wall beside her and bent his head to hers. He captured a lock of her hair and tugged hard.

"You know, me and my boys, we got a rule. Don't matter which one of us she's fuckin'. If she ain't married, she's fair game." Again the dry, woody stench of whiskey engulfed her.

"You're a little fatter than I like, but you sure look sweet." He stepped back a fraction to look at her, and inside his vile gaze, Debbie saw all the sick and twisted things he wanted to do to her.

"Wh-where's Angel?" She stammered. Wishing for her pocketknife, Debbie cursed herself for no longer carrying it.

"Who?" he asked and laughed again. His hand dropped from her hair to her chest, just above her breasts. His fingers dipped between her cleavage and cold panic lodged in her throat, freezing her in place.

Then Rocky was suddenly gone. Wrenched away from her and shoved up against the opposite wall. Preacher quickly advanced on Rocky and gripped him by his shirt collar.

"Don't you ever touch her!" he shouted, his voice quaking with rage. "Not fuckin' ever!"

"Get your fuckin' hands off me," Rocky growled.

Dark eyes stared into dark eyes, and both men's features tightened further. The tension between the two was tangible, rolling off them in menacing waves.

"You don't touch her," Preacher repeated coldly. "Ever."

All around them Road Warriors had paused in their debauchery and were watching the exchange with wary expressions. Crazy-8 and Knuckles had also joined the fray. Fists clenched, bodies taut with aggression, they met the wary gazes of the surrounding Road Warriors with hard, unyielding stares.

It was Rocky who relented first. Smirking, he put his hands in the air. "Whatever you say, *Prez...*"

Preacher took a halting breath and released Rocky with a shove. Quickly straightening, Rocky turned and stalked off down the hall, but not before winking in Debbie's direction.

Then Preacher turned his blistering gaze on Debbie. His eyes were on fire. The tendons in his neck and arms were bulging, straining beneath his skin.

She shrunk back against the wall as he advanced on her, but made no move to stop him as he grabbed her arm. Holding tightly to her, Preacher marched her down the hallway. As pregnant as she was, she had to practically run to keep up with his long-legged stride.

He brought her to a sudden stop outside of the room he always kept locked, and after fumbling with his keys, threw open the door. One look at the lethal expression still marring his handsome features and Debbie hurried inside. Preacher slammed the door shut behind them, pitching the room into near darkness.

A light flickered on, brightening the room and high-lighting the thick layer of dust coating nearly everything inside it—a desk and chair, numerous family photos, and a long, rectangular table with enough chairs around it to seat every member of the club.

While the rest of the clubhouse smelled lived in, this room smelled stale and unused. Debbie's stared briefly at the desk in the corner and the framed photograph resting on top—a black and white snapshot of a young Gerald and Ginny, a swaddled baby in Ginny's arms, and the clubhouse towering behind them.

"What the fuck are you doin' here?" Preacher snarled.

"And where the fuck is Tiny?"

"Who are all those women?" she countered, her voice trembling—with anger or fear, she didn't know. She gestured toward the door, residual panic making her movements jerky and uncoordinated.

Preacher's frown deepened, making the angry lines in his face appear twice as pronounced. And Debbie was once again struck by how different he seemed.

"I told you not to come here. You bein' here is doin' the exact opposite of what I told you to do!"

"I thought you had business to take care of!" she shouted. "But you're throwing a party? Is this what you do on the road?"

"What happens here or on the road isn't any of your business."

Shocked, Debbie blinked. Her eyes filled with tears. "Is this what you want, then?" she whispered.

"Is what what I want?"

"Those disgusting women!" She thrust a finger toward the door. "I saw Knuckles and Crazy-8, and I saw you!"

Preacher regarded her coolly. "I don't know what you think you saw, but those women are hookers, bought and paid for. And I haven't touched a single one of 'em."

"Then why are you here?" Her bottom lip trembled relentlessly as she tried desperately not to cry. "And why can't I be here with you?"

Preacher's eyes flashed, and his expression turned deadly once more. "Those men are monsters," he said quietly through clenched teeth. "Do you get that? They are fuckin' monsters and I don't want you anywhere near them."

"They why are they here?" she demanded. "Why are

they in your clubhouse? You say they're monsters, but they're here because you let them in! Are you a monster too?"

Silence followed her words—the sort of stillness that steals everything within its reach, strips it naked, and swallows it whole.

Debbie's thoughts jumbled. And as her emotions overflowed, so did her eyes.

"Is it because I look like this?" Tears streaming down her cheeks, her hands flew to her stomach. "Because you did this! You did this to me!"

"I know what I did." Preacher's tone was as unyielding as the look on his face. "I didn't mean for it to happen, but I ain't gonna keep apologizin' for it, either." His jaw locked. "I want my fuckin' kid."

"That makes one of us!"

Preacher's nostrils flared wide. "What is wrong with you?" he demanded. "Look at your fuckin' stomach! You need to own up to what happened and get your damn head on straight! We are havin' a kid, you're gonna be a mother—"

"Shut up!" Debbie cried, slapping her hands over her ears. "Just shut up!"

Preacher took a threatening step towards her, his hands clenched into fists. Debbie scrambled backward, taking refuge behind a chair.

Surprise flashed in his eyes. Shaking his head, he threw his hands in the air. "What am I doin' wrong? You got a place to live, don't you? Food, clothes, money? When was the last time you had to jack a wallet or scam a meal?"

"Screw you!" Debbie continued to cry. "At least I wasn't pregnant!"

Preacher stared at her. "Are you tellin' me that you'd rather be out there on the street, livin' like a goddamn rat, than here with me, havin' my kid?"

A bolt of clarity flashed through the roaring storm that was Debbie's emotions.

No, God no. She wouldn't trade her life with Preacher for anything that had come before. But she wasn't about to admit to it—she was far too upset at what she'd seen going on inside the clubhouse tonight.

Preacher closed the remaining distance between them and grabbed hold of the chair Debbie was hiding behind. "What the fuck do you need that I ain't givin' you? More clothes? More money?"

"Screw you," she whispered hoarsely. He could take his clothes and his money and shove them up his ass for all she cared. All she wanted was him.

The chair between them disappeared, and Debbie flinched as it crashed into a wall.

"Answer me!" he demanded. "What else do you need?"

"I need to not be pregnant!" she screamed. "I don't want a fucking baby! I don't want to be a mother! I don't want this, Preacher!"

Her explosion startled them both into silence.

Preacher recovered first, his surprise quickly reverting to anger. "Too late," he ground out.

His refusal to hear her, to even acknowledge her fears, sent her into another emotional tailspin. "Fuck you!" she cried, "*Fuck you!*"

Nostrils flaring wildly, rage stamped into every line on his face, Preacher stepped closer, forcing Debbie up against the wall. "Fuck me? Is that what you need? You're jealous of those whores out there? You wanna get fucked in front of everyone too? Want me to pass you around?"

Debbie's breath hitched, her heart skipped a beat, and then her hand cracked across Preacher's face. His head whipped to the right under the force of her slap.

He turned back to her slowly, flexing his jaw.

Debbie brought her throbbing hand to her mouth and squeezed her eyes shut. "I'm sorry," she rushed to say. "Oh God, Preacher, I'm so sorry."

She flinched when he touched her wrist, and gently tugged her hand away from her mouth. "Wheels, open your eyes and look at me."

She shook her head, and he sighed loudly.

"I'm protectin' you, don't you get that? But I can't protect you if you don't listen to me." Preacher's voice was a soft, tender rumble.

Eyes still closed, Debbie continued to shake her head. She didn't understand anything regarding the club. And with tonight's revelations, she wasn't sure she ever wanted to.

Preacher bent his head to hers. Forehead to forehead, nose to nose, his warm breath mingled with hers. Debbie breathed in the familiar and comforting scent of him, hating that it was mixed with the noxious smell of cheap perfume.

His hands captured the sides of her head. "The less you know, the safer you are."

She opened her eyes. "Are you safe?"

The corner of his mouth lifted. "How many times do I gotta tell you? You don't need to worry 'bout me."

It was such a small thing—a single extra blink—that Debbie almost didn't notice it. And probably wouldn't have if she hadn't been looking directly into his eyes.

"Lie," she whispered.

He stared at her for a long time, a mix of emotions passing over his features—guilt, sadness, and pain. The same pain she always glimpsed in his eyes when she found him roaming their apartment at night.

"Oh, Preacher," she whimpered, and kissed him—a soft brush of her lips. He drew in a deep, ragged breath and then covered her mouth with his.

Then she poured everything she was feeling—all her shock, her anger, and her fears—into their kiss. All her love too.

And when they broke apart, and Preacher's hands fell away from her face, gone was the pain in his eyes. Instead, they burned hungrily.

"Come on," he said, taking her hand. "We're goin' home."

No sooner had they'd turned toward the door when Knuckles burst through it. Smoke and music filled the room. "Sylvie's gonna kill Joe!"

"Sylvie's here?" Frowning, Preacher looked at Debbie. Biting down on her bottom lip, she nodded.

"Preacher, man, she's got a gun!" Panic-stricken, Knuckles was hopping from foot to foot, while both nodding and shaking his head back and forth. "She's really gonna kill him!"

"A gun?" Again, Preacher looked at Debbie.

Mouth hanging open, she only shook her head.

Preacher looked instantly ten years older and markedly more exhausted than she'd ever seen him before. "Jesus Christ," he muttered. "Jesus. Fucking. Christ."

"Knuckles, you stay with her." Preacher pointed at Debbie. "And lock this fuckin' door behind me. None of the trash out there gets anywhere near my girl, you got that?"

Knuckles nodded. "I got it, boss."

Locking the door behind Preacher, Knuckles turned to Debbie, a strained smile on his face. "You ain't got no gun, right Debbie darling?"

He pointed to the words on his T-shirt—PEACE, LOVE, AND PUSSY.

"'Cause, I'm a lover, not a fighter."

Preacher found Frank waiting for him at the bottom of the first-floor stairwell. In sharp contrast to the others, Preacher could always count on Frank to be sober and ready for anything that came their way. The man had zero distractions—he didn't drink, didn't use drugs, and didn't mess with women outside of his marriage. Back when they were kids, Preacher used to rag on him for his inability to let loose and run wild. Now though, as a grown man with the responsibility of the entire club resting solely on his shoulders, he was glad for Frank's steadfastness and reliability—even if it was sometimes to the point of neurosis.

"All clear?" he asked.

Frank gestured to a small cluster of half-dressed people being ushered down the stairs by Whiskey Jim. "That's the last of 'em."

"It's only the three of them still up there," Jim called out, shooting Preacher an irritated look. He'd been doing that a lot lately—irritated looks, exasperated sighs, and eye rolls. All blatant signs of disrespect that Jim would never have dared with The Judge.

Preacher was aware that Jim wasn't happy about the changes being made to the club, mainly the addition of the Road Warriors. But that decision wasn't up to Jim or anyone else.

Having had enough of Jim's blatant disregard for his authority, Preacher held Jim's stare, silently conveying his displeasure until Jim had the good sense to look away. Satisfied, he turned back to Frank.

"Did he say three? Who else is up there?"

"Sylvie won't let the whore leave."

Preacher cursed the entire way up three flights of stairs. He expected this shit from Max—eighteen years old and newly patched in, he was a ticking time bomb, ready to blow his load over every pair of tits that so much as jiggled in his direction. But Joe? With a wife and kid at home and another kid on the way, Joe should be spending less time at the club, not more.

To make matters worse, Joe rarely put the bottle down these days. More often than not, Preacher would find him passed out somewhere in the clubhouse, sans clothes and with no memory of what had happened the night before. With the arrival of the Road Warriors, Joe had only gotten worse.

Maybe it was time to start rethinking Joe as his vice president. Maybe he should have told tradition to go fuck itself and given the job to someone better suited. If things continued on this way, if Joe couldn't get his shit together, eventually Preacher was going to have to give the position to someone else—someone up to the task.

They climbed higher up the stairs, and soon Sylvia's

hysterical ranting filled Preacher's ears. Frank flicked his gaze down the empty hallway. "They're in Joe's room. You want my help, or you want me standin' guard?"

"Wait here. Make sure no one else comes up."

Leaving Frank at the end of the hall, Preacher crept cautiously toward Joe's room. Keeping against the wall, he peeked inside.

Sylvia stood just inside the doorway clutching a small revolver—a .38 special that Preacher recognized as one of several guns he'd given specifically to Joe. Preacher ground his teeth. His brother wasn't just careless, he was a bona fide moron.

"Where'd you get the gun, Sylvie?" Preacher called out.

She spared a quick glance over her shoulder, long enough for Preacher to see that her face was streaked with makeup and tears. "Mind your own damn business, Preacher!"

"This is my business," he replied. "That's my little brother you're pointin' a gun at."

Sylvia let out a strangled sob. "Your little brother is a rotten two-timin' whore!"

Preacher sighed. If Sylvia didn't shoot Joe, he just might do it himself. "Yep, Sylvie, he sure is. But that don't mean you can shoot him."

"He never comes home!" she cried. "I can't come to the club anymore, and he never comes home! And then I find him with this—*this whore!*"

"I didn't know he was married!" a new voice cried out.

"What did you say?" Sylvia turned toward the voice, and the gun in her hand began to quake.

"Sylvie, no!" Joe shouted. "Point the fuckin' gun at me!"

Preacher quickly shifted to the opposite side of the doorway, allowing him a better view of the room. A young woman with messy brown hair and red lipstick smeared across her cheek was sitting up in Joe's bed, clutching a blanket to her chest.

A few feet away Joe stood naked, cupping his crotch with both hands.

The gun swung back to Joe and Sylvia exploded. "What? You care about this whore? You can't make time for your own son, but you care about her?"

"Please, Sylvie," Joe pleaded. "You've got to calm down. That ain't what I meant!"

Preacher's eyes were on the gun wobbling precariously in Sylvia's unsteady grip. One wrong twitch on the trigger and Joe was going to end up with a hole in his chest.

Out of time and options, Preacher lunged, grabbing Sylvia from behind. Quickly gripping her wrists, he squeezed until she cried out in pain, and the gun clattered to the floor.

"No!" Sylvia thrashed in his arms, twisting her body and flailing her legs. Wrapping his arms around her middle, Preacher dragged her into the hallway.

"Frank! The gun, the girl!" he roared needlessly. Frank was already there, rushing past him into the room.

"Listen to me, Sylvie!" Preacher had to shout to hear himself over Sylvia's hysterical screaming. "Joe doesn't love you! You hear me? He does not fuckin' love you!"

Sylvia went still and silent.

"He didn't want to marry you, either." Preacher lowered his voice and softened his tone. "He did it 'cause our old man told him he had to."

Sylvia heaved brokenly. "No," she whispered hoarsely. "No..."

"You know it's true. You know I'm right, Sylvie."

"I thought he was gonna change. I thought he could love me... oh God, I'm a fool..." Shoulders shaking, she began to sob. Preacher held her until she quieted and then he turned her in his arms and set her back against the wall.

"Joe ain't ever gonna be faithful," he told her. "Not ever. But I can't have you at the club pullin' guns on people and makin' a goddamn scene, can I?"

Sylvia's bloodshot eyes filled with fresh tears. "No."

"Good girl. So I'm gonna need you to make a decision, Sylvie. Right here, right now, okay?"

Nodding limply, Sylvia's gaze dropped to the floor. "Okay," she whispered.

"You got two choices. You take my piece-of-shit brother as he is—you raise his babies and stay the hell away from the club, no questions asked. You do that, and I promise you Joe will be comin' home most nights, and he won't be bringing any of his bullshit with him."

"Preacher—"

"Shut the fuck up!" Preacher spun around and collided with Joe. Shoving Joe up against the wall, he pressed his forearm to his brother's throat.

"I don't give a flyin' fuck what you've got to say right now. "You're my goddamn VP, and you know better than anyone what's at stake right now! But instead of makin' sure shit goes smoothly, I'm up here disarming your fuckin' wife 'cause you seem to keep forgettin' you have one!"

Beneath Preacher's arm, Joe's Adam's apple bobbed. "No," he rasped. "You don't—"

"Are you thick?" Preacher growled, putting more pressure on Joe's throat. "Your president just told you to *shut the fuck up*! Say another fuckin' word and I will tear that patch off your cut and put you out on your ass."

Joe's mouth snapped shut and Preacher released him with a slap upside his head.

"Or you can leave him," Preacher told Sylvia. "Forget about Joe and go find a man who's gonna do right by you."

Sylvia's bitter laughter rang out through the hall. "Who's gonna want me now?" Tears rolled down her cheeks as her hands dropped to the swell of her stomach. "You fucked me, Joey. You really fucked me."

Glancing over his shoulder, Preacher found Joe staring at Sylvia, hopelessness and misery etched in his expression.

Not feeling the least bit sorry for him, Preacher barked, "Get dressed, and get Sylvie outta here. And I don't want to see your face for at least a week, you got that? Fix your fuckin' family or don't come back."

No one said a word as Preacher turned away and stalked off down the hall. Halfway to the second floor, Frank appeared out of nowhere—just like the apparition he'd been nicknamed after.

"The gun?" Preacher asked.

Frank produced it from inside his cut. Taking it, Preacher tucked it into the back of his jeans.

"The whore?"

"Taken care of. Where you headed?"

"Gonna go grab my girl and take her home. Then I'm gonna fuck her 'til she sleeps for a week and forgets she's pissed." Sighing, Preacher scrubbed a hand down his face. "You got this mess covered?"

"You know I do."

Preacher clapped his friend on the arm. "Don't know what I'd do without you, brother."

The corner of Frank's mouth lifted in a rare smile.

"You don't ever gotta worry about that."

CHAPTER 29

EBBIE'S WATER BROKE ON A THURSDAY AFTERNOON, exactly one week before she was due to give birth.

One minute she was standing in the kitchen making a grilled cheese sandwich on the stovetop, and the next she was gripping her stomach as a painful cramp rippled through her abdomen. She didn't think anything of it at first—she'd been cramping all morning—until she felt a rush of liquid between her legs.

For a moment she just stared down at the puddle at her feet, wide-eyed and unblinking. Then as realization dawned, a chill slid up her spine. Fear curdled in her stomach. She'd been starving just a few minutes ago, but now she felt hot and shaky, and like she might vomit.

No.

Horrified, she slowly backed away and glanced at the

calendar on the wall, zeroing in on the circled date.

No, no, no, not yet.

"Tiny!" she called, her voice trembling. "Tiny! Help!"

There was a crash inside the bathroom, followed by shouted curses. Tiny was still zipping up his pants when he came flying into the kitchen. "What? What's wrong?"

Debbie pointed at the puddle on the floor with the spatula in her hand. Tiny squinted at the mess. "You spill somethin'?"

"My water," she whispered.

"You spilled your water?"

"Tiny! My water broke! The baby!" She gestured frantically at her belly. "*The baby*!"

Tiny stared at her. "The baby," he repeated dumbly. "The baby…" His eyes widened and his mouth fell open. "Jesus fuck, *the baby*?" Panic filled his plump features. "It's comin'? Like, right now? Jesus!" Hands in his hair, he glanced wildly around the kitchen. "I'll go get my bike!"

Debbie squeezed her eyes closed, fighting for calm. "I can't ride on your bike," she hissed. Tossing the spatula into the sink, she pushed passed him. "You go call Preacher. I'm going to go change."

Inside the bedroom, Debbie changed out of her night-dress and into one of the many shapeless maternity shifts Sylvia had loaned her. Finished, she glanced around the room, catching sight of her reflection in the mirror.

Her shaking hands went to her stomach. She was nothing but stomach—as if the baby had taken her over completely. She was ridiculously pale, too—her wide eyes looked glaringly dark against her too-white skin. Staring at herself, she shook her head slowly.

She couldn't do this. She wasn't ready.

Biting down hard on her bottom lip, she breathed in deeply through her nose. And then out a moment later. Air raced through her lungs, cold and cutting, doing nothing to lessen her fear. Every breath felt like an extra helping of dread until her lungs felt too full and her breathing turned shallow.

Abruptly, Debbie turned away from the mirror and took a seat on the bed. Staring helplessly at the bare, cream-colored wall, she placed her hand on her chest and attempted to breathe normally.

This couldn't be happening. It wasn't time yet.

Oh God, she needed Preacher.

Covering her face with her hands, she breathed noisily into her palms. She needed Preacher. He should be here with her. She couldn't do this without him. He wanted this baby—*not her.*

"Please no," she mumbled. She dropped her hands and looked helplessly around the room to the wall. "Please God, no. I can't do this."

She definitely couldn't do this with Tiny.

Another cramp rippled through her, worse than before. Pain radiated from her back to her front and she rolled onto her side, clutching her stomach. Once the discomfort subsided, she blinked blearily across the room.

"Debbie?" Tiny appeared in the doorway, scratching at his head. His nervous gaze flicked nervously around the room before landing on her. "Preacher ain't at the club and Max says he don't know when he's gettin' back. Want me to grab a taxi?"

"No!" Debbie cried, violently shaking her head back

and forth. "Call Sylvia!"

She wasn't going anywhere without Preacher. She would stay right here until he showed up.

Tiny looked as scared as Debbie felt. "But, uh…" He swallowed hard. "Shouldn't we get you to the hospital?"

"Tiny! Call Sylvia—right now!"

Eyes wide and head bobbing frantically, Tiny disappeared down the hallway.

Minutes passed, maybe hours; time had ceased to exist in Debbie's current state. Panic continued to worsen her nausea, causing her to periodically dry heave. Her contractions persisted, coming closer together. Several times Tiny poked his head in to ask her if she needed anything, and she'd only managed to groan in response.

"Where is she?" Sylvia demanded.

Debbie jolted at the sound of Sylvia's voice and cried out. A moment later Sylvia rushed into the bedroom.

"I'm here, I'm here!" Sylvia was breathless as she dropped down on her knees beside the bed. Her hands covered Debbie's—cold against Debbie's sweat-drenched skin. The familiar, overly sweet scent of Sylvia's perfume filled Debbie's nostrils, causing her stomach to roil.

"My water broke," Debbie moaned.

Sylvia smoothed a hand over her forehead. "Oh Debbie, that's the least of it. From the looks of it, you're in labor." She glanced around the room. "Now where's your bag?"

Debbie blinked at her, confused.

"Your bag," Sylvia repeated. "Your hospital bag? Clothes for you and the baby?"

Debbie shook her head. "I forgot."

She hadn't really forgotten; she just hadn't done it. She

hadn't been able to bring herself to do anything baby related. Everything the Sylvia had purchased for the baby was piled inside the closet, still wrapped in its store packaging.

Sylvia smiled at her—a kind and gentle smile that looked out of place on the always-scowling Italian. She squeezed Debbie's hands. "Don't you worry, I'll take care of it."

Debbie watched through blurry eyes as Sylvia hurried around the bedroom, grabbing handfuls of things from inside the dresser and shoving them into Debbie's canvas backpack. Throwing open the closet, Sylvia began yanking items off hangers.

Finished, she turned to Debbie. "We gotta get you to the car now, okay? Can you walk?"

Debbie's tears spilled over. "Sylvie," she whispered frantically, "I'm scared. Please, I don't want to do this. Please..."

If Sylvia answered her, Debbie didn't hear it. Another cramp pulsed through her, ten times more painful than the last. Eyes squeezed shut, Debbie twisted the bed sheet in her grip.

"Breathe, Debbie, breathe!" Sylvia shouted. "Like this! Remember how I showed you?"

No, Debbie did not remember. And even if she could remember, she couldn't fathom how anyone could expect her to breathe through this god-awful pain.

"Oh God," she panted, rolling onto her back. Clutching her belly, she blinked up at Sylvia's looming face. "It feels like I'm falling apart!"

"Oh Debbie, that's normal." Sylvia smiled anxiously. "They tear us open coming out and then their sweet faces put us back together."

Not wanting to hear about babies and their sweet faces, Debbie turned her head. "No," she moaned, pushing herself further across the bed, away from Sylvia.

"Oh God, oh God, it hurts so bad." She clutched her belly. "I can't do this, Sylvie. I can't do this—not without Preacher."

"Of course you can! Women have been givin' birth since the dawn of time. It's like pushing out a watermelon! And I'll be right there with you. And then Preacher will— oh shit, Debbie you're bleeding!"

Debbie felt Sylvia's hands on her legs, pushing them apart. She heard a gasp, and then, "Tiny! Tiny! We need to get her to the car, *now*!"

Pulling on his leather riding gloves, Preacher strode inside the warehouse, Rocky beside him. Dark and damp with humidity, the crumbling structure stunk of mildew and rot.

They turned the corner into a larger, somewhat lighter area, the shattered windows letting in what little light the overcast afternoon offered. The smells were different in this room, metallic in nature, along with the pungent aroma of gun smoke.

A half dozen or so bodies littered the large space—Rossi foot soldiers. Blood seeped from various wounds, pooling around the dead and dying men, further discoloring the stained cement.

Somebody groaned—a wet, gurgling chest rattle that pinged distractedly through Preacher's thoughts before lodging firmly in his consciousness.

He would always remember that sound. It was the

sound of death—live and in stereo.

Preacher passed Frank, who was standing among a handful of Road Warriors. Then Joe, who stood alone, a gun in his hand and body at his feet. He passed more Road Warriors and more of his men. He didn't look at a single face, either living or dead. His sole focus was on Hightower, and the man kneeling at his feet.

Rocky veered off, leaving Preacher to continue on alone. The blade at his side was heavy—a freshly sharpened piece of stainless steel that had once belonged to The Judge. It banged against his hip in time to his steps. In time to his heartbeat. In time to the quickly forming lump pulsing inside his throat.

Reaching Hightower, Preacher peered down his nose at the man on his knees. With a head full of white hair, a face full of wrinkles, and wearing a pressed black suit with a red pocket square, Salvatore Rossi looked less like the head of the Rossi crime family and more like an impeccably dressed grandfather.

Salvatore's ancient eyes flicked up, meeting his, his expression blank, his demeanor strangely calm. "Damon," he greeted him, his Italian accent rolling and thick.

Preacher blinked at him, not comprehending Salvatore's cool composure. It was hardly the attitude Preacher would have expected from a man who had to know he was about to die.

Especially when his own heart was flapping wildly inside his chest.

It was also another thing Preacher would never forget. Much later in his life, when his body count was plentiful and he'd long forgotten what it felt like to solve his problems with mere words, he would still remember the look on Salvatore Rossi's face.

"Are all my boys dead?" Still so absurdly, unnervingly calm, Salvatore raised one bushy white eyebrow.

Preacher dropped down on one knee and stared into the old man's eyes. "Your sons, your grandsons. All of 'em."

Weeks ago Preacher had finally managed to appropriate the Rossis' Columbian connection right out from under their noses. With the Road Warriors now under Preacher's control, and ready to form Silver Demon clubs all over the country, the Columbian's potential to increase their revenue by 200% was too lucrative an offer to refuse.

Then today, after months of strategic planning, putting every player in place, the Silver Demons and the Road Warriors had taken out the Rossi underboss, each Rossi caporegime, and any foot soldiers that had been with them at the time of their ambush. With only scattered foot soldiers remaining, the Rossis wouldn't be recovering from this anytime soon—if ever.

Ending the life of the Rossi family Mafioso, Salvatore Rossi, was Preacher's job. A blow he'd long been dreaming of delivering personally.

The corner of Salvatore's mouth quirked. "I knew you'd do great things, Damon. You always were a hungry boy. I could see it in your eyes."

Preacher's nostrils flared. His chest caved and his heart quaked. "You killed them."

Salvatore's expression didn't change. "No. I did not. But that doesn't matter anymore, eh?"

Preacher jumped to his feet and snarled, "No, it fuckin' doesn't."

Pulling his blade from its sheath, Preacher moved to stand behind Salvatore. Gripping a handful of the old man's hair, he wrenched his head back and pressed the edge of the blade to his throat. A thin red line welled amid his wrinkled, sagging skin.

Salvatore didn't make a sound, didn't move a muscle. Neither did Preacher.

Preacher had gotten into countless fights during the course of his life. He'd broken men's bones and beaten men into unconsciousness. He'd done some sketchy things in prison to ensure his own safety—things he wasn't proud of.

But he'd never killed a man before.

The finality of this moment barreled into Preacher like a freight train. There would be no going back, no do-overs, no time to press pause and just drift along while he sorted through his bullshit.

He made the mistake of glancing up. All across the room, all eyes were on him, waiting for him to finish it. He knew he couldn't look weak, not in front of his own men, and especially not in front of the Road Warriors. Not if he expected to take control of them, to lead them.

So he did the only thing he could think of to do. He flipped his fucking switch and let it all back in—everything he'd long shut out.

He let his mother's face fill his memory.

And he thought of his father.

He saw the smear of blood on the trailer door.

And then he recalled the day he was forced to watch as their matching coffins were lowered into the ground.

And just when he wanted to scream… he slid the blade across Salvatore Rossi's throat instead.

The mob boss slumped to his side, wide-eyed and clawing at his throat. Both horrified and fascinated, Preacher watched as thick, dark blood spurted and gushed from the gaping wound in his neck.

"It's done, then? You're gonna patch us in?" Rocky's booted feet drew precariously close to the blood creeping across the floor.

Preacher cleared his throat and prayed his voice didn't shake. "I need you and your boys to lay low for a while, wait and see if we get any blowback. But yeah, it's done."

Rocky started to smile, and Preacher turned his attention back to Salvatore. The old man had gone still, though his mouth still worked soundlessly.

Preacher was suddenly struck with a memory.

When his he and his brothers were little, The Judge would take them fishing at the pier. He taught them all sorts of things—various fishing line knots, and what bait worked best for which fish. The fish they'd catch, The Judge would slap across the dock, killing them instantly.

They should never be needlessly cruel, The Judge had told them.

Again Preacher saw the smear of blood on the trailer door—an image that would never leave him.

And then he walked off, leaving Salvatore gasping for air.

Inside the clubhouse, half his club trailing behind him, Preacher headed into the kitchen. Quickly peeling off his gloves, he tossed them onto the countertop and moved toward the sink. Behind him, his men filed in. Nobody said a word.

Turning on the faucet, Preacher cupped his hands and splashed several handfuls of cold water on his face. Dripping wet, he gripped the counter and bowed his head. Preacher's arms began to quiver.

He'd done it. He'd actually fucking done it.

It was so fucking surreal, this entire day. He'd avenged his parents and effectively ended the Rossi family. Him. Just a no-good kid from the neighborhood.

"Preacher?" Frank leaned his elbow on the counter. "How you doin'?"

Preacher's eyes slid to Frank. His longtime friend had killed men today with the same ruthless efficiency that he did everything else. He didn't appear bothered in the least. In fact, he seemed almost... tranquil.

Preacher couldn't even begin to comprehend that kind of calm. He was... hell, he didn't know what he was feeling, exactly.

Killing Salvatore—it had felt horrible.

And yet, also exhilarating. Powerful.

Preacher ran a hand over his face and blew out a breath. "I'm good," he lied.

Frank stared at him, his gaze full of speculation and doubt. Straightening, Preacher folded his arms across his chest. "I'm good," he growled.

"Good. 'Cause they aren't." Frank's gaze shifted.

Preacher turned, facing the kitchen and the four men spread throughout. Still no one spoke or even looked at one another.

"Smokey and Jim come back yet?" Preacher quietly asked Frank.

"Not yet."

Preacher nodded and pushed away from the counter. After grabbing two bottles of liquor from a nearby cabinet, he handed one to Hightower. "You okay?"

Hightower often bragged about his many kills in Vietnam. Still, Preacher couldn't imagine that killing men in a firefight was anything like the carefully calculated, up close and personal hits they'd exacted tonight.

His expression unreadable, Hightower nodded slowly. "Right as rain, Prez," he drawled.

Preacher clapped him on the arm and turned to Bullet. Unable to hold his gaze, Bullet stared down at his boots.

"I ain't sweatin' it, my brother," Bullet muttered. "There ain't nothin' so bad in this world that a wet, warm pussy can't fix."

Suddenly laughing, Hightower wrapped an arm around Bullet's neck and squeezed. "You know it!"

Across the room, Knuckles was seated at the dining table, pale-faced and staring at his hands splayed out in front of him. Joe sat beside him, staring vacantly across the room, an unlit cigarette quivering between his lips.

Setting the second bottle down on the table, Preacher gripped Knuckles' shoulder and bent down beside him. "You did good today."

Bloodshot eyes lifted and narrowed. "Yeah?" Knuckles' voice was small and timid.

Preacher squeezed his shoulder. "Yeah, man. Real fuckin' good."

Knuckles let out a breath, then another, and then he grabbed the bottle. While Knuckles drank, Preacher pulled Joe into the hallway and lit his cigarette for him.

"Get some girls over here," he said. "Smoke some shit, snort some shit. And you make sure you fuckin' call me when Smokey and Jim get back."

When Joe didn't respond, Preacher slapped him lightly on the cheek. "Hey, you hearin' me?"

Joe blinked several times. "Yeah, man, yeah. Get some girls over here. Call you when Smokey and Jim get back. Got it." He continued to smoke—quick, successive drags. Sighing, Preacher turned to leave.

"You headed home?" Joe called after him, "You gonna make me go home to Sylvie tonight, too?"

"I'm goin' home. You do whatever the fuck you gotta do."

"Preacher! Shit! Preacher!" Shouting excitedly, Max swung his long body over the first-floor stair railing. "Debbie had the baby!"

As if he'd been punched in the gut, all air fled Preacher's lungs.

Max rushed down the hall. "Debbie, she had the baby! She's at the hospital! Sylvie's with her—Tiny, too!"

"She's at the hospital," Preacher repeated dumbly. His heart thudded in his chest. He shook his head as if to clear it. "Is she... okay?"

Max skidded to a stop and gripped Preacher's shoulders. "She's fine. They're both fine."

Preacher stared at his brother. "Both?"

Max grinned. "Yeah, both. Preacher, you've got yourself a daughter."

CHAPTER 30

SANDWICHED BETWEEN MAX AND SMOKEY ON THE sofa, Preacher swallowed the last of his beer and got to his feet. On a chair nearby, Crazy-8 held Louisa in his lap and was whispering something in her ear. Preacher winked at her as he passed, and she burst into giggles.

Across the room, Preacher stopped beside the group gathered around the television. A baseball game was on, the New York Yankees vs. the Detroit Tigers, but instead of watching the game they were arguing over which Hendrix album had the better lineup.

"*Electric Ladyland* tops 'em all," Preacher interjected, smacking Bullet upside his head.

Knuckles raised his beer. "You know it, Prez!"

"Fuck you, you crazy white fools!" Bullet shouted. "*The Jimi Hendrix Experience*, hands down!"

"It don't count if he was already dead!"

"Dumbass kids," Jim complained. "What about the greats? What about Sinatra?"

"Here we go again," Anne muttered. "Sinatra this, Sinatra that."

Knuckles made a face. "Man, screw Sinatra. The only Frank I'm listenin' to is Zappa. And you, Ghost." Knuckles nudged Frank. "If you ever come up with somethin' useful to say."

"Nice shirt," Frank said wryly, eyeing the slogan printed across Knuckles' chest—MY FACE LEAVES AT 10:00. BE ON IT. "That about sums up your thought processes, huh?"

As more insults were traded, Preacher moved into the hall and turned the corner. He paused briefly as he passed the kitchen, hearing Debbie's soft laughter over the clanking and clattering of dishes. Preacher started to smile, then frowned as Sylvia's horse laugh drowned out nearly every other sound.

Up ahead, amid a cloud of smoke, Tiny and Joe were seated at the breakfast table, sharing a joint. A bag of chips and a small handheld radio sat on the table between them, Fleetwood Mac's *Go Your Own Way* playing.

On the floor nearby, little Frankie was pushing his toy trucks around a very frustrated-looking Trey. Not yet able to walk, Trey was relegated to making mad grabs for the trucks each time Frankie brought them near, only to have Frankie snatch them away at the last second.

Preacher bent down beside the boys and held out his hand. "How's it hangin' over here? You two gonna gimme some skin?"

Grinning, Frankie slapped his little hand down on top

of Preacher's. Trey, his face screwed up in concentration, batted furiously at Preacher's arm.

"Preacher, brother, you look like shit," Tiny called out.

Feeling like shit, Preacher staggered toward the table and sat down with a thud. Resting his head on the tabletop, he said, "Man, I haven't slept in days. My kid does nothing but eat, shit, and scream."

A little over a week had passed since Preacher had brought Debbie home from the hospital. An entire week of feeling overwhelmed, completely out of his element, and borderline delirious from sleep deprivation—even more so than usual.

Joe's eyes slid to where Frankie Jr. was now running circles around Trey. Trey's face was quickly turning red, while his bottom lip trembled and his eyes filled with frustrated tears.

Joe snorted. "Yeah, that sounds about right."

"And you got another one on the way."

"Don't remind me."

"Stop fuckin' her," Preacher offered. "No more nookie, no more kids."

"I stop fuckin' her," Joe shot back, "and she starts screamin'. And then I got screamin' kids *and* a screamin' wife."

"*Poor Joey*," Tiny taunted, "who's got a smokin' hot wife who likes fuckin' him." Tiny rolled his eyes. "Cry me a goddamn river. I can't even pay a bitch to like fuckin' me."

Eye wide and dancing with laughter, Joe looked at Preacher. It was the first hint of a smile Preacher had seen on his brother's face in… hell, Preacher couldn't even remember the last time he'd seen Joe smile.

"Smokin' hot?" Joe asked, then laughed. "Tiny, you got a thing for Sylvie... 'cause I'll fuckin' pay you to take her."

A shrill wail rang out through the apartment, causing all three men to cringe. A moment later Debbie appeared in the kitchen entryway. She moved into the hallway utterly oblivious of Preacher's presence, her sole focus on the bundle in her arms. If he'd been worried about Debbie coming to terms with being a mother, he wasn't anymore. Every day he had to beg to hold his own daughter.

Preacher's eyes roamed her body. Her dark hair hung over her shoulders in loose, messy waves. Wearing his Led Zeppelin tour T-shirt, a pair of loose-fitting track shorts, and a pair of tube socks pulled up to her knees, she looked damn good for a girl who'd just given birth. She hadn't gained much weight while pregnant—she'd been all stomach. But what she had gained, Preacher was hoping she'd keep. He'd always appreciated a little extra when it came to a woman's curves.

Slapping his hands down on the table, he pushed himself to his feet. "Speakin' of smokin' hot girls..."

Humming Fleetwood Mac, Preacher followed Debbie into the bedroom. Closing the door behind him, he joined her on the bed.

"Remind me to find us a bigger place," he muttered. Resting his head against Debbie's shoulder, he glanced down at his daughter and smiled. She was perfect—ten fingers, ten toes, full, fat cheeks and a tuft of dark hair on her head. Her tiny hands were currently curled into itty-bitty fists, one resting on the swell of Debbie's breast while she suckled. Her eyes—big, expressive eyes framed in dark lashes—were on him.

Looking into her eyes, a lump of emotion swelled in his throat. While the shape and size of his daughter's eyes were similar to Debbie's, their color—a deep, smoky gray—belonged to Ginny.

Gently he closed his hand around her bare foot and ran the pad of his thumb over the tops of her toes. "Hi baby girl," he murmured. "Is it your nap time yet? 'Cause it damn sure is mine."

"If you'll be quiet she'll fall asleep."

He glanced up at Debbie and snorted. "If I had your tit in my mouth, I wouldn't be sleepin'."

Debbie's lips twisted adorably. "Shut up."

"Make me."

"I would… if I didn't have a baby in my lap."

"Excuses, excuses…" Noticing his daughter's eyes had drifted closed, Preacher chuckled. "Look at this shit. How the hell do you sleep and eat at the same time?"

"I don't know… why don't you ask Tiny?"

"I'm tellin' him you said that."

Debbie shrugged. "Go ahead. He ate more than I did these last nine months. I can't believe how much ketchup he eats. Did you know he eats it right out of the bottle? Do you know how many bottles of ketchup we've gone through?"

Shoulders shaking, Preacher buried his face against Debbie's arm to muffle his laughter.

"Preacher?"

He looked up. "Hmm?"

Peering down at him, Debbie's eyes were shining with emotion. "I'm glad you've been home," she whispered.

Guilt swamped him. He knew full well he'd been neglecting her these last few months—that she'd been spending more time with Tiny than with him. But as much as he wanted to apologize, to tell her things were going to be different from here on out, he knew he couldn't. Especially now, with the added responsibilities of the Road Warriors and the acquisition of the Columbian imports, the club would have to continue to come first.

"You think of a name yet?" he asked, changing the subject. "We can't call her baby girl forever."

They'd left the hospital with a nameless baby. Debbie had spent her entire pregnancy unwilling to discuss anything baby-related, and Preacher had been so busy with the club that when it had come time to name their daughter, neither of them had known what to say.

Debbie looked down—sound asleep, their daughter was nuzzled between her breasts, mouth agape and snoring softly. "I still like Ginny," she said, glancing sideways at Preacher.

His lungs constricted. Every muscle in his body involuntarily tightened and twitched.

Debbie hadn't been the only one to suggest naming the baby after Ginny. Nearly everyone had suggested it, and each time they did, Preacher had the same gut-churning reaction.

Suddenly awash with uninvited images and feeling restless, Preacher shoved himself upright and scrubbed a hand down his face. The surprise birth of his daughter had been enough of a distraction to keep his darker thoughts at bay, but they were slowly, surely creeping back in.

He'd killed a man—albeit a man who'd killed countless others, his own parents included. But no matter which way he spun it or justified it, he'd still killed a man.

And because of it, Preacher couldn't think of his mother without seeing the blood on the trailer door, a coffin being lowered into the ground, and the gasping, dying face of Salvatore Rossi.

He didn't want any of that ugliness associated with his daughter.

Hell, he didn't want any of that ugliness associated with *him*. But he'd made a choice—as if there'd been any other option for him—and now he had to learn to live with that choice. There was no room for men with regrets in his world.

Debbie slipped her hand beneath the hem of his T-shirt and up his spine. Her palm paused on the space between his shoulder blades—a comforting reminder that he still had something good and pure—and Preacher eventually found his breath.

"We don't have to name her Ginny. We could name her Evangeline instead? Or maybe just... Eva?"

Preacher shook his head. "I don't know."

Debbie continued to rub his back. "Sylvie wants to name her Marie." She laughed softly. "And Anne is convinced that Anne is the perfect name."

Preacher wrinkled his nose. "Yeah, that's not gonna happen. What about you? Is there anyone you wanna name her after? A grandma? A great aunt? A friend?"

His questions were met with silence. Glancing over his shoulder, Preacher found Debbie staring out across the room, her bottom lip tucked beneath her teeth. "Wheels?"

"No," she said, looking at him. "I don't have anyone."

Preacher turned around and faced her. "You don't have anyone? What the fuck are we?" He pointed between him and their daughter. "Chopped liver?"

Debbie rolled her eyes. "I didn't mean it like that. I just meant I don't have any family."

"Yeah you do. You got me and her. And you've got all them assholes, too." He nodded at the bedroom door. "We're your family now."

Debbie's chin began to wobble, and her eyes filled with tears. Cursing, Preacher leaned in and kissed her lips. "No cryin'," he said, and kissed her again. "Can't have both my girls cryin' all the damn time." Another kiss. "Gonna drive me crazy."

Debbie laughed through her tears. "I'm sorry. I don't know what's wrong with me. I'm just…"

"Emotional?" Preacher kissed her three more times. "Sentimental? Over-tired? Half-fuckin'-crazy?"

Debbie continued laughing. "Yes. All of that."

There was a knock on the bedroom door. "Preacher?" The door cracked open and Frank's voice filled the room. "We've got a problem."

"Hold that thought," Preacher said, and kissed Debbie twice more before rolling out of bed.

Laying her daughter down beside her, Debbie leaned over and pressed a kiss to each of her rosy cheeks and a third to her forehead.

"I hope your daddy agrees," she whispered, "because Eva is a beautiful name. A beautiful name for a beautiful girl."

She continued to nuzzle her cheek. Happily breathing in her clean, sweet scent, Debbie marveled at how much she already loved her. Every day, it seemed, she loved her more.

Sylvia had been right—giving birth had been horrible, and Debbie had felt as she was splitting in two. But once it was over, and Debbie was holding her daughter in her arms, staring down at her sweet little face, her pain became a distant memory.

Every single misgiving she'd had about becoming a mother had instantly shifted. Anxiety had turned to awe. Resentment had turned to protectiveness.

That wasn't to say that she wasn't still afraid. She still felt fear. She was terrified of making a mistake or doing something wrong, or accidentally hurting this little life entrusted to her. But this fear was different; this fear had a purpose, a reason, and was ultimately overshadowed by joy.

Debbie brushed a fingertip over the soft swell of her daughter's cheek, admiring her. With dollish, delicate features and flawless porcelain skin, she really was a beautiful baby. Her eyes, though, were downright entrancing.

The sudden urge to draw her had Debbie reaching across the bed and plucking her sketch pad and pencils from the bedside table. Setting the pad in her lap, she flipped it open to a clean page. The tip of her pencil hovered over the page while she looked at her daughter, deciding on what to draw first.

Slowly, carefully, Debbie drew the soft curves of her closed eyes and then, with quick flicks of her wrist, added her dark lashes. She'd just set to work on her little pink mouth, pursed in the shape of a bow, when the bedroom door opened.

"… There's room at the warehouse in Greenpoint." Still talking to Frank, Preacher backed slowly into the room.

"Put another couple of Rocky's boys on watch."

"Consider it done," Frank replied. His dark eyes shifted, landing on Debbie. Unnerved, Debbie quickly looked away.

Since learning Maria's heartbreaking secret, Debbie could hardly stomach even the briefest of glances in Frank's direction. She felt culpable now—as if keeping Maria's secret somehow made her every bit the monster Frank was.

The door clicked closed and Debbie looked up to find Preacher leaning against it.

"You okay?" She mouthed the question, fearing Frank was still in earshot.

"Fuck," he muttered. "There's just so much shit. Every day there's more and—*fuck*."

Pushing away from the door, Preacher reclaimed his seat beside her in bed. Holding his arm out, he gestured for her. Scooting over, Debbie tucked herself against his side.

"Sometimes I think I shoulda never gone to Four Points." Preacher's words were calmly spoken, though his heart pounded furiously beneath Debbie's cheek. "Sometimes I wish I'd just put you on the back of my bike and… and just gone wherever the wind took us."

"We could have joined the circus," Debbie said.

Preacher snorted. "Yeah? What would I do in the damn circus?"

"Lion tamer?" she suggested. "Tightrope walker?"

Laughing, Preacher pressed a kiss to the top of her head. "What about you? What would you do in the circus?"

"Oh, I wouldn't work *in* the circus, I would *work* the circus. Imagine all the wallets." Grinning, Debbie glanced up, expecting to find Preacher laughing. Instead, he looked thoughtful.

"Wheels?"

"Yeah?"

"Marry me."

Debbie froze. "What?"

Preacher dropped his chin, bringing them nose to nose. "Marry me," he repeated.

She blinked several times, then shook her head. "What?"

Preacher's eyes crinkled at the corners. "You heard me."

"Yeah, I heard you," Debbie breathed. "I just—are you serious?"

"Am I serious?" he laughed. "Of course I'm serious. I wanna do this right, you know? You and me and—" Preacher paused to glance at their daughter. "And Eva."

He gave Debbie a lopsided grin. "We're already a family, right? We should make this shit official."

"I, uh…" Debbie didn't know what to say. Preacher had caught her entirely off guard—she'd never pegged him for a big proponent of conventional institutions.

"Shit," Preacher muttered, running a hand through his hair. "Shit. I did this all wrong."

Untangling from Debbie, Preacher jumped out of bed and dropped down on one knee. Then he gestured for her hand.

In something of a daze, Debbie gave it to him, watching slack-jawed as he pulled her butterfly ring off her index finger and slid it onto her ring finger.

Holding up her hand, she looked at the ring as if she'd never seen it before.

"I promise I'll get you somethin' better," he rushed to say. "A big, fat rock or somethin'. Whatever the fuck you want." He grinned up at her.

He looked so young, she thought. Happy, too. His eyes were lighter—there was no trace of tension in his expression. Reaching for him, Debbie tucked a handful of loose hair behind his ear.

"Wheels, you gonna say somethin' or you gonna leave me hangin' 'round down here like a goddamn fool?"

She hurried off the bed and into Preacher's arms. Wrapping her arms around his neck, she pressed a kiss to his lips. "Yes," she whispered and kissed him again.

"What's that?" he asked. He pulled back to look at her, still grinning.

She shoved at his chest. "Yes, I'll marry you! Yes, yes, yes!"

He kissed her hard, laughing against her mouth—a deep, happy rumble that vibrated between them.

"I got another really important question." Preacher broke their kiss. Holding Debbie's face between his hands, his expression suddenly grave, he searched her eyes.

"Was that shithead doctor serious? Do we really gotta wait *that* long before havin' sex again?"

CHAPTER 31

"**W**HAT ABOUT THIS ONE?" SYLVIA HELD UP AN infant-sized dress—pink, with a white lace bib, and thick white tulle lining the underside.

Earlier this morning Sylvia had phoned Debbie in a panic—she'd been overwrought, desperately needing to prepare for the quickly approaching birth of her second child, claiming she didn't have nearly enough clothing, or bedding, or toys.

Debbie, having still not mastered the art of talking her way out of something Sylvia had her mind set on, found herself inside Macy's department store, rifling through racks of overpriced infant clothing.

Debbie eyed the dress skeptically. "You don't even know if it's a girl. What if it's a boy? You're going to dress him in that?"

Sylvia shrugged. "Who's gonna know when they're that young?" She laughed. "Besides, I just got a feeling about this one."

Tiny pried his eyes away from the blonde he was ogling. "You can't be puttin' boys in dresses, Sylvie."

Scowling at Tiny, Sylvia slammed the dress back on the rack and huffed. "I just want a little girl so bad," she said. "I can't very well be doin' hair and nails with this one!"

They both glanced at Trey—seated in his stroller, he was grabbing fruitlessly at the clothing on the racks. In a covered carriage beside him, Eva lay sleeping soundly.

Debbie reached out and touched Sylvia's arm. "I know you want a girl, but a little boy is just as good... and you'll always have Eva. I'm sure she'll love having an aunt to do hair and nails with."

Smiling, Sylvia covered Debbie's hand with her own. She opened her mouth to speak, then frowned. Eyes wide and mouth falling open, she grabbed Debbie's hand and squealed.

"That's the ring?" she shouted. "Oh my God, Debbie, it's huge! Why didn't you tell me that fool had finally gotten you a ring?"

Embarrassed, Debbie snatched her hand back. "He just gave it to me last night."

Weeks had passed since Preacher had asked her to marry him, and Debbie had all but forgotten his promise to get her a ring. She'd been shocked when he'd come home from the club early last night and proposed to her all over again.

Shaking her head, Sylvia's eyes gleamed with envy. "It's just gorgeous," she breathed. "How many carats is it? Two? Three?"

Debbie glanced down briefly at the sparkling diamond adorning her ring finger, then at the butterfly ring on her index finger, and shrugged. "I don't know. I didn't ask."

In truth, she much preferred her own ring—the little silver butterfly that Preacher had proposed with meant more to her than a diamond ever could.

"So when's the big day?"

Debbie looked up. "What day?"

"You're wedding, silly! When are you and Preacher planning on gettin' married?"

Debbie bit down on her lip. "Um..."

"Oh, and you've got to let me go dress shopping with you! My aunt owns a boutique in Jersey City—she can get you whatever you're lookin' for... What kind of dress are you lookin' for?"

Debbie only stared at Sylvia.

"Well, it's gotta be beautiful," Sylvia continued. "And white. Or, maybe pink? I was reading this magazine the other day and... oh! Speaking of beautiful things, did you see Burt Reynolds on the cover of *People*? Mm-mm-mm. I don't know what it is about a man with a mustache. I keep tryin' to get Joey to grow one."

"What kinda mustache we talkin' 'bout here?"

Sylvia's eyes were like ice, frosting over as her gaze snapped to Tiny. "Who asked you?" she bit out. "Mind your own business."

Whereas Debbie had long since grown used to Tiny's presence, Sylvia had begun to resent it and made no effort to hide her feelings about what she perceived as a needless nuisance. Coupled with her contempt for the club, Tiny didn't stand a chance.

Shrugging, Tiny stroked his cheek. "I'm just sayin', I think it all depends, you know? Are we talkin' about a Fu Manchu or a John Holmes? And is this mustache on a big guy or a little guy? 'Cause us big guys can pull off most mustaches, but those scrawny little assholes can't do it. They're walkin' around lookin' like a broomstick with a squirrel on top. But I'm thinkin' Joe could probably pull off a John Holmes—he ain't so scrawny."

Fighting to keep a straight face, Debbie slapped her hand over her mouth. Beside her, Sylvia made a choking noise.

"Somethin' funny?" Tiny glanced between them, genuine confusion crinkling his features. "You bustin' my chops, Debbie darlin'?"

"It's nothing," Debbie remarked, still fighting a laugh. "I just never realized you put so much thought into men and their facial hair."

"It's not nothin'," Sylvia practically growled. "Here we are talkin' 'bout dignified men like Burt Reynolds and this idiot is talkin' about John Holmes—a goddamn porn star!"

At that, several fellow shoppers glanced in their direction. A woman holding a small child gasped and hurried away.

"Whatever," Tiny muttered. "I gotta take a leak. You two wait here." Turning away, he noticed the nearby shoppers eyeing him—their expression ranging from amusement to disgust.

"What?" he shouted. "All you uptight broads wanna pretend you ain't never watched a skin flick before, that's fine with me!" Throwing his arms up, he stormed away.

"Debbie," Sylvia groaned, "Preacher has got to give you

a new babysitter. I can't take that revolting man another second. Tell him anyone *but* Tiny."

Debbie watched as Tiny disappeared down the escalator. "I don't really mind him so much anymore. He kinda grew on me."

"Like fungus or something?" Rolling her eyes, Sylvia patted at her perfectly coiffed curls and sniffed imperiously. "I've known that man for years and I still can't stand him. You know he smells like ketchup, right? Tell me I'm not the only one who smells ketchup on him!"

While Sylvia continued to rant, Debbie turned away, laughing and shaking her head. After browsing through several racks of clothing and nothing catching her eye, Debbie continued on. Noticing a nearby doll display, a slow smile split her lips. Eva was still too young to enjoy a doll, but Debbie hadn't yet bought her anything frivolous—something she suddenly wanted to remedy.

"Mama's going to get you a dolly, baby girl," she said, pushing the carriage toward the display.

Plucking a box from the shelf, Debbie peered through the plastic covering at the creamy-skinned, dark-haired doll. "If only she had gray eyes," she murmured and set the box back on the shelf.

She traveled further into the toy department, looking over the fun, colorful displays until something caught her eye. Going up on her tiptoes, Debbie reached for a porcelain doll dressed in an elaborately beaded gown.

"Miss Reynolds."

Dropping down on her heels, Debbie whirled around. An older man stood nearby. Tall and slim, he wore a dark gray suit. His hands and face were spotted with age, and he was nearly bald, with only wisps of gray hair remaining.

Debbie gripped the baby carriage and jerked it in the other direction. Another man was fast approaching—short and stocky, he had messy brown hair and thick sideburns the same dull brown color as his suit coat.

Debbie's eyes bounced between the two men, alarm bells going off inside her. She thought she might recognize them, though she couldn't recall from where.

"Agent Willis of the Federal Bureau of Investigation, Miss Reynolds," the older man said, briefly flashing the identification he'd pulled from his pocket. "And this is my partner, Agent Parker. We just need to ask you a few questions."

The FBI? Debbie's reeling thoughts fell into place. She had seen them before—parked outside the clubhouse. Preacher had told her to never look their way, to act as if they weren't even there.

"Or should we say 'Miss Stephens'?"

Debbie's shocked gaze swung to Parker. His condescending smile told her she hadn't misheard him—he had, in fact, called her Miss Stephens.

Her name. He knew her name—*her real name.*

"Do you have any idea how many people go missing every year, all over the country?" Shaking his head, Parker smacked his lips together. "Too many to keep track of. Like finding a needle in a haystack. Lucky for us, sweetheart, you're a high-profile case."

Gooseflesh rippled up and down Debbie's arms and legs. Still clutching the baby carriage, she pressed her back against the display behind her and tried hard not to shake.

"That big-shot daddy of yours put up a pretty penny for

your return, you know that?" Parker pulled a folded piece of paper from inside his suit coat and shook it open.

It was a "missing" poster with Debbie's face on it—a grainy black and white copy of a school photo taken nearly three years ago. Beneath the photograph was her full name, city and state of residence, her date of birth, her height and weight, and a hefty reward sum—the size of which sent shockwaves through Debbie.

She pressed her hand to the space below her neck and swallowed hard. "He's not my dad," she heard herself croak. It was an odd thing to say, given the situation, but she felt compelled to say it anyway. She wanted a clear distinction between the two men. One had been a good man who'd loved her, and the other... his polar opposite.

"Dad, stepdad. Don't matter to us what he is," Parker continued. "Only that he wants you back. And according to this..." He tapped his fingertip on the flyer directly over Debbie's birthdate. "... you're still a minor."

He wants you back. He wants you back. He wants you back.

The silent screaming began. White-hot panic filled her belly. Those four dread-inducing words played on repeat in Debbie's mind. Living nightmares crept free from the dregs of her memories. Her breaths grew thin and her vision went spotty.

"Please," she rasped. "Please, you can't do this. You don't understand—you can't send me back there."

"Parker." Willis moved to stand beside Parker. Eyes filled with concern, he placed his hand on the younger agent's shoulder. "Ease up—"

Parker jerked away and took another step toward

Debbie. "Oh, we can, sweetheart. You don't turn eighteen for another couple of months. Your parents still have legal rights to you. And what you've been doing here in the city, underage and playing house with the likes of Damon Fox—"

Smacking his lips again, Parker's eyes dropped down to the baby carriage, sparking with malicious intent.

"Preacher doesn't know!" Debbie cried softly, wishing she could shield Eva from his view. "I haven't told him anything about me!"

Parker's answering smile was callous and cold. Shaking his head, he waggled a finger back and forth. "Well aren't you a little minx. Doesn't matter, though. Your parents could still make a whole lot of trouble for him if they wanted to. They got the money to do it, that's for sure."

Debbie began to shake, shivering despite the suffocating heat she was feeling. It was too much—it was all too much. Her palms were clammy, and her mouth had gone dry. Her heart was racing, her mind spinning, tears threatening. She wanted to shove past the agents and run. Run out of the store and disappear among the crowded streets of Manhattan.

For the first time since meeting Preacher she was aching for the safety and anonymity living on the road had afforded her.

But it wasn't just her anymore. She had Eva and Preacher. She had a family now, and she couldn't just leave them. But neither would she allow these men to send her home.

She couldn't go home—she couldn't go back to *him*. She wouldn't survive it.

"There's another way." Willis stepped forward, moving to stand in front of Parker. Eyeing his partner with distaste, he plucked the flyer from the younger man's hand and crumpled it beneath his slim fingers. "We could forget we ever saw this, and you can go back to being Debbie Reynolds from Akron, Ohio."

Debbie stared up at him—scared, confused, and barely breathing. Why would the FBI follow her here, intimidate and threaten her, if they were just going to retract their threat? Something else was going on, something that went beyond her.

"Here's the thing, *Debbie*," the younger agent sneered. Elbowing Willis aside, he leaned over the baby carriage, close enough that Debbie could smell the stale coffee on his breath.

"We don't want you. We don't care about you and whatever it was that sent you running across the country. We want the Silver Demons. *We want Preacher*. You help us make that happen and we'll leave you be."

"I don't know anything," she hurried to whisper. "He doesn't tell me anything!"

Parker made a clicking noise with his tongue. Straightening, he smoothed his hands down the front of his jacket. "That's a damn shame," he said. "Then it looks like you're headed back to—"

"Please!" she cried. "You don't understand." She shook her head frantically. "Please, you can't send me back there. Please. *Please*."

She suddenly couldn't seem to find enough air in her lungs. "H-he's a m-monster," she barely managed to finish.

"A monster?" Parker spat. "You've been spreading your

legs for a fucking monster. Do you have any idea what that man of yours has done? How many men he's—"

"Parker!" Willis's tone was harsh, infused with warning.

Parker's eyes shot to Willis. "You know it was them," he growled, shoving his finger in the older man's face. "You know it."

Willis gritted his teeth. "We've got no proof. Stay on the task at hand."

Willis faced Debbie. "Anything you can think of—a name, a location, anything at all."

"Please, no," she whispered, shaking her head again. Even if she did know something, how could they expect her to betray Preacher?

"You don't seem to understand the gravity of your situation." Willis's voice was firm, and his expression hard. "You are, quite literally, in bed with a known criminal. Damon Fox is under suspicion of racketeering, money laundering, and drug smuggling, and that's just the tip of the iceberg. On top of that, you're a runaway and considered a minor in the state of New York. You don't have a leg to stand on here. Either you help us, or *we will* take you in and contact your parents."

Willis glanced down at Eva, still sleeping soundly in her carriage. "What that'll mean for your little one, I don't know. Social Services might—"

"There's a warehouse!" Debbie blurted out. "In Green… Green something—I can't remember!"

If she could have, if she hadn't been pinned against the shelving unit behind her, she would have thrown her body over the baby carriage. They couldn't take Eva from her— they'd have to kill her first.

The agents glanced at once another. "Greenpoint?" Willis asked.

"Yes!" Debbie nodded emphatically. "Greenpoint. But that's all I know. I swear it."

The two men exchanged another look. "I knew it," Parker hissed. "I knew—"

"We'll be in touch." Willis grabbed his partner's arm and practically shoved him down the aisle. Just as suddenly as they'd descended upon her, they were gone.

Debbie stared after a moment, before dropping to her knees beside the carriage. Bowing her head, her threatening tears slipped free.

"Are you alright, dear?" An elderly lady was peering curiously down at her.

Swiping at her eyes, Debbie nodded jerkily and hurried to her feet.

"Yes, fine," she said. "Thank you."

Blurry-eyed and shaking, Debbie gripped the baby carriage and hurried away. She sped blindly through the store, nearly knocking into several people. Everything felt wrong. Her previous life and her current life had just come to unexpected blows in the middle of Macy's—one second she'd been shopping and laughing, and then the next... everything had crumbled to pieces at her feet.

She remembered this feeling well—the unrelenting, heavy hand of fear pressing down upon her. She'd lived with it every day for years—afraid to go home, afraid to speak so as not to be noticed, afraid to tell the truth, afraid to lie, afraid of what lay in wait for her in the dark, afraid of her own reflection, even.

Debbie brought her hand to her mouth, stifling a sob.

She should have told Preacher the truth when she'd had the chance. Now… it was too late. Her truth had just been used against her, and against Preacher. Debbie's pace quickened. The hand over her mouth tightened. Her vision blurred further. She had to get out of here. Out of the city. Out of New York. She had to get away—as far away as possible.

"There you are!"

The sight of Tiny jogging toward her had Debbie skidding to a stop. Dropping her hand, she quickly composed herself.

"I told you to stay put!" Tiny wheezed. Huffing and puffing, Tiny was red-faced, and his brow was dotted with sweat. "You tryin' to give me a heart attack?"

Despite herself, Debbie managed a nervous laugh. "Sorry Tiny. I got distracted."

"You can't do that to me, Debbie! What if somethin' happened? You know Preacher would kill me, right? He still hasn't forgiven me for that shit you pulled months ago—runnin' off with Sylvie to the clubhouse after I fell asleep? I lose you again and he's gonna have my head—"

Only half listening, Debbie followed mutely behind Tiny. Appearing calm and collected on the outside, her insides were a twister of emotion—anxiety, fear, and an ominous sense of foreboding swirled to new heights inside her.

Feeling nauseated, she pressed a hand to her stomach and swallowed hard.

Oh God, oh God, what had she done?

CHAPTER 32

HUMMING VAN MORRISON'S *BROWN-EYED GIRL*, Preacher cradled Eva in his arms, softly swaying her. Sucking on a pacifier, she stared up at him from beneath heavy, fluttering eyelids. Looking at her angelic features, one would never know just how truly diabolical she was.

Death by insomnia was his baby girl's superpower, as Preacher was fairly certain he hadn't gotten a full night's sleep since her birth.

He was so exhausted he was daydreaming about sleep. So goddamn exhausted that he'd chosen to stay home today rather than head to the club. Although considering the sort of bullshit that awaited him at the club, choosing to stay home hadn't been a hard decision to make.

With the gaping absence of the Rossi family, the Columbo family was now the reigning mafia in New York.

Typically Preacher wouldn't have given them a second thought—they were just a school of sharks in a vast sea filled with predators. Only these particular sharks had recently severed what little business relationship the Silver Demons had with them and gone radio silent—an aggressive move he translated to mean that a storm was brewing off in the distance. Another storm that Preacher didn't want to have to face just yet.

Still humming, Preacher moved into the living room. Dancing past the windows, he grimaced as the bright sunlight streaming in through the slatted blinds temporarily blinded him. His feet made quick work of the floor, eating up the distance between him and the crib in the corner.

"You need your own room, baby girl," he whispered. "Can't be sleepin' in the living room forever, can you?" Preacher had meant to have found a bigger place by now, at the very least an apartment with two bedrooms. He just hadn't yet found the time.

Glancing down at Eva, he found her eyes closed and her pacifier dangling precariously from the side of her mouth. Shoulders sagging with relief, he slowly lowered her into the crib.

Don't wake up, don't wake up, he chanted silently, half expecting her eyes to flip open at any moment and the ear-splitting yowling to begin again. When she remained sleeping, he blew out the breath he'd been holding.

"You need to sleep for at least five hours," he scolded quietly. "Shit, I'll even settle for three. You gimme three hours of sleep, and I'll buy you whatever the hell you want—a car, a pony, a goddamn golden diaper. You name it, baby girl, and it's yours."

Turning away, he'd managed only a few steps when the phone rang. Horrified, Preacher darted into the kitchen, yanked the phone off the wall and the cord out of the jack, and tossed the entire contraption into the sink. Cursing, he closed his eyes and waited for the crying to begin.

Seconds passed without a sound, and Preacher cracked one eye open. Still nothing.

Relief flooded him. "Crisis averted," he muttered.

Heading down the hall toward the bedroom, Preacher's only plan was collapsing into bed and getting as much shut-eye as possible before Eva woke up. Instead, he found himself leaning against the doorjamb, admiring the girl in his bed.

Debbie was laying on her side, her back to him. The windows were open, and muted sounds of the city below filled the room. A warm breeze caused the hem of her T-shirt to billow, giving Preacher a nice glimpse of her backside. His eyes slowly traced the curve of her hip down to the seam where ass meets thigh. Then lower, admiring the full length of her legs.

Moving into the room, Preacher took a seat beside her on the bed. She twitched as he palmed her calf, and then shivered as he ran his hand up the length of her leg, pausing on her hip.

Smiling, he leaned over her, and was startled to find her eyes red and her cheeks wet. The moment their gazes collided, she hurriedly swiped at her cheeks and attempted a smile.

Preacher shifted onto his stomach beside her. "Wheels, what the hell?"

She only stared back at him, her bottom lip trembling,

looking for all the world like the sky was going to come crashing down around them at any moment.

"I have to tell you something," she eventually whispered. Swallowing thickly, she cast her eyes aside. "You're going to be angry."

"Why? You steal my wallet again?" He winked at her. Only his joke didn't have the intended effect, and instead of laughing, Debbie's eyes filled with fresh tears.

"Hey," he said gently, grabbing her and swiftly tucking her partially beneath him. Situating his leg between hers, he lowered his head, bringing them nose to nose. "Whatever it is, whatever's wrong, I'll fix it, okay? I'll fuckin' fix it."

She made a noise—a choking sob, and her eyes squeezed shut. She attempted turning away, and Preacher quickly rolled over top of her, caging her beneath him. "Wheels," he growled, growing frustrated. "Baby, talk to me."

Her eyes opened tentatively. Worry lines creased her brow. Breath shuddered from her lungs.

"Please don't get mad," she whispered.

Eyes narrowed with concern, he shook his head. "I promise."

Another breath shuddered free and then, "My name isn't Debbie," she whispered in a rush.

He blinked, and then pressed his lips together, fighting a smile. Brows lifted, he murmured, "You don't say..."

"It's Elizabeth," she continued. "My real name is Elizabeth."

Debbie held his gaze, and surprise rippled through Preacher. She was telling the truth. After all this time, she finally trusted him.

"Elizabeth Taylor?" he asked—an attempt to lighten the mood.

She choked on her laughter, laughter that quickly turned to a sob. "Preacher," she whispered frantically. "I'm sorry I lied to you. I should have told you the truth from the beginning. I should have—"

Moving off her, he helped her to sit and pulled her into his arms.

"Wheels, I don't give a shit what your name is. Never did, still don't. You think names matter to me, then you don't know me at all." He shook his head and shrugged. "Far as I'm concerned, I'm Preacher, you're Wheels, and everything else can go—"

There was a knock at the front door—a heavy, frantic pounding. Debbie jumped and Preacher rolled quickly out of bed, cursing.

"Goddammit," he muttered, stalking down the hallway. "I'm gonna kill whoever that is if they—"

Eva's cry rang through the apartment.

Still cursing, Preacher flipped the locks on the door and flung it open.

"Preacher!" Joe burst inside and grabbed Preacher's arms. His one eye was wild, and a light sheen of sweat covered his face.

"Why the fuck aren't you answering the phone?" he demanded. "We're in the middle of a fucking shitstorm! The Feds found the house in Greenpoint! Preacher, man, they raided it this morning! Killed two of Rocky's guys when they stormed the place!"

Pain flared hot in Preacher's neck, and his temples began to throb. He shoved Joe away. "Shit," he breathed, running his hand over his mouth and beard. "Fucking shit." He swallowed hard. "What about the others?"

Joe shook his head. "The other two guys got away. They made a beeline for Rocky, and now he's movin' all his boys outta the city as we speak."

"No, idiot, *the other warehouses*. Did the Feds find 'em?"

"No, man, no. Everything else is solid. But… Rocky's pissed. He wants to move the—" Joe's mouth snapped shut, his eyes flicking to something past Preacher.

Glancing over his shoulder, Preacher found Debbie standing just outside the living room. Wide-eyed and pale-faced, she was bouncing Eva gently in her arms.

"They can't trace the warehouses to us," he muttered quietly, turning back to Joe. "We made sure of it."

"They can trace the fuckin' Road Warriors to us!" Joe hissed.

His headache worsening, Preacher grabbed Joe by his shirt collar and brought them nose to nose.

"Do you ever pay attention? The Road Warriors ain't patched in. All the Feds found was a couple nomads inside a warehouse. Owning a motorcycle and wearing a cut doesn't automatically make those men mine, does it? Greenpoint is gonna lead them to the Rossi family, and dead men don't tell tales. Worst case scenario, the Feds raid the clubhouse on a hunch, hoping to find a connection, and you know the worst thing they're gonna find? Tiny's fuckin' stash of special brownies."

Joe's shoulders slumped. "Jesus, Preacher… I thought we were up shit creek for sure."

Gritting his teeth, Preacher released Joe with a shove. They were still up shit creek. Never mind the Feds,

Preacher's concerns lay with the Columbians. With the loss of the Greenpoint warehouse, the Silver Demons had just lost a great deal of product they'd been entrusted to move.

"Man, I don't get it." Joe kept his voice low. "We had that shit locked up tight. There's no way the Feds coulda found Greenpoint on their own... unless we can't trust Rocky, or *fuck*, what if it was one of our boys?"

Preacher's head all but exploded with pain. While massaging his temples, he wracked his brain, trying to think of when, or with whom, he might have screwed up.

"Preacher."

He turned to Debbie. Still holding Eva, she'd plastered herself against the wall. Tears streamed down her cheeks.

"I'm s-sorry." Her lips trembled and her words shook. "I'm so sorry."

Preacher stared at her.

"I should have told you the truth." She continued to cry.

"Preacher?" Joe moved to stand beside him.

"Go downstairs." Preacher's tone was clipped and hard. "Wait for me there."

"But—"

"Now, Joe. Right fuckin' now."

Preacher stayed quiet until he heard the door close.

"What did you do?" he bit out, and when Debbie didn't respond immediately, he shouted, "What did you fuckin' do?"

Startled, Eva began to cry. Blanching, Debbie shrunk against the wall. "There were two agents!" she blurted out. "And they told me—"

"I don't give a shit what they told you!" he raged, advancing on her.

"They knew who I was!" she cried. "Preacher, they said they were going to send me home! They said they'd take Eva away! They—"

"Stop!" he roared. "Fuck!" Running his hands agitatedly through his hair, he turned away.

His eyes darted in every direction—he didn't know what to do, where to look, what to think. How had this happened? His girl had betrayed the club—shit, *his girl had betrayed him*. Adrenaline-fueled anger took root inside of him. His hands clenched into fists, and he spun around to face her.

"Whatever they said, whatever they threatened, you should have come to me first! Now two men are dead because of *you*, and if I can't somehow make back the money for everything the club just lost, I'm gonna be next!"

Debbie's tear-stained face crumpled, and she sank to her knees on the floor. "I didn't know," she gasped. "Please, I didn't even know what Greenpoint was. I was scared—I didn't know—"

"What else did you tell them?" he demanded tersely through clenched teeth.

"Nothing! I swear it, Preacher, nothing! I don't know anything!"

Jaw locked and twitching, muscles coiled and ready to spring, Preacher lost the battle he was waging with his temper and sent his fist hurtling into the wall, smashing through the plaster. Twice more he punched the wall, the action doing nothing to soothe the waves of aggression rolling through him.

Worse, Debbie was still crying, and Eva had progressed to wailing. And Preacher needed to get the fuck out of there.

He moved quickly to the door, snatching his wallet and keys from the table as he passed.

"Preacher—wait!"

Whirling around, Preacher pinned Debbie with the full weight of his fury. "I have to go," he bit out. His chest heaved with angry breaths. "I have to fix what *you* did."

Shaking, Debbie got to her feet. Clutching a still-crying Eva to her chest, she took a tentative step forward. "Please," she whispered brokenly. "Please don't let them send me back home. I can't go—"

"Stop!" he shouted, "just stop! I can't—fuck, I can't deal with you right now!"

Turning away, he shoved into his boots, wrenched open the door, then slammed it shut behind him.

Debbie's sobs followed him down two flights of stairs before fading away.

It took Debbie over half an hour to settle Eva down, and then nearly another hour to calm herself to the point where she could think clearly—if a panicked stream of consciousness could be considered thinking clearly.

She moved around the apartment feeling jittery and itchy, alternating between wringing her hands and scrubbing mindlessly at her cheeks and arms. Occasionally she'd sit, only to end up fidgeting, growing frustrated and jumping up again.

"Oh God," she whispered as she wandered. Two men had been killed, and all because of her. Preacher was right; she should have gone to him first. No, she should have told him the truth from the beginning. If only she wouldn't have lied, maybe this could have all been avoided.

Her heart began to pound, and her tears spilled over. What good was wondering what might have been when she'd already ruined everything?

Finding herself in the bedroom, Debbie glanced around blindly. What would Preacher do when he returned? She'd never seen him so angry—all of his anger directed at her. Would he throw her out? Force her to leave?

Hot tears slid down her cheeks as she stared at their bed, unable to conceive of never sleeping beside him again.

Could he forgive her for this? And if he did, would he ever look at her the same way again—as if the mere sight of her made his day better?

A sob escaped her. Had she really ruined everything? Hopelessness and helplessness engulfed her, and she sank to her knees on the floor. Hugging her chest, she rocked herself while she cried.

Gazing miserably across the room, she noticed her canvas backpack hanging on the doorknob. Her scrambled thoughts paused—she could disappear for a little while. She wouldn't leave for long, just until she turned eighteen and the FBI could no longer use her against Preacher. And maybe some time apart would give Preacher the time he needed to calm down... and hopefully forgive her.

Scrambling to her feet, she retreated quickly into the hallway and practically ran to the living room. Peering inside Eva's crib, Debbie's heart painfully squeezed. Tentatively she reached out and ran her shaking fingertips down Eva's cheek. Tears blurred her vision.

She couldn't leave her daughter. She just couldn't.

"I love you so much, baby girl," she cried softly.

But maybe she should leave…

Just for a little while.

Just long enough to make everything right again.

Preacher elbowed his way past the many men crowded outside the office, then slammed the door shut in their faces. Right now, his head was a mess of problems without solutions, and he didn't have the patience to deal with everyone at once.

He took half a second to eyeball the desk he'd sworn he'd never sit behind before kicking the chair out from under it and collapsing into it. Uncapping the bottle in his hand, he guzzled at least two inches worth of gin before looking up and acknowledging the others in the room.

Rocky stood in a corner, arms crossed over his chest, head lowered, black eyes flashing beneath a heavy brow. Joe and Frank sat at opposite ends of the meeting table. While Joe appeared distraught, tapping his fingers anxiously over the oak slab, Frank was as stiff and as unreadable as ever.

"Two of my men are dead," Rocky spat angrily. Everything about the man was threatening—the menacing edge in his tone, his wide stance, and the clenched fists at his sides.

"Aren't they my men now?" Preacher growled. In an effort not to punch something, he picked up a pen lying on the desk and spun it between his fingers.

Rocky took a deliberate step away from the wall. "Am I missin' something? Did I sleep through bein' patched in?"

Preacher raised an eyebrow. "It's a damn good thing I didn't patch you in, or we'd all be in fuckin' cuffs right now."

Grimacing, Rocky shook his head. "Who's this *we* you're so concerned about? Your men or mine? Seems to me like you're thinkin' mine are expendable."

Preacher shot up out of his chair. The pen in his grip snapped in half, and ink dripped from his clenched fist onto the desk. "In case you forgot, I've got two dead men myself." He stared at Rocky, hard and unblinking. "At the end of the day, we're all fuckin' expendable."

Preacher didn't bother bringing up his mother. Rocky didn't place the same value on women as he did men and wouldn't consider her death as any great loss to the club.

Unconsciously, Preacher's gaze slid to the family photograph on the desk. Avoiding The Judge's disapproving stare, he looked instead at his mother, and he couldn't help but feel that when the club had lost Ginny, they'd lost everything.

He turned back to Rocky. "Greenpoint is gone. Your two men? Gone. Now we can sit here screamin' about it, or we can get down to business and make sure this shit doesn't happen again. What's it gonna be?"

Seconds passed in silence while Preacher and Rocky stared each other down. Rocky looked away first and retreated to the wall, looking only slightly less lethal than before. Tossing the broken pen away, Preacher wiped his ink-stained hand on his jeans and took his seat.

"Good choice," he muttered, "Now let's fix this shit."

"It's like I told One-Eye over here." Rocky jerked a thumb in Joe's direction. "We need to get the goods outta the city. Couple of my guys got some land over in Illinois—a pumpkin farm with a barn. It's the perfect place for long-term storage. Middle of fuckin' nowhere."

Preacher nodded. "That solves one problem. Now what

about Greenpoint? How're we gonna make back what we lost?"

"We jack up prices for a while," Frank offered. "Columbians won't ever need to know what happened."

Joe scrubbed at his jaw. "We can do that with the metal, but it ain't gonna fly with the drugs. We're gonna need to cut up what we've got left, stretch it as far as it'll go." He shrugged. "Fake it 'til we make it all back."

Frank frowned. "That's risky."

What Joe was proposing was very risky. If buyers caught on to what they were doing, which someone undoubtedly would, people were going to get pissed—and when people got pissed, things had the potential to get messy. *Messy and bloody.*

But not nearly as messy as losing their heads at the hands of the Columbians.

"No shit, Sherlock." Joe rolled his eyes at Frank. "But it's either that or we start robbin' banks."

Frank slowly turned in his seat, his deadpan stare landing on Joe. "Your old lady likes guns, don't she? You two gonna be the next Bonnie and Clyde?"

Snorting, Joe flipped him off.

Preacher grabbed his bottle of gin and took a long swallow. "Nobody's robbin' any banks. Nobody's givin' Sylvie any guns, either." He pointed between Joe and Rocky. "You two, get the fuck outta my office and go tell the rest of 'em what they need to know."

When the door had closed behind them, Frank faced Preacher. "You're really gonna make Rocky your sergeant?"

Sighing, Preacher eyed the office door. "For now."

"He's a loose cannon."

"I know."

"He's gonna be trouble."

"Not much I can do about it."

"Yet," Frank said.

"Yet," Preacher agreed and took a swig.

"We got any leads on who tipped off the Feds?"

Preacher chugged another several inches of gin. "It was Debbie," he said tightly.

"What was Debbie?"

"Greenpoint. She ratted us out to the Feds."

A subtle flaring of his dark eyes was Frank's only reaction.

"They scared the shit outta her... threatened her with... somethin'." Preacher shook his head. "I don't know specifics."

"If she folded once, she could do it again."

Preacher sank down further into his chair and took another swig of gin. "I'll figure it out," was all he said. *Just not right now*, he added silently.

Right now he was going to drink himself into oblivion and hopefully forget the never-ending, ever-expanding pile of problems heaped at his feet... for just a little while.

"Here." Frank set down an unopened bottle of rum in front of Preacher. "You're lookin' a little low."

Muttering his thanks, he continued to drink, hardly noticing when Frank left.

Sometime later, Preacher staggered out into the hall looked blearily toward the living room. Music was playing, and he could hear chatter and laughter. Rum in hand, he stumbled forward.

The bright colors in the living room made his head hurt,

and he sat down on the first empty seat he came across. Someone called out his name, though he wasn't quite sure who.

Eyes closed, he rested his head against the back of the sofa and continued to drink.

Feeling disoriented, sluggish, and blissfully numb, Preacher almost didn't register the sudden extra weight on his lap. He cracked one eye open and waited until his spinning vision fell into focus.

He recognized her, or rather he recognized the ring in her nose and the safety pins dangling from her ears. She was new to the club, had been hanging around only this past month or so. Her name was Jenny or Jessica—he couldn't remember which. With her ripped-up clothing and bleached blonde Mohawk, she looked better suited to standing outside CBGB's, screaming about anarchy and animal rights, and flipping off anyone who didn't look like her.

"You look sad, Mr. Preacher President," she said, then giggled.

Preacher thought her speech might have been slurred—or maybe it was just his hearing that was slurred.

Her hand appeared on his chest and dragged slowly down the front of him. Gripping his belt, she yanked hard. Her lips split into a sly smile—a blur of bright red lipstick and gleaming white teeth. "You want me to cheer you up?"

"No." He tried swatting her hand away—a piss-poor attempt that had her giggling.

She grabbed him again, this time below his belt. "Lemme make you feel better," she purred, stroking him through his jeans. "I promise you, your girl ain't ever gonna know."

His girl. Bitter laughter lodged in his throat. His fucking girl was the reason two men were dead and a third of their goods had just been confiscated by the goddamn FBI.

But she hadn't meant it. She hadn't known. She was a good girl. She was his good, good girl.

And this was his fault. All of it. He'd kept her in the dark thinking he was protecting her from his world. Instead he'd ended up being the reason she'd been tossed into this sea of sharks, head first and without a lifejacket.

Are you a monster, too? Debbie's voice echoed in his thoughts.

He lifted the bottle to his lips and chugged until his head was heavy, bobbing involuntarily, and rum was spilling from the corners of his mouth.

"I'm a monster," he whispered brokenly to the girl on his lap.

"I like monsters," she said, and grinned. And the next thing Preacher knew, she was nose to nose with him, licking the rum from his lips. He made a half-hearted attempt to push her head away while his own lolled backward, hitting the wall.

Giggling, she resumed tugging at his belt.

Too tired to move, too drunk to care, Preacher's eyes began to close, and soon... everything faded to black.

CHAPTER 33

Present Day

PREACHER RELEASED A SHUDDERING SIGH, AND AS THE air fled his lungs, the light leached from his eyes. He slumped back against his pillows, looking shaken.

"Daddy?" I whispered. "What happened next?"

He turned his face just a fraction, enough for me to see the tears in his eyes. "I went home the next mornin' and found you in your crib screamin' something fierce. Hungry, diaper hadn't been changed."

I was gripping the bedrail so hard my knuckles had turned white. "Where was she?"

He shook his head. "She was gone, Eva."

"Gone? As in—"

"As in half her shit was gone and so was she."

I glanced up at Deuce. Standing beside me with one hand on my back, he was watching Preacher intently, every bit as captivated by the story as I was. Releasing the bedrail, I wiped my sweaty palms down the front of my jeans. "So she did run off, then?"

"Never woulda guessed she woulda left me—or you—like that." Preacher's voice began to quiver. Blinking rapidly, he swallowed several times. "But I fucked up, Eva. I said some shit I shouldn't have. None of that shit was her fault. It was mine—it was all my fault."

"Did you ever find out anything? Anything at all?" My voice was hoarse—strained with desperation. And my skin felt too tight, my lungs and throat, too—as if my last shreds of hope were strangling me.

"I kept thinkin' she'd show back up after she cooled off. I kept thinkin' that she had to come back… for you, at least."

Tears burning in my eyes, emotion lodged in my throat, I could hardly speak. "So she didn't come back?" I managed to ask. Deuce's hand on my back began to move in soothing circular motions.

Preacher stared off across the room. "I was a mess—couldn't sleep, couldn't eat. I had Tiny stayin' at the apartment, gave you to Joe and Sylvie, and I went lookin' for her. Looked everywhere. Even filed a missing person's report. That's when the Feds came knockin', tryin' to say I did somethin' to her. And that's when I found out who she really was."

Preacher released a chest-rattling sigh. "Elizabeth Stephens—that was her real name. Born and raised in Southern California. Parents were Linda and Daniel Stephens—blue-collar family. Daniel died in a car crash

367

when she was only three years old. Fell asleep at the wheel. Linda worked odd jobs for a few years until she remarried some hotshot real estate developer from Newport Beach. Name was Bruce Holtz. Guy was loaded. And a real fuckin' scumbag."

Listening to Preacher, it sounded as though he'd memorized a file on my mother—which, knowing my father, he probably had.

"A few women filed rape charges against him over the years." His eyes on the ceiling, Preacher shook his head. "Ain't nothin' ever came of any of it—the charges were always dropped. Back then, things being the way they were, him being as rich as he was, I figured either nobody believed those poor girls, or he'd paid 'em off."

"Rape," I repeated numbly. "Did he—"

"She never told me," Preacher interrupted. "But with him bein' such a fuckin' scumbag, and her bein' so damn scared of bein' sent home, it wasn't hard to put it all together."

I closed my eyes and just breathed—an attempt to clear my head of the uncomfortable, painful images filling it. Just like my mother, I knew what it was like to be violated by someone who'd been like family to me. Had she blamed herself, too?

It certainly wasn't something I was glad to share with her, but it did help me understand why she'd been so secretive, and why she lied to everyone. Even the fear that had caused her to betray Preacher to the FBI made sense.

"What happened to Holtz?" It was Deuce who spoke. The hand on my back stilled, and I opened my eyes to find my husband staring at my father, a menacing gleam in his eyes.

Looking between them, seeing a similar expression on Preacher's face, I swallowed hard. It was easy to forget the kind of men they were—how cold and detached they could be when it came to those who'd wronged them or dared to hurt the people they loved.

Preacher smiled faintly—a slight baring of teeth. "He died the followin' year. Got carjacked at gunpoint, and took a bullet in each eye."

"The followin' year?" Deuce sounded amused.

Preacher's expression turned indignant. "I couldn't do anything right away. The club, the goddamn Feds—I had too much heat on me. One wrong move and I was goin' away for life."

"How'd you get the FBI off your back?"

"I made them an offer they couldn't refuse."

"You helped them take down the Columbo family, didn't you?"

Preacher shrugged. "They wanted a notch on their belt and the recognition, and I figured I was better off havin' the Feds owe me one, rather than them beatin' down my door every other second."

"Jesus, Fox. You're half the fuckin' reason the Italian's operation fell apart." Deuce sounded impressed—a rare occurrence.

"And her mother—my grandmother?" I interrupted, faltering over my words. I couldn't have cared less about anything to do with the mob or the FBI. Tears were still threatening and I was finding it increasingly hard to hold them back. Deuce's hand moved from my back to my shoulder and gave me a comforting squeeze.

Preacher's eyes shot to mine. "Don't you cry for her,

baby girl," he growled. "That bitch wasn't your grandmother; she was a goddamn drunk and a piece of shit. I kept tabs on her over the years. She got all that bastard's money and drank herself to death. Died when you were fourteen. Was a better death than she deserved, and she damn sure wasn't worth your tears."

I shook my head, and a single tear slipped free. I wasn't crying for her. I wasn't even crying for my mother.

I was crying for Preacher.

I'd thought I'd known who he was. But I hadn't. I hadn't known him at all.

It isn't easy to see your parents as people, separate from you. To think that they once had a life before you, that they'd lived and loved and lost, and everything in between, all before you'd ever existed.

The Preacher I knew, the one I'd loved my entire life, was a driving force in the criminal underground. He was a hard man, steadfast, who brooked no arguments from anyone—with the minor exception of those he loved.

But he'd also been so much more than that, more than I'd ever dreamed. I'd never known the young Preacher—full of self-doubt, lost in the world, and wishing for something more. I hadn't known the son who'd struggled to free himself from the life his father had laid out for him. Neither had I known the man who'd loved the girl.

I only knew the person he'd become after he'd lost so much, the man he'd become because he'd lost so much. I was suddenly feeling as if he'd been shortchanged—as if we both had.

"Ah, shit, Eva." Preacher reached over the bedrail, his hand quivering. "Never could stand seein' you cry."

I grasped his hand between mine and bowed my head. And then I cried. I cried for all of us. For Preacher, for The Judge and Ginny, for Elizabeth Stephens, and... for me.

"Why did you wait until now to tell me the truth?" I eventually asked, wiping away the last of my tears. "About all of it. I still don't understand, Daddy. Why did you keep it from me?"

Preacher stared at me for a moment, considering. "Back then a lot of people thought I took out my own parents, and I didn't bother correcting them. They thought I was crazy, they were afraid of me, and that served me well over the years... but I didn't want you knowin' any of that—thinkin' that of me." He paused, his chest heaving with heavy, painful-sounding breaths.

"I might have told you the truth once you were old enough to understand. But as it turned out... I didn't even know the truth."

Tears filled his eyes. "And then... I couldn't tell you, Eva. I couldn't face it. It was all my fault... all my fuckin' fault. It was right there in front of my face the whole goddamn time and I never saw it."

Eyes narrowed in confusion, I squeezed his hand harder. "What was your fault?"

His sunken features contorted. Pain blazed in his eyes. "Everything, baby girl. Every goddamn thing."

The click-click of footsteps across the floor startled Preacher awake. He'd fallen asleep slumped forward in one of the two uncomfortable chairs in Frank's hospital room. Pushing upright, he peered at the newcomer in the room through

blurry eyes. Petite, with long blonde hair, the young nurse gave Preacher a sympathetic smile.

Approaching Frank, she began systematically checking the machines surrounding his hospital bed. Muted red and green lights flashed from one; a soft, steady beeping came from another. And in the center of it all lay Frank—heavily sedated, an oxygen mask covering his nose and mouth, he lay utterly still save for the slight rise and fall of his chest.

It had been three days since Preacher had gotten the call—Frank had been involved in an accident on the Long Island Expressway. The pileup had sent a Mack truck skidding straight into Frank's bike, dragging him across three lanes of traffic and crashing through the median before dislodging him.

Glancing at the empty chair beside him, Preacher wondered where Tiny had disappeared to. He looked to the window—at the black sky beyond the brightly lit skyline. Then at the clock on the wall—it was nearly midnight.

Scratching idly at his stubbled jaw, Preacher got to his feet and approached the bed. "How's he doin'?" he asked.

"It's too soon to tell," the nurse replied. "He's suffered so many injuries. His body needs time to heal."

He glanced down at his friend's unrecognizable face— bruised and swollen and missing skin on his left cheek. Most of the skin on the left side of his body was in similar condition—mangled and shredded. Frank had also broken his left arm, both of his legs, and nearly all his ribs. There was internal damage, too—some brain swelling and a punctured lung that he'd since had surgery to repair.

"If it makes you feel any better, I've seen people recover from far worse."

Eyes flicking up, Preacher nodded slowly. He knew Frank would recover. He and the rest of the club would see to that.

Finished checking on Frank, she started across the room. Pausing at the door, she glanced over her shoulder and flashed Preacher a smile—an interested, flirtatious smile.

"You should go home and go to bed," she said.

Fully awake now, Preacher took a moment to look her over. She was cute, but nothing special. There was nothing remotely interesting about her face or body, nothing that stood out and made him take notice. Still…she'd do.

"Yeah?" He raised his brows. "You gonna join me?"

Her answering blush was contrived—an attempt to look innocent when her body language told him she was anything but. Head tilted to one side, neck exposed, her slim fingers tapped along the side of her white dress uniform, purposely drawing his attention to her tilted hip.

Not in the mood for games, Preacher regarded her plainly. "What time do you get off?"

A breezy shrug. "Two."

"My place or yours?"

Her smile turned coy. "We'll see," she said, and then slipped into the hallway.

Smirking, Preacher turned back to Frank. "It's the leather, brother. Gets 'em every time."

Staring down at his disfigured friend, his humor quickly faded. Preacher hated hospitals. The dead and dying aside, he hated the smell of them—a god-awful mixture of urine and cleaning solution. He hated the feel of them, too—so suffocating, and restricting. It wasn't all that long ago that he'd finished up his second stint in prison, and tiny rooms such as this one never failed to make him feel like he was right back inside.

But he wouldn't leave, at least not until Tiny returned. He'd promised Frankie Jr. as much—the poor kid had already lost his mother to cancer a few years back. And if something should happen to Frank during the night, Preacher didn't want Frank to be alone. He'd made that crystal clear when the hospital staff had demanded he leave and return during visiting hours. Fuck their rules. He had a duty to his road chief, as his president and as his friend, to stand by his side.

Sighing, Preacher shoved his hands into the front pockets of his jeans and began meandering around the room, stopping every few minutes to glance out the window at the illuminated city below. Always awake, that was New York. Wide awake and ever changing.

The city reminded him of Eva—astoundingly adaptable, and with a solid foundation regardless of the fast-moving, always-changing world around her. Despite her young age, his baby girl had handled his time in prison like a champ and his homecoming just as well. She was well suited to this life, he thought proudly, even as the very same thought caused a sinking sensation in his gut.

Shaking his head to clear it, Preacher turned away from the window and his gaze snagged on a large plastic bag—a patient belongings bag shoved into a corner.

Picking up the bag, he pulled it open, grimacing as the acrid scent of blood and body odor filled his nostrils. What remained of the clothes Frank had been wearing during the accident had been stuffed inside—two mangled boots and what was left of his leather cut.

Preacher set the destroyed leather aside. He would have someone salvage the patches and sew them onto a new vest.

Pulling the boots from the bag, he found Frank's wallet tucked inside one, while something shiny glinted from inside the other. Preacher's hand disappeared inside the boot, closing around something hard.

"What the fuck," he muttered, pulling free a heavy metal key ring.

Squinting in the dimly lit room, he held up the throng of, not just keys, but jewelry. Mostly rings, but also charms and the occasional earring or bracelet. He turned the key ring in his hand, his eyes roaming the odd mix when he suddenly stopped.

The boot in his other hand fell to the floor with a hard 'thwap'.

He moved quickly across the room and flipped on the light—the overhead fluorescents flickered on, brightening the room.

His heart pounding in his chest, Preacher stared down at the ring squeezed between his thumb and forefinger—a World War II United States Marine Corps ring, its ruby center glinting brilliantly. Slowly he rolled the ring between his fingers, exposing the inscription inside: THE JUDGE.

Preacher's heart hammered wildly inside his chest. He'd forgotten about this ring until this very moment, forgotten that his father had almost never taken it off. It had been a permanent fixture on his right ring finger.

How had Frank—

Why did Frank—

Releasing the ring, Preacher began searching frantically through the rest of the jewelry, pausing briefly to study each piece. He wasn't entirely sure what he was looking for, only that he was thinking of his mother.

Piece by piece, he stared down at the unfamiliar scraps of metal. For all he knew, any number of them could have belonged to Ginny.

It had to be a fluke. There had to be an explanation. For whatever reason, Frank had The Judge's ring, and Frank would have a reason. A damn good reason for having this— this key ring full of things that so clearly didn't belong to him. And Frank's reason would make perfect sense, and Preacher's world would stop spinning and—

Preacher froze.

He stopped moving, stopped breathing.

Everything stopped.

His heart, his breath, the whole fucking world went skidding off the road, headed straight for the unforgiving wall of what was to become his new reality and shattering everything he thought he'd known.

"No..." he whispered hoarsely. "No, no, no, no, no."

Staggering backward, his back found the wall.

He shook his head, refusing to believe his own eyes. Maybe it wasn't hers. Maybe it was just a coincidence.

With a shaking finger, he touched the tiny silver butterfly—spotted and tarnished.

A strangled noise slipped past his lips. "Wheels," he rasped.

Preacher hopped out of bed and dropped down on one knee. Then he gestured for Debbie's hand. Looking adorably bewildered, she gave it. Twisting her butterfly ring off her index finger, he pushed it onto her ring finger.

"I promise I'll get you somethin' better," he told her. "A big, fat rock or somethin'. Whatever the fuck you want."

She only continued to stare down at him, wide-eyed and

gaping. Several seconds passed, long enough that Preacher was starting to wonder if he'd made a mistake by springing this on her. Hell, he hadn't even known he was going to ask her. It had been a spur of the moment decision brought about solely by the way she made him feel—like she was it for him. Like there couldn't possibly be another her out there, and so he needed to get his fucking shit together and do right by her.

His brow rose. "Wheels, you gonna say somethin' or you gonna leave me hangin' 'round down here like a goddamn fool?"

Debbie slid quickly off the bed, dropping onto his lap. Wrapping her arms around his neck, she kissed him. "Yes," she whispered against his mouth.

"What's that?" he asked. He pulled back to look at her—into the eyes that never failed to bring him peace. And at those sexy-as-hell lips that he couldn't get enough of.

Laughing happily, she shoved at his chest. "Yes, I'll marry you! Yes, yes, yes!"

Feeling wetness on his cheek, Preacher blinked. Then he blinked again, and more tears fell.

Unsteady and trembling, he turned to look at Frank. The sight of his friend—disfigured and lying broken in a bed—didn't have quite the same effect on him as it had before.

He looked at Frank as if he'd never seen him before.

Why? The one-word question pounded through him, as unrelenting and demanding as Preacher's thrashing heartbeat.

Why—

How—

He didn't—

He couldn't—

Breath purged from Preacher's lungs. His eyes squeezed shut and tears rained down his cheeks. He didn't know where to begin. How to process. What to think. How to feel. He knew nothing—absolutely fucking nothing.

He wanted to rationalize this, wanted to slap some sort of reasonable explanation onto this discovery, but the truth wouldn't relent. It pushed against each barrier Preacher tried to erect, battering wildly, shouting loudly, refusing to be ignored.

The key ring felt suddenly too heavy in his hand, this key ring full of... fucking trophies. Heavy and pulsating, pulsing like a beating heart. The beat echoed in his ears, in his veins.

Those rings weren't just rings. They were people. Dozens of people.

The smear of blood on the trailer door flashed in his mind over and over and over again, until he felt drunk and dizzy.

Preacher choked on his thoughts. Choked on the memory of a sweet, young face. Full lips split into a wide smile. A pair of big, beautiful brown eyes.

He'd thought she'd left him. All these years he'd thought she'd run from him.

Rage—pure, unadulterated rage flowed through him. Every muscle in his body tensed until his skin felt ten times too tight, and his breath was coming in short, angry bursts.

Preacher didn't recall crossing the room. One second he was flush against the wall and the next he was bent over the hospital bed, tearing the oxygen mask away, and gripping the swollen face of a man he'd considered his brother.

His fingers squeezed Frank's nose while his palm covered his mouth. Frank's body hiccupped even as Preacher felt slithers of air escape the confines of his hand. He clamped down harder. His rage swirled higher. His tears fell faster.

Another machine began to beep, faster and louder. Then an alarm went off, ringing loudly through the room.

Preacher blinked and snapped to attention. He slapped the mask back over Frank's face and was quickly backing away from the bed when two nurses burst inside the room.

Mouth agape, barely breathing, I could do no more than stare at my father.

Much like Preacher had, I was having an equally hard time processing the truth. I didn't even know where to begin. My grandparents, my mother, *fucking Frank...*

"I just lost my fuckin' mind," Preacher croaked. "She'd already been gone so long, and I'd already guessed somethin' wasn't right. And then I saw those rings, and I knew what he'd done, and I just... lost my fuckin' mind."

He turned to me, his red-rimmed eyes wet with tears. "It was all my fault, Eva. I didn't see it... I didn't see it... I didn't know... and it was too late. Lookin' back now, I can see it all. Things were wrong. Frank was... wrong. I see it clearly now. Don't know why I could never see it back then."

Preacher squeezed his eyes closed, and tears ran freely down his wrinkled cheeks. "And Jesus, Eva," he whispered, "You gotta know that I only took Frankie in because I felt so goddamn guilty. I was only thinkin' about what Frank musta put him through... especially after Maria had passed."

Recalling Frankie's nightmares and his inability to sleep without me, I clasped my hand over my mouth, stifling a sob. He'd been beyond help—beyond anything I could have done for him, at least. Still, my heart broke for him all over again—for the broken little boy I'd loved as a brother.

There was a touch to my back, and I glanced up to find Deuce staring down at me, his features pinched, his eyes darker than normal, violence shimmering in their depths. Fighting for calm, I attempted to school my features. But it was too late, and Deuce knew me too well.

When it came to my relationship with Frankie, there was only so far Deuce could be pushed before he started pushing back. He couldn't understand it—why I loved Frankie despite all he'd put me through. And that was okay, because most of the time neither could I. Love was irrational like that—irrational, uncontainable and unexplainable.

"I'm gonna go get some air," he growled softly.

Feeling guilty, I watched him walk stiffly away.

With a sigh, I turned back to my father.

He was fumbling with the collar of his hospital gown, his unsteady fingers tugging his gold neck chain free. With some effort, he slipped it over his head and offered it to me.

I could only stare at the tiny ring dangling from the chain. No longer silver, it was heavily tarnished, but there was no mistaking the butterfly setting.

"I knew she was gone," he said, "I knew I wasn't ever gonna see her again, but I never stopped thinkin' that maybe she'd show back up one day. All my life, that feelin' never left me. I kept thinkin' maybe I'd been wrong. Maybe she was still out there somewhere."

Trembling, he began shaking his head. "Maybe if I coulda known exactly what happened, I coulda moved on. Maybe if I coulda buried her..."

"*Oh Daddy.*" Fumbling with the bedrail, I found the mechanism that allowed me to lower it. Scooting my chair forward, I grabbed Preacher's hand and brought it to my cheek. The necklace and ring dangled between us.

"You forgive me, baby girl?" Eyes full of pain and bright with tears implored me, and my heart shattered for the hundredth time that day. Vehemently I shook my head. "There's nothing to forgive, Daddy. Frank—he did it. He did all of it."

Preacher looked at me with such tenderness, with such love, and with more sorrow than I'd ever imagined him capable of.

"I don't deserve you," he whispered hoarsely. "I didn't deserve her, either. I should never have touched her. I did this, Eva. I brought her into my world, and it killed her." His voice cracked and his eyes filled again. "I killed her."

"No Daddy." I attempted to sound firm, despite my grief. "Frank killed her. Frank did this."

Preacher either didn't hear me, or he was unwilling to believe what I was telling him. He only continued to whisper, "I didn't deserve her."

Wrapping an arm over his chest, I buried my face against his side and just held him as tightly as I could.

CHAPTER 34

AT THE CLUBHOUSE, SHUT INSIDE PREACHER'S OFFICE, I absentmindedly traced the dark ink stain on his desk. Much like everything else inside this room, the stain had been there all my life.

It was late yet the clubhouse was full, friends and family were filling nearly every room. I knew I should be out there visiting, but there were other things weighing heavily on my mind.

Leaning back in Preacher's chair, I closed my eyes and inhaled deeply. It smelled like my father in here—leather, his favorite brand of cigarettes, and hints of the cologne he sometimes wore. And I wondered how long it would be before it no longer did.

The door opened, hinges squeaking. Opening my eyes, I sat up and squinted through the dimly-lit room. A head full of dyed black hair, fashionably streaked with gray and white and curled to perfection, peeked inside. A wrinkled hand tipped with long red nails waved hello.

"Hi, baby girl." Sylvia's rough-hewn, nasally voice filled the room. "Can I come in?"

I gestured her forward, and the door opened, revealing a large metal box clutched between her arms. Elbowing the door closed behind her, she hurried across the room and placed the box on the desk in front of me.

Wringing her hands together, she took a step back. "I've always wanted to tell you the truth about her, Eva. So many times. Your mother, she was my friend, you know?" Taking a breath, Sylvia shook her head. "She was such a sweet girl and I loved her very much."

Sylvia nodded at the box. "Your father—he threw so much away. He was hurting. He wanted to forget, I think. But I kept as much as I could get my hands on."

With my heart in my throat, I stared at the box, already imagining what might be inside.

"I'll leave you alone." Sylvia moved toward the door.

I jumped up. "Aunt Sylvie, wait!"

She paused and turned, and I noticed the tears in her eyes.

"I don't think I've ever thanked you," I said.

Confused, Sylvia shook her head. "For what?"

"For helping him take care of me. For helping him raise me. You and I both know he couldn't have done it without you."

Sylvia's hand went to her throat. "Oh God, Eva, it was my absolute pleasure." Again she nodded at the box. "You come find me when you're done, okay?"

As the door closed softly behind her, I looked down at the box before me. With shaking hands, I lifted the heavy lid and peered down at the contents inside—a short stack of notebooks, a few articles of neatly folded clothing, a small brown purse, and a couple of books and trinkets.

I bypassed all of it for the notebooks.

Laying the first one on the desk, I opened to the first page. The drawing had yellowed and faded some, but not so much that I couldn't make it out. One hand flew to my mouth while the other hovered just above the page, quivering. It was just as Preacher had described—a smiling man with a little girl on his lap.

Carefully I flipped through the pages, finding hand-drawn illustrations of the story my father had told me. I saw Preacher, young and handsome, stretched out on a bed, sound asleep. And Sylvia, heavily pregnant with Trey. I saw Joe and Max, and my grandparents—Ginny with a cigarette in her hand, smiling, and The Judge with his arms crossed over his chest, his squared jaw and proud nose reminding me so much of Preacher.

I pulled another notebook from the pile, finding page after page of what I assumed were my mother's first impressions of New York City—sketches of the clubhouse, the neighborhood, the Statue of Liberty, and the Empire State Building.

I touched the next drawing tentatively. Beneath a shock of dark hair, wide eyes set above plump cheeks stared back at me. "Frankie," I whispered, my eyes filling.

There were more sketches of Frankie, of Tiny, of my uncles, and other club members—some of whom I knew, and others I only recognized from photographs I'd seen.

I paused on a drawing of Preacher, standing inside a room I didn't recognize. Standing beside a window, his gaze was fixed on something the artist couldn't see. He was shirtless, his arms folded across his chest. His long hair was unbound, hanging loose around his face.

The detail was incredible.

She'd drawn him so carefully. So exquisitely.

She'd drawn him as if she'd loved him.

I flipped to the next page and instead of a drawing, I found a discolored Polaroid photograph tucked into the binding. As I pulled it free, my hand began to shake.

In my hand, I held the family I'd never gotten to have. A handsome young man grinned at the camera, his arm wrapped protectively around the beautiful girl smiling beside him—a tiny baby swaddled in her arms.

That beautiful girl was my mother and that baby is me.

Tears clouding my vision, I found myself stumbling backward, nearly tripping over the chair behind me. Oh God, I couldn't breathe. It was too hot and I couldn't fucking breathe.

Clutching the picture to my chest, I hurried across the room, threw open the office door, and burst into the hallway, gasping for air. The hall was thankfully empty, and I sagged back against the wall, breathing hard.

Glancing around, I felt as if I were seeing the clubhouse for the first time.

Everything felt different now—foreign.

And everywhere I looked, I felt her—the ghost of a girl I'd never gotten to know.

I could see her now, walking down this very hall. Young and beautiful. Pregnant with me yet still just a baby herself.

And utterly without a clue as to the kind of world she'd stepped into. I wanted to reach out and grab her, pull her to me, and keep her close. Keep her safe from those who would try to take her from me.

I followed her ghost until my eyes stopped on a familiar shape skulking in the shadows by the stairwell. "Tiny?" I called out, squinting. "What the hell are you doing?"

Tiny shuffled out from stairwell, his eyes on the floor. "I'm sorry, Eva," he whispered, his sad eyes finding mine. "I never wanted to lie to ya. 'Bout your mom and 'bout your old man bein' so sick."

I shut my eyes for a moment and then let out a sigh, and with it any residual anger I was harboring. There was no use in yelling at a bunch of old men who'd only been doing what they were told. It would only hurt both them and me, and it wouldn't change a damn thing. My mother was still gone, and Preacher was still dying.

"You can make it up to me," I told him.

His head bobbed in earnest. "Anything, Eva. You name it, it's yours."

"You spent so much time with her—my mother." I lifted the picture, showing him. "Will you tell me about her? I want to know everything about her, Tiny. Every single thing."

A wobbly smile stretched across his sagging jowls. "Is that all? Where do ya wanna start? Shit, I still remember the day you were born like it was yesterday."

He offered me his arm and I looped mine through it. Arm in arm, we headed toward the living room.

"Scariest fuckin' thing that ever happened to me," he said.

I bit back a laugh. "I love you, Tiny," I murmured,

shaking my head. "With extra sugar."

It was nearly four in the morning by the time I dragged myself up to my old room. Pushing open the door, I cringed when it creaked, and then smiled, unable to remember a time when it hadn't creaked.

The television was on, bathing the room in muted, flickering light. I took a moment to look over the familiar space—the posters on the wall, the framed photos, the rows of shelves filled with cassette tapes and CDs. It felt like home and yet… didn't.

Eventually my gaze landed on Deuce. Lying on his stomach in bed, he wore only a pair of boxer shorts. His lack of snoring told me he wasn't sleeping.

We hadn't spoken since we'd left the hospital and he'd disappeared within minutes of our arrival at the clubhouse.

I sat down beside him, visually tracing the many tattoos covering his broad, muscular back, marveling at his beautiful body. Whereas my father looked ten years older than he should, Deuce looked at least ten years younger than he was. Not that it mattered what age he looked—Deuce would never not be beautiful to me.

"Baby? You awake?"

"Nope."

"Are you ignoring me?"

"I'm fuckin' talkin' to you, ain't I?"

A smile tugged at my lips, and I bent down to press a kiss between his shoulder blades. His warm, smooth skin twitched beneath my mouth, and a shiver shook through Deuce.

"We can talk about it if you want," I whispered. "Don't let it fester."

Deuce sighed heavily, his big body lifting off the mattress. Flipping onto his back, he folded his arms beneath his head—a move that caused his impressive biceps to shift and swell beneath his colorful skin.

"There ain't shit to say," he muttered. "You know I hate this fuckin' city, hate this fuckin' house, hate this motherfuckin' room. But those are my demons, darlin', and you've got bigger shit to be dealin' with."

I stared at him a moment, hating him for clinging to things that couldn't be changed, while also loving him at least a hundred times more for always being so glaringly, unapologetically him.

"I don't want to deal with my own shit right now," I told him. "Right now I want to pretend that I don't have any shit to deal with at all."

"That still don't mean we should talk about mine."

We fell silent, watching each other in the semi-darkness.

"Are you coming with me tomorrow—back to the hospital?"

"That's a dumbass fuckin' question, Eva."

Again the silence stretched between us, my gaze wandering away with my thoughts.

"He loved her, you know," I said suddenly.

"Babe." Deuce's tone gentled. "He ain't never stopped."

I nodded distractedly. "She loved him, too. I know she did."

When Deuce didn't say anything, only continued to watch me, I bent down and pressed a kiss to his lips. His large hand cupped the back of my head, and his mouth

388

covered mine. Demanding lips, rough strokes of his tongue, he nipped my bottom lip before breaking the kiss.

"That was so fucking hot," I told him breathlessly, eyeing him hungrily. "What gives you the right to be so old and yet so fucking hot?"

He snorted. "You are one crazy bitch."

Straightening, I laughed at him. "That's all you got? I'm a crazy bitch?" Brow lifted, lips twisted, I blew him a kiss. "You are getting soft, aren't you? Old, and soft, and *sweet*."

Grabbing my wrist, he set my hand on top of the bulge in his boxers. "Yeah? That feel soft to you?"

I shrugged. "Kinda…"

Deuce let out a low growl, and a heartbeat later I was laid out flat on the bed, his big body hovering over mine. His hips dipped and mine arched, and our mouths met in an explosion of need. Clothing was shed, as were any reservations. Frenzied, we touched each other in ways we hadn't touched in years. My staccato breaths joined the fray.

I couldn't remember the last time I'd felt like this, so turned on, so crazy needy. Nothing more than a thrashing mass of flesh and bone, desperate for more of him.

"I wanna see you," he said, reversing our positions.

Straddling his hips, I watched as Deuce's eyes traced a greedy path over every inch of my bare skin. Lips parted and breathing hard, his hooded gaze met mine and the way he looked at me? I felt young again. And beautiful. And *oh my God*, so fucking alive.

One hand planted on his chest, I rushed to guide him inside of me. And as our bodies connected, a gasp and a growl collided in the space between us.

I bent to kiss him. Our mouths fused together, I

snapped my hips forward, eliciting a throaty groan from Deuce. Panting and eager, I began to move.

His thumbs hooked beneath my hip bones. Calloused fingertips dug into my backside, stilling me. My eyes fluttered opened, finding his.

"Babe," he said, low and raspy. "I want it fuckin' slow."

Shivers raked up and down my spine, and I sighed against his mouth.

Then I gave it to him slow.

EPILOGUE

A LIGHT BREEZE BLEW LAZILY PAST ME, BRINGING WITH it the scents of freshly cut grass and newly blossomed flowers. Several strands of my hair lifted, and the remaining tears on my cheeks dried up and disappeared. A short ways off in the distance a small flock of geese had congregated, occasionally honking as they shuffled through the cemetery.

Preacher's funeral had ended hours ago, and it had been a service any biker would have been proud to receive. Bikers from all over the country had come to pay their respects. Personal stories had been shared—some happy, some sad, and others so vulgar I'd felt compelled to cover my young son's ears. Then my teenage daughter Ivy had sung one of Preacher's favorite songs a cappella, only managing a few lines before everyone else joined in.

Later at the graveyard, hundreds of motorcyclists had lined their bikes along the narrow pathways, engines revving. "Preacher!" they'd shouted, their fists raised. "Preacher, Preacher, Preacher..." Louder and louder they'd chanted his name as if the louder they shouted they might somehow reach him.

I glanced over my shoulder, scanning the remaining motorcycles parked along the cemetery path. Only family and Silver Demons remained now. They talked quietly amongst themselves, leaving me to my grief.

Turning back to the simple cement tombstone before me, my gaze traced the engravings. Beneath Preacher's name and the years he'd lived, BELOVED BROTHER AND FATHER was inscribed. And below that, "Ride forever free" had been etched in scrawling cursive.

My eyes filled with tears for the hundredth time today.

Memories assaulted me.

Preacher lifting me up onto his broad shoulders, showing me the world from new heights.

Inside the clubhouse, Janis Joplin on the stereo, standing on Preacher's feet while we danced around the living room.

The first time I'd ridden on the back of his motorcycle, putting on a brave face while my hands fisted in his jacket, squeezing him as tightly as I could.

My chest grew suddenly tight, and my vision swam. Unable to catch my breath, my hands flew to my chest and I gasped, forcing my lungs to fill.

When you're little, your parents are your whole world. But as you grow, you change. You become your own person, create a family of your own, and you start to forget.

What a cruel, cosmic joke the world plays on us, causing us to remember... by taking them away.

"Oh, God, Daddy," I whispered, swiping at my wet cheeks. "I don't know how to do this. I don't know how to be in this world without you."

"Mom?" Ivy's familiar hand slid into mine and squeezed. I squeezed her back, always glad for her company.

"I'm okay, baby," I lied, fighting back another wave of tears. Kids will do that to you—force you to be strong when you feel anything but. Although as I looked over at the beautiful young woman beside me, I could hardly call her a kid anymore.

She flashed me a sad smile that caused her dimples to deepen. Blonde and blue-eyed, she was every bit Deuce, and yet I could also see so much of me in her. In her eyes that were just a bit too big, and in her lips, thicker and wider than most. And in the generous curves of her body.

These were all traits I'd once thought I'd inherited from Ginny. I'd only just learned the truth—that I looked more like my mother than I did anyone else. What a difference a day can make. The turned-over earth beneath my feet was proof enough of that.

"I meant to show you this." I pulled the faded photograph from my coat pocket and handed it to Ivy.

"This is my mother. Your... grandmother." The foreign words tumbled awkwardly from me.

"Wow," Ivy breathed, her eyes widening. "Is that you she's holding—the baby?"

Pressing my lips together, I nodded sadly.

My daughter's gaze darted between the picture and me,

and another smile split her lips. "Oh my God, Mom, you look so much like her."

My damned eyes filled again.

"And Grandpa was super hot..." Ivy's nose suddenly wrinkled. "And I can't believe I just said my grandpa was hot."

Laughter bubbled up inside me. "He was, wasn't he?" Wrapping my arm around Ivy's waist, I laughed through my tears.

Deuce appeared on the other side of me. He ran a hand down the center of my back. "You ready to ride, darlin'?"

Instead of flying home, Deuce and I had decided to ride back to Montana on my father's '69 chopper. Preacher had loved that bike more than any other and had kept it in pristine condition all these years. And I knew nothing would make him happier than knowing I was keeping his girl on the road.

But I wasn't ready to leave just yet. To turn away from Preacher's grave, to leave this cemetery... it felt so final. I wasn't ready to let go yet. I needed another moment with him.

Who was I kidding? I needed more than a moment. I needed to see his crooked grin once more. I needed to hear his smoke-roughened voice call me "baby girl" just one last time.

"I need a few more minutes," I told Deuce. "Where's Damon?" My eyes roamed the remaining people, searching for my son.

"Last I saw he was runnin' around pickin' out graves for everyone."

While Ivy choked on her laughter, my brow shot up.

"Seriously?"

Deuce shrugged. "Your son, babe."

"Our son," I snapped. "I didn't make him by myself."

Deuce's hand disappeared from my back and appeared on my ass. Lightly smacking me, he said, "I'm only takin' credit for the not-crazy ones."

He moved to Ivy and tugged on her arm. "Give your mom a few more minutes with her old man."

Ivy slid her hand into Deuce's and grinned up at him. "That means you're only taking credit for me, right Daddy? Because I'm definitely not as crazy as Danny... right, Daddy?"

"You're all fuckin' crazy," he muttered. "Every last one of you."

Smiling, I watched them for a moment before turning back to my father. My smile falling away, I found myself dropping to my knees in the dirt. Placing my hand on the tombstone, I tried to think of something to say. Anything at all. But words eluded me.

What was there to say?

I miss you?

I love you?

Both of those sentiments went without saying. I would love him and miss him until my very last breath.

"Daddy," I whispered as my eyes filled again and more tears fell. "I hope you... I hope... I wish..."

I never finished my thought. Preacher's story had ended, and no amount of hoping or wishing would change that.

"Goodbye Daddy," I finally said.

Standing, I squeezed my eyes shut and pictured him as

I would always see him, as the strong, powerful man from my youth—tall and lean, his long brown hair pulled back, his warm, handsome smile, and his striking brown eyes full of pride and love.

Goodbye, baby girl...

ABOUT THE AUTHOR

Madeline Sheehan is the *USA Today* bestselling author of the Holy Trinity series and Undeniable series. She has also co-authored with Claire C. Riley the Thicker Than Blood series, and *Shut Up and Kiss Me*.

Welcome to her world of fantastical romance, full of unconventional love and unscripted emotions.

www.MadelineSheehan.com

OTHER WORKS BY
MADELINE SHEEHAN

UNDENIABLE SERIES
Undeniable
Unbeautifully
Unattainable
Unbeloved
Undeserving

HOLY TRINITY SERIES
The Soul Mate
My Soul to Take
The Lost Souls: A Novella

Co-Written with Claire C. Riley

THICKER THAN BLOOD SERIES
Thicker Than Blood
Beneath Blood and Bone

Shut Up and Kiss Me

Made in the USA
Monee, IL
18 February 2025

12503328R00233